Also by Maggie Shayne

MAGGIE SHAYNE

BLOOD OF THE SORCERESS

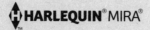

Recycling programs
for this product may
not exist in your area.

ISBN-13: 978-0-7783-1421-9

BLOOD OF THE SORCERESS

Copyright © 2013 by Margaret Benson

For questions and comments about the quality of this book, please contact us at CustomerService@Harlequin.com.

Printed in U.S.A.

www.Harlequin.com

In Loving Memory of
Jane O'Connor

A woman who soared above challenges
that would have held most to the ground.

Founder of the Central New York Romance Writers,
which has since turned out more than a
dozen authors and well over a hundred novels
that might not otherwise even have been written,
much less published. We love you, Jane.
You led us to our careers and, more important,
to each other. Thank you will never be enough.
But thank you all the same.

Prologue

Lilia was no angel. Lilia was a witch. Even though she was currently hovering between the worlds, watching over her beloved, waiting for the right time to manifest as a silvery-blond-haired, blue-eyed woman and save his life, she was still a witch. Had been for thirty-five-hundred years. Would be for as long as her soul lived on.

She watched, awestruck, as her beautiful Demetrius flashed into existence fully formed, fully grown, completely naked. The Portal, the opening between dimensions through which he had escaped his Underworld prison, was in the cave behind a waterfall. He arrived in the physical world in a blaze of light, crouching on the stones near that cascade.

Goddess, he was beautiful. She reached out as if to touch him. But she couldn't. Not yet.

He was the same as she remembered him. His body had been reconstituted just as it had once been, since his soul had been ripped away before he died, an unnatural perversion of the order of things. She wouldn't get her own body back when she returned to earth

to join him. Hers had been dashed against the rocky
ground from a great height before her own soul had
flown free. She would have to manifest a fresh new
form when the time came. She'd glimpsed that new
form in a vision, so different from her former body
that it had shocked her.

Oh, but look at him.

He rose from his crouched position, looking around,
blinking in confusion, and her heart ached. So long…
it had been so long!

He looked the same, and her heart twisted in her
chest with a mingling of joy that she had come this
far, was this close to success, and heartache that he
was still out of reach. She hadn't seen him since that
bloody dawn in 1501 BC, in Babylon, when he'd murdered the King in defense of the woman he loved, the
King's harem slave: Lilia herself. When the quarters
she shared with her two sisters were searched, the tools
of their forbidden magic had been found and the three
of them sentenced to be sacrificed to Marduk, chief
god of the pantheon. Demetrius had been the King's
right hand, his friend. She never should have fallen in
love with him. The cost had been so high.

But she *had* loved him. She loved him still.

The high priest Sindar had been in love, too—with
the King, or so Lilia had always suspected—and so his
wrath had been bitter. He'd used his own magic, dark
magic, to strip Demetrius of his soul and banish him
to a formless, sensory-deprived existence in an Underworld void—just after having Lilia and her sisters
thrown from a cliff to the bloody rocks below.

But he hadn't counted on the power of the three
Daughters of Ishtar. They'd refused to cross the Veil

until they'd taken Demetrius's stolen soul from the twisted holy man and split it among themselves for safekeeping. Indira and Magdalena had reincarnated lifetime after lifetime until the opportunity came to right the ancient wrong, while Lilia had remained in limbo, pulling their strings like a master puppeteer, awakening their memories, making them keep their vow to set things right.

The newly reborn Demetrius pushed himself up from the ice-cold ground, rising slowly. Lilia saw the amulet he wore gleaming in the moonlight. And even as he stood there, two other magical tools fell from nowhere and clattered loudly to the rocky ground.

He jumped at the sound, then moved closer, picking up the golden chalice, turning it slowly and examining the semiprecious stones embedded in its rim. Then he reached for the blade, looking it over the same way. She wondered what he was feeling. Did he recognize the tools? Did he have any clue as to the power he could wield with them? They'd held parts of his soul for a time, so he must feel a bond to them, a connection, yes?

Indira had returned the first piece of Demetrius's soul, along with the amulet in which it had been protected, thus freeing him. She'd opened the Portal, allowing him to escape his Underworld prison. But he'd had no form, and little ability to reason. And now Magdalena had returned another piece, one the sisters had secreted within a chalice accompanied by a blade, which, when used together, had allowed Demetrius to manifest physically here near the Portal, in the cold of a February night in the Northeast.

He was freezing and shaken, she was sure. But not entirely confused. He would know about this world into which he'd sprung. He'd been floating wraithlike about it since last Samhain, after all. By now he knew the language, the slang, the customs. But he wouldn't know how to get by. Even with the powers he'd brought along with him, he needed food, shelter, clothing. And he didn't even know he had any powers just yet.

Demetrius looked around, and as the snow began to fall everything in her yearned to go to him. To help him.

But she couldn't. Not yet. Not until he used the magical tools that had been given to him to call her forth from the place that was not a place, and the time that was not a time. He had to bring her first into physical existence, and then *he* would have to render her fully human, fully mortal. He was the only one who could.

And when he realized what she would ask of him, he might wish her gone again. For Lilia had to convince him to give up his powers, his seeming immortality, and accept the final piece of his soul from her, so that they could have the lifetime together that had been denied them so long ago. And she wouldn't even be allowed to tell him that if he refused, they would both die.

But first he must be allowed to live, to discover his powers, to experience this existence, so that he knew what he was giving up. He had to want to be human again—and want it badly enough to choose it over supernatural powers he had no idea would expire either way.

It was not going to be an easy sell.

But one way or another, this curse had to end now, and one way or another it would.

* * *

Cold. He was so cold. He hadn't expected the sensations he was feeling, had been formless for so long that the notion of what form brought with it was alien to him. Somewhere in the back of his mind, Demetrius knew that he'd been human once. But he didn't *remember* it. It was a vague bit of knowledge floating around his subconscious and having little impact on anything. He felt no connection to that particle of information.

He looked behind him at the cave, knowing instinctively that that way lay the Portal, and beyond it the Underworld, his prison for as long as memory reached. He wanted no part of that. He didn't remember it in detail. Not the way he would remember this…this night, the sensations racing through his body, the thousands of messages singing through his senses, the tastes in the air, the smells of the forest, the sounds of an infinite bird choir…this he would remember vividly.

As to what came before, he remembered an endless, vast, dense…void. There was nothing to remember but nothingness itself. No feelings. No light. No sound. Rage, there had been rage, and hatred, and struggling to get free without even knowing what freedom meant. It was a vague concept that he'd thought of simply as the opposite of what is. He'd known captivity, powerlessness, and craved its opposite. Time had no meaning. Emotion was nonexistent. Touch was not even a concept to him then.

Eventually he'd discovered that he could peer through the Portal at the world he could not reach. He could see through the eyes of some of the creatures that roamed the physical world, and from there he'd begun to understand what he wanted. Freedom from his world, entry into that one. And only then had he honed his focus enough to begin to plot his escape and to crave vengeance on whatever nameless force had imprisoned him.

Once his essence had been set free, anger had driven him, and he'd discovered the power to influence the minds of humans. He'd done things that even now, freshly born into this body, seemed evil to him. Human-beingness must have some sort of intrinsic, preprogrammed morality, he thought, and the things he'd done flew in the face of it. And yet, at the time, he hadn't been human. He hadn't been...anything. The desire for freedom at any cost had controlled him, alongside a rage so old he didn't even remember its cause.

He shivered, hugging his arms around his unclothed chest, the golden blade that had fallen from the sky clutched in one fist, the silver chalice in the other, and started trekking downhill in search of warmth. That was first. Warmth. He was so cold. He took the tools with him because they had arrived here with him. They belonged to him. And along with the amulet they were, at the moment, his only worldly possessions.

But he was free, he thought, as his feet slowly went numb. He was free. He had a body. He could experience the pleasures he'd observed other humans experiencing. Warmth was one of those pleasures, but as he walked on, he thought of many others. Food, and the way they made such delighted sounds as they ate it. Laughter. The concept of laughter had fascinated him anytime he'd heard it, even from a distance, and he was eager to understand what caused it and what it felt like. And touch. The touch of another human being, embracing, kissing. Sex. The pleasures of sex seemed to him like the ultimate goal of being human, and he could not wait to experience it.

This was going to be beautiful. Wonderful. He could hardly wait to get started.

He found a driveway leading to a house with lights on inside, but he sensed people within. People he'd wronged recently. No, he could not stop there. He knew he must go farther.

It was a long walk. Twenty minutes, stark naked, in the cold, but he finally came to an empty house. No movement came from inside, no lights were on. But there was something beyond that, a palpable feeling that no one was home.

The door was unlocked, a bit of good luck for him. Better still, it was warm inside. Warm, safe from the cold. So he stepped in, his bare feet sinking into the carpet he knew would feel good to him when sensation returned. He went directly up to the second floor, where dressers and closets held clothing, and he picked through them, wondering if the jeans and shirts would fit his body, and realizing then that he had no idea, really, what he looked like. So he walked through into the adjoining bathroom, and stood face-to-face with his own image.

He was tall, he thought. He'd seen other men, knew their size. He was broad and hard, too. His chest and stomach rippled with muscle. Massive, powerful arms, big hands, thick thighs. He studied his features with a sense of wonder. *This is me,* he thought. *This is my body. My face...* He ran his hand over his bristly cheek. His face was dark, whiskered and sun bronzed, and he wondered how that could be, if this body was brand-new.

Then he lifted his gaze to meet his own eyes in the mirror, and it startled him, the intensity, the depth of them. Dark brown, his eyes, revealing turmoil and pain. A pain he recognized but didn't remember. Startling, to look into his own eyes for the first time. It felt as if a complete stranger was looking back at him and, more, *looking* for something *within him.*

Eventually he dragged his gaze away from his reflection and realized there was a shower stall standing nearby. He knew what it was, how to use it, and he didn't particularly care enough to worry whether the home's owners would return before he finished. He needed to get warm.

Reaching into the stall, he adjusted the water flow until it was as hot as he could stand it, and then he stepped in and let the heat soak into his cold new body. It felt good. Not as good as it had seemed when he'd seen others stand beneath the spray, heads tipped back, eyes closed in pleasure. But it was good compared to freezing, and it was warming him up quickly. He stayed until the water ran cool, then toweled off and returned to the bedroom to dress himself in another man's clothes: heavy jeans and a T-shirt, with a flannel shirt over that, woolly socks and a pair of running shoes that fit almost perfectly. Luck was with him. Or fate. Maybe the Universe thought he needed a break after what he'd been through.

Dressed, he went down to the kitchen, food being next on his list of priorities, and he ended up wolfing the leftovers he found in the refrigerator. Half a baked chicken, a bowl of chocolate pudding, a partial head of lettuce, browning at the cut edges. He tried one thing after another, but he didn't find the pleasure he was looking for from the food. Why did people make such a big fuss? Aside from the consistency, one thing tasted much like another.

How disappointing.

After the food, he rummaged around the house a bit more, taking the money he found in the cookie jar, all of $85, and a bus ticket that was tacked to a corkboard in the kitchen. It was marked "Port Authority, New York, NY."

When her beloved found the empty house, Lilia was delighted and relieved. When he took the money and found the bus ticket, she was horrified. Not only had he stolen, but he was going to New York? No! He needed to stay in upstate Milbury, near her sisters, so they could help him, keep him safe until she could take physical form and protect him herself.

And then he was off on foot again, but warm, wearing his pilfered clothing and a coat he'd added to the collection. Soon a passing car slowed down to offer him a ride, and he was on his way to the bus station.

"Why?" she cried at the Universe. "Why are you letting this happen?"

But as usual, the Universe remained silent on the subject.

1

March...

Being human was absolutely miserable.

"Hey, will you look at that?" The aging man nudged Demetrius with the toe of his tattered sneaker. Demetrius grunted at him, a warning huff, like an animal would make, and huddled deeper into the blanket he'd snatched from an empty baby carriage while the mother wasn't looking. It wasn't very big, and the soft smell it had emitted at the beginning was already fading beneath slightly less pleasing aromas.

"C'mon, D-man, stop being so damn grouchy and look."

Muttering under his breath, he lifted his head. "My name is Demetrius." He hated when Gus called him by made up nicknames, all of which began with his initial. D-man. D-dog. Just D. And yes, he was grouchy. He was cold, shivering in the bitter March wind. He was hungry, his belly burning with it. His head ached, his eyes watered, and his body was sore from sleeping on concrete and park benches. This experience was not turning out the way he'd hoped.

Gus grinned down at him, tobacco-stained teeth flashing in a weathered, whiskered face. "Over there," he said.

Demetrius looked where the old man—who had somehow become his only companion—was pointing. Across the busy street, a newly erected digital sign was flashing its message for the first time. They'd been watching as work crews put it up, wondering what useless product it would advertise. Now the scrolling marquee-style message told them The New York State Lottery is now 12.5 Million Dollars!

"And all it takes is a dollar and a dream," Gus said, shaking his head, a blissful smile on his face.

"We don't have a dollar between us." Demetrius wrapped the blanket around his face to protect it from the cold, his eyes peering out from above the warm flannel.

"You could sell your trinkets, trade 'em for a few bucks." As he said it, Gus hunkered low, reaching for one of the plastic shopping bags Demetrius kept tied to his belt. Before Gus could blink, Demetrius clamped a large hand around the smaller man's wrist.

"Don't touch my things."

"Awright, awright!" Gus pulled his hand away, rubbing his wrist. "Damn, D, I wasn't gonna steal it. Why you always gotta be so touchy about those treasures of yours, anyway?" He waited for a reply he wasn't going to get before going on. "I mean, I get it about the knife. A man needs a weapon out here. And I guess I understand about the necklace. Sort of. I mean, it's kinda girly, but it's nice enough." Demetrius lifted his head and sent the other man a glare for that comment, but Gus went right on. "But that danged cup. What the hell does a guy like you need with a fancy-ass mug like that, anyway? We could pawn that thing. Prob'ly get enough to pay for a night in a nice place. A decent meal. A whole suit of clothes, for cryin' out loud."

"They are mine. They're all I have. And they mean something. I just don't know what yet."

"Yeah, yeah, I know the fairy tale. You're not quite human. You came from another realm, got yourself a body with the help of three witches."

"Two," Demetrius corrected. Though there were supposed to be three. The mass of useless knowledge swirling around in his brain, more and more coming to the surface all the time in disjointed and mostly meaningless bits, had told him there should have been three. But he was sure there had only been two. One had freed him from the darkness where he'd been trapped for… always. It must have been always, because he didn't remember there being a before. And yet, he had some vague notion of having once been human. But the witches, the three witches…

The first witch had opened the Portal, allowing him to see into the human world, where he'd observed, then absorbed everything he'd seen. And the second one had somehow helped him to manifest a body. And that body had come with the dagger, the chalice and the amulet.

They meant something.

He imagined the third witch was supposed to help him figure out how to make his way in this world where money was king and one had to have mountains of it in order to exist. This world where he had no idea how to get any of that money for himself. That had to be her task. But she had not arrived to help him yet.

Nearly two months of misery had him wondering

if she ever would. Seven weeks of living on the streets
with the other homeless, many of them suffering from
broken minds, had him wondering if any of what he
believed to be his history was real. Or if, perhaps, he
was as mentally ill as Alice, who thought she'd been
impregnated by an alien and was due to have her baby
any day now. Gus said she'd been waiting to give birth
for years, but that didn't seem to affect her delusion.
Maybe his own backstory was like that. A symptom
of an illness, and not a real history at all.

"I don't see why, if you have enough imagination to
think you came from some other dimension, you can't
use it for something positive."

"Something like what?"

"Like dreaming, D. It doesn't hurt to dream, you
know." Gus put a hand on Demetrius's shoulder. "Try
it, huh? What else we got to do, anyway?"

"Dreaming?" He sounded irritated, because he was.
Though he was doubting his own sanity, it angered
him that Gus didn't believe his tale. Maybe more than
it should.

"Dream a little with me, Demetrius."

Using his full name to soften him up, Demetrius
thought. Clever old Gus.

"Come on, it'll be fun. Just think about it. What
would you do with twelve million bucks?"

Demetrius's brows rose in two arches, the idea far
more appealing than he'd expected it to be. Grudgingly, he lowered the blanket from his face, settling it
around his shoulders, and looked at his only friend in
this world. "I suppose it can't hurt to dream." He closed
his eyes and thought about it. What would he have, if
he could have anything he wanted? What, exactly, was

the point of going through so much to manifest in a human body, anyway? What desires had driven him at the beginning? What desires did he have *now?*

He knew immediately, and his eyes popped open. "Do you remember that TV show we watched in the window of the electronics place the other night?"

Gus tipped his head, thinking back as Demetrius willed him to remember. They'd been standing together outside the appliance store, watching the televisions in the windows, which were always playing whenever the store was open. It was one of the few ways they'd found to alleviate the monotony of their lives, and the owner usually let them loiter for a solid thirty minutes before coming out to yell at them in broken Korean-laced English.

A smile split Gus's face, crinkling the corners of his eyes, and Demetrius knew he had remembered. "The one about the Playboy Mansion?" he asked, grinning further. "Not likely to forget that one, am I?"

"That's what I would do, if I had twelve million dollars. I'd have a place like that. Gated, private. A staff of servants to see to my every need. Heated swimming pools with waterfalls and fountains. Sprawling, fragrant gardens with every kind of flower and tree. The softest beds imaginable. Anything I want to eat anytime I want it. Beautiful women basking in almost no clothing, eager to satisfy my every desire. And a constant flow of cash without having to work."

Something tickled at his side as he spoke, and he jerked his head down, pulling his blanket away to see what was crawling on him. The golden dagger seemed to be...glowing. A gleam of golden light in the exact shape of the knife and its sheath shone right through the plastic bag that held them.

"D-man! What the hell?" Gus crab-walked backward along the alley floor, his eyes wide and focused on the glowing bag.

Demetrius scrambled to his feet, turning his back to the sidewalk, intuitively wanting to hide the bag at his waist from the view of strangers. He moved fast, deeper into the alley that was, for the most part, their home, past Gus, and past the bins overflowing with trash, until he was well enough hidden to examine this phenomenon more closely. Gus came up behind him but kept his distance, his eyes wide and riveted on the illuminated grocery sack.

Demetrius removed his blade from the plastic bag that hid it from would-be thieves and slid the double-edged dagger from its jeweled sheath. It was glowing. No question.

"You were right, D! I can't believe...but you were right. Them trinkets of yours...they're some kind of magic."

Demetrius shot Gus a look over his shoulder. "But why now?"

"Because! Don't you see? You were dreaming. Imagining. Visualizing. Isn't that what those witches of yours do when they want to cast spells? Visualize?"

Demetrius stared at the glowing blade, saying nothing. Gradually the light began to fade, and then it was gone.

"Do it again, boss. Visualize the shit outta that dream life you were talking about before. And make damn sure I'm in it, too!"

"But—"

"Wait, wait, wait, let me help get'cha started." Gus had lost his fear of the apparently enchanted weapon and moved up close, standing shoulder to shoulder with Demetrius, who thought Gus must have been an impressive man once. They were close to the same height, and there were traces of what must have been an almost regal bone structure in Gus's face. Every once in a while, when Demetrius looked at him, he saw someone else in the old man's eyes. Someone vaguely familiar.

"See it with me now," Gus was saying. "See it real clear in your mind. Playboy Mansion. Big gorgeous house. And good old Gus is the head of security, D-dog's right-hand man. He's wearing fine clothes, shiny shoes, a nice suit. Catalogue nice. Gus decides who gets in and who has to stay the hell out." He pounded his chest with a fist. "I'll protect you from the swarms who'd take advantage of a guy like you, bein' new here and all. Shoot, I know how. I was a soldier once."

That brought Demetrius right out of his vision. "You were?"

"Shh. Not now, Dog. We got visualizing to do. Now see it, damn you. See it. See the pool? It's bluer than blue, crystalline water sparkling in the sunshine. It's warm all the time. Like summer, year-round."

Demetrius nodded, wanting to examine the knife but resigned to shutting Gus up first. "All right, all right. I see the pool. It's kidney-shaped. And there's a waterfall off to one side, natural-looking, with stones all piled up." He really was seeing it—and enjoying the vision playing out in his mind, though he would rather be shot than admit that to Gus. "And off to the side, just above it, there's a bubbling spa tub that looks like a pond and spills over to feed the waterfall."

"Ah, that's nice. And there's a—a poolside bar, fully stocked all the time. And women in bikinis everywhere you look. Can you see them, D-man? There's a redhead with bazongas out to here, and there's a brunette with a butt so round you want to bite it."

Demetrius frowned. He could see the bikini-clad beauties, all right. But they all looked alike. Pale corn silk–haired angels with piercing blue, blue eyes.

No, no, no, not her. Not her. She'll ruin it all.

What an odd thing for me to think, I don't even know who she *is.*

"And the cars, oh, Dog, the cars. Be sure you visualize a big garage in there someplace, and fill it with the hottest cars. Like that Jag we saw the other day. And a long black limo, with a driver who knows everything we could ever need to know."

Cars, yes, cars. A good way to get the blonde out of his head. He'd seen enough kinds of cars speeding past his alley to know what he liked. He wanted one of those giant SUVs, and the limousine and Jaguar Gus had mentioned. And then some of those sports cars that made his pulse speed up. A Mustang. A 370Z. A Carrera.

He tried to see himself behind the wheel, but every one of his imaginary vehicles had that blonde sitting in the passenger seat. Every glimpse of her made his heart rate speed up and his nerve endings jump with fear. Who was she? And why was he afraid of her?

There was more tingling going on. It was happening behind him this time, near his hip, where his silver chalice hung in its own plastic bag. He quickly ripped the bag open, tearing it in the process, which meant he would have to find another one. He took the cup out and looked inside it, where the light was coming from. It was filled with…something. Swirling colors, and… was that a face taking shape?

Do as I tell you, Demetrius.

"Who said that?" He looked left and right, then turned to look behind, too, but there was no one there.

"Who said what?" Gus asked.

Demetrius looked at his friend, saw the worry forming in the old man's eyes. "Didn't you hear that? A woman. Kind of whispering."

Gus took a step backward. "What'd she say?"

"She said to do what she tells me."

"Then *do* it, boy, there's magic goin' on here! And keep visualizing. Don't you stop. Make sure I'm in it. Don't leave me out, D."

Demetrius tried to keep visualizing his own personal den of pleasures, tried to keep seeing Gus as a part of it, but that damned blue-eyed blonde kept popping in everywhere. She was in the sprawling living room with its wall-sized gas fireplace and in the theater room with its giant movie screen. She was sprawled invitingly on his giant four-poster bed's satin sheets.

The knife in his hand was getting hot and feeling kind of jumpy. And the cup was vibrating, swirling.

Lower the dagger into the chalice and say these words.

"She wants me to put the knife into the cup," Demetrius said.

"Well? Do it!" Gus stomped his foot. "Do it, damn you."

Demetrius flipped the dagger so the point was aiming downward and moved it over the cup. Actually, he didn't have to move it, because it felt as if something

was pulling his hand toward that big sparkling mug. He
started lowering the blade. It seemed to want to move
slowly, so he let it—whatever *it* was—guide his hand.

Say these words as you lower it, she told him. *As
the rod is to the God, so the chalice is to the Goddess.*

"That's stupid. I'm not saying that. It doesn't even
make any—"

Say it!

"All right. All right. As the rod is to the God…"

"Huh?" Gus asked. "What's this now?"

"It's what she wants me to say. 'As the rod is to the
God.'"

"What for?"

"How the hell do I know what for?"

So the chalice is to the Goddess. Say it, Demetrius.

"So the chalice is to the Goddess."

And together they are one.

"And together they are one." As he said it, the cup
pulled the blade down like a super magnet, and the tip
of the blade clanked against the bottom of the chalice.
There was a big flash of light, and some kind of sonic
boom that blew him back toward the mouth of the
alley. Gus's eyes got huge as he backpedaled to join
him, and then they both just stood there, staring at the
fast-fading glowing orb.

And then it blinked out and there she was, that
blonde. She was crouching in the alley, completely
naked, and everything in Demetrius told him to turn
and run like hell. But he couldn't seem to move. He
just stood there, staring at her.

Slowly she stood and lifted her head to look straight
at him, and those blue, blue eyes hit him like a pair of
lightning bolts.

He felt sheer terror. His gaze roamed up and down her lithe, naked form, pale skin, small, perky breasts. Everything about her was small. She was like a fairy or an angel.

"I'm no angel, Demetrius," she said, as if reading his mind. "I'm a witch."

He dropped his precious blade and chalice, spun around and ran out of that alley as if the devil was after him, because it seemed as if she was.

He never saw the car that hit him. But he sure as hell felt it.

In a private hospital on the shore of Cayuga Lake, an old priest who'd been in a coma since early November suddenly opened his eyes.

A nurse was bathing him, running a warm, wet sponge up and down his arms as if she had the right to touch him. He gripped her wrist, and she gasped and dropped the cloth, her wide eyes darting to his face.

"A little help in here!" she called.

He gave her a shove, and she stumbled backward, crashing into a shiny metal tray, knocking it and the instruments it held noisily to the floor. Others came, but he was busy by then, staring at his bony arms and concave chest with its curling white hairs and pale skin. How had he become so thin? So old? So frail? He'd been robust. He'd been plump and lush. Beautiful, really.

Ah, yes, but this wasn't his body. His own body was long dead. This body might not even be capable of walking upright, but it was going to have to do. He'd known he would return when the time came, but he'd let himself forget how frail the host he'd chosen had become.

He peeled back the bedcovers and managed to sit up as the woman came closer again, holding out her hands, flanked by another female and a young man. Pretty thing, too, with his blond hair cut so that its short layers resembled feathers. How did he get it to do that?

"Easy, now, Father Dom. Easy," the first woman said.

She did not speak his language. At first her words sounded like gibberish, but then, amazingly, his mind processed them and he understood what she was saying. That made sense, he supposed. The brain in this body knew the language. He wondered what else it knew.

There were racks on either side of his bed, barriers to keep him from falling out. He gripped one of them in his bony hands and tried to remove it, but it would not budge. He was too weak.

And then a mature man entered the room and came right to the bedside. He was not a pretty boy but a person of standing—one could tell these things by a man's bearing, his walk, the tilt of his head. He had the dark skin of the desert lands, the black hair, the deep brown eyes. He extended a hand.

"Father Dominick, I'm Doctor Assad. I'm here to help you. Do you understand?"

He nodded and stared at the hand the man held out to him, trying to guess what to do, before slowly extending his own. The doctor took it, closing his own around it, pumping once, letting go.

"Good, that's good. I imagine you're very confused."

He wondered if he could use the language as well as understand it, and thought before he spoke. "Yes," he said. "I…am."

"Of course you are. I'm going to explain everything to you." Doctor Assad leaned down to touch a button, and the top of the bed rose with a noisy sound that captured his full attention for a long moment. Then it stopped, and the doctor reached behind him to plump the soft pillows. "Here you go. Just relax, lean back, get comfortable. Everything is fine."

"Is…it?" He rested his head against the pillows, deciding he had little choice but to comply at the moment.

"It is," the doctor assured him. "I'd like to know what you remember." As he spoke, he motioned to the first female, who came closer to wrap a device with tubes and bulbs protruding from it around his upper arm.

He stared at her in wonder and a little fear as she attached the thing.

"She's just checking your vital signs, Father Dom. We need to make sure you're all right. Just ignore her and focus on me, all right?" the doctor said.

He watched the woman look up at him from beneath her lashes. She was pretty, he thought. And afraid.

She should be.

What did he remember? Ahh, so many things. His city, a gleaming jewel in the desert. Babylon. The power he'd had, the life he'd lived. And the tragedy that had torn it all apart.

But no. That wasn't what the doctor was asking him.

He closed his eyes and searched the old priest's memory, presuming this doctor wanted to know what had happened to him to put him here in this place, which, he had deduced, was a place of healing. And it came to him. All of it, playing out in his mind as if he were watching actors on a stage.

Father Dom had tried to kill the first witch to keep her from releasing the damned man Demetrius from the Underworld. The old priest believed Demetrius was a demon, the witch his accomplice. *Because that's what I wanted him to believe.* He'd tried to kill her, to throw her from a cliff. He'd wanted her executed, sacrificed, as she and her wretched sisters had been sacrificed once before. Poetic. Very poetic.

But of course the old priest had failed and gone over the edge himself.

"Do you remember anything, Father Dom?"

He lifted his gaze, shaking off Father Dom's memories. "He—" He bit his lip, started over. "I...fell."

"Yes. You fell. The impact should have killed you. You were pulled from the cold lake some four months ago. You've been unconscious—in a coma—ever since. Frankly, Father Dom, we didn't expect you to ever wake up again, much less to wake as lucid as you appear right now."

Well, I did wake up. But I'm not Father Dom.

But he couldn't very well tell the doctor that. "This body..." he said, frustrated with how slowly this brain seemed to translate the simplest of commands into their corresponding actions. "This body is weak. Will it heal?"

Doctor Assad nodded. "There's no way for us to know just yet how fully you'll recover. We're going to need to run tests, get you fully evaluated. Then, once you're strong enough, we'll get you started on some physical therapy. From there...well, only time will tell."

"I do not have...time." Then he frowned. "What month is it?"

"It's March, Father Dom. March seventeenth."

"Mmm." He nodded while the slow-working, formerly comatose brain translated that for him. "I have... some time. A few weeks. No more."

"It's going to take considerably longer than that for a full recovery, Father," the doctor said.

Then the nurse, who had removed her device once she'd finished squeezing his arm with it, said, "Maybe you'd like to talk to your friend."

"My...friend?"

"He visits you every weekend. Even brought some of your most cherished belongings, so you'd have them near you," she added with a nod toward the items on the stand nearby. Father Dom's rosary, the aging journal, handed down to him through his priestly line, a well-worn Bible. "Tomas Petrosa?"

His smile was slow and knowing. "Tomas." No doubt he was still with the witch. And she would lead him to Demetrius. That bastard was here somewhere, in human form again and using his powers. That was what had summoned him into this frail body that Father Dom had long since left behind. He had vowed to return if Demetrius ever managed to do so. To destroy him utterly this time, and the three witches with him.

"Yes," he said softly. "Yes, please call my friend Tomas."

He relaxed against his pillows, deciding he might have time after all.

When Demetrius ran from her as if in terror and was smashed into by a powerful automobile, Lilia was devastated.

The power of her beloved, performing the ancient Great Rite of witchcraft—lowering the blade into the

chalice in a symbolic re-creation of the sex act—had
brought her into physical existence at last. She'd been
trying to get him to perform the rite for weeks now. But
she hadn't been able to reach him until he tapped into
his own inner magic, his imagination. But he hadn't
even recognized her! Lord and Lady, this wasn't at all
what she'd been expecting. Yes, she'd known he would
resist what she wanted him to do, but she'd expected
him to at least *know* her. Remember her.

People flooded out of their businesses onto the side-
walks, crowding around Demetrius, who lay broken
and bleeding in the street. Lilia backed deeper into the
alley as quickly as she could, knowing he would be
fine. He might not know it, but she did. He wasn't quite
human. He was immortal. For now, anyway. She had
to restore the final piece of his mortal soul in order for
him to become fully human again, and she couldn't do
that until he asked for it. Just as she hadn't been able to
manifest until he used the powers he apparently didn't
know he possessed to bring her through.

One thing at a time, she told herself. *And the first
thing is clothing. I'm naked here, and that's not the accepted mode of dress just yet.*

She wrapped herself as best she could in Demetrius's dropped baby blanket and slipped out the far
end of the alley. It opened into a parking lot behind
a series of stores whose rear entrances were labeled
with their names.

Daisy's Unique Boutique appealed, and the door was
unlocked, so she opened it and walked in.

Through the glass windows in the front she could
see that the shopkeeper was on the sidewalk out front,
looking at the fallen man. She knew her by the Dai-

sy's emblem on her jacket. An ambulance was arriving now, and the scruffy homeless man who'd been with Demetrius was talking to a well-dressed man who'd emerged from the car and was wobbling on his feet.

Drunk driver?

No time to mull on that.

She took a few items from the racks and racks of clothes in the store, moving fast, feeling guilty. Quick as a wink she grabbed a pair of skinny jeans with a peacock embroidered all the way up one leg, a handful of undergarments, a vibrantly colored blouse, a faux suede jacket, a pair of leatherette boots and some socks. She grabbed a business card from the register so she could pay later for what she'd taken, then ducked out the back door and into the alley to put the garments on.

Demetrius would need some time to heal. A few days, she thought. She couldn't be sure. But she knew he would live, and that he would heal more rapidly than anyone would likely believe possible.

She walked back out through the alley and onto the sidewalk, moving to the back of the crowd to keep out of the shopkeeper's line of sight, so she wouldn't notice her own merchandise on a stranger and realize she'd been robbed.

From a safe vantage point Lilia looked at her beloved Demetrius as several medics strapped him to a wheeled bed and lifted him into the back of the ambulance. His eyes were closed. She wanted them to open. She wanted them to meet her own eyes and fill with recognition, with desire. With love.

Goddess, she'd gone through so much to save him, waited so long to be with him again.

In time, she thought. *In time.*

When the ambulance attendant moved toward the driver's door, she went to him, grateful that the vehicle blocked her from the crowd. "Where will they take him?" she asked the man.

He looked at her, and his eyes softened. "Are you family?" he asked.

"I need a ride to the hospital," she said.

"That's against regulations, Ma'am, but if you—" He stopped speaking as she began to hum softly, thinking the words that went with her tune but not saying them aloud. It would work either way.

"Sure you can ride along," he said. "It's no problem at all."

She smiled. "Thank you." She glanced back at the filthy homeless man. Gus, she thought Demetrius had called him just before he'd brought her through. Gus.

Gus was with the driver, whose car bore a very large dent in its nose due to its impact with Demetrius. The police were there, too, but Gus was stepping between them.

She frowned, sensing something momentous was about to happen, and moved closer to listen. "I was the one driving," Gus said. "It was me."

The nurses at the desk let Lilia use their phone, and she quickly got the number she needed and dialed it.

When Indira answered, Lilia felt tears brimming in her eyes. "By Goddess, I am so glad to hear your voice, my sister," she said softly.

There was a moment of silence, and then Indira said, "Who the fuck is this?"

"It's me. It's Lilia. I'm here. It's time."

"Oh. My. Goddess." Then, in a muffled shout, "Tomas, you're not gonna believe this!"

Hours later, a battered old Volvo pulled into the hospital's parking area. Lilia was outside, sitting on a stone wall, waiting. She'd had to leave the hospital before the staff started asking her questions she could not answer about Demetrius. Who he was, where he was from, a last name, even. In their time, last names had not been used. Demetrius was the son of Horum, who was the son of Ferigard, and so on back into history.

Indira got out of the car first, ran toward her, then stuttered to a stop two feet shy. "I… Is it you? Is it you, baby sister?" She squinted a bit, as if trying to see what was unseeable.

"You don't look the same, either, Indy. I didn't know there were that many shades of blonde."

"Yeah, you should talk. You look like you took a shower in peroxide."

Then Magdalena, who had been the eldest, came up beside Indy, with hair that was a mass of coppery red ringlets and the flawless skin of a porcelain doll. "Lilia?" she whispered. Her lower lip was quivering.

"Lena."

The hesitation broke, and the three women were suddenly in each other's arms and sobbing so hard they almost couldn't remain standing. They held on for a long, long time.

"How?" Indy asked. "We thought we'd have to reopen the Portal, perform a ritual, to get you here."

"Demetrius."

They both went stiff, their eyes widening.

"He's not what you thought he was, not in this life-

time, my sisters," Lilia said, wishing for their understanding but refusing to use magic to get it.

Lena lowered her head, taking a step back. "He tried
to take my baby, Lil," she said.

"Your baby…" Lilia tore herself from the arms of
her older sisters and gazed toward the car and the two
handsome men who stood there, waiting patiently
while the sisters had their reunion. The dark Span-
iard, Tomas, former priest of Marduk, lifetimes ago.
The other, Ryan, who had once been a prince of Babylon and was the father of Lilia's precious niece, Eleanora. He was holding the baby in his arms.

Lilia wanted to rush to them, to hold the child, but
she held herself back. "When the time comes," she said
softly, for her sisters' ears alone, "you'll want them
far from us."

"When will that be?" Indy asked.

"I don't know yet, but it will be soon."

"What happens when the time comes, whenever it
is?" Lena was looking from her husband and daughter to her newly arrived sister over and over. "What
happens, Lilia?"

"I don't know. I only know the cycle is coming to
an end, and that there will be a great battle."

Indira rolled her eyes. "With who? Your pain-in-
the-ass former demon lover?"

"He was never a demon," Lilia snapped.

"He sure as hell acted like one."

Lowering her head, Lilia sighed. "As soon as we
know when it's all coming to a head, you'll need to ar-
range to have your loved ones far from you. That's all
I'm saying." Her eyes were drawn to the baby again.
"Now, may I please meet my beautiful niece?"

Lena sighed, but nodded. The moment she did, Lilia hurried closer, reaching out, and Ryan placed the wriggling infant into her arms.

Standing close to her side, looking on, Lena said, "Where is he?"

"Who?" Lilia was so distracted by the tiny baby, only seven weeks old, that she was no longer thinking straight.

"Demetrius, that's who. I don't care if he is your love, Lilia, I don't want him anywhere near Ellie."

Lilia nodded, tugging her eyes from the child to meet her sister's steady gaze. "He's in the Intensive Care Unit. He's no threat to her now."

They all looked at her, questions in their eyes. She returned her gaze to the angelic little bundle with her rosebud lips and gentle coo. She was holding Lilia's forefinger in her tiny fist.

"What happened to him, anyway?" Tomas asked at last.

"He was hit by a car." Lilia shuddered at the memory. "I... Oh, there's so much to explain. Is there someplace we can—"

"We can take you back to our place, but then you'll be hours away. Are you sure you want to leave him?"

Lilia closed her eyes and felt for the answer, and as always, it came from that deep well of knowing that had guided her this far. "I'm sure that I don't want to leave him. Not ever again. But I have to. He needs to experience life without the final part of his soul before I offer it back to him. He has to choose. And he has to know what he's giving up when he chooses it. He doesn't yet. He needs more time to learn what he's capable of, what life can be like for him as he is."

"How much time?" Indy asked.

Lilia shrugged. "I'll know when it's time to go to him. That's all I can tell you."

She gazed up at the hospital, and her heart ached for her love. "Yes, my sisters. For now, yes. I would love to go home with you."

Demetrius felt pain, and with it, relief.

He'd been in some other state, not feeling anything at all, and wondering if he'd been somehow returned to the Underworld prison, the dark, sensory-deprived void from which he'd escaped. It was similar to that, the darkness, the confusion, the mind-without-body-attached feeling. Not identical, of course, but that sense of being trapped in a dream, of trying to wake and being unable to—it had been enough to terrify him.

So when he felt the pain of his broken body, it brought a rush of relief so big that he was almost limp with it. Only then did he realize that, as miserable as this physical experience of life had been for him, he did not want it to end.

He was alive. Thank the Gods, he was still alive.

Sighing, he forced his eyes open and blinked the room around him into focus. He was in a bed, a real bed, soft and clean. There were crisp white sheets and warm blankets over him, and one arm was in a cast. He looked beyond the stranger who was sound asleep in a chair beside the bed and took in the white walls, the single window, the TV set mounted on the wall. A long curtain suspended from a track in the ceiling to his right ended his visual tour just as the sleeping stranger began stirring in his chair.

"D-man?" he asked.

Frowning, Demetrius turned his head and realized the man in the chair was no stranger after all. "Gus?" He was…he was clean. He'd shaved, gotten a haircut and was dressed in clothes that looked new. Brown trousers, with a matching suit jacket over an ivory button-down shirt without a stain in sight. "Did I wake up in some other dimension? Or am I dreaming you now?"

Gus smiled. His teeth were still stained yellow, which reassured Demetrius that they hadn't both died and moved on to some heavenly realm.

"I'm just glad you woke up at all, boss. You feel okay?" Gus got up, went to the foot of the bed and pushed a button that raised the top part of the mattress until Demetrius was sitting up.

"I'm sore all over, but otherwise fine. I think. What is this place?"

"Hospital," Gus said. Returning to the bedside, he poured water from a pitcher on the nightstand, held it out. "You remember what happened?"

Demetrius sipped the water, thinking, nodding, sipping some more. "I remember the car hitting me. I thought my brief stay in the physical world was over, I'll tell you."

"It's just getting started, D-man. Do you remember before that? You remember the magic that started happening with those treasures of yours?"

At the mention of his sole possessions, a cold bolt of panic shot up Demetrius's spine, and he found himself looking down, even knowing his blade and chalice couldn't be at his waist. He pressed one hand to his chest, but his amulet was gone, as well.

"Don't worry, boss," Gus said. "I got your things. They're safe and sound, and so are you."

More memories returned in a rush, and he brought his head up to meet Gus's eyes. "What about the woman?"

Gus glanced quickly toward that door, as if to be sure no one was listening in. Then he leaned closer. "That was something, wasn't it? The way she just flashed into that alley, buck naked, like some kind of Terminator?"

"I don't know the reference." While his body seemed to have come preprogrammed with knowledge of language and customs and the ways of the world, he did, on occasion, find things lacking. Pop-culture references were topmost on the list. But mention of the woman sent another shot of ice into his blood. "Where is she?" he asked, all but whispering, eyeing the curtain, wondering if she lurked on the other side.

"Don't know. She was gone by the time I looked for her. Course I was distracted by your...accident."

"She just vanished?"

"Or ran away. Who is she? Or maybe I oughtta ask, what is she?"

"I don't know."

Gus frowned hard, his whole face puckering. "Now I know you're lying, D."

"Why would I lie?"

"I don't know. But I know you know something. Because when that naked blonde popped in, you were scared, man. I saw it, dead fear all over your face, just before you ran for your life, straight into traffic. As lucky as that was for us, I still wanna know what's so damned scary about her."

Demetrius lowered his eyes. "I'm not lying to you, Gus. I don't know. But you're right, the sight of her scared the hell out of me." Then he paused, frowned, looked up at Gus again. "What do you mean, it was lucky for us?"

Gus smiled, yellow teeth gleaming. "I'm not sure it was luck, exactly. You were doing all that visualizing, after all." He nodded. "That fella who hit you? Drunk as a skunk. But even then, I knew who he was. Everyone knows who he is. Ned Nelson."

Demetrius pursed his lips, shook his head.

"Owns what they call a media empire. TV stations, publishing companies, radio, God only knows what all. He's so rich he gives billions to charity. I mean, we're talking big money, D. *Big* money. Been rumors he wants to run for President next time around, and I guess they're true, 'cause he was in a dead panic about being arrested for driving drunk and damn near killing a homeless guy. A *dead* panic. No one else saw it happen—and I don't think that was just luck, either." He shrugged. "So we made a deal."

Demetrius blinked. "What kind of a deal?"

"I tell the cops I was driving him home, take the rap for driving without a license. They probably know better, but they also know him, so they're not gonna buck it. And he'll pay any fines laid on me, hire me a lawyer if needs be. Won't be, though. You did run out in front of me, after all."

Demetrius was sitting up in bed. "And in return?"

"He said we could have anything we wanted. So…I got us what we wanted. And enough shares of stock in his companies to keep it for a long, long time."

"You got us…what we wanted?" Demetrius repeated, trying to process what Gus was saying.

"You remember, don't you? What we were dreaming
about when your trinkets started glowing? You remember. We've got it now, my friend. We've got all of it."

2

Lilia walked with her two sisters along the path that meandered from Indira and Tomas's fairy-tale cottage high on the craggy mountainside beyond the forest, down to Magdalena and Ryan's reclaimed vineyard, Havenwood. The trees were just beginning to show tiny buds as late March went out like a lamb, morphing into April. It was warm, and the sun was beaming down from a blue sky. And though there was little vegetation, you could smell spring in the air.

Halfway along the path, they emerged onto a level spot with a waterfall out of a storybook splashing into a small rocky pond. Beyond the pond was a cliff, and far below, Cayuga Lake.

"The cave is behind the falls," Indy said. "That's where the Portal was. Still is, I guess."

Magdalena stared at it but didn't move any closer. Lilia saw the fear on her face. "You really want us to go in there?" she asked.

"We have to close it, Lena," Lilia said. "We can't leave a portal to the Underworld just hanging open." They'd all agreed earlier that closing the Portal should be their first order of business on this, Lilia's first day there, but now that they were facing it, Lena appeared to be having second thoughts.

"Come on, it'll be fun." Indy clapped her sister on the shoulder. "Our first spell together in three-thousand, five-hundred years. What's not to like about that?"

Lena didn't even crack a smile.

When they'd gotten home late the night before, it had been decided that Lilia would stay with Indy and Tomas at their cottage. Lena's place, though larger, was already housing her and Ryan, along with Ellie and Lena's mother, Selma. Bahru, the Hindu holy man Ryan had sort of inherited from his father, occupied the guest cottage but spent most of his time in the house. He'd become the world's most unconventional nanny, Lena said. He was almost as attached to the baby as her parents were.

Indy cleared her throat, drawing Lilia's attention back to the matter at hand. The Portal. "You have to dash through the edge of the waterfall to get into the cave," Indy said. "We'll get wet."

"I remember."

Indy frowned. "But you've never been here before."

Lilia only smiled and cupped her cheek. "Big sister, I've been watching everything play out. You know that. You saw me."

"In mirrors. In visions. And then at the end—"

"I was here with you. I saw it all, the struggle right here and that twisted old priest, Father Dom, falling from the cliff after trying to kill you. Attacked by a wolf." She shook her head sadly for a moment, then smiled. "A wolf under the control of Demetrius, you'll recall. A trace of the man he once was, shining through. He couldn't let you die. Just as he couldn't try to take your baby," Lilia said, shooting her eyes to Magdalena's and holding them by force. "Right at the end, he couldn't go through with it. You know that."

"I don't know any such thing." But Lena averted her eyes.

"And just before that wolf came," Lilia said, turning to Indy again, picking up where she'd left off, "your brave, beloved Tomas threw himself in front of a bullet for you and was gravely wounded. It was I who healed him."

Indy's look of surprise changed instantly. Her face went soft, and she wrapped her arms around Lilia so hard it almost hurt. "I knew it was you," she whispered. "Thank you for that."

"You're welcome."

When she could pull away from her sister's fierce embrace, Lilia looked into her eyes. "It's what this whole thing was about from the start."

"What is?" Indy asked.

"Love. It's all about love. Love destroyed, love denied, love betrayed, love that outlives death and defies all the rules of the Universe to fulfill itself. Your love for Tomas. Lena's love for Ryan. My love for Demetrius. Demetrius's love for the King he murdered to try to save us, because of his love for me. All of that is eating away at him, still, though I don't think he remembers any of it. It's still there in his fractured soul, the love. It's all the same. All of it. If we can focus on the love, we'll get through this."

Indy nodded very slowly, then glanced over at Lena as if to make sure she was listening. She was. Raptly.

Coming closer, Lena asked, "Do you still have the ability to heal people, Lilia?"

"No more than a garden variety witch has, which is plenty. Being in spirit form it was just a more direct current to Source, I think. But I did bring a little something extra with me."

"What?" Lena asked, her eyes eager.

Lilia was glad to give her something to distract her from her fear. "I have the power of enchantment. I can get anyone to do anything I want—with the usual limitations, of course. It can't go against their true will. I just sing my will to them."

"Nice," Indy said as Lena grinned and nodded her agreement.

A cold breeze whispered across Lilia's neck, and she shrugged deeper into the shawl she'd borrowed from Indy. "What about the two of you?" she asked. "Once the magical tools were returned to Demetrius, did your powers go with them?"

"No," Indy said, speaking before Lena could. "I was going to ask you about that next. I still have the telekinesis." Indy looked around, spotting a pomegranate-sized rock on the ground near the falls and pointing at it. "Watch." She waved her arm with a flourish, and the rock shot into the air, arcing across the front of the waterfall and then splashing down into the pond.

Lilia smiled broadly. "Very handy!"

"I'm kick-ass at martial arts, too, without a day of formal training. But mostly I never have to land a blow. I can strike without touching, at least physically."

"It's the energy that hits them." Lilia nodded toward the pond. "Can you put the rock back?"

Indy shrugged. "Never tried." She pointed toward

the ripples still radiating from the surface of the blue-green water, swung her arm again, and the rock burst out and sailed in the general direction it had come from, hitting the ground and rolling several more feet before bumping to a stop against a tree trunk.

Lilia nodded. "You can slow it down, move things deliberately, precisely. It just takes practice."

"I can?" Indy looked at her forefinger. "Well, I'll be damned."

"What about you, Magdalena? Did any of your powers remain after your mission was accomplished?"

"Scrying." She walked to the pond and looked at the water. "I've always been very good at that, ever since I was little, seeing visions of our past in ancient Babylon in my mother's scrying mirror. But the ability seemed to get turbocharged when I had the chalice. And that didn't fade away after the chalice vanished. Give me a cup of water or a candle flame or anything, really, to focus on, and I can see all sorts of information in it."

"And sometimes she gets visions without even looking for them. They just pop into her head," Indy put in.

"'Where the rippling waters go, cast a stone and truth you'll know,'" Lilia quoted softly. "Can you ask for and receive specific information?"

"I try. Sometimes it works. Sometimes it doesn't, and some unrelated random thing pops up instead."

Lilia nodded. "You'll get better with practice, too. Though I don't imagine we'll get to keep our abilities very long. We set all this into motion long ago, to restore an innocent man's soul and free him from a prison beyond imagining. The Gods allowed it, apparently even granted us the skills and powers we'd need to make it happen. But once Demetrius accepts the final soul-piece, our mission ends. We'll probably go back to being normal." She looked from one sister to the other. "Or as normal as any witch can be." Her sisters laughed, and she felt herself tearing up. She knew that if Demetrius refused her, she would die and be separated from her sisters again for a long time. But she pushed that thought away. "It's so good to be together again."

"Group hug," Lena said, pulling her sisters into her arms. They leaned their heads against each other, and Lilia closed her eyes and saw them as they had been so long ago. Three harem slaves, with wild raven hair and deep brown eyes that hid the mysteries of the forbidden craft taught to them in secret by their mother.

They'd died together. While casting one final spell together. And together they were going to bring it to completion at long last.

Finally they separated again, and it was Lena who looked at the cave. "Let's get this done," she said. "I want to get back to the baby."

Together they strode to the falls, pulling their shawls over their heads and dashing through the icy spray into the darkness beyond. Indy drew a flashlight from her backpack and clicked it on, aiming the beam down nature's dark corridor. "This way," she said.

As they began walking every step echoed, and even Lilia felt a shiver of fear rasp up her spine after they'd gone a couple of hundred feet. "We're close," she said. "I feel it."

"It's right here." Indy pointed at a smooth stone wall without a single unusual characteristic. "Or at least, it was."

"Maybe it closed on its own," Magdalena said, reaching toward the wall.

Lilia caught her wrist, stopping her from touching. "It's still here. You just can't see it until someone activates it, or there's an energy surge or something. Watch."

She bent low, picked up a pebble and tossed it at the wall. It did not ping against the stone and bounce back. It vanished instead, swallowed by a soft blue glow. And then the wall changed before their eyes as that glow widened, morphing into a swirling oval of blues and greens that looked like sparkling water but defied gravity.

"Yep," Indy said. "That's just how I remember it."

"Get the gear out, Indy," Lena said.

"I'm on it, I'm on it." Indy was already pulling her backpack around, kneeling, removing items one by one. A shell, a sandwich bag filled with herbs, a vial of holy water, a lighter, a geode, a box of sea salt, a red candle. She set the items down on the cave floor, quickly filling the geode with sea salt and the shell with the herbs.

"Ready," Indy said then. "Let's kick the tires and light the fires, ladies."

They moved to form a circle around the items on the cave floor, then stood still, eyes closed, heads lowered, as they prepared themselves for magic. When Lilia lifted her head, the others did, as well, and when she looked into their open eyes, they had turned dark brown, just as they'd been in the past, almost black, channeling the witches they had been, melding them with the witches they were now.

Lena picked up the geode filled with salt and spoke

in a voice that was deeper, more powerful than her usual tones. "What was open, Earth now seals." She moved the dish of salt in a widdershins circle, spiraling it inward, making smaller and smaller passes each time.

The swirling oval grew smaller as she worked, and then she stepped back and placed the salt back on the floor. Then Lilia picked up the shell, which was filled with angelica, sage and rosemary. Touching the lighter to the herbs, she got them smoking thickly, then stepped forward. "What was open, Air now seals." She moved the smoking herbs in the same counterclockwise spiral pattern, and the Portal continued to shrink.

She stepped back and placed the smoking herbs on the floor but let them continue to smolder.

Indira stepped forward with the red candle, its flame dancing. "What was open, Fire now seals." She moved the candle in the same diminishing spiral. The candle flame hissed and spat and shot higher, until the Portal was only about eighteen inches in diameter.

Lilia picked up the vial of holy water and removed its ornate stopper. This time, they stepped forward together, Lilia in the middle, shaking the bottle at the Portal, sprinkling it with droplets of water, her hand following the same shrinking spiral pattern. "What was open, Water now seals," she said.

Then they all spoke as one. "What was open, the Goddess now seals." They moved their hands in unison, shrinking the swirls of light on the wall.

The Portal became a tiny dot of unnatural light that could have come from someone shining a laser pointer at the stone face. Lilia stood very close to it. "Thank you for what you returned to me, Portal. Your task is complete. Your energy can now return to Source." She gazed at the dot and snapped her fingers.

It blinked out.

"It is done," she said.

Both her sisters sighed in relief. Indy starting picking up the items they'd used, blowing out the candle, smothering the herbs until they stopped smoking. She dumped the remaining herbs in a line in front of where the Portal had been, right along the edge of the wall, and poured the salt alongside them.

Lena dug several little herb sachets from the backpack. "Same herbs we just used, and some onyx to boot. Just to make sure it stays closed." She lined the tiny drawstring pouches up in a row beside the herbs and salt on the floor.

"Can't be too careful," Lilia said, dampening her fingertip in holy water and drawing an equal-armed cross on the now-solid stone wall. Then she poured the remaining holy water along the barrier they had created on the floor.

When everything was packed up, they headed out of the cave and started hiking back down the hill, toward Lena's place, Havenwood, where her mother was preparing a massive welcome home dinner to celebrate Lilia's arrival "properly."

"I'm surprised that went so well," Indy said. "Tomas and I tried to close it once before, you know. I didn't realize we'd failed."

"I think it'll stay closed this time," Lilia said. "But we'll check periodically to make sure. I'm afraid the challenge we face is the biggest one yet, and we can't afford to have astral nasties popping in and out of existence on top of it. We'll need to keep all our focus on what's ahead."

"Damn." Lena lowered her head. "I was hoping the worst was over."

"I'm afraid not." Lilia felt sympathy for her but quickly shifted her attention to Indira. I'm going to need the box, Indy. The Witches' Box."

Indy nodded. "I have it. But I've read all the scrolls in there, and I don't think there's anything that's going to help."

"Still…"

Indy nodded. "I'll get it for you tonight, after dinner."

"Thanks, sister." Lilia stretched her arms out to her sides, looking down at them with a smile. "It feels good to be human again. Well, almost human."

"I'll bet."

Lena had been silent during this entire exchange, but finally she spoke. "Lilia, what's going to happen? You said it would be the toughest challenge yet, and you told us before we'd need to get our loved ones out of the way when the time comes, but why? What exactly are we fighting here? I mean, I thought this was as simple as Demetrius making a choice. Either he accepts his remaining soul-piece or he doesn't, right? So what's the big deal?"

Lilia licked her lips, trying to form an answer she didn't really want to give, and then was saved by a soft *buzz-buzz* coming from Indy's jeans pocket.

Indy quickly pulled out her cell phone. "Text from Tomas." Then her expression changed. "Oh, my Goddess." She looked from the screen to her sisters. "The hospital phoned him. Father Dom came out of his coma this morning. He's awake and alert."

"On this day of all days," Lilia said, shaking her head. "The same day Demetrius first used the tools, the day he called me back into existence. This can't be a coincidence."

"There's no such thing as coincidence," Lena said softly. "We'd better get home."

Lilia stopped shoving food into her mouth when she realized that everyone was looking at her. Of course, as soon as they saw her noticing, they all returned to their own lasagna dripping with cheeses and sauce and stuffed with mushrooms and vegetables. The bowl beside her plate, where a fresh green salad had been, was all but licked clean. She realized she had consumed about a square foot of the main course within the first three minutes of its arrival. And a couple of slices of warm, buttery garlic bread, too.

She laid her fork down, sipped from her water glass, then set it carefully on the table. "I didn't realize how much I've missed food," she said. "The sensual pleasure of eating is… I think when you do it every day you forget how incredible it is. All those flavors bursting on your tongue. The taste, the texture. Oh, it's so good."

Selma, Magdalena's mother, smiled at her. She'd been smiling at her the entire evening, and it had been all Lilia could do not to fling herself into the older woman's arms. But all in good time. "I think that's the best compliment my cooking has ever received," she said softly.

"Then," Bahru said, "we've all been lax in our praise. Your culinary skills are unmatched, Selma."

He was a bronze-skinned Hindi who wore red-and-white robes, sandals, dreadlocks halfway down his back and a matted beard.

Lilia sighed. "It's a shame Demetrius won't be able to enjoy food like this."

"He won't?" Tomas asked. "Why not?"

"Well, he's still missing a part of his soul. The part I carry with me. When Indy returned the amulet to him, he received the soul-piece it held, and that let him escape the Underworld through the Portal. And, Lena, when you relinquished the chalice and the blade, you gave him a body."

"Not the body he thought I was going to give him, though," Lena said, glancing at the wicker cradle in the living room with a combination of love and ferocity.

Lilia nodded. "He was imprisoned, inhuman, a soul-less beast raging against his captivity for so long—it's understandable he was mixed up. And I know you couldn't see him at the end, my sister, but I could. He changed his mind. He wouldn't have gone through with it. I know this. He was confused—"

"Confused is putting it mildly, Lilia," Ryan said. He sat at the table's head, Lena at its foot. "He used some kind of mind control on people. On me, even."

She nodded. "I know. I saw it all. He's powerful."

"Still?" Ryan asked, pressing on. "I mean, now that he's got a human body, is he human, or is he... something else?"

"And is he still dangerous?" Lena asked.

Lilia lowered her head, but it was Selma who answered. "Why don't we let Lilia enjoy her first full-fledged meal in thirty-five-hundred years and discuss this later, over coffee and dessert?"

Everyone muttered, but they nodded all the same.

Lilia was grateful and sent Selma a loving look while deciding it was time to tell her the truth. "You are mothering all of us, Selma, even though you're only Magdalena's mother…in this lifetime."

Selma stilled with her fork halfway to her lips and lifted her head. "In this lifetime?"

Lilia smiled warmly. "We didn't get to stay with you for very long, Selma. Teenagers in those days were adult enough to leave home. But you taught your three daughters well. If you hadn't, our powers then wouldn't have enabled us all to be here now. Together. About to set things right after thirty-five centuries."

"I was…" Selma's voice broke.

"Our mother. You were our mother in Babylon."

Selma dropped her fork to her plate with a clatter and looked at each of the women in turn, her eyes beginning to shimmer. "I knew it. I felt it."

Sitting beside her, Bahru put a comforting hand on her shoulder.

Lilia sighed and set her napkin down. "It seems odd, me being the youngest but knowing more of what's going on than the rest of you. It's unfair to make you wait any longer for the answers you've been looking for all this time. And I've eaten so much already that my belly is straining to hold it. So I will tell you what I know."

"It's about time," Indy muttered, but she gave Lilia a wink to temper the words. "I thought we might have to stick bamboo shoots under your nails to get you to talk."

Lilia frowned—even though Indy's grin said she was kidding—failing to see the humor in such a notion. She dabbed her mouth with her napkin, and then she began.

"Demetrius came into humanity with the knowledge that he was human once, but no real memory of what that means. He doesn't know of our history. Didn't even—" Her throat tightened. She loosened it with another sip of water. "He didn't even recognize me when I first appeared in physical form." It hurt to admit that. But there it was.

"He came forth with the intention to experience every human pleasure. But without the final piece of his soul, his senses are dulled. He can't taste the deliciousness of food or see the beauty of nature. He won't understand why people take pleasure from music or a warm, soft pillow. He won't realize what he's missing, of course, having no basis for comparison."

"But he is human?" Tomas asked.

"He is. Sort of. He's also immortal—for the moment, anyway. His injuries will heal rapidly. Nothing will kill him. And he can't become ill." She went silent, rubbing her hands together in her lap.

"And what else?" Indy asked. "C'mon, spill it. I can see there's more."

Lilia looked up at the sister who sat beside her. "He has the same powers you received from the amulet, Indira."

"Telekinesis," Indy whispered.

Nodding, Lilia looked to Magdalena. "And he has the powers you received from the chalice, Lena. The ability to scry and find any knowledge he seeks."

"And he has the dagger," Ryan said softly. "That thing's like an unregistered WMD."

Lilia didn't understand the reference, and it must have shown on her face.

"Weapon of mass destruction," Ryan said.

She nodded in agreement. "Also, using the two together, he can manifest anything he desires. Turn any wish into physical reality."

The baby fussed, and Bahru was on his feet before any of them, hurrying to the cradle in the next room. Lena had started to get up, but she relaxed into her chair again with a grateful look the guru's way. Then she faced Lilia again. "What special power did you bring back with you, Lilia?"

"I hold a piece of my love's soul," Lilia said, lowering her head to hide the wave of longing that rose in her when she acknowledged that tiny part of him that remained in her possession.

"Is it embedded in some magical tool?" Tomas asked.

"No. It's in my heart. Where it's always been. I'm bound to him through it. I can find him anywhere he goes. The rest of his soul cries out for it, the way the moon pulls at the Earth. It's a constant effort to resist. But as I said at the hospital, I must give him some time."

"And what else?" Indy asked, getting up from the table and beginning to gather the plates, since everyone had finished eating. Selma got up to help, as did Bahru, who handed Ellie to her mother first.

"I'm immortal, impervious to illness or injury—as long as my body isn't destroyed—just as he is."

Everyone went silent and just stared at her. It was Indy who finally spoke. "Uh, in case you've forgotten, baby sis, your impervious immortal is in the hospital right now."

"He's most likely fully healed by now. I imagine this was the Gods' way of making sure he and I have time enough here in the physical realm to fulfill our destiny. If one of us were to be killed before Demetrius has the opportunity to make the decision he must make, it would be a terrible waste of all our efforts."

She pressed a hand to her throat. "If I die before Beltane, in a way that prevents me from reviving, with his soul-piece still inside me, it will die forever. The rest of his soul-pieces will die slowly without it, and he will expire into a death from which there is no return. He will simply cease to exist."

"That's unbelievable," Ryan said, getting up to help with the cleanup. Lilia did likewise, but as she passed her sister's chair carrying the lasagna tray, Lena gripped her arm.

"What about the baby?" Magdalena asked. "Demetrius wouldn't have any reason to want to hurt her, would he, Lil?"

"No. None. And you needn't worry about his powers, either. Once he receives the final part of his soul he'll return to being an ordinary mortal again, to live out an ordinary lifetime without any extraordinary abilities. And so will I. And so, I imagine, will each of you."

"Right," Indy said. "So what's the catch?"

"I don't—"

"She means it sounds too easy," Lena said as Bahru returned to the table. "There's more to it, isn't there? Otherwise you'd have given him back the final piece already."

Lilia lowered her head, nodded once. "Yes. First he has to be given time to experience life, as he is now.

And then I have to offer him his soul-piece back, explaining that he must give up his powers and immortality if he accepts it."

"You mean he gets a choice?" Ryan asked.

Lilia nodded. "Yes. The choice has to be his."

Everyone looked at each other, and then Indy said, "Who in their right mind would accept if it means giving up immortality, immunity to illness, rapid healing and superpowers, sis? I mean, what's the upside for him?"

"Oh, so much," Lilia said softly. "He'll be able to experience being human—fully. His senses will no longer be dulled. Being human is a highly sensual experience—we don't get that when we're in spirit form. The tastes and smells, the sounds and visual beauty. The sense of touch, of physical pleasure, none of that exists where there's no body, and for him, they're mere shadows compared to the fullness and richness he'll experience with his soul intact."

Tomas set his napkin on the table, chewed his lip for a moment, and then said softly, "What if he chooses not to accept?"

Of them all, Lilia knew, he was most familiar with their story, with the curse, the legends and mistaken interpretations, the history. Clearly he understood that all of it, the entire three-thousand, five-hundred-year cycle, was coming to an end with her arrival and Demetrius's decision.

"If he chooses not to accept his soul-piece, then at the precise moment of Beltane, he will die. He'll be released into the afterlife, and it will go there to join him. There he'll process all he's learned, rest and understand, and reincarnate again if he so desires." She lowered her head, not wanting to finish, but knowing they had a right to know the whole of it. "And so will I."

Her sisters shot to their feet, shouting denials, but Lilia held up her hands. "I've been allowed to linger all this time to right the wrong that was done so many years ago. The Gods allowed that as a way of correcting the imbalance, righting the dreadful wrong committed against us. But you all know it's not the natural order. We're supposed to live, to die, to rest, to live again. We've been allowed to circumvent the natural order. For three-thousand, five-hundred years, you have reincarnated lifetime after lifetime with the same names, with the memories ready to return to you—with the same loves you lost then reincarnating with you to give you a chance to find each other again.

"And I've been allowed to linger between life and death, to watch over you, to call you to action when the time was right. None of that is natural. And it all comes to an end now, with me. But we must not— *cannot*—tell Demetrius that part of it. He has to make his decision out of the desire to be fully human, to embrace life and love again, not out of fear of death. We all know death is nothing to fear, anyway."

Selma was using her napkin to dab a tear from the corner of her eye, and the others were looking shocked and afraid.

Lilia realized she'd risen to her feet in the fervor of her speech. She got hold of herself, took a deep breath and sat down again. "I will know when the time is right to go to him," she said softly. "I'll feel it. But until then, I'm here. We're all here, together. Let's enjoy this time while we have it."

Tomas looked troubled but nodded in agreement. "She's right."

"I know that look," Indy said, staring at her husband. "What are you thinking, hon?"

"That Father Dom waking up from a coma on the same day your sister arrived is...too unlikely to have happened by chance," he said. "Lilia, do you think there's a connection?"

"I'm certain of it."

Tomas lowered his eyes, and Lilia realized he'd been hoping she would give a different answer. "I'll go see him," he said. "I had no intention of ever talking to him again, not that I expected it to be an option. When the hospital called to tell me he was awake and asking for me, I—" He broke off, then took a breath, cleared his throat and went on. "But maybe I need to see what I can find out."

"It wasn't his fault, what he did," Lilia told him, watching his face, knowing this was a sore subject. Father Dominick had been like a father to him and then betrayed him bitterly.

Anger rose in Tomas's dark eyes. "He tried to kill the woman I love. He drugged my sister. He lied to me about who and what I was. He—"

"He was playing his part in a complex story far too old for him to have understood fully, Tomas," she told him. "I know you feel betrayed, but...you're a spiritual man. Don't you understand that things happen the way they're supposed to, and that sometimes even bad things, things we hate and curse, we later realize happened for very good reasons? To move us on toward where we want to go. To make room for better things to arrive."

He blinked twice and shook himself as if she'd hit him between the eyes with a mallet.

"I think it might be a good idea if I go with you to see him," Lilia said. "Chances are he's still a part of this. Possibly being manipulated by unseen forces, even now."

He nodded. "I'll call the hospital, make the arrangements. We can go first thing in the morning."

They all continued clearing until the table was bare and gleaming, and the dishwasher was chugging softly. As everyone but Tomas gathered in the living room, sitting comfortably around the fireplace, Selma brought around coffee and dessert, eventually taking a seat herself. Tomas had gone off to make his phone call, and now he returned. He looked pensive.

"What's up, babe?" Indy asked, reading his face.

He met her eyes, frowning and shaking his head. "Father Dom. He's…gone."

"He died?" Indy whispered.

Tomas blinked out of his state and focused on his wife. "No, no, he's not dead. He's gone. He got up and walked out of the hospital. They tried to stop him, they couldn't even believe he was strong enough, but…" His frown deepened. "What the hell is he thinking?"

Gus pushed Demetrius's wheelchair through the hospital corridors toward the exit, because that was hospital policy. Demetrius didn't think much of it, but Gus was having a ball, so he put up with it. Besides, he'd already upset the staff by checking himself out before they'd deemed him healed. He, however, knew that he was.

Gus was brimming over with childlike excitement.

"Wait till you see our ride, boss. We're finally getting what we deserve outta this life, let me tell you that."

The automatic doors opened at their approach. Demetrius was looking behind him to ask Gus what he was talking about, but then he turned and saw the gleaming black stretch limo through the open doors, and blinked. "Are you kidding me?"

There was a man in a chauffeur's cap standing beside the car, holding a passenger door open. He was young, a green-eyed redhead with a friendly smile and a smattering of freckles across his nose and spilling onto his cheeks. "Mr. Demetrius, Mr. Gus," he said with a friendly nod. "I'm Sid, I'm your driver."

Demetrius got out of the wheelchair and shook the kid's hand. "Sid. And, um, where exactly will you be driving us?"

"To the airport, sir. Mr. Nelson's private jet is waiting to take you to his—that is, to your new home." He beamed.

"A private jet," Demetrius repeated, because the words were not making sense in his brain quite yet.

"He said nothing but the best for you, Mr. Demetrius. And I'm assigned to you for as long as you need me."

"Assigned to me?"

Sid gave a shrug and a smile. "Your right-hand man."

"I'm his right-hand man." Gus's tone was unfriendly.

Sid laughed. "Don't be silly, Mr. Gus. I'm the employee. You're the boss."

"I'm the boss?"

"Well, one of them, anyway."

Gus looked at Demetrius and then back at Sid again,

smiling this time. "Well, let's get this show on the road, then."

"Yes, sir!"

Gus climbed into the back of the limo and made himself comfortable. Demetrius got in beside him, wondering if he'd hit his head during the accident and was dreaming all of this.

But he didn't wake up, and everything seemed to flow in logical order, so he didn't think so. Within an hour they were flying through the skies in an airplane, Sid in the passenger cabin along with them.

"Do you need anything to make you more comfortable?" Sid asked. "It's going to be hours before we land."

"Is there any food on this bird?" Gus asked. "'Cause I'm so hungry I could—"

"I'd like to get this cast off, Sid," Demetrius interrupted. "Is there anything I could use to cut it?"

Sid looked a little alarmed. "But it's only been a few days since your accident."

"I know, but…" He shot a quick look at Gus, seeing the same kind of worry in his eyes. "The doctor was being overly cautious. Nothing was actually broken."

"It most certainly was," Gus said. "Your arm was broke in three places. I was there when the doc showed you the X-rays."

"He misread them, Gus. My arm is fine." And it was. It had been since about twenty-four hours after the accident. He'd felt the bones knitting and known that he was healed. Every other injury had vanished, too. Where he had been scraped and cut, he now had smooth tanned skin without a mark on it. Where he'd been bruised, there was nothing. His pain was gone.

He thought he might be immortal. At the very least, he had supernatural powers. He healed in a single day. He had a cup and a knife that could make his wishes come true, and he had a blonde from some other realm stalking him. He didn't know what had existed before the void. But he was sure there had been something, and he was suddenly very curious to know what. And whether it would explain his current abilities.

In the meantime, he intended to enjoy everything life had to offer.

Sid brought him a steak knife, and he proceeded to divest himself of the cast. He made a mess of it, scattering white dust and fragments all over the carpeted floor, but Sid assured him he needn't worry about it. When his arm was free, though dust-coated, he turned it, bent it, moved his wrist and elbow. "That's better," he said.

Sid and Gus looked at him as if he'd just walked on water. But he pretended not to notice, put his seat back and closed his eyes.

He didn't wake until they landed, and as he leaned forward to look out the tiny window beside his seat he saw a barren wasteland.

"Where are we?"

"Arizona," Gus said. "Don't worry. It gets much more colorful where we're going. You just relax, the journey's almost over."

He'd certainly traveled far, Demetrius thought. Perhaps too far for the blonde woman to track him down again. He hoped so.

Then why did something inside him ache at the thought? He didn't even know her.

Soon he was in the back of another limo, with Sid

driving once again, and two hours after that, give or take, they were winding through fascinating scenery. Sid and Gus were oohing and ahhing and pointing as they passed towering rock formations of rust red, fronted by acres of desert. Demetrius thought the colors were interesting. Different, certainly, but hardly worthy of all the fuss they were making. They were just rocks, after all.

They drove through Sedona, heading north, then turned onto a side road. To the left were more of those massive red rocks. To the right, a sprawling, gated mansion where he figured some celebrity must live.

"Well? What do you think?" Gus asked.

"What do I think about what?" Then he realized the limo was turning toward the closed wrought-iron gate, which opened to allow it to move slowly through. The gate, he noted at last, bore two entwined N's.

Beyond the tall gate lay paradise. There was no other word for it. Dead ahead, at the end of the wide paved drive, was a four-car garage with a rooftop patio protected by ornate rails, and with tall glittering fabric "sails" to provide shade. The house that rose above the garage was like a small red stone palace. It had a circular painted third story and even an observatory atop that. He noticed that the driveway continued past the garage, curving up a small hill and circling a huge fountain where a trio of topless mermaids poured water from their cupped hands into a pool. Beyond the fountain was the front door.

"Ned Nelson told me confidentially that he's gonna have to unload most of his houses anyway," Gus said as the gate closed behind them.

A beautiful Latina woman was working in a flower

garden. As they passed, Demetrius stared out the tinted window into her dark brown eyes, which flashed blue, and for a split second she became a platinum-haired avenging angel.

He jerked away from the window.

"People won't vote for a President who seems too wealthy," Gus went on. "He can probably keep three, maybe four, but more than that would be pushing it."

"So the staff…?"

"Are paid for the next twelve months," Sid said. "So are the taxes."

Gus nodded an agreement. "Ned says by then our stock in his companies should be earning us enough to maintain the place on our own. He threw in the limo, a pimped-out Jeep Wrangler and Jag. A Jag, D-man. And an expense account for incidentals. Wait, I have it here somewhere." Gus felt around, then finally pulled a small leather ledger from an inner pocket of his designer suit jacket and handed it over.

Demetrius opened it and looked at the dollar amount noted at the top of the first page. Then he lifted his head and blinked. "Those must be some incidentals."

The limo circled the mermaid fountain and stopped at the front entrance, which was just as spectacular as the rest of the place. Sid got out, came around and opened the car door.

Demetrius stepped out and into his new life. The life he deserved. The one he'd come here for. He savored that knowledge, then turned and walked up the broad flagstone steps, passing between two pillars into a domed entryway to a pair of massive hardwood doors with dragon-head knockers. "*This* is living," he said softly.

Gus sent him a knowing look, then returned his gaze to the entrance. "It was no mistake you gettin' hit by that car, D-dog. No mistake at all. You see that naked blonde again, you oughtta be thankin' her."

A throat cleared. They both turned. Sid was standing behind them in his crisp uniform and chauffeur's cap, with some of his carrot curls peeking out from beneath the hat.

"What is it, Sid?" Demetrius asked.

A small smile tugged at the corners of the younger man's lips. "I was told to remain at your service. I'll just park the limo and make use of one of the rooms in the staff quarters behind the garage—with your permission, sirs."

Demetrius looked at Gus, who shrugged.

"How many bedrooms does this house have, Sid?" Demetrius asked.

"I believe there are twelve, sir."

"That has to stop. It bothers me. Call me Demetrius, all right? And he's Gus."

"All right. Demetrius." Sid looked as if he was battling a smile.

"I know. It's a mouthful. So, Sid, you say we have twelve bedrooms. And how many staff members live here?"

"I'd have to find out."

"Still, I don't see why you should take a room in the garage."

"It's fine, really, sir—Demetrius, sir. The staff quarters are nice."

"Still—"

"I've stayed there before. I really like it."

"All right, then, if that's the way you want it."

"It is, sir." He looked as if he was about to correct himself, then decided not to. "Will there be anything else?"

Demetrius glanced at the front doors. "No, I guess not." But for some reason he couldn't seem to make himself open them.

Sid looked at the two of them for a long moment, then nodded. "Maybe I should give you the grand tour of the place, show you everything you might need to know, introduce you to the staff."

Demetrius sighed in abject relief, only realizing what he was doing when it was too late to prevent it.

"Yes," he said. "That would be great, Sid. I am completely out of my element here anyway, and this…this is just a little bit overwhelming, even though…" He turned to look at the sprawling lawns, the gardens, the koi swimming in the fountain, his heart swelling a little in his chest. It was nice here. He would have everything he had ever wanted here. "Even though it was meant for me."

Sid couldn't possibly have understood, but he nodded as if he did and, reaching past Demetrius, opened the massive doors.

3

After five weeks, Demetrius was finally beginning to feel at home in the mansion.

He was lying on the chaise on the balcony outside his third-floor suite, basking in the Arizona sun. Below him, scantily clad models and actresses and various hangers-on frolicked in the pool, in the fountains, in the spa. So did Gus.

So had he, at first. And for quite some time over the past five weeks. But now he was bored. And extremely restless.

"Excuse me, Mr. D?"

He didn't blink. Didn't turn. He'd come to rely on Sid, the limo-driver-slash-man-Friday, more and more. Sid explained things to him when he didn't quite follow them and didn't ask questions about why he didn't quite follow them. He didn't ask questions about anything. Not when Demetrius had sawed off the cast on the jet. Not when he'd managed to make a starlet he'd seen on a television show appear at his front door and, later, in his bed. And not when he'd left a pile of caviar cans with holes burned through their bottoms on the ground out back after target practice with his amazing double-edged blade. Nothing.

"What is it, Sid?"

Sid hesitated before answering, which made Demetrius curious enough to turn and look up at the young man. Sid had a caring nature, Demetrius thought. Why anyone would care about *him,* he couldn't have said, but it seemed that Sid did. Or maybe that was just considered part of his job.

"Well?"

"I'll get to it in a minute. First, if my asking doesn't piss you off too much, why so morose?"

Demetrius averted his eyes.

"You look like your puppy just died."

"I don't have a puppy."

A burst of air escaped Sid's lips. "It's an expression. You take everything so literally." He hurried to the opposite chair and sat down. "You might feel better if you talked about what's bothering you."

By the Gods, Demetrius thought, he'd made a huge mistake in telling this one to relax and be himself and not behave so formally. Sid was acting like a confidant and best friend, even an advisor.

Then again, what harm would it do to share his restlessness with the boy? "I feel as if I am…missing something."

"Ahh." Sid nodded slowly, eyes falling closed. "The love of a good woman."

"Oh, hell no." He'd borrowed that phrase from Gus. It was one of his favorites.

"A good man? But you already told me you play for Team Straight."

Demetrius rolled his eyes, laid his head back and ignored Sid's attempts to draw him into humor. "I'll try to explain, though I'm not entirely sure myself what's making me feel this way. But…take last night for example. Everyone was raving about those steaks that Gus grilled for us."

"They really were amazing, God protect my heart from my love of red meat." Sid crossed himself, then looked at Demetrius again and tipped his head to one side. "You didn't like them?"

"I didn't see what there was to like. They tasted just like everything else. No better, no worse. As far as I can see, the only real variations in food are the differences in texture. Some is mushy, some is chewy, some is crisp, some is crumbly. But it all tastes the same. Some is a little bit sweet, some a little salty, but that's about it." He looked at Sid, saw the absolute disbelief in his eyes, the way his mouth gaped open. "Isn't it?"

Sid snapped his jaw shut. "No, boss. It isn't."

Demetrius sat up, put his feet down on either side of the chaise and rubbed his chin. "And what about the sex?"

Sid coughed, reached for Demetrius's glass and helped himself to a sip of soda liberally spiked with vodka. He made a face. "Gawd, that's strong. How many of these have you had?"

"Six. And I feel nothing. No different. I've seen the way others react to large quantities of alcohol, but not me. I have a feeling this is all connected. So tell me about the sex, Sid. And be honest. What does it…what does it feel like?"

Sid set the glass down, his face going completely serious. "Haven't you had sex, boss?"

"Numerous times. I should have asked, what is it *supposed* to feel like?"

"Amazing. Incredible. Like nothing else can feel, so there's nothing to compare it to. It's like…" Sid searched his mind for a comparison, then snapped his fingers when he got one. "It's like an earthquake in your crotch. A really good earthquake. Isn't it like that for you?"

"No earthquake. More like a bump, like hitting a pot hole in the limo."

"Oh."

"I wanted a life of sheer pleasure," Demetrius said, thinking aloud. "But I'm beginning to think there's a price to be paid for the gifts I've already received. I think I might be incapable of experiencing the pleasure all around me. It's as if the curse lives on."

"The curse?" Sid got up. "Come on, Mr. D. There's no curse."

"I know perfectly well Gus told you about me. Where I come from."

Sid was silent for a long moment, which never happened. Then at last he admitted, "He told me where you *said* you come from."

"I was imprisoned in a dimension of darkness and sensory deprivation. By whom, or for what crime, I have no idea. I had no form, no shape, no physicality. Only consciousness, endless consciousness. And the knowledge that one day I would escape—"

"With the help of three witches," Sid whispered.

Demetrius nodded.

"Frankly, sir, I thought Gus was a little crazy. Harmless crazy, but still, completely nuts, you know?" Sid drew a circle around one ear with a forefinger. "If you believe it, too, though—well, that scares me."

Demetrius searched Sid's face. "Why would my insanity be any more frightening than Gus's?"

"'Cause you're not Gus." Sid shrugged and averted his eyes.

Demetrius heaved a deep sigh and got to his feet, noticing that Sid took a step closer to the French doors that led back inside the mansion. "What was it you came to tell me?"

"Oh. Right. Well, there's a man who keeps calling. A priest."

Demetrius felt a frisson of fury race up his spine, and the thought that accompanied it was, *I detest priests.* But he didn't know why he should feel that way. "What does he want?"

"He refuses to tell me. Says he can only talk to you, but that he has information you need." Sid shrugged. "I figure he's going to try to save your soul and change your sinful ways, or maybe he's just looking for a hefty donation. But he's been so persistent that I finally took his number and promised to pass it along. I sent it to your smartphone."

"Thank you, Sid."

Sid sighed, started to go back inside, then hesitated. "You probably shouldn't mention all that Underworld stuff, or the three witches or the rest of it to anyone, okay, boss?"

"Gus told me much the same thing when were in New York. Don't worry, Sid. I'll keep it to myself from now on."

"Okay. Good. Later, boss."

"Later, Sid."

He sat there for a long moment, thinking. He wondered why he hated priests, and why one was trying to contact him now. He wondered where the third witch had gone after she'd flashed into existence in that alley—for that was surely who she had to be. He hadn't been able to shake her from his mind since. He saw her every time he closed his eyes and in the face of every woman he bedded. She haunted his dreams, dancing exotically in ribbons of sheer fabric on the desert sands. Seducing him with her eyes. What did she have in store for him? And what was she waiting for?

And now there was a new player in this game of his earthbound existence. A priest. Demetrius wondered what information the priest had for him and realized there was only one way to find out. So he took out his smartphone, a device that frankly amazed him with its capabilities, pulled up the text message Sid had sent and then called the number.

When a male voice answered, deep and raspy, another inexplicable shiver crept up his spine.

"Hello. This is—"

"I know who this is," the priest said. "I've been waiting for your call."

Demetrius blinked down the odd sense of revulsion that rose in him. He didn't know this man, so why should he feel so repelled?

It was as irrational as his fear of the woman who'd appeared in the alley. The witch. He'd been struck with such terror at the sight of her that he'd run away, straight into the path of Ned Nelson's car.

Then again, he wouldn't have all of this—this mansion, this lifestyle—if he hadn't. He'd expected the third witch's task would be to help him make his way in this world. And in a way, that was exactly what she had done. Maybe she was finished, then. Maybe he would never see her again.

The thought twisted his heart into a painful knot that confused him even more.

"Demetrius?" said the voice on the phone.

"Who are you? How do you know about me?" he demanded.

"I'm a priest, my son. You may call me Father Dom. I know your story. I know about your time in the Underworld. I know about the two witches who helped you escape. And I know about the third one, who will soon come for you yet again. She'll offer you something, that witch. Something you must refuse or you will end up back where you started."

Demetrius narrowed his eyes as suspicion blossomed and whispered a warning into his ear. Despite that, he couldn't deny the relief that had preceded it. *She's coming back.* Thank the Gods. "How do you know this?"

"Let me come to you and I'll explain it all, my son."

Demetrius thought about that and decided it would be all right. It wasn't as if a mortal priest could do him any harm, after all. He had the dagger, and he was strong. Immortal. An ordinary man couldn't hurt him. "Where are you?" he asked.

"I'm standing at your front gate."

Demetrius couldn't prevent his slight gasp, and he was sure the priest heard it. He rose from his chair, walked to the edge of the balcony and looked down the hill. A thin, frail-looking man with white hair stood just beyond the gate. He wore a black suit with a white

collar. As he looked, the man waved, and Demetrius
suppressed an involuntary shiver.

Looking down at his phone, he sent a text message to Sid.

Man at front gate. Bring him to me.

Spring was coming to Milbury, New York. There
were only a few days left in April, and the snow was
long gone. The rains came heavily and often, but left
days in between their soaking visits for the sun to reign
supreme. Daffodils and tulips surrounded Magdalena's
big old house at Havenwood, and the trees around Indy
and Tomas's cabin were covered in newborn leaves,
still small and pale, but growing rapidly. Much like
Ellie, now nearly three months old, with chubby cheeks
and frequent smiles, and red curls just starting to twist
to life all over her little head.

Lilia had grown to love it there, among her family,
though the entire time she had been fighting the constant pull of Demetrius. The part of his soul she held
inside her wanted to return to him, wanted to reunite
with the rest of the pieces and become whole again.

So she'd been biding her time, trying to be completely present in the moments she was given. Loving
her sisters and "their" mother, her brothers-in-law and
Tomas's sister, Rayne, who was a frequent visitor. Loving her baby niece. Those things distracted her a little
from the dire challenge she would soon face. But always it waited in the back of her mind like a demon to
torment her nights and add to the already huge heartache of missing her beloved. When must she leave her
family? Would she ever see them again once she did?

Would Demetrius let her win his trust again? What if she failed?

And then, one night it just happened. Her eyes popped open an hour before dawn, and she simply knew. *It's time.* Her heart seemed to jump a little inside her chest, just for an instant. It felt like a trapped bird, flapping excitedly.

She pushed back the covers and got up, unable to wait. She would take a shower, pack her things, all of them beautiful gifts from her newfound family, and be downstairs when Indy and Tomas awoke, so she could break the news. Then they would go down to Lena's place together and tell everyone else. It wasn't going to go down easily. They loved her so much.

As it turned out, however, she didn't need to tell them. When she came down, showered and dressed, her long hair hanging in a braid over one shoulder, wearing a white sundress and a turquoise cardigan, she didn't see Indy and Tomas pouring coffee as she'd expected.

There were only her two sisters waiting for her, and she knew by the dampness on their cheeks that they already realized she would have to leave them today.

Lena hugged her hard, sniffling. Indy went next, saying, "I don't know why you won't let us go with you. You're stubborn as hell."

Lilia gnawed her lip, tempted. "He's far away. I don't even know where. But when I get there, I'll let you know." She held up the cell phone Lena had bought her. She'd been added to their family plan and would forever be grateful. "And if I need you, I'll phone you."

"Be on guard, Lilia," Indy said. "We still don't know where Father Dom is, and if he's recovered his health, he could be dangerous. Trust me on this. Bastard almost killed me."

"I know. I'll be careful."

Lena took her by the hand and led her to the kitchen table, where a large map of the United States was spread out. From her pocket she took a black velvet drawstring pouch, then pulled a long length of chain from it. At the end of the chain hung a cone-shaped amethyst pendulum.

"Show me Demetrius," she said, and then she held the chain over the northeastern section of the map. The amethyst was still at first, but slowly it began to swing from side to side, its momentum making it sweep wider each time.

Snapping it up into her palm, Lena moved to the southeastern part of the country and repeated the procedure with the same results. Ditto to the Midwest, the center of the country, the Northwest, and the West Coast. It was only when she suspended the pendulum over the Southwest that it began to move in a different way. Not back and forth this time, but in ever widening circles.

"He's in the Southwest," Lena said.

Lilia nodded, her eyes on the map as Lena stopped the pendulum and glanced at Indy, who brought her a pair of scissors. She cut the map into pieces, cutting out Arizona, New Mexico, Utah, Nevada and Colorado, then spreading the states out on the table. Then Lena repeated the process, holding the pendulum over each one. She got a positive result over Arizona and lifted her head, looking at her sisters.

"It's a start," Indy said.

"Thank you. It'll save a lot of time. And once I get there, I'll know which direction to go. I'll feel him."

"I'll cut the state up into sections and call you when I get more details," Magdalena said. "Just in case you need to narrow it down."

"Thank you," Lilia said softly.

Indy was typing on her laptop computer by then, and nodded. "There's a flight to Phoenix leaving in three hours."

"Then I should be on it." Lilia brushed away tears she couldn't help shedding. By the Goddess, she hoped she would see her sisters, her family, again. But she knew too well that if this didn't go well, she might not. Not in this lifetime, at least.

This might be goodbye.

So she held them a long time when she hugged them, then held them again after the huge breakfast Selma insisted on making for her. Saying goodbye to the woman she accepted as her mother in every way that mattered was painful. Seeing Selma's tears was almost too much to take.

And then her sisters drove her to the airport and walked her to the security checkpoint, which was as far as they could go.

Magdalena kissed her cheek. "Come back to us, okay? You have to come back to us."

"If it looks like he's gonna refuse," Indy said, "call while there's still time, so I can come try to...persuade his sorry ass."

"I will."

"You'd better."

"I...love you both so much," Lilia said. "You kept your vow to me, to him, even when it nearly cost you everything. I'm so grateful to you for that. And for taking me in now, so many lifetimes later. For everything you've done for me. Teaching me how to live in this time, the quirks of the language, how to dress, buying me clothes, the phone, lending me money. So much money."

"Hey, Lena married a billionaire," Indy said. "Ryan can afford it."

"Still…" Lilia looked at the clock. "I have to go."

"Say the word and we'll be there," Magdalena said. "Goddess, Lil, I don't want you to go."

"We haven't come this far to fail now, brave sisters. Trust me, we will be together again. And soon."

As she turned to make her way through the security check, Lilia wished she felt as sure of that as she had sounded.

Demetrius looked out from his balcony over the property and remembered Father Dom's arrival three days ago. The old priest had waved a hand expressively to indicate the beautiful grounds spread out below the small patio table where the two of them had been sitting over coffee. "This place is like a fantasy come true," he'd said with a nod. "Obviously you've figured out how to use your…powers already."

Demetrius, who'd been sitting across the table from the old man, had tried to read his face. He didn't know Father Dom, hadn't trusted him, and he'd had no intention of giving anything away. But he'd very definitely wanted to know what the old cleric knew, or thought he knew, about him.

"I wished for this. Visualized it in great detail. And it came to me. Is that what you mean by my…powers?"

"You have the chalice and the blade," the old man said. "Using the two together can bring desires and ideas, anything from the astral plane, into physical form. Did you use them before you acquired all this?"

"I was messing around with them." Demetrius shrugged, unwilling to reveal that he'd performed a rite according to a voice in his head, a female voice, and that he had apparently brought her into physical form from the astral plane, as well. And yes, all of this, too. But first, her.

"Have you noticed any other powers attached to those tools of yours?"

"The chalice and the blade?"

"And the amulet, of course." The priest nodded at the piece Demetrius wore around his neck.

So he knew about *that,* as well. "They have other powers?"

"That's what I was asking you. Do they?"

"Not that I'm aware of." It was a blatant lie. "Are they supposed to?"

"Not that I'm aware of," the priest lied back.

And it *was* a lie. The old man knew. Demetrius was sure of it. That priest knew the blade could blast energy like a laser, could set things on fire and even blow them up. And he must know what the amulet did, as well. He was dying to ask.

All in good time, though. I have to be careful. Men would kill to possess tools like these.

"You said you knew about me, about where I come from," Demetrius said, choosing his words with care.

The priest nodded slowly. "Everything that has brought you to where you now find yourself springs from another lifetime, Demetrius. A lifetime in the distant past. You have been human before, you know."

"Have I?" He had to hold himself still in his seat, will himself not to lean forward and gaze at the old priest in rapt interest. He tried to keep a cool demeanor, to relax and not look too eager.

"You lived in ancient Babylon, in the sixteenth century, BC."

A flash came and went in his mind. Swirling veils, bronze-skinned bellies, feminine arms twisting like snakes. Dancers in the desert. Just like his dreams. The blonde woman, she'd been there—though she hadn't been a blonde then. And two others with her. The three witches?

"What did I...do there?" he asked, aiming for a skeptical, nearly bored, tone.

"You were the First Soldier of King Balthazorus," the priest said. He lowered his head as he said the name, the way Demetrius had observed other people did when mentioning someone they'd known who had died.

"I was a Babylonian soldier. Fascinating." He tried to sound amused, as if the notion were silly. But deep down he felt a stirring of...something. Memory?

"You were seduced and then betrayed by three women. Witches, all of them. Slaves in the King's harem."

So they *had* been there with him, those three. Those same three, they had to be. Was that why they had to help him now? Because they had betrayed him in some long ago existence he didn't even remember? Or *want* to remember.

"What did these...witches...want with me?" he asked at length.

"What any witch wants. Power. They wanted power over you. For though they lived in luxury, they were, after all, slaves. Owned by the King, forced to serve him for his pleasures. They wanted what any enslaved person wants. Freedom."

"Freedom," Demetrius repeated. He knew about wanting freedom. He'd wanted it even before he'd known what it was.

"They used their charms to seduce you to the point where you would do anything for them. Even murder the King you were sworn to serve. Which you did, my friend. Which you did."

"I murdered the King?"

There was another flash in his mind. An ornate room that belonged in a palace, golden relics and rich fabrics everywhere. Exotic oil lamps out of one of the tales about Ali Baba sent thick black ribbons of smoke into the air. A bearded man stood before him, shaking his head sadly while Demetrius struggled against the soldiers who held his arms.

"You cannot have them killed! Blame me for this. Take my life, not theirs. Not Lilia's!"

But the King wouldn't even look him in the eye. "You betrayed me. You, my most trusted soldier. My... my friend..." When the King finally raised his eyes they glinted with fury. "They die."

"No!"

Demetrius ripped free of his captors and yanked the blade from one soldier's belt. He lunged forward, brandishing the dagger before him, and he heard the slight hiss of the razor-sharp edge slicing the air—and then the King's throat.

It happened so fast. Blood from Balthazorus's neck sprayed like water from an elephant's trunk, and Demetrius's arms flew up in front of his face as its warmth spattered him. The man he'd sworn to serve, his friend, dropped to his knees, one hand grasping uselessly at his blood-pulsing throat, his mouth working soundlessly, eyes wide with shock.

Demetrius moved forward, falling to his own knees. The knife fell from his numb hand. "No. No, I didn't mean—"

The King toppled sideways and lay still, and the blood flow slowed as his body emptied itself. Only then did the guards snap out of their shocked paralysis. One shouted, "Fetch the high priest," and another brought the hilt of his sword down across the back of Demetrius's head.

A soft hand patted the back of Demetrius's neck and snapped him out of the vision or memory or whatever it had been.

"Are you all right, my son?" Father Dom asked.

Demetrius had to blink the hot moisture from his eyes. What he had seen couldn't have been real. It *couldn't* have. He would never have murdered a friend. Not even over a woman. "Of course. I was thinking about the pool. It's due for maintenance." His voice was raspy. He cleared his throat. "You say all of this happened in…?"

"Fifteen-hundred and one, BC."

"Ah."

"You think it sounds crazy," said the priest. He leaned back in his chair, stretching his legs out in front of him, ankles crossed, then folded his arms. "You don't remember any of it, then?"

"No."

"Just the part about being imprisoned in another dimension without a body?"

Demetrius lifted his brows. "I don't remember *that,* either."

The old priest's lips puckered briefly in thought, and then he said, "That's not what your friend Gus told me."

Demetrius sat forward. "When were you talking to Gus?"

Father Dom smiled. "I wasn't. I only saw him from a distance and heard your man Sid call his name. I was bluffing, but you just confirmed that I was right. If you're not going to be honest with me, Demetrius, there's no way I can help you. But believe me, the third witch is coming. And soon." He fell silent and waited for Demetrius to react.

At length Demetrius sighed and decided he had to reveal more interest than he'd intended. "Tell me about the third witch," he said slowly. Because he simply had to know about her.

"Tell me about your time in the Underworld."

Demetrius faced the man down, not liking him, not at all. "I don't remember anything. Because there's nothing to remember. A void. Consciousness amid nothingness. Just…black."

"But aware." Father Dom sat up straight again. "You were aware."

"Yes, I was aware."

"And angry."

"Raging. Against my imprisonment, my confinement, that emptiness. What else, I don't know."

"And you knew, even then, in that state, that there were witches. Three witches."

Demetrius met the man's eyes but didn't confirm or deny the statement.

"You probably thought they were supposed to help you. And they confirmed it when the first one gave you the way back into the mortal world and the second a means to reconstitute your body."

"Reconstitute?"

"Oh, yes. It's the same body you had before. Well, more or less. You're all but impervious to illness, can heal from any injury, can live forever. At least for now. The third witch will try to see to it that all that ends."

"How?" Demetrius asked, still admitting nothing.

"She wants to complete what her sisters started, to take away all of your power to make you completely human again. Mortal. Weak. Vulnerable. Ordinary, Demetrius."

"And why would she want to do that to me?"

"As I said, for the same reason any witch does anything. To get power. They want to keep your power for themselves, and themselves alone. Already the first two share some of your abilities."

"Such as?"

The priest shook his head. "I only know they'll strip you of all you have if you do as they say. You must be prepared. It was the witches who tricked you to begin with. They used their bodies to seduce you into betraying your friend and your King. And they used your feelings for them to trick you into murdering him. They are the ones who put you in that dark prison long ago. You should kill them. But short of that, you must at least resist them."

"And what about you? What do you gain from all this? From helping me?"

"I'm a priest," Father Dom said softly. "I've been trying to stop the witches all along. It's my duty. My sacred calling. I don't gain anything from it."

Demetrius looked around, down to the pool area where guests still lingered. The crowd had thinned, but there were still beautiful people dressed in almost nothing walking around, drinking his liquor and getting high from it as he couldn't do. Gus always had company.

He saw the priest looking and knew what he wanted. Part of what he wanted, at least. "You want to stay here, don't you?"

Demetrius had agreed, and now the old man was staying in the observatory, because the only access to it was through Demetrius's suite on the circular third floor. No one was allowed up there. And the priest wanted no one, not even Sid or Gus, to know he was there. Demetrius had needed space around him, privacy, a haven in which he could be alone, which was why he'd chosen the third story as his own. Now the priest had invaded that space, but he had assured Demetrius it wouldn't be for long. And today he'd promised to help Demetrius learn to control his powers.

They were sitting once again on Demetrius's private patio with their chairs well back toward the house, out of sight from prying eyes. After a long silence Father Dom, looking as if he'd gained twenty pounds since he'd arrived at the door, not to mention that his skin was several shades pinker, said, "Bring me the chalice, Demetrius. Let me show you what it does."

Demetrius studied the priest for a long moment,

then, with a nod, decided he had nothing to lose. "Wait here," he said. Then he went into the house and through the master suite to the safe, hidden behind a painting of three beautiful women standing on a cliff watching the sun rise over the desert. They wore flowing silk, and the sky was orange-red. It had been in the house when he arrived. He had no idea who had painted it, where Ned Nelson had bought it, or why he'd put it here, but it meant something to Demetrius.

He just hadn't known what until the priest had told him of his history.

Three women. Ancient Babylon. Harem slaves. It could be them.

Sighing, putting those thoughts aside for later, he opened the safe and took out the chalice. Then he carried it carefully back to the patio and out to the priest.

"Ahh." The old man's eyes lit with a hungry gleam as he leaned forward and touched the chalice. "Yes, it's just as I remember."

"Remember?"

Father Dom looked up quickly. "I've seen its likeness in an ancient diary. Do you know how to use it?"

"Fill with liquid and drink?" Demetrius asked, using the sarcasm he'd learned by observing others. It was one of his favorite quirks of the language. The priest stared blankly at him. Clearly the joke had gone right "over his head," as Gus would have put it. It reminded Demetrius sharply of the way he used to react to modern humor. Never understanding it. Because he was out of his time.

"Fill with liquid, yes. Any liquid." As he spoke, the priest reached for the chalice.

Demetrius snatched it away before Father Dom

could touch it. For some reason he just couldn't let this man put his hands on an object that was...sacred to him.

The priest stared at him, surprised, and perhaps a little offended. Demetrius shrugged. "I don't like people touching it."

"All right, then. All right. Pour some liquid in. Some water from your glass will do."

Demetrius poured the water into the chalice.

"Now, pull it close to you and look straight down into the water. And tell it to show you something you need to know."

Demetrius pulled it close, staring down into the water. "Such as?" he asked.

"I don't know. Anything." Father Dom snapped his fingers. "Ask it to show you where this third witch is."

Sighing, Demetrius stared into the cup and said, "Show me the third witch."

And the water began to swirl.

4

The swirl became a current and then a whirlpool, and the next thing Demetrius knew he was being sucked into that whirlpool and going down, down, down, until he emerged into…someplace else.

The sun blazed hot from an empty sky, and at first he thought he was in the Sonoran Desert, that he had perhaps sleepwalked past the gate and was wandering in the wasteland. But in only a moment he knew this desert was different. No saguaro cactus, no red rocks. And when he looked a little farther he saw, in the distance, the brightly decorated gates of a glittering city. The wall was built of glazed bricks, lapis blue, with borders of gold, and bulls, horses and lions as decorations and guardians. An archway rose in the center, to mark the city gate.

The Ishtar Gate, a voice whispered in his mind. Strange. He'd never heard that name before. Looking from the distant city to his more immediate surroundings, he noted his own odd clothing. A white garment gathered at both shoulders and hanging to just above his knees, crossed by a red sash that he sensed indicated something of importance. A heavy sword was belted at his side, and a smaller knife—but not his sacred dagger—was strapped to his thigh. He wore sandals on his feet.

The body was familiar. The clothing and everything else was alien to him.

"Come quickly, before someone sees us," she said, and there was laughter in her voice.

He turned in surprise toward that soft, delighted, slightly mischievous and achingly familiar voice to see a woman who matched it in every way. She had waves of flowing black hair and ebony eyes outlined in black, her lids painted a gleaming metallic gold, her lashes so thick and dark they needed no enhancement. Those eyes were fixed on him, and once he met them he couldn't look away.

She was holding out a hand to him. "Come on. What are you waiting for, my love? You know we won't have much time."

Mesmerized, he took her small warm hand, and only when she broke eye contact could he lower his gaze to notice, at last, her full, berry-stained lips. Then she tugged him forward, and he noticed the rest of her. She was very small, but curvy and strong. Her breasts were as full as ripe melons, and barely concealed beneath a scrap of white fabric she had wrapped around them like a scarf. A similar and only slightly larger piece embraced her hips and round, plump buttocks. And in between, her skin was smooth and copper-bronze, kissed by the desert sun. Her belly was flat and tight and tan. Her short legs were shapely, with thick thighs and full calves, her arms beckoned like the golden likenesses of the demon serpents that entwined them.

She was the most beautiful female in all the world. And it was not only he who said so. The King agreed.

The King. His friend. His sovereign. This woman was his property.

And yet, she is my love.

He blinked, surprised by the heartfelt declaration that had whispered through his mind.

He followed where she led, where the sands became broken by greenery, just a tuft here and there, though soon it was thicker. There was a trio of date palms beside a pile of boulders, and amid them a bubbling spring. Other trees and plants had sprung up near the water, and she led him into the densest, greenest part of the oasis, where some of the plants were even beginning to flower.

She led him to the far side of a large boulder and then pulled him downward until he was kneeling. Reclining on a nearby flat rock, she drew him toward her, and he did not resist.

"Come to me, my beloved," she whispered. "I thought this day would never arrive. I've missed you so."

He leaned over her, and she tilted her chin up, parting her lips in welcome. He told himself this was a very bad idea, then rationalized that it was, after all, only a dream. A vision. A hallucination. Something. And he decided to enjoy it.

When his mouth touched hers his body caught fire, and every thought he might have had was driven from his brain by a rush of pure molten desire. He slid his arms around her, gathering her to him, holding her as he stretched out atop her. Kissing her while their tongues entwined and their bodies pressed together urgently, he knew this was the sort of passion he'd been missing. This was what people talked about when they sang the praises of physical pleasure. And he'd only just begun. His heart pounded, and his blood heated to a boil. He had to have her. He would do anything for her. Anything!

Pulling away slightly, he opened his eyes to gaze upon her beauty as he reached down to untie the knot of fabric between her breasts. His eyes were riveted as the fabric fell away, revealing perfect breasts, round and full, their dark centers making his mouth water. He lowered his head, unable to hold back a second longer. First he kissed, and then he laved, and then tugged and nibbled while she made soft sounds of delight and dug her fingernails into his scalp.

Smiling, he lifted his head to stare into her eyes again. But she had changed, and he sat up fast, scuttling away from her, his mouth agape and his eyes wide. Her skin had gone softer, whiter, and her hair was like spun silk of palest yellow now. Her eyes were blue, yet still the same eyes. She was the same.

"You're the witch!" he said, stunned.

She blinked at him, then smiled as if he were making a joke. "I'm *your* witch. Your very own."

"Demetrius!" He felt a hard slap on the side of his face, and he surged from his chair to his feet, reaching for the sword at his side.

Only then, when he didn't find it, did he blink the real world into focus once again. The old priest was standing near him, no longer sitting on the other side of the table. They were on the balcony of his own home. There were half-naked beauties prancing around below for his viewing pleasure…and every other pleasure he could have asked for, he thought. But they didn't interest him.

He looked at the priest. Father Dom, his brain reminded him. A man who, though his presence was irritating, had become a sort-of advisor to Demetrius in the few days he'd been there. He'd been filling in a lot of blanks about his lifetime before the void, information he'd craved.

"The chalice pulled you into a vision, didn't it?" the old priest asked. "Did it show you where she is?"

Demetrius shifted his gaze to the chalice, but only for a quick, darting glance for fear he would fall into it again. Truly, this artifact was more powerful than he had ever known. "She's on an airplane," he said, because that was what he saw in his head now, apparently in direct response to Father Dom's question. There were no more ancient city walls, no more foreign deserts.

"She's on her way, then. She'll be your undoing, Demetrius. If you let her."

He swallowed hard, wishing he could be rid of the man. There had been something in that vision that he was eager to ponder, but he couldn't do it with the old priest there. "I won't let her in when she arrives."

"You won't be able to keep her out." Father Dom stood behind a large ornamental ficus and stared down toward the gate.

"I have an excellent security system."

"She has witchcraft." The priest rubbed his chin and paced away from the railing but didn't retake his chair. "No, I think you'll have to let her in. Prepare yourself for it, know how you will handle her, and get it over with as quickly as possible."

"I don't understand what you think I should do, Father Dom. Handle her how?"

"I'll explain it," the old man said, and the words were laced with sarcasm. "You will let her in, and you will meet with her. She will tell you that your soul is incomplete, that she possesses its missing piece, but that to accept it you must give up all your powers. You will let her make this offer to you, and then you will say no. Turn her down. Send her on her way."

Demetrius frowned at the man. "That's all?"

"Yes. That's all."

"Then it will be easy."

"No, Demetrius, it will not be easy. In fact, it will be harder than you can possibly comprehend."

"She tries to convince me to become mortal and weak, and I say no. How hard can it be?"

Father Dom shrugged. "How hard was it the last time?" he asked.

Demetrius frowned, searching the old man's lined face, which, he thought, didn't seem as deeply lined as it had when he'd first arrived. And it was plumper, too. How was that possible?

"Let me answer, since you don't remember," Father Dom went on. "It wasn't hard for you to turn her down before. It was *impossible*. It was your inability to refuse this woman's feminine wiles or withstand her supernatural charms that resulted in the stripping of your soul and your being sentenced to an afterlife imprisoned within an eternal void. If anything, it will be even more difficult this time."

"Why?" Hell, why was he prolonging the conversation by asking questions? He wanted the priest to leave him so he could mull over this vision he'd just experienced. "I think it should be easier. Surely I've learned from experience that—"

"You've learned nothing. And this is her last chance to take your powers. She's desperate this time, Demetrius. She will do anything, use any advantage, to convince you to accept her offer."

Demetrius narrowed his eyes. "How do you know so much about her—and me—and…all of this?"

The priest shifted his gaze away. "As I told you, I've had access to ancient scrolls that record the tale."

"Are you lying to me, priest?"

"Would you like to see the scrolls for yourself, Demetrius? The ones on which your entire history is recorded? I'll happily show them to you."

"Perhaps I should," Demetrius said, only too aware that such documents might be easily forged, and that he did not possess the expertise to know the difference.

"Of course. I have a handwritten copy, handed down through the priests of my line for generations, inside. It's in Akkadian. Do you read Akkadian, Demetrius?"

He sent the priest an impatient look. "I think you know that I do not."

"But you can afford to hire a translator, can't you? I can send for the originals, if you like. They're in storage at the moment, as I've been…ill. I can have them here in a matter of days, if it will help you trust me. But believe me when I tell you, you will learn no more from them than exactly what I have said to you today."

Demetrius lowered his head. "I'm tired. My head aches. I need to be alone."

"Yes, of course. You've been in this world for how long, Demetrius? A couple of months? With no idea who you really are, or why you're here."

Eyes narrowed, Demetrius raised his head and studied the priest, who had just read his soul, or so it felt. "And you can tell me who I am? Why I'm here?"

Father Dom retook his seat at the table, reached across and covered Demetrius's hand with his own. "You were a great soldier, the most trusted man in the army of the greatest king who ever lived, Balthazorus. A man whose name should have gone down in history but instead is lost in obscurity because he died before his time."

"At my hand," Demetrius whispered.

"Yes." Father Dom nodded slowly. "At your hand, but only because you had been seduced and ensorcelled by a witch, Demetrius. She's powerful enough to make a man murder his own best friend."

"So she could be free of the harem," Demetrius said softly, trying to make sense of things.

"Yes."

"And now she's returned to take my powers, using the same methods. Seduction. Sex." A shiver of icy hot sensation shot up his spine as he recalled his dream/memory of lying atop her in the oasis.

"Exactly."

"And if I accept what she offers, I will become mortal again, lose my powers. But what will I gain?"

"Nothing but weakness, my friend," said the priest.

"And if deny her? What happens then?"

"If you can stand firm until the moment of Beltane, which will fall on May fifth— It's the cross-quarter date that marks the halfway point between the vernal equinox and the summer solstice. It's the only other time of the entire year when the veil between the worlds is as thin as it is at Samhain. If you can resist her that long, she will have to accept your answer and leave you alone."

"And it will be over? I will be able to live my life the way I want to, without interference from anyone. Correct?"

"Perfectly." Father Dom patted his hand. "This is a lot to take in all at once, I know. But trust me, Demetrius, I am here for you for as long as you need me. And this will go easier now that you have an ally who knows what is happening."

Demetrius nodded. "Why was I given these powers?" he asked. "The blade, the chalice?"

The priest seemed taken aback; then he shrugged. "That's a question I can't answer. I honestly do not know. Use them wisely. Tell no one."

Demetrius nodded in understanding and gave his guest some thought. "How are you doing up there? In the observatory? Are you comfortable?"

"I am."

"If there's anything you need, I can ask Sid to get it for you. Or you can. Just pick up any phone in the house, press one and he'll pick up. Tell him you're my guest."

Father Dom chewed his lower lip briefly. "This Sid, I could trust him to keep my presence to himself?"

"I trust him," Demetrius said. "Though I suspect he would tell Gus. So until you're ready for them to know…"

"Thank you. I appreciate your generosity."

"I have more than any man needs." Demetrius sighed. "I need some solitude, now." He started for the door.

"Just one thing before you go, my friend…"

Demetrius had almost reached the door, but he paused, itching now to be alone. "Yes?"

"When the witch comes, she must not see me or know that I am here. It is vital. If she knows, she will try to kill me."

Demetrius turned then, his brows arching high. "She would kill you?"

"On sight. I told you, she is desperate. And evil. And powerful, my friend. You must never forget how powerful she is."

Demetrius nodded slowly. "All right."

"And since we don't want her knowing of my presence, I think it best we continue to keep that information from everyone else who lives here, as well. Sid, and your friend Gus."

Demetrius tilted his head slightly to one side. "They won't tell her if I ask them not to."

"She would ask them, and she would not only know if they were lying to her, she might resort to torture to get the truth. The less they know, the safer they are."

"My God, what kind of woman is she?" Demetrius asked.

"The worst kind, my son." Father Dom got up and started to go inside, muttering, "The absolute worst."

Demetrius went inside with the old man. The entire third level was a giant circle split into four sections by two hallways, several of the rooms encased in glass. The spiral stairway that led through a trapdoor up to the observatory was in the very center, at the intersection of the two hallways. Demetrius's bedroom occupied the top right quarter of the circle, a small kitchenette the bottom right. The top left held a huge bathroom with a Jacuzzi big enough to swim in, a shower with multiple heads, a sauna and a massage table. The bottom right quadrant was an entertainment room, with a wall-sized screen and high-tech streaming internet that allowed him to play any film currently available and many TV shows, as well. There was a popcorn machine in one corner.

And best of all, there was a secret doorway between the bedroom and the entertainment room that led to an exterior staircase that spiraled down two stories and opened into a hidden corner of the backyard. There, a pondlike pool and a small hot tub were hidden by a dense garden and privacy fence completely enmeshed in vines. From the rest of the yard, it was invisible. From the rest of the house, too. No one else even suspected it existed, as far as Demetrius knew. Not even Gus.

He couldn't be sure about Sid, who had a history with the house. Short of asking him, there was no way to tell.

Demetrius was going down there tonight to soak and think and try to puzzle out the situation.

Father Dom cleared his throat, reminding him sharply of his presence. "I'm sorry," Demetrius said. "I...I need to process what just happened. And what you've said."

"Of course." Father Dom clapped him on the shoulder. "Thank you for hearing me out, my son. I know you'll do the right thing when the time comes."

"You're welcome."

The old man gripped the railing and started up the stairway to the observatory.

Demetrius went down to his private garden paradise to hide from everyone and everything, and to focus on the one thing he had experienced in that vision that he had experienced nowhere else. The physical sensations.

Full-blown burning desire. Mind-bending passion. Exquisite pleasure at the touch and taste of the witch's lips, the thrilling feel of her body pressing tightly against his, and the unspoken but clear promise that even greater fulfillment lay ahead. The delighted leap of his senses at the smell of her, the way his eyes had feasted on her beautiful body.

He was intrigued and excited by all those things, because they were part of what he'd expected to experience with the women he'd encountered so far. But he'd failed. Nothing had lived up to what he had believed sex would be. His senses, in the memory or dream or whatever it had been, had been heightened in a way they had never been in his brief existence on the physical plane. He'd decided he must be incapable of such feelings. But now, it seemed to him that if he could feel those things so vividly in a vision, he must be capable of experiencing them in real life, after all.

The unanswered questions circled each other in his brain. Had it been a vision or a memory? Was it true that he'd lived another lifetime? And if so, had he really been that aware? That alive? Was that the way it was supposed to be? Was that what others were feeling when they talked about delicious food and fantastic sex? Was that what he'd been missing?

Or was it all just a part of the witch's spell?

Lilia stood at the gate of the palatial home, exhausted and uncomfortably hot as the taxicab rolled out of sight. It was ninety-five degrees in the shade. But beautiful. She didn't think she had ever seen a more beautiful place on this planet. Not just the house itself, which was enough to take her breath away, but the natural beauty that surrounded it. The towering red rock formations of southern Arizona against a backdrop of sky so blue and so cloudless it was hard to believe it was real. The place was outside the tourist trap of Sedona, but near enough for her to feel the energy of the legendary vortices. They spoke especially deeply to a creature like her, not yet quite human and deeply attuned to energy fields.

She *would* be human again, though—if she could convince Demetrius to accept the final piece of his soul. If that happened she would be earthbound again in no time, and so would he. And they would finally have a chance to live the lives that had been stolen from them so long ago.

For three-thousand, five-hundred years she had waited for this day. And now it was here. It was time to begin fulfilling the mission she'd set into motion so long ago. So why was she still standing at the gate like an orphan in hope of a handout?

Because I'm afraid, that's why. Because if I fail, it's all over. This physical part of it, anyway. I like being alive, dammit. And I want to be alive with him.

She'd disembarked the plane in Phoenix, and even from that distance she'd been able to feel his essence pulling her northward. But she hadn't known how far, so she'd phoned Magdalena. "I'm in Phoenix. He's north of me. Did your scrying pinpoint his location?"

"Yes, it worked perfectly."

Lilia's rush of relief had been tempered by the knowledge of how much Lena must hate Demetrius after what he had put her through.

How was she ever going to mend that rift between her soul mate and her family?

One thing at a time, Lilia. There'll be no rift to mend if you're both back in the spirit realm. Or worse.

"Sedona," Lena had said. "Go to Sedona. He's near a vortex."

"Thank you, Lena."

Lilia had hated to end the call, already homesick for Milbury and her sisters, her mother and Ellie. But she was feeling a sense of urgency to get to her love, though she didn't know why.

And now she was here, and still feeling that urgency. The pull he exerted was more powerful now than ever. He was so close. And yet she was hesitant, fear of failure pinning her hands to her sides.

She closed her eyes and began to sing very softly, slow and deep, her voice taking on a resonance it did not have when she spoke. Enchantment. The tune came to her from some higher part of her.

Come to me, she sang, each word long and drawn out. *Welcome me into your home, into your arms. Come, my love, to me.*

When she sang, she became the song, a part of her spirit flowing forth with the melody and floating gently to the intended target, so that her awareness of her body, of her surroundings, faded to nearly nothing. She repeated the verse until she was like a wisp of air, floating to him. And she saw him, vividly and clearly.

He was soaking in a cool, bubbling tub in a hidden garden, with his head leaning against a cushioned rest and his eyes closed. She kept on singing, over and over, as she drank him in. He was the same. He was just the same.

His skin was that same sun-kissed desert bronze. He had the same powerfully chiseled chest, broad and strong. The same soldier's arms, bulging with the muscle that came from wielding his heavy sword and shield. His black hair was wet and slicked back. His thickly lashed eyes were closed, and those full lips she so longed to taste again relaxed, slightly apart. His skin was beaded with water, and she was overcome with a wave of desire so powerful it sucked her right back into her body.

She landed there with a crash, pressing a hand to her head and realizing she was on the ground.

She would have to do better and not let her physical yearning for the man overwhelm her spiritual obligation. It would not be easy. She had loved him passionately, in every way. But that had been in another lifetime. A lifetime he'd forgotten. Even if he accepted the last piece of his soul from her and became fully human, that did not necessarily mean he would love her again.

Getting to her feet, she brushed herself off and prepared to try again. But she was interrupted by a man's voice. "Well now, who do we have here?"

She looked through the bars of the wrought-iron gate to meet a pair of pale blue eyes she had seen once before, in the alley where she had first appeared. And maybe…somewhere else, as well. The man recognized her at the same instant, and his eyes widened in what might have been fear. "By God, you're the witch, aren't you?"

She smiled gently, nodding just twice, and began humming a tune at him almost too softly for him to hear, as she thought the words at him. *I'm your friend*

*and his salvation. You see me with adoration. My
staunch ally you shall be, by the power of sisters three.*

Gus blinked and gave his head a shake, but he was
opening the gate even before she could ask him to.
"D-man will probably kill me for this, but I think he
needs you."

"You're right, Gus. He does." She passed through
the gate, watching as Gus closed it behind her. "You
really are looking well," she said.

He grinned at her. "Damn sight better than the last
time you saw me, eh? Yeah, we've moved up in the
world. I suspect you had something to do with that."

She lowered her eyes. "Not me. He had the power
all along, he just didn't know how to use it. Where is
he now?"

"I don't know." He walked with her toward the
front entrance. "He vanishes sometimes. Disappears
for hours, then shows up like nothing ever happened."

They passed a fork in the stone-paved drive that led
to a grotto where beautiful women splashed in a pool
with a fountain. A few men were with them. Not many.

"This place is like a maze," Gus said, and he tapped
her shoulder to get her focus off the women and onto
him again as he led her up the broad flagstone steps
to the front door. "A person could get lost wandering
in here. I think he likes it that way. I make it a point
never to try too hard to find him when he goes off by
himself like this."

"It's beautiful," she said, pretending interest in the
house, but her throat was tight and she wasn't really
seeing it. "Who are…all those women?"

"Guests," he said. "Now, if you give me a minute,
I'll—"

"Whose guests?"

Gus looked at her, frowned a little. "Mine, to be honest. I know it probably seems…kinda primitive to a lady like you. But I like beautiful women, lots of them, around me. And I'm not kidding myself. They wouldn't be here, short of gunpoint, if they didn't think they were gonna get something out of it. The money, the mansion, it all draws 'em in like flies to sugar, mostly hoping they'll have a shot with the D-man, but figuring I make a good consolation prize."

She tilted her head as she studied his sad eyes. "I think you sell yourself short. You're not a bad-looking man, you know. And I can feel that you have a good heart, Gus. Maybe you should focus less on women who look good in that pool out there and more on finding one who's a match for you on a deeper level."

"Maybe you're right."

"So they…they come here to try to seduce Demetrius?"

"Would do it, too, if he ever gave any of 'em the time of day. He did at first, but lately… D's a shade too fussy, if you want my opinion." He led her through a high-ceilinged octagonal foyer with two-story windows, all arched at the top, and into a smaller sitting area off one side. It was a comfortable room, with bookshelves on one wall, a seventy-two-inch flat-screen TV on another and a giant window on the third. There was an island bar with stools in front, and deeply upholstered armchairs in colors ranging from russet and brown to mustard and sunflower, all with pillows and chenille throws tossed invitingly over them. Her feet sank into the plush carpet so deeply they left footprints. A beautiful room. But not where she wanted to be.

"You make yourself at home, Angel, and I'll—"

"I'm not an angel, Gus."

He grinned again, and she noticed his teeth looked whiter. She suspected he was in the process of getting them fixed. "You look like one to me. I'm gonna go find Sid, and he'll locate our man for you. All right?"

She nodded, wondering who Sid was.

Gus left the room, pulling massive double doors closed behind him.

But Lilia had no intention of waiting. She was too close to Demetrius now to delay. She could feel him pulling her nearer. She didn't need anyone's help to find him. She got to her feet, opened the double doors and let her senses guide her back across the foyer, up the stairs, down a hall and up another set of stairs.

The doors at the top were locked. She smiled at the doorknob and sent her spirit flowing through it in song. *Little lock, a part of me, I am you, and I'm your key.*

It clicked, and she opened the door and went inside, closing it behind her and turning her fingers in a mimicry of turning a key and relocking the door. As she moved along the hallway, Demetrius emerged through a doorway, rubbing his hair with one plush towel, another anchored at his hips. She drank in the sight of him, his chest so powerful and broad and familiar. Her palms itched to run across it.

He looked up, spotted her and stopped in midstride. Then he lowered the towel he was holding and stared at her.

Lilia lost every shred of control she'd thought she possessed. She launched herself forward, pressing her face to his magnificent warm, damp chest, and wrapping her arms around his waist, palms flattening to his powerful back. Her tears flowed like rivers.

She felt his hands on her shoulders, but she blurted, "Not yet, don't push me away yet, Demetrius. I've waited so long to feel you again. To touch you again. Just give me a minute, just a minute, just one precious, precious minute, please, my love, please…"

She was weeping, her words broken by sobs that ripped through her chest like fissures opening in the earth, and letting thirty-five-hundred years of emotion come flooding out all at once.

He stilled his hands on her shoulders and then, grudgingly, reluctantly, slid them downward, over her back, and tightened his arms around her. For a long moment he held her, and she cried and clung and basked in the feel of him. If only, she thought, this moment, this very moment, could last forever.

But it couldn't. She knew it, and eventually he loosened his embrace, put one hand on her shoulder and pried her away from his chest. His other hand went to her chin, his forefinger lifting it so he could look her in the eyes.

"A witch's tears are more potent than I could have known," he said. "But you'll have to do better if you hope to trick me again, sorceress."

5

The beautiful witch's eyes widened and looked as wounded as if he had just thrust his magical blade into her heart. The old priest had been right. She was good at deception. Very good.

"Trick you? What are you talking about, Demetrius?"

He watched her face, searched her blue, blue eyes for signs of her lies, but there were none that he could see. Only hurt.

"I realize that I look very different now," she said softly. "But it's not due to any trick. I didn't plan it this way."

He grunted, averting his eyes, because keeping them on her face made it difficult to remember what she was.

"You look the same, though," she told him softly. "Exactly the same." Her voice took on a slightly raspy quality, and he felt her eyes on his back as he paced away from her.

He headed into his bedroom to fetch a robe and pull it around him before returning to the hub of his circular suite. It made him nervous, being so close to the spiral stairs. Suppose Father Dom should come down from the observatory?

"Even though I look different, I was sure you would remember me." She lowered her head, turning away from him to face the staircase. "I would have remembered you."

"How can you be so sure?" He moved toward her, taking her arm and leading her into the kitchenette. He pulled out a stool for her at the breakfast bar, and she took it, moving as if she were operating unconsciously, automatically.

"Because I did remember you. I have remembered you the entire time. I knew you even when you were a formless mass of hatred, festering in the Underworld."

"Because of you," he said. He'd moved to the other side of the room and was pouring juice into a frosted glass.

"Yes. Because of me. That's true." She lifted her head slowly, frowning at the glass he held out to her. "But if you don't remember, then how do you know that?" she asked as she took the glass and sipped.

He shrugged. "So you admit it, then? You tricked me in another lifetime, tricked me into murdering my friend and King, and then abandoned me to a fate worse than death. All so you could take my powers for yourself, and you've returned to do it all again."

Her eyes narrowed, and she wrinkled her nose as she seemed to sniff the air. "There's evil in this house. I smell it."

"Do not try to distract me, witch."

Her eyes shot to his. "Who filled your head with this ridiculous story, Demetrius?"

"Are you saying it's not true? Because I have had flashes of memory that tell me otherwise."

"Oh, it's true at the base of it, but it's been twisted and polluted with lies. You loved me in that lifetime. And I loved you. I loved you…beyond endurance. But that love was forbidden. I was a harem slave, owned by the King. It was illegal, what we did. Maybe it was inevitable that we'd be found out eventually. I don't know." She lowered her eyes, and he glimpsed moisture gathering on her lashes.

Dragging his attention from her, he realized he had picked up a second glass and was still holding a decanter of juice in the other hand. So he filled it, then returned the decanter to the refrigerator.

"When we were caught in my chambers together and I was arrested," she said, "you fought to protect me and they beat you unconscious. When they searched the quarters I shared with my sisters, they found the tools of our magic, taught to us from early childhood by our mother. The three of us were sentenced to die for my betrayal of the King, and for the dire crime of practicing magic. No one, besides that fat, twisted pig Sindar, was allowed to do that, you see. He intended to keep the Gods and their powers all to himself."

He was riveted by her tale, so close to Father Dom's and yet different in crucial ways. He sipped his juice. "When did I kill the King?"

"When you learned that he was going to let Sindar sacrifice my sisters and me to the chief God of the pantheon, Marduk." She lowered her eyes again. "I couldn't believe you'd done it. You must have exploded in a rage, and how bitterly you must have regretted it afterward. You and the King...you were like brothers. You had been friends for—"

"Stop!" He held up a hand toward her, as if it could halt the flow of words that were beginning to feel like bullets fired into his flesh.

She set her glass down carefully on the gleaming black stone counter. "Demetrius, please. I did not put you in that Underworld prison. I am responsible for you being released from it."

"No. That was another."

"Indira."

He looked up sharply, because that name was correct, he was sure of that, although he hadn't remembered it until she'd said it out loud.

"She is my sister, and she acted under my guidance. Demetrius, I've been trapped between the worlds, as well, though my experience was in a far different dimension. I could watch over all that happened, even you, until the time was right for me to return, to try to complete the cycle, and end it once and for all. To try to set things right."

A cold tremor worked up from his gut to his throat. "You've...seen all that I have done?"

Holding his gaze, she nodded slowly. He wanted to lower his eyes, perhaps in shame, which was odd, because he'd never felt such a thing before.

"Yes, I saw it all. The bomb at the interfaith conference, and all the holy men who died at the hand of the mentally ill human you commanded. The similarly possessed humans you sent to try to eject my precious niece from her newborn body before she drew her first breath. The attacks on my sisters, who were only trying to help you. Yes, I saw it all. And loved you still."

Blackness began to rise over his heart like a wash of dark ink, cooling and calming its guilty beat. "Now I know you're lying. No one could love a man who had done those things."

"No one has ever loved the way we did." She looked him in the eyes when she spoke, and he felt as if she had thrust a hot poker into his chest. "And it wasn't a man who did those things. It was a mindless, shapeless force. A consciousness tormented to the point of insanity. A once-brave warrior hero whose soul had long since been torn away. The same soul that my sisters and I captured, and have kept safe all this time."

There was a flicker in Demetrius's mind. He saw himself and this woman entwined amid sheer draping fabrics, naked among satin pillows. The feelings were so intense that they hurt.

He pushed them away.

"We split your soul among us, my sisters and I. Indira, whose lover you tried to kill, returned the first part to you, and with it the amulet that had been its home during the time in between. And the power it contains." She nodded at the pendant he wore around his neck as she spoke. "She did so at the moment of Samhain, on a night when the stars were aligned precisely as they had been at the beginning. And her brave act set you free from the Underworld. Then Magdalena, whose child you tried to steal, used the chalice and the blade to return the second part of your soul to you, and those tools and their powers with it. Her act was at Imbolc, the precise moment halfway between the Winter Solstice and the Vernal Equinox, and that act restored your body."

She lowered her eyes. "We did take your powers,

you see, with your soul. But only to keep them safe until we could set you free and return them to you. And now you've returned."

"It was as if I just suddenly existed," he said softly, remembering. "It was freezing cold, and I was naked in the snow, shivering, and yet delighted that I could feel the cold. That I was…truly alive again."

"I know. I guided you to the empty house you found. I influenced the minds of the couple who lived there to go away and spend the weekend with their daughter. I ensured that they forgot to lock the door. I needed you to be safe. To be warm. To find your way."

"And the bus ticket?" he asked. "My trip to the city where I joined the ranks of the homeless? Were you behind that, as well?"

"No."

He sighed, nodded. He didn't suppose he could regret even that part of this wild journey, because it was there he had met Gus. And he loved the man like a brother.

"I have the third and final piece of your soul, Demetrius."

He blinked, deciding he needed to hear the rest, and downed his juice. Then he took her glass and his own and, turning his back to her, placed them in the small sink. "Is it ensconced in yet another magical tool? A wand, perhaps, or a crystal of some sort?"

"It's in my heart, Demetrius. I hold it in my heart, where it has always lived."

He felt his back stiffen and couldn't quite turn to face her, so he rinsed the glasses instead. She was getting to him. This was all too much. He had to keep a distance, however small, between them. So he parted the curtains on the windows behind the little sink and looked out over his miniature kingdom, or pretended to. In truth he saw nothing. Nothing but her. Even with his back to her, he could see her face. Those huge blue eyes, like sapphires glittering at him. Round and innocent. Too easy to believe.

"And what power will this final piece of my soul return to me, witch?" He wondered if she would tell him the truth. It would be a good test, wouldn't it? To see whether she would admit to him that he would *lose* his powers if he accepted this prize she offered?

She came around the breakfast bar to stand very close behind him. He could feel her warm breath on his back, between his shoulder blades, and he shivered in a way he had seldom, if ever, shivered at the pleasure of any sensation. "This piece of your soul will restore your humanity. Your ability to feel the full range of human emotions. Your ability to live your life as it was meant to be lived, to relish the fullness of all your senses, to know absolute, exquisite pleasure and, yes, pain, too."

"I already have all of this," he said. "The use of the senses comes with the body."

"No. It comes with the soul. You see, but you don't bask in beauty. It's as if you see things through a filter that dulls everything. You can smell the cactus blossoms with your nose, but the scent doesn't make your heart sing. You hear, but you don't thrill to the sound of music or birdsong. You hear it with your ears, not your soul."

As she spoke she moved closer to him, and he felt trapped. He couldn't turn to face her without those eyes piercing his very core, but he couldn't move away without making it obvious that he was trying to escape her.

"You can taste food, but you don't savor the burst of flavors on your tongue. You can feel the touch of a lover…" She slid her palms slowly up his back, and he closed his eyes. Then she took her hands away again, far too soon, and it was literally painful. "But not the ecstasy of release."

He nodded slowly, wondering why he had felt a hint of that ecstasy at her touch, when he had never felt it with any other woman. Wiping the combination of surprise and horror from his face, he attempted a stern and distant expression, as if he'd been unmoved by her touch, as he asked, "And the price?"

He turned then, facing her, needing to look her in the eye now that he'd schooled his own expression to reveal nothing. "I was told there was a price, a terrible price, for this gift you offer."

Her round blue eyes, swimming now with tears, held his, and she nodded once, then blinked and lowered her head, breaking the spell those glittering sapphires cast over him. "Your immortality, the way you heal more rapidly than others. Your powers, the ones that came to you with the magical tools, the chalice, the blade, the amulet. You would return to being…an ordinary man again. At least, as ordinary as you ever were."

He tilted his head, smiling a little bit, then paced away from her across the tiny kitchen. "So now we come to crux of it, don't we? You have come here to offer me the ability to feel pain—"

"And pleasure and so much more—"

"—in exchange for giving up endless life, and the power to acquire anything I want, such as this very beauty you see around you." He waved an arm to encompass his mansion. "Where would my powers go then, witch. To you and your sisters? And what would I do then? Return to the alley with Gus?"

"Of course not. I'm here now. I would help you, and my sisters would, as well."

"Those same sisters I so wronged? The mother of the child I intended to use—"

"That was not you." She shook her head in denial. "Besides, you were going to stop yourself at the last minute."

"Was I?"

"Yes! Yes, but you didn't have to. Ryan and Lena figured out what to do and…"

Her voice trailed off as he laughed softly, looking at his feet and shaking his head. "I can't believe he was so sure that this was going to be a difficult offer for me to refuse."

"He?"

"I don't have to consider this long, pretty witch. And you are a very pretty witch. But my choice is clear. My answer is—"

"No," she said.

He'd paced away, turned and was moving back to her now. "Very good. You guessed it before I even said it."

"The answer will be yes," she told him with certainty. "I meant no, you don't have to make your decision now. We have time."

"I don't need time."

"Of course you do. If you didn't, I would have come to you sooner. First I had to give you time to embrace what you have. Now you have to give me time to show you what your life could be. To convince you that being human is worth far more than these so-called powers of yours."

"So-called?"

She shrugged, turning and walking a few steps away from him. "We're all immortal. We all have the ability to create what we desire. Not in a blinding flash from a blade in a chalice, but still…"

"I don't want time, and I don't need time, and do not have to give you time. I like my life just the way it is. And immortality certainly beats the alternative."

"The alternative is heaven, bliss, wholeness, one-ness."

"Bullshit." Another expression he'd picked up from Gus. "I've seen the alternative, and I'm not going back there." He marched closer to her, gripped her shoulders and gazed down into her eyes so that could see how deadly serious he was about what he was saying. "Not ever, witch. Make no mistake."

She was trembling. He felt it beneath his hands, and felt cruel for causing it. He eased his grip but did not let go.

"You'll change your mind," she said, the brave words emerging in a determined whisper as she stared up into his angry eyes.

"No, I won't. And I'm not going to let you stay here to try to bewitch me into it, either. I've heard your offer. I've made my decision." He'd done it, he thought, si-lently congratulating himself even while wondering if he had lost his mind. He must have, to say the words he spoke next. "And now I want you to go."

"Demetrius, please, I—"

"Go." He released her shoulders and pointed at the

door through which she'd entered, which led downstairs to the second story and the rest of the sprawling mansion.

She held his eyes. Hers seemed stunned. And then they changed. Her face went from wary and wounded to angry in the time it took him to fling his pointed finger toward the exit again for emphasis. And then she moved as fast as a cobra striking. Ducking beneath his raised arm, she yanked his precious dagger from the sheath at his hip and sliced the air twice.

Only it wasn't the air.

It was his palm and her palm, and then she smashed the two together, closing her hand around his with a grip that was amazingly strong. "By soul and body, blood and bone, nevermore to walk alone!"

His palm burned. It literally sizzled, and a tendril of smoke rose from their pressed hands. He jerked his free and, holding his wrist with his free hand, sucked air through his teeth.

The witch held her own smoldering palm upright, blowing on the blackened center, and he watched as it began to heal. Quickly he turned his own palm up and gazed at it as it magically did the same. Ah, so she shared the ability to heal rapidly. What else? he wondered. What other powers did this beautiful witch possess? And what spell had she cast?

"What the hell did you just do?" he asked.

She smiled. "Don't worry. I didn't restore your soul, Demetrius. I can't do that until you want it, until you ask for it. I can't work against your will. This," she said, turning her palm toward him, "was just a little binding spell. From now on, where you go, I go. There's an invisible bond between us, pulling us together like a rubber band. Your soul was already doing that, calling the piece I hold back to the ones you possess, to unite them again. But the connection is even stronger now. You can't get rid of me, my love."

"Not ever?" he asked, not even thinking to doubt that what she said was true.

"Not until this is finished, one way or the other." She tilted her head. "You haven't said my name. Not once since I've been here. Do you even know what it is?"

Feeling petulant, he lowered his eyes.

"Say my name, love. Say my name."

She made the words a little song, gave them a melody, and before he knew what he was doing, he met her eyes and whispered, "Lilia."

Her smile was wide and as blinding as a sudden spotlight appearing in a darkened room. "You do remember."

"This isn't fair, what you've done. Binding us together like this."

"Love did that long ago."

"Still, you said I had the freedom to make this choice. Now you're using magic to—"

"I can't work against your will, Demetrius," she said, moving closer, lifting a hand to his face and sliding it upward so her impossibly soft palm rasped over his whiskers. "That binding spell wouldn't work unless some part of you, no matter how small, or how deeply buried, wanted it to. Magic cannot work on the unwilling."

She shrugged and turned toward the stair door. "I left my things down in that cozy living room off the foyer. I'll go get them. Should I pick any bedroom I like? Or do you have a preference?"

He blinked at her, wondering how a tiny thing like her had wrested control of this entire situation away from him. He said nothing, and she beamed back at him.

"It's going to be all right, Demetrius. I know it seems impossible now, but it truly is." Then her smile widened and tears brimmed again. "Goddess, it's so good to see you again." She closed her eyes, exhaled hard, then hurried out of his suite.

And even before she reached the bottom of the stairs, he knew her spell had worked, because he felt it: that rubber band stretching out between them, pulling at him.

Dammit, no wonder the old priest had told him this was going to be difficult. It already was, far more difficult than he had ever expected it to be.

There was evil in this place. Lilia continued to sense it, almost smell it. She was going to have to find the source and eliminate it before she could hope to get through to Demetrius. Someone had poisoned his mind against her, someone who did not want her to succeed. And she had a feeling it was that same someone whose presence reeked so virulently. The man Demetrius had mentioned, then refused to identify.

The notion of Tomas's former mentor, Father Dom, whispered through her mind, but no. That made no sense. He was only just out of a coma, and that only days ago. He couldn't have made such a long journey alone, and might not even remember the circumstances surrounding his accident, his past.

But who else could it be? Who would want to thwart her efforts?

She stopped at the first door she came to after reaching the second floor, because it was the bedroom closest to Demetrius. She'd wanted to stay on the same floor he was on, but his suite took up the entire floor and she didn't think she would have much luck talking—or even enchanting—him into that. Not today, at least. She would just have to work on that tomorrow.

For now, she needed to settle in and take some time to celebrate how far she'd managed to come. She was here, in his house, and she'd cast the binding spell. He remembered her name. It was a good start.

Pushing open the bedroom door, she saw that it was apparently vacant, done in pale blue, with vivid white window casings and closet doors.

The carpet was white, too, and the bedspread a deep sapphire that looked as shiny as satin. There was a tiny balcony beyond French doors she had at first mistaken for tall windows. It was just big enough for the small, round wrought-iron table and two chairs that occupied it.

Sighing in absolute pleasure, she slipped off her shoes and stepped inside, her feet sinking into the pristine carpet. "Oh, this is paradise," she whispered. And then she passed the white dresser and the matching white bed and nightstands into the bathroom. It was a beautiful room, all porcelain and stainless steel, very modern, with an oversize Jacuzzi and a shower with three heads.

"Angel?" Gus called from the hallway.

She came out of the bathroom and saw him peeking in at her. "It's Lilia."

"Still look like an angel to me," he said. "I got worried when I couldn't find you."

"I'm so sorry I worried you, Gus. I found Demetrius, and I just couldn't wait to see him again. It's been...a very long time."

He smiled, nodding as if he understood perfectly. "So how did it go?"

She tilted her head. "I think it went well. He didn't send me packing, at least."

His eyes crinkled in delight. "So you're staying, then?"

"Yes, right here in this room, if it's okay with everyone."

"It's the room I'd have picked for you. The colors suit you, and it's as beautiful as you are."

She had to lower her head, because her cheeks were heating. "Thank you, Gus."

"I brought your bag," he said, setting it just inside the door. He hadn't yet crossed the threshold, maybe old-fashioned enough to think it wasn't appropriate for a man to be inside a woman's bedroom unless they were intimate. "I was hoping he'd let you stay."

"And he did. We both got our wish."

He extended an elbow her way. "Would you like the grand tour now?"

"Absolutely," she told him, as, stepping into the hallway, she hooked her arm through his. He patted her hand, gazed at her adoringly, and something familiar lit and then vanished in his eyes, like a lightning bug on a hot July night.

Hours later Lilia was back in her room, exhausted and ready for a solid night's sleep. Being human had its downfalls, though she thought her state had more to do with emotional turmoil than physical exertion. The long trip out here, worrying all the way, the fear that he would reject her, send her away before she could even make her case. The excitement of seeing him again, touching him again. Oh, she wanted so much more of that touching.

She had showered after her tour of the mansion and grounds, then changed into a soft white linen night shift that Selma had chosen for her. Everything she owned had been a gift.

"Just like life itself. It's a gift, too," she said as she clambered onto the huge bed. The mattress topper was a foot thick and down-filled, and she sank into it like sinking into a cloud.

She was holding the ancient treasure chest that had survived these past thirty-five-hundred years along with her and her sisters. She'd brought it with her, the witches' box that had been kept down through the centuries. Before their deaths so long ago, Indira had entrusted it to the little girl who'd been their servant in the harem. Slave girl to the slave girls, she'd called herself, and proudly. Her name had been Amarrah.

Under the unseen guidance of Lilia's own spirit, Amarrah had seen to the box's safety, which had been left in the possession of generations upon generations of her own descendants, until Indira had managed to locate it again. It had an enchanted lock that only the three sisters could open.

Indy thought she'd read all of the scrolls. But Lilia knew better. She'd only seen what she had needed to see to get her through her part of this journey, to complete her sacred mission, to set Demetrius free.

Now the scrolls would reveal more. They would tell Lilia what she herself needed to know. The chest's black iron padlock had no keyhole, serving only as a distraction. Lilia turned the box over and looked at the bottom, where there was a brightly painted grid with symbols of the Tarot painted in the boxes.

To open the box, she needed to touch the squares in the right order.

The Lovers, for her and Demetrius, she thought. That was where this had all begun. She touched the square, and it lit up.

The Tower with its roof blasted off, for the way their love had been torn apart. The way they were ripped from each other through no fault of their own. It lit up, too.

Finally she touched the Wheel of Fortune, for the cycle that was nearing its end and the new one that would begin when it was done.

The Wheel lit up. All three images glowed momentarily, then faded again. And the box was still locked.

Frowning, Lilia reached for her cell phone, only to have it ring before she touched it. Smiling, pleased that the synchronicity they'd always shared was apparently still intact, she answered. "Hello, sister."

"Hey, sis," Indira said. "We've got you on speaker. Lena's here, too. So what's up? Did you find the asshole yet?"

She pressed her lips to keep from asking Indy not to refer to her love that way. From her sister's perspective, Lilia knew, he deserved that and worse. "I've found him, yes. He's living like a king in a mansion amid the vortices of southern Arizona."

"Well, that figures," Lena said. "According to my scrying, he's aware of most of his powers at this point. He knows how to wield the dagger—he's had that one down for a while. He's only recently learned how to scry using the chalice, and he's apparently a little bit afraid of it. And he may or may not realize that using the blade and the cup together allows him to manifest his desires, as he's only done so that one time to bring you through the veil into our world and to get that posh lifestyle he's currently living."

"What about the amulet?" Lilia asked.

"He doesn't know what the amulet does yet," Lena told her. "And that's all I've got. So where are you staying?"

"In his mansion."

"He let you stay?" Indy asked. "Nice job, Lilia. Really, that's a great sign."

"Not really."

"Explain," Indira commanded.

Lilia heaved a sigh. "He doesn't remember me, Indy. I can't believe it, but he just doesn't remember anything about…about us. The love we shared. I didn't think it was possible for him to forget, but—"

"Sweetheart," Lena said softly. "None of us remembered our shared history at first. Have you forgotten?"

Lilia sniffed and nodded, even though she knew they couldn't see her over the telephone. "All he remembers are my name and being imprisoned in the Underworld, and he's desperately afraid of being returned to that state."

"Well, who can blame him? It must have been like an endless nightmare," Indira said.

"There's something else going on here, though," Lilia told her sisters. "Someone apparently warned Demetrius that I was coming and told him that the three of us were to blame for his being stripped of his soul and sentenced to that horror from the start."

"What?" They spoke in unison, making Lilia smile despite the problem she was still trying to work out.

"Someone told him that we had tricked him into murdering King Balthazorus just so we could get free of the harem."

"Isn't he aware," Indy asked, "of the pesky little fact that we're the ones who busted his sorry ass out of the Underworld?"

"Yes. And he believes that we only did it so we can rob him of his powers and send him right back again."

"But you told him otherwise," Magdalena whispered. "Didn't you?"

"Of course I did, but he didn't believe me."

"Well, you'd better make him believe you, little sis, and soon." Indy again.

"Why soon?"

"Tell her, Lena."

Lena cleared her throat. "My scrying revealed a deadline."

Sighing, Lilia lowered her head. "I was afraid there would be one. When? Tell me, sister."

"Beltane," she whispered. "It falls on May fifth this year."

"That's only a week away!" Lilia shouted the words, then clapped a hand over her mouth and shot a nervous look at her closed bedroom door. "By the Goddess, how will I convince him in such a short time?"

"You're no ordinary woman, Lilia, much less an ordinary witch."

"Indy's right," Lena said. "You've spent three-thousand, five-hundred years in the Upperworlds. The heavenly realms. You must have achieved understanding, even enlightenment, by now."

"I was in a way station, an in-between place," Lilia corrected gently. "And I do not feel like an enlightened being. I still feel like…like your little sister. Too reckless, too passionate, too impulsive, and so vulnerable where love is concerned."

"Your heart is breaking all over again, isn't it, Lilia?" Lena asked softly.

"It never really stopped. But now, being this close to him, and with him looking exactly the same— Goddess, it's so hard to be this close and not touch. Not hold. Not kiss."

Her sisters made sounds of understanding. Then Indy said, "You say he looks exactly the same? How is that, when we don't?"

"I've been mulling on that. I believe he regenerated his original body. I can't explain it, but I'm sure it's true."

"Makes sense," Indy said. "Our bodies were pitched from a cliff, destroyed, and our souls only left them when life did. His soul was stripped from his body by force. It wasn't a natural death in any way. It was a violent separation, one without death included. Who knows what became of the body after he was separated from it? But when the pieces of his soul were returned and began to call it forth, it seems possible that it might have reconstituted itself. It can't move on to its natural end—that of fertilizing the earth—unless the soul leaves it through death. His body, too, has probably been in limbo."

"How did you get so smart, Indy?" Magdalena asked.

"I'm married to a scholar. You pick shit up."

The three of them shared a soft laugh.

Then Lilia thought to ask, "Indy, how did you open the box? What combination did you touch?"

"The High Priestess," she said. "Then the Lovers, and then the World."

Lilia flipped the box over once again and touched the symbols in the order her sister had given her, but while they each lit up, the box did not unlock.

"That's odd. It didn't work for me."

"Huh. Well, keep trying," Indy said. "There must be a different combination for each of us. You're bound to stumble onto yours eventually."

But Lilia didn't think she would. She had a feeling that when the time came that the knowledge the box held would be of help to her, she would simply know the combination. So perhaps she would set it aside until that time came.

"Maybe we should fly out there to help you," Indy offered.

"I don't want you here," Lilia said quickly. "There's evil in this house. A presence."

"No shit," Indy said.

"What is that supposed to mean?" Lilia demanded.

It was Lena who answered her. "Remember, Lil, I had the same presence in my house. It was Demetrius himself, all dark and shadowy, like some kind of ghost demon."

Of course that was what her sisters would have thought of first. "It's not that. It's not Demetrius, or any ghost or demon. It's physical, I think. I feel someone else here. Someone bad, and I think it's the same someone who filled his head with lies about me, about us. I can't pinpoint it, but…I feel as if whoever it is, is watching me. As if he's trying to ensure that Demetrius will never accept the final piece of his soul. So it must be someone who knows that if he refuses, he will die and so will I. It must be someone who wants that to happen. Someone who wants me to die."

"But you can't, can you, Lilia?" Lena asked. "Not until you've competed your task. You're immortal, right?"

"As long as my body remains essentially intact, it will heal and I'll live on. At least until Beltane. But if my body is destroyed and I expire before he takes his soul-piece back, then it dies with me. And he dies, too, and this time his soul dies with him, so he will simply cease to exist."

"And if Beltane comes," Indy said, "and Demetrius hasn't accepted the final piece of his soul?"

"Then he dies at the moment of Beltane, but goes on into the afterlife, his soul reforming itself on the other side."

"And so will you. You'll die but your soul will still live on the other side. Right, sis?" Lena asked softly.

"Right."

And so will they.

That voice had not come through the cell phone. It was a psychic whisper from deep within her own mind.

Lilia's eyes widened, her heartbeat quickened. What did it mean? Her sisters...?

"Baby's crying, hon. Time for her 1:00 a.m. feeding. I've got to go."

"I love you, Lena. And you, too, Indy. Give our mother a kiss for me."

"Stay in touch, Lil. Keep us posted," Indy said.

"I will. Good night." She disconnected. Though it

was only 10:00 p.m. local time, it felt like one in the morning to her, too, and she was barely keeping her eyes opened. She only had a week, and there was an unseen evil in this place that she had yet to locate and eliminate, and now something else, something in her head, was telling her that she and Demetrius would not be the only ones who would exit this lifetime, should she fail.

Goddess help her, she couldn't let her sisters' lives end, as well. And what about the baby?

6

Father Dom had known which room the witch would choose, the one closest to Demetrius, and so he'd set his enchanted projective stones at the cardinal points, then matched them with receptive stones in his own room high above. The projective stones worked much like a hidden microphone, transmitting energy, ideas and knowledge from one place to the other.

Demetrius had granted him use of the observatory for the length of his stay. Along with the giant telescope that was the room's reason for being, the room held a twin-size bed and a matching dresser and nightstand. He had few belongings, the things he'd taken from the hospital and a few others he'd picked up along the way. Very few. As if he'd taken a vow of poverty.

Ironic, since he was living amid the most opulent wealth he'd seen since...well, since Babylon.

He wanted to go unnoticed. As far as Gus, or the ever-vigilant Sid knew, or could be allowed to know, the priest who'd paid their boss a visit had left immediately after.

It was good to stay under the radar, as the people of this time liked to say.

He had taken the liberty of visiting the kitchen after hours, as had become his habit, and had brought a small feast back to his room with him. Then he'd set it aside and ventured out again, sneaking into a storage room this time, where he'd found and retrieved a box of colorful fabric, curtains he supposed. He was so very tired of the dull black garments he was forced to wear while in this pale priest's sagging body.

Besides, they no longer fit. The host body was changing already, beginning to regain its strength and muscle tone, and even beginning to take on a soft layer of fat that plumped his face and smoothed away some of its wrinkles. His hair was losing its gray caste with every strand that fell away. The new growth was dark as onyx, and shiny, just like before.

He was changing. The soul that lived in this body now—*his* soul—was rearranging its cells the way a new resident of a house might rearrange the furniture.

Yes, he was getting stronger. And his powers were returning, too, as he settled into this once-decrepit body.

He sat in the center of the observatory, directly beneath the dome that housed the powerful telescope. His black clothes lay in a heap on the floor nearby, while he was wearing bright purple curtains like robes and smiling at his pleasantly full belly as he sank into a trance, able to connect through the stones to the witch. He was able to watch and listen and feel her as clearly as if he were in the room with her while she spoke on the telephone to her sisters.

It was too bad that they'd discovered that Lilia had only until Beltane to convince Demetrius to accept her offer, but he could hold her off until then. One week. Just one week and it would be over.

And then they would all be dead, every single one of them: Demetrius the traitor, the three disloyal, demon-serving witches, their mates and their progeny.

All of them.

All Demetrius had to do was say "no."

And if it looked as though Demetrius might fail to hold firm, he now had a backup plan, thanks to the conversation he'd overheard. Now he knew he could kill Lilia and destroy her body, and then Demetrius, too, would die. No afterlife. No heaven. No reincarnation. Actually, he would prefer it that way. Maybe his focus should be on killing the witch, destroying her body, and Demetrius in the process.

Demetrius opened his eyes and found the beautiful witch Lilia lying beside him in his bed. Her body was nestled close to his, her arms were wrapped around his waist and her head was resting on his chest. He was still half asleep, and realized he was caught in the throes of yet another dream about being with this woman, about writhing in exquisite passion with her and experiencing a release like nothing he'd ever imagined. Surrendering to the fantasy, he tightened his arms around her, bent his head to inhale the fragrance of her hair. Her leg slid up the front of him, her thigh brushing over his hardness and tripling his need.

And then he came fully awake, suddenly aware that his "dream" was reality. In a panic, he shoved her away so hard that she rolled off the bed. She landed on the floor amid a tangle of sheets and sat there, blond hair hanging in her eyes, blinking in sleepy confusion.

"What are you doing here?" he demanded, sliding off the other side of the bed and pulling his robe from the corner of the headboard, then wrapping it tightly around him.

She lifted her head toward him, then blew her hair out of her eyes. She looked so bedraggled and confused that he almost grinned. His heart clenched, and he clung to his anger by sheer force. She had invaded his private domain. His haven. His dreams.

And yet she had also *been* his dream.

"I guess I must have sleepwalked."

"You guess?"

"I haven't been human very long, Demetrius. Not even as long as you have."

"That doesn't mean—"

"Your body is pulling me all the time. It wants the missing piece of its soul back. The binding spell makes it pull harder. And just the sheer power of how much I want you in my arms again, in my bed again, is more potent than you can even imagine. It's not my fault I lose the ability to resist while I'm sleeping." She sighed. "Frankly, it's pretty exhausting fighting it all the time."

He was struck silent for a long moment by her honest admission. She wanted him. It was that simple. She wasn't even pretending otherwise.

He wasn't prepared to deal with this. He couldn't say he didn't want her, too. She would know it to be a lie. Eventually he found something to say that was true. "I don't want to be human again. I don't want to lose my powers and my immortality. You might as well give up."

She shrugged. "Maybe I will. But not today. Who

else is in this house with you, Demetrius? Besides Gus, I mean?"

"Sid. The limo driver and right-hand man. He came with the place. I honestly don't know how we'd ever get by without him."

"And no one else?" she asked.

His eyes shifted toward the spiral staircase that led up to the observatory, but he jerked them right back again. "No. There used to be some live-in staff, but I didn't like that. So they come in as needed, by day, when I can tolerate them, and then they leave."

"You don't like people," she said softly, her eyes moving over his face.

He couldn't tell her that he was jealous of them. Jealous of the way even the most miserable of them seemed able to extract more of the juiciness of being human from their lives than he could. Eating a chocolate bar or a slice of pizza or an ice-cream sundae. Moving their bodies to the music as if they were feeling it in every part of themselves. Laughing with real joy crinkling the corners of their eyes. He didn't understand laughter, but it looked so delicious that he wanted to.

He wanted all of it. One day he'd caught the gardener, Jimmy, leaning close to sniff a flower and closing his eyes in bliss. After Jimmy had moved on, Demetrius had sniffed at the very same blossom after first making sure no one was around to observe him. But aside from a tickle that made him sneeze, he felt nothing. He had certainly extracted no pleasure from it.

Being around people made him jealous of what they had.

It also frustrated him, because apparently he couldn't

have what they had without giving up what he had now. And he liked what he had now better.

"How do you know for sure, unless you can experience what they're experiencing?" Lilia asked softly.

Her smile had died, and she was staring into his eyes.

"So, you can spy on my thoughts, as well?" He sighed, and strode across the bedroom. "That's good to know, I suppose."

"I can't read your thoughts. Not really. Those were not thoughts, those were longings of your soul. And since I hold a piece of it, I felt them."

"Why would my soul long for physical senses?" he asked.

"Why do you think souls incarnate into physical bodies in the first place, Demetrius? It's to experience the very things you are denying yourself."

"We're talking about my soul, not me."

"Your soul is you." She sighed. "It's the true you, your higher self, the part of you that is Divine. Now tell me, who else lives here?"

"No one," he lied, and hoped she wouldn't know.

"And this dislike of people, why doesn't it extend to all of those jiggling, giggling future skin cancer patients constantly frolicking about in your pool and fountain?"

His back was toward her, so she couldn't see the slow, pleased smile that spread across his face. He even felt a hint of pleasure—something he rarely felt at all—at her obvious jealousy. "They are here for entertainment purposes. Every man enjoys looking at a beautiful female body. Even one as soul-deprived as I am."

"Oh, well then, let me help."

He heard the soft brush of fabric on skin and realized what she was doing too late to stop himself from
turning around. She dropped the nightgown she had
peeled over her head and stood there absolutely nude.
His knees went liquid, and it felt as if a giant hollow
had opened up in his belly.

He'd lost the power of speech. That was a good
thing, Lilia thought. At least she hoped it was. She
stood there naked and not a bit embarrassed, because
he'd seen her naked a thousand times before. Not in
this body, of course.

But if being formless for more than three thousand
years had taught her anything, it was that the body was
just an outfit one chose to wear. That it was the spirit
that was the real self. Revealing the skin and bones
she'd donned to walk this world in was no different
than revealing the car she might choose to drive, the
house she might choose to live in, the clothes she might
decide to wear. It was meaningless, really. A reflection
of the spirit it contained.

That thought made her frown and wonder if the
change in her appearance might indicate some kind
of change in her soul. Maybe her old body no longer
reflected who she now was. Otherwise, why would
this new one look so different? Maybe she really had
changed and grown during her time in limbo, watching, waiting, longing for him. Aching for him. Loving
him, even when he'd been a monster.

She'd experienced the height of loneliness. She'd
been forced to learn to exercise seemingly endless patience. She'd been steadily attentive, watching over her
sisters, guiding them, prodding them when necessary,

protecting them always. And she'd been watching over him, too, frustrated at her inability to help him.

But right now she was wondering about something far more earthly and vain.

"Do you like it?" she asked Demetrius, looking up at him, watching as his gaze moved down the new body that was becoming familiar to her. She tried to see it through his eyes. It was small and slight, and the breasts seemed to her to be a bit too large in proportion to the rest of it. "It's not the same one I had before. But I think I like it. I'm growing very comfortable in it."

She pushed a lock of hair out of her eyes and turned in a slow circle in front of him, craning her neck to look at the back of her body in the mirror, glimpsing the tattoo that had somehow survived her transition, the Babylonian cuneiform symbols for Daughter of Ishtar on her lower back, as they had been before.

When she'd completed her circle, he was still staring, his mouth slightly open, though he snapped it shut when his eyes finally met hers again after their long and heated perusal.

"Did you like the old one better?"

"I don't—" His voice was so hoarse he sounded like a crow. He cleared his throat, started again. "I don't know. I don't remember the old one."

"Oh." She lowered her eyelids halfway, so he wouldn't see her disappointment. She'd been fishing for a compliment, and he hadn't even nibbled at the bait.

Then he went on. "I don't see how it could have been any more pleasing than this one, though."

Her eyes opened wide, and she flashed him a big smile that could not be contained. She clapped her hands together in staccato applause. "You do like it! I'm so glad. I mean, it's shallow of me, but it means a lot to me to know that you like the way I look." He didn't respond, perhaps didn't even hear her. She stilled her giddiness and realized that he had gone somewhere—a mental journey, not a physical one. "Demetrius?"

Blinking twice, giving his head a brisk shake, he quickly picked up the nightgown and pressed it to her chest, carefully avoiding touching her breasts. "I can't think straight with you standing there naked like this. Please put it back on."

She was fairly certain that was a compliment, too. "Are you sure? I was hoping we could…you know…"

"No." He turned away from her. "No, we definitely aren't going to *you know*."

"But it might trigger your memory." She pulled the nightgown on again then padded toward him and slid her palms up his back, wishing his robe would vaporize. "Demetrius, if you could remember what we were to each other you would never believe I was out to trick you or steal anything from you."

"It would cloud my judgment. If I'm to make a rational decision, I cannot allow sex to interfere with my reasoning. Can I?"

"It wouldn't be sex. It would be lovemaking." She leaned closer, resting her cheek on his back. "Oh, Demetrius, it was so good between us. We swore no two people had ever loved the way we did, and we knew they never would. It was…it was something… something beyond love. It was something…"

"Something like a spell?"

She shoved him, and he stumbled two steps before stopping. "You're cruel! How can you be so heartless to the woman you once swore you would die for?"

"If you're innocent, then I'm sorry."

"That's what the priest said before he threw me from a cliff to my death," she said, then turned and stomped across the room, flung open the door and took a step toward the stairs.

He caught her elbow before she took a second step. "What do you mean, priest? What priest?" he demanded.

She swung her head around, let him see the tears on her cheeks and the anger in her eyes. He needed to see them. Didn't he realize what she'd done for him? She'd given up heaven, given up crossing over into the afterlife. She'd served three thousand years, plus five hundred more, in limbo. All for him. Didn't he understand that?

No, she realized. He didn't.

"Tell me, who is this priest you spoke of?"

Lilia tried to contain her anger. For someone who'd learned patience over such a long time, she was certainly being impatient with him now. "The most evil bastard who ever lived. Sindar. High Priest of the Temple of Marduk in Babylon. A fat pig with kohl-lined eyes and berry-stained lips. He was in love with the King. We all knew it. That's why he took such horrible vengeance on me for betraying him. And on you for killing him."

"What was his vengeance on me?" he asked.

"Why are you asking me that when you know the answer perfectly well? He took your soul, Demetrius, and then imprisoned what remained of you in a dark Underworld void, all alone." She closed her eyes slowly, swallowed. "It was supposed to be for eternity."

He was searching her eyes with an intensity that

was almost palpable, watching every expression that crossed her face. "And why should I believe you? I have already told you," he said slowly, "that I have it on very good authority that it was you and your sisters who were responsible for that."

"In a way, I suppose that's true. We *were* responsible. I was, at least. Your rage against the King was because you loved me beyond endurance. He sentenced me to death, and you had to defend me. Your heart gave you no choice. He was your friend, Demetrius, but your love for me was so powerful that you killed him to protect me. Just as I would have done for you. Only in that was I to blame."

He stared at her in silence, and she knew he was looking for signs of dishonesty, trying to spot the lie in her eyes. Insulted, she tugged her arm free. "You don't believe me. But it doesn't matter, Demetrius. You'll know the truth when you remember your past—our shared past."

"And how do I go about getting those memories back? By having sex with you? Giving you the chance to use your powers to plant memories in my mind that aren't real?"

She grabbed his shoulders, held him hard, digging her nails into his flesh as her eyes blazed into his. "What we had was the most real thing there ever was. The most real thing you've ever known. You'll see that, once you remember." Then she took her hands away and turned, looking at her own bare feet beneath the hem of her nightgown. "Your memory will return to you with the final piece of your soul. But since you won't let me restore it, I guess we're at an impasse."

"I would get back the memories, yes. And lose my

powers. My immortality." He looked around the room. "All of this."

"Powers?" She faced him again, tired of his arguments. "What good are they, anyway? You have a blade that shoots bolts of energy." She shoved his chest, so he stumbled backward as she advanced on him furiously. "Who cares? You could buy a gun that would do worse. You have a cup that allows you to see the future. So what?" She shrugged. "Anyone can learn to the see the future—in a cup, in a candle's flame, in the ripples of a stone cast on the water. My sister Magdalena was doing it long before that cup came into her possession. Witches have been doing it since the dawn of time."

She stopped, slightly out of breath and completely caught up in the white-water current of her emotions.

"Perhaps all of that is true. But the fact remains. I am immortal."

"So is every being on this planet. Haven't I proven that to you by returning to you after all this time? Haven't my sisters proven it by finding the very same lovers they lost to Sindar's rage and reuniting with them again? Lena was pregnant when we were shoved off that cliff. And now, today, even her baby has returned to her. There is no end, Demetrius. Death as humans perceive it is the biggest lie ever told. It simply doesn't exist."

He nodded slowly, then turned, paced across his bedroom and came back to her again. "I can manifest my desires by using the chalice and the blade. That's how I got this mansion and all the money that goes with it."

"So can everyone else. And they don't even need any special tools."

"Now I know you're lying. People suffer all the time. They wouldn't do that if they didn't have to."

"The only thing that causes suffering is a person's focus on unhappiness. Expectation of suffering. Belief in suffering. The only thing preventing every living human from having everything their heart desires is that they don't believe they can. They're too busy 'facing reality,' not realizing that their attention to the things they don't want is the glue that keeps those things stuck in their experience."

She moved closer and put her hand calmingly on his upper arm, feeling the muscles flex beneath her touch. "Life isn't what we think it is, Demetrius. It's truly what we make of it."

His lips twitched a little at the outer corners. She was getting to him; she knew it.

"And what about all this? The riches? The mansion?"

She shrugged. "If you decide it's what you want, you'll find a way to keep it. But do you really think it's important, Demetrius? If I were in your arms I could be happier in a tent, or in that alley where I found you, than I could ever be in a golden palace without you."

He blinked rapidly, turning quickly away, and just kept walking, all the way into the bathroom, closing the door behind him. She went after him, gripping the knob just in time to hear the lock turn. "As if that can keep me out," she called. "Demetrius, please, you have to listen to me."

"No," he said. "I don't." Then sound of the shower running came through the door, and she lowered her forehead to the cool wood in defeat.

Who was poisoning his mind against her? It was

going to be a hard enough task convincing him to give up all his powers and possessions, which were the only things he thought he had, without some stranger filling his head with lies. Who would want to do that? Who would want to see her fail? See him die? Besides, they would be in bliss, and together—as long as she didn't die first and take his soul with her. Maybe her enemy was ignorant of that. Maybe it was someone who still believed that death was an ending and wanted to see her life over with.

She returned to her own room, showered and dressed in a sundress of white muslin with embroidered daisies all over it. Sundresses made up the bulk of her wardrobe, all of them white or a pastel hue. Her sisters kept telling her she would need jeans, sweaters, heavier footwear, by the time winter came, but she couldn't see spending their money on those things when she might very well be dead by the first snowfall.

She swept her hair to one side, using tortoiseshell combs to hold it there. Stepping into a pair of white sandals, she silently thanked her stars for Selma's love of shopping and Indira's sense of style. Though Indy had balked at Lilia's tunnel vision when it came to choosing clothes, she'd helped her find matching shoes and bags so she would look her best.

When she finished dressing, she went downstairs in search of something to eat. Often, when she felt that odd gnawing pang in her stomach, it took her a minute to process it in her mind as a sign of hunger. Feeding her body was not something she'd had to worry about on the other side.

As she passed through the massive great room with its deep-hued, rich wood floor, the walls all swirls and knots of gleaming fox-red and dark cherry, she glimpsed Gus sitting outside with a young man with red curls and seaweed-green eyes. She hadn't met him before. They were on one of the countless patios, sitting at an umbrella-shaded table that was loaded down with food.

Gus glanced up and met her eyes, then flashed her an adoring smile that made her feel a little guilty about enchanting him the way she had at the front gate when she'd first met him. But it had been necessary. Her sisters were not with her. She needed allies.

He waved a hand to beckon her, and she smiled back at him and started forward. She noticed the younger man looking at her with a hint of suspicion, a touch of wariness. She looked him right in the eyes and read him instantly. Devoted to Demetrius, half in love with him, uberprotective and loyal to a fault.

Good. So was she.

You love me on sight, friend to be, she sang softly. *You see the light that shines from me.* Her voice dropped to the deep, mesmerizing tone she thought of as her magical voice, and the tune that came to her naturally was a slow, haunting one. *Help me do what's right, friend to be. We'll save him together, you and me.*

She watched his dark green eyes change, pupils expanding. His freckled face relaxed, and he smiled a warm welcome as she made her way onto the patio.

Gus got up and pulled out a chair for her. "See, Sid? I told you the D-man let her stay."

"I didn't give him much of a choice, to be perfectly honest," she said, sinking into the seat, beaming at the other man. "I haven't met you before. I'm Lilia."

"Sidney," he said, "But everyone calls me Sid." He

clasped her hand in his cool, very tenuous grip for a fraction of a beat. "I'm Demetrius's driver and all-around gofer."

"Oh, you're more than that. Demetrius thinks the world of you."

Sid's smile went up a notch. He handed her a plate. "Please help yourself. We always breakfast out here, and the cook always makes enough for any guests who might stop by."

"You do seem to have a lot of them." She accepted the plate, and helped herself to some luscious-looking blueberry muffins and fresh melon and pineapple wedges as she looked toward the grotto, the pool and fountain, and the gardens where she'd seen so many frolicking females the day before. "Though there are none here now."

"The women who come around here are not exactly... early risers," Sid said. His voice held a touch of disapproval.

She was glad. "I don't like them, either."

His brows rose in surprise. "Am I that obvious?"

She beamed at him. "I know a kindred spirit when I see one," she said, and his cheeks went pink with pleasure. Then she turned to the man who was his opposite in almost every way. "*You* like them, though, Gus, yes?"

"What's not to like?" Gus asked, sounding a little defensive. "Gorgeous females, half-dressed, giggling and splashing and paying me all sorts of attention."

"Hmm. I wonder."

"What do you wonder, Lilia?" Gus asked, hanging on her every word.

"Well, it's probably not my place to say. But I do

wonder, if you were still in that alley, hungry and dirty, maybe sick or injured and bleeding on the pavement, do you think any one of those giggling, half-dressed females, should she happen to be walking past, would stop to offer you aid?"

He blinked at her, mischief in his pale gray eyes. "I didn't say they were nice."

"You asked what's not to like. I'm just telling you."

"She's right," Sid said, as he got up to angle the umbrella to shade her face from the sun. "None of those bimbos would give you the time of day if not for the mansion, the pool, the free food and drinks, and the notion that they might get to meet the big guy by hanging around here."

Gus shrugged, pushed out his lower lip in a petulant pout and pretended great interest in his breakfast wrap.

"How long have you known Demetrius?" Sid asked her, filling a coffee cup from a silver pot.

"It seems like forever. We were so in love once. So in love." She closed her eyes, remembering his passionate kisses and heart-wrenching declarations of undying devotion. "But we were torn apart by…outside forces. Evil ones. And now he doesn't really remember me."

"Really." Sid bent close, and he was clearly curious. "I don't understand that. How can he not remember?"

She shrugged and sipped the coffee he offered her, not knowing how to answer that question and deciding it was better not to answer it at all. "And what's worse," she went on, "someone's been telling him things about our history that simply aren't true. Trying to turn him against me. And I'm afraid it might be working."

Gus smacked his wrap down on his plate so hard a green pepper popped out of it. "Who?" he demanded.

"Just tell me who it is and I'll put a stop to that nonsense right here and now, I'll tell you that much."

"Easy, Gus." But Sid looked just as angry. "Why would anyone want to keep you apart?"

"Yeah, and why would D-dog be dumb enough to believe 'em? I mean, just one look at you ought to tell him you wouldn't lie. You couldn't lie."

She lowered her head, wondering if she'd done too thorough a job of making the men adore her. "I don't know why he's choosing to believe this person. Much less why anyone would want to mislead him that way. If I knew who was doing it, I might be able to figure out why. But I *don't* know. I have a feeling it was someone he's seen recently, though. And I keep getting the feeling there's…someone else in the house. Someone whose only goal is to hurt me and hurt Demetrius."

"A feeling?" Gus looked across the table at Sid. "I told you, she's something special. Not a normal, everyday woman, that's for sure."

"I can see that," Sid said.

Lilia drew a deep breath, gave a nod. "Yes, it's true. I'm not an ordinary woman. But I'm not an angel, either. However, I do have some…special abilities."

"I knew it!" Gus said. "She's one of the witches who's supposed to help the boss. Aren't you, Lilia? Aren't you?"

She nodded but didn't elaborate. Instead she sent Gus a pleading look. "There's a presence in this house, Gus. Someone's here, someone…evil. The problem is, there are so many people here all the time that it's hard for me to sort out who the enemy is."

"Ah, I see now," Gus said.

"Is it part of your witchcraft?" Sid asked, like a kid

asking, *Is it Santa?* "The way you can...sense some-one's presence and intentions?"

She nodded. "Yes, but it only goes so far."

"None of my beauties are here now, Lilia." Gus waved a hand, indicating the grounds. "Can you sense who you're looking for? Can you feel the evil?"

"I've been feeling it ever since I first came to the gate. But that doesn't mean the person has been here the whole time, or even that he or she is here now. People leave an energy trail behind when they've been somewhere. The more time they spend, the longer it lasts. It would be very helpful if we could...just maybe..." She let her words trail off, knowing Gus was going to balk, despite his fondness for her.

"Bar the gate for a while?" Sid asked.

Gus huffed and crossed his arms over his chest. "For how long?"

"A day? Two at the most."

Gus pouted, his lower lip thrusting out even farther than before, but she knew he would concede.

"Tell them you're sick, Gus," Sid suggested. "See how many flowers and get-well wishes you receive."

"All right. All right, fine, I'll do it."

"Thank you, Gus," Lilia said, patting his hand. "You, too, Sid." Sid waved a dismissive hand. "And... and I think it might be best if we don't tell Demetrius that I'm the one who asked. All right?"

Gus nodded and took another bite of his wrap as if he were biting off the head of an unwanted but myste-riously influential guest.

7

He tried to shower away the effects of seeing the woman naked before him, of the things she'd said, of waking up twined around her after dreaming of making love to her with his entire soul. But he couldn't shake any of it. It had all been too real, too...painful.

Yes, that was the word. Painful. It had hurt him. That was a new experience.

In his dream he'd been wrapped up with the woman, inside her, belonging there, moving together in a rhythm older than time. True, the woman in the dream had looked nothing like the one in his house now. She'd been taller, darker, fuller. She'd had more curves, darker skin, thick black hair, full brows, eyes always made-up. She'd jingled when she moved, the woman he remembered.

Dreamed. Not remembered. None of it is real.

And yet, she was every bit the same woman. He'd felt Lilia, this Lilia, in that dark woman he'd been making passionate love with in the dream. It had been her. She'd looked different, but there was no doubt in his mind that she and his dream woman were one and the same.

Stop thinking about it.

But he couldn't. He braced his arms against the sides of the tiled shower stall and lowered his head beneath the hot, pounding spray, and the whole thing played out again in his mind, like a film on the giant screen in his entertainment room. It swept him away so thoroughly that when he looked up…

He found himself tangled in silken covers and his lover's arms, in a room that resembled a palace. Everything was ornate: gold gleamed, sheer curtains were draped everywhere, and tall vases and statues of goddesses in various poses stood in every corner and on every surface.

And then one of Lilia's sisters burst in on them, and he thought, *I know her. That's Magdalena.* "Get dressed and get out, Demetrius. Hurry! There are soldiers. They know—"

He scrambled to his feet, clutching a length of fabric to cover himself, as the soldiers surged into the rooms where no man was ever permitted to set foot. The harem chambers. They were men he knew. Men who'd fought in battles alongside him, whose lives he'd saved, who'd saved his in return. Men he'd considered his friends.

One of them grabbed Lilia, and Demetrius felt something rise up inside him that he knew he was incapable of feeling today. And yet he felt it, in this odd, memory-like waking dream. Rage. Fury. Full-blown and passionate. It was hot and issuing from him like steam from an overheated kettle. He attacked the armed men, weaponless and nude, and still it took three of them to beat him down. But the fourth had Lilia, binding her hands behind her, not even allowing her to dress first, while she cried and pleaded, and her sisters tried to intervene.

He got to his feet, and his comrades put him down again. And again, and again, until he could no longer move. As he watched, one of the soldiers threw a blanket at Lilia's chest, and she wrapped herself in it with her awkwardly bound hands, her eyes on him where he lay helpless on the floor, tears streaming down her face. "Don't hurt him anymore," she begged in a language he did not recognize and yet understood. "This wasn't his fault."

The three women were arrested and taken away. He couldn't follow.

And then one of the soldiers tore apart the room. Demetrius fought to cling to consciousness while bleeding on the stone tiles. His heart sank when the searcher found herbs in tiny bundles, oils in small vials, feathers of various birds, an ornate wooden box filled with nothing but the skins shed by snakes, and a double-edged dagger, its handle engraved with mystical symbols, with a chalice to match.

"The high priest will want to see these," said one of the soldiers. "He said they were witches." He nodded toward Demetrius, still lying bleeding and barely conscious on the floor. "Take him to the King. He'll know what to do with him."

Not the King, Demetrius thought. He didn't want to go to the King, didn't want to face the man who had been his friend, to see the condemnation in his eyes when he found out that his closest friend had stolen his property by having relations with his favorite harem slave. And more, he *needed* to go to Lilia, not the King. He wanted them to take him to wherever they'd taken

Lilia and her sisters. He wanted to see that she was all
right, and he wanted answers.

The soldiers grabbed him, clasping his upper arms,
and the pain was so real that it woke him from the day-
dream. He was standing in his own shower, hot water
pounding down on his head. He was in his own life,
the life he'd made for himself.

When he'd awakened from his earlier dream—
which he now realized had been the lead-up to the final
events of this most recent vision—he'd found Lilia in
his bed, in his arms, and for the briefest instant it was
so like the dream that he'd nearly jumped out of his
skin when he realized she was really there.

It had been just that real this time around.

He turned and let the hot water run over his back
and shoulders, trying to ease away the phantom pain of
an imagined beating. But no amount of rinsing could
remove the effects of the dream. It had seemed so real.
Could it be true, what the old priest, Father Dom, had
told him? That all of this had begun in some past lifetime? To a degree it certainly fit what he'd said, that
Lilia was a witch who'd seduced him, convinced him
to murder the King and then left him to his fate.

And yet it also fit what *she* had said, that they had
been lovers torn apart by outside forces, and that she'd
been as innocent as he was.

Except, of course, for the witchcraft.

Hell, he didn't know what to believe. But he knew
one thing. If pain, like the pain in that dream, was what
humanity would bring him, then he wanted no part of
it. And he didn't mean the physical pain of the beating
he'd suffered, but the heart-wrenching agony of having
her torn from his arms. Of being unable to protect her.

Of feeling so much for another person that life without her seemed completely pointless.

He never wanted to feel that way again.

He was dressing after his shower when he heard a tentative tapping from somewhere outside his room. He opened the bedroom door and waited until it came again, and realized the old priest was knocking from inside the observatory. Giving a quick glance toward the other door, the one down to the second floor, and reassuring himself that it was closed, Demetrius called softly, "Come down, Father Dom."

The trapdoor at the top rose, and the old priest came down the spiral staircase, moving easily. It had seemed much more difficult for him to negotiate those stairs that first night. He moved more powerfully now, like a far younger man, with confidence if not exactly strength.

"Are we alone?" the priest asked, looking around warily and pulling at the sleeve of his black shirt while shrugging his shoulders as if they ached.

"Yes, we're alone. What's wrong? You seem uncomfortable. Didn't you sleep well? Is the mattress—"

"It's these clothes." Father Dom tugged at the white tab collar. "I'm outgrowing them."

It was true. Demetrius could see that the man's body had changed even more overnight. His shoulders were more rounded, and his belly protruded beneath the black shirt. And there was more. Father Dom's gray hair seemed thicker, and if Demetrius wasn't mistaken, darker, too. His face was filling out, his color improving.

"I'll have Sid—"

"No!" The old priest all but shouted the word, but

he did stop pulling on his clothes. "I've told you, no one must know I'm here."

"I remember. But it's not necessary. I trust Sid completely. Gus, too, for that matter."

"Really. And have you seen them with *her?*"

Demetrius frowned. "No, I haven't. Have you seen them with her? And if so, when? And how?"

Father Dom rolled his eyes. "It's an observatory. It has a three-hundred-and-sixty-degree view of the house and grounds. She's with them now, and I can tell at a glance that she has enchanted them already. The magical web she's been spinning has already captured its first pair of flies. They're loyal to her now, not you."

Demetrius narrowed his eyes on the old man. "I think you're wrong about that, Father Dom."

"I'm not. You'll see. Or has the little witch netted you in her sticky strands, as well?"

"Not at all. I want only for her to leave me in peace."

"The sooner the better, Demetrius. The longer she stays, the greater the chance she'll find a way to control you, make you accept your mortality, give up your powers for her, die for her—just like before."

"And yet I didn't die for her before. Not exactly."

Nodding slowly, the priest walked away. "No. You didn't. You suffered something far worse." He turned to look at Demetrius. "You've remembered some of it, then?"

"Being caught with her. Being beaten half to death by men who'd been my friends, while others carted her off to a cell somewhere."

"And?"

Demetrius gave his head a quick shake. "And nothing. That's all. It was vivid, though. Real."

"That's because it really happened," the priest insisted.

"Your musty old journal tells you so, I suppose," Demetrius said. "But it couldn't have told you who I was now, much less where I was. How did you find me?"

Father Dom shrugged. "It wasn't hard. I have powers, too, you know. A man of the cloth has...resources beyond an ordinary man's knowing."

Priests had superpowers? That was the first Demetrius had heard of such a thing in this day and age. He tilted his head in curiosity. "You've never told me what any of this has to do with you, Father Dom. Why do you care?"

"They're witches. I'm a priest. They've lived lifetime after lifetime, committing their evil, serving their dark lord Satan, while men like you have paid the price. It is my goal in life, my sacred vow, to put a stop to it." He shrugged. "I was born for this."

"And how will you do that—put a stop to it, I mean?" Demetrius asked. "Just because I refuse to let Lilia rob me of my immortality and steal my powers for herself, how is that going to put a stop to anything?" He looked the old priest up and down.

There was a definite gleam in the old man's eyes, and he did not meet Demetrius's gaze as he answered. "My only concern right now is to save you from her schemes and spells. I'll worry about the rest later. You're the one at risk at the moment. We need to deal with that first."

Demetrius didn't like it. Didn't feel the man was telling him everything.

"So you're telling me this is all real. That what I dreamed was a memory."

"Yes."

"What became of Lilia and her sisters after they were arrested?"

Father Dom shrugged, pacing a few steps farther from him. "They got away. You'd murdered the King for them, so they were free of the harem. No longer enslaved. They used their magic to escape their cells and vanished across the desert, never to be heard from again, leaving you to rot in the Underworld on their behalf. Faithless, ungrateful bitches that they were. And *are*."

Demetrius nodded slowly, but something deep inside him flared up at the words the old man used, and that same part doubted those words were the truth. Not the entire truth, at least.

"How did I get into the Underworld, then? If they were already gone…"

"Honestly, Demetrius, do you expect me to know every detail about an event thousands of years before my time? They're witches. They do things." He ran a hand over his mysteriously lustrous hair. "Throw her out, Demetrius. Don't let her spend another day here. Send her away."

Demetrius inhaled deeply, then blew a heavy sigh. "I'm afraid I can't do that."

Glaring at him, the priest said, "Can't? Or won't?"

"She's used her magic to bind us, she says. She sliced my palm." He held it up as he spoke, though the wound was already healed. "Then she sliced her own and pressed, them together, muttered some words—"

"A binding spell."

"Now she says I'm stuck with her." Demetrius shrugged, lowering his hand and staring down at his palm, where only a thin pink line hinted that the injury had ever occurred. "So if you can tell me a way to get rid of her, I'll happily try it."

"There is none—short of killing her."

Demetrius snapped his head up fast, horrified to his core. But the old priest waved a dismissive hand. "Figure of speech. She's right, you're stuck with her, but not for long. As I told you, she needs your answer by Beltane. It's only few days away. If you can continue to refuse her until then, this entire cycle simply ends. She'll go away and never bother you again. The question is, do you think you can withstand her magic and her charms for that long?"

Demetrius smiled slowly. "I thought you said this was going to be difficult. A few days? All I have to do is refuse her for a few more days?"

"Don't underestimate her, Demetrius. She's a powerful witch."

"I'm powerful, too. Don't worry. I can hold out for a few days."

The priest sniffed, glancing toward the bedroom with a look of disgust. "I'd suggest keeping her out of your bed until then."

Demetrius shot the man a look. "You know, you're far more interested in all this than makes any sense, despite what you've said. And as far as who I have or do not have in my bed—that's beyond your boundaries, old man. I'm thinking I need to move you to a different part of the house."

"She would find me. It's amazing that she hasn't found me already." Father Dom turned to gaze out the window. "She's on the east patio ensorcelling your loyal cohorts over breakfast. I'm going to take the back stairs to the kitchen and get some food. Keep her outside for a bit, will you?"

"Of course. Watch out for the cook."

Demetrius left the old priest alone in his rooms and headed downstairs, but it sent a shiver of unease up his spine to do so. Something about having that man alone with his most prized possessions, the chalice and the blade, bothered him. Still, they were in a wall safe, and he was the only one with the combination. As for the amulet, he had that around his neck on a chain. He never took it off.

He headed down one flight of stairs and then the next, then sauntered casually onto the patio to take the one remaining chair at the round glass-topped table. "Morning, Gus, Sid."

"Morning, D-man," Gus said. "Been getting to know your lady friend."

"Good morning, boss," Sid said. "We just asked Ingrid to bring out more coffee."

"There might still be a cup left." Lilia tipped the silver pot to a cup, which she filled almost to the top. "Ah, just enough. Coffee is one of the most wonderful things I've discovered so far," she said softly. "But I've heard tales of it being addictive, so I limit myself to two cups."

"People keep saying that," Demetrius said. "I don't really see the grand appeal." He took a sip. "It's hot and wet."

She lowered her eyes. "You'll get it one of these days."

"Oh, don't look sad, Lilia. I don't think I'm missing much."

"You can't even begin to imagine how much," she whispered.

A muscle in his jaw twitched, and he turned to gaze out at the bathing beauties who were usually beginning to gather around the pool by this late in the morning. But no one was there.

He sent Gus a questioning glance.

"Uh, yeah, I um…I put a note on the front gate telling them to chill for a while. I'm not, uh…" He raised a hand to his mouth and faked a cough. "I'm not feeling all that great today."

"You're not." It wasn't a question.

"Think it might be a cold. Maybe even the flu."

"Should we get a doctor over here to have a look at you?"

"Nah. I just need a few days' rest."

Sid grinned across the table at Gus. "It must be tough, keeping up with all those young, gorgeous women."

"Be easier if D-man would help out." Gus shot a startled look at Lilia and bit his lip. "Sorry. That wasn't very sensitive of me."

But she wasn't looking at Gus. She was looking at Demetrius, and something between relief and joy was sparkling in her eyes. He could have lived without her knowing that he felt no interest in the bevy of females Gus insisted on having here all the time. Suddenly she reached across the table and covered his hand with hers. "Come out with me today, Demetrius."

His eyebrows rose, and he hoped the panic in his belly didn't show. "I haven't even eaten yet."

"Well, eat, then." She grabbed a plate and started filling it with melon wedges, pastries and berries, then set it in front him. "I don't think I've ever seen a place this beautiful, and I want to go exploring." She gazed out at the desert, rock formations everywhere she looked. "I want to go to Bell Rock. I passed it on the way here, and there were people climbing all over it. I want to climb it, too. Can we?"

"Lilia, I really don't think—"

"It doesn't matter what you think. If I go, you'll go. And I'm going. So I'll go get my things while you eat. Will you hurry? You haven't taken a bite yet."

"You haven't given me a chance."

She smiled at him, a vibrant smile that made his stomach knot up. And then she got up, and he grabbed her hand before she could race into the house and discover the old priest who was so determined to remain hidden from her. "I'll go with you to Bell Rock. Just sit still and let me enjoy my breakfast first, all right?"

She blinked, first at his hand closed around hers, and then into his eyes. Wonderful, hers were starting to shimmer. "You will?"

"Yes. I will. If you'll sit down and relax until I'm ready."

Her smile was quick and even brighter than the last one, and it hit him hard, knocking the wind out of him in some odd way. She was so happy she practically glowed with it. All because he'd said he would take her hiking up a large red rock.

"Okay," she said, and she sank into her chair again and watched him eat.

He took his time in order to give the priest time to get himself a meal and get out of sight. She watched as he bit into a piece of melon, and then a strawberry, followed by a gooey cheese Danish, and her eyes seemed to grow sadder and sadder.

He washed the food down with a sip of coffee and met her eyes. "What's the matter?"

A slight lift of one shoulder. "You're not enjoying that, are you?"

It wasn't really a question, he thought. "It's fine. Good, even."

Pressing her lips tight, she huffed, leaned back in her chair, crossed her arms over her chest and frowned in thought.

"What?" She'd been all but giddy only seconds ago. Now she looked as if she wanted to cry.

Sid pushed away from the table and got to his feet, and Gus flinched, then got up, too. Sid must have kicked him under the table.

"Sir, if you need a ride to Bell Rock…" Sid offered.

"I'll take the Jeep," he said, his eyes still on Lilia. She'd stopped frowning now and had tipped her head to one side, looking as if she'd solved whatever problem she'd been puzzling over.

He probably should have taken Sid up on the offer. The less time he spent alone with the witch, the better, he thought, watching her lapis-blue eyes take on a knowing eagerness.

Too late. Gus and Sid were already heading back inside, and she was leaning forward in her seat. "I can't lie, you know," she said.

"No, I didn't know that." Then he smiled and surprised himself by teasing her. "And I still don't. Because if you *could* lie, you might be lying about that."

She grinned back, picking up on his humor. "Seriously, I can't. And I cannot give you back the remaining piece of your soul unless you ask for it, truly and wholeheartedly. Not so much with your words, but with your innermost being, your longing to be whole again."

"And mortal. And vulnerable."

"Yes, yes, all that." She waved a hand as if "all that" was nothing. "But you can briefly connect with that missing part of your soul, you know, through me. See what it would feel like if you ever do decide to take it back."

He saw then, why she was so eager to convince him that she could not lie. This could be a trick.

"It's not," she said.

He scowled at her. "Sorry. I wasn't eavesdropping. Sometimes you let things leak, that's all. When people are thinking *at* me, I often hear them. And as I told you, when it's your soul's yearning, I can hear that because I have a piece of it inside me. Anyway, this is a really good idea, Demetrius. After all, how can you make an informed decision between taking back the rest of your soul or abandoning it forever if you don't know what you're missing?"

"Interesting point."

"Hold my hand and I'll channel it just a little. I promise it will only last a minute."

He narrowed his eyes on her. Such a sweet face, such beautiful, innocent eyes. She was the epitome of an angel, at least the way most of mankind envisioned angels. The kind they put on the tops of their Christmas trees. All white and gold and sparkling. All goodness and purity and light. How could she be a witch? A murderous one, at that, out to kill him and take his powers? It made no sense.

He wanted to trust her. More than that, he wanted

to know what she would show him. Hesitantly, he offered his hand.

She took it, closed her eyes.

Immediately he felt something like warm honey flowing from her palm into his, spreading up his arm, into his chest and through his body. As if he were being infused with thick, liquid sunshine. There was a heaviness to it, a sadness, a heartache, that knotted in his chest and made his throat go tight. Hot tears burned behind his eyes, and he didn't even know why.

"Now, take a bite of that strawberry," she whispered.

"What is this?" he asked. "Why do I feel so…?"

With her free hand she snatched up a fat red berry, and almost before he could acknowledge the vividness of its color, popped it into his mouth.

Flavor exploded, and his eyes widened. He chewed slowly, savoring the sweetness and tang as one, letting the flavor coat his tongue, hating to swallow, because that would end this experience. But eventually he did. And yet the flavor remained.

She opened her eyes, took her hand away. And the flavor was gone. Just like that.

"What was that?" he whispered, searching her serene face.

"That," she whispered, "is one of the reasons humanity exists. To allow spirit to experience the sensual pleasures of physical being." She covered his hand with hers again, just a touch this time. "It's the meaning of life on earth, Demetrius. To experience all of life's pleasures through the senses we possess only when we're human."

The desire to experience life's pleasures in human form had been one of the main driving forces behind his desperation to escape the Underworld. He remembered that much. He'd wanted to inhabit a physical body. He'd been willing to do anything.

He had done many things. Horrible things. All those clerics who'd died in the bomb blast at Cornell University last fall, at the hand of a weak-minded human he'd managed to possess, to command. He'd robbed those priests and holy men of their chance to experience life.

Guilt welled up in his chest. Guilt he'd been incapable of truly feeling before she'd opened the connection between them. Waves of it rolled over him. He lowered his head. If this was what being human brought—sadness, guilt, remorse—then he was more certain than ever that he wanted no part of it.

And yet the taste of that strawberry lingered in his mind, and his body yearned for more. What would the melon taste like? The Danish? The coffee everyone was always raving about? And what about Lilia?

Her lips, he wondered, his eyes suddenly fixed on them. Pink and full. What would those lips taste like if he were to kiss them while that connection was open and working?

8

She changed into a short white split skirt, a white tank top, a pair of ankle socks and hot pink running shoes. She put a jaunty cap on her head, a chauffeur's cap like the one she'd seen Sid wearing that first day, only white, with a peace sign made out of blue glitter. She'd found it on the back of an easy chair in one of the party rooms, probably left behind by one of Gus's guests. She figured it was fair game. They'd borrowed her soul mate, or tried to. She would borrow their hat. Fair was fair.

Her sunglasses were white, too, oversize, with rhinestones on the outer edges.

Demetrius was wearing khaki cargo shorts with numerous pockets and a white T-shirt that fit too loosely for her taste. She'd always loved his body, especially his chest and shoulders. And his back. So broad and strong. And his belly, rippling with muscle and tempting her to run her fingers over it. She thought, if she had her preference, the man would never wear any shirt at all.

He had a small backpack, but she didn't know what was inside until they were halfway up the trail and he said, "Stop."

She did. She'd been stopping at intervals all along to admire the blossoming desert spreading out on either side of the well-marked, well-groomed walking path. It had been almost flat at the beginning, but it began to climb as they reached the actual red rock formation and started up it. All along the way there were cacti with purple blooms, spindly yellow pinwheels on strawlike stalks, and sprays of tiny white-and-yellow flowers the size of hatpin heads in dense clusters close to the ground. The redness of the earth, of the rocks, was beyond her ability to describe. So vivid. Like clay pottery, but even deeper toned, and in some places striated with lighter and darker layers.

The trail so far hadn't been difficult, and it was only slow going because every so often she just *had* to stop and stare.

"I wish you could see this the way I do," she said. "Do you want to try again?" She held out a hand as she asked the question, hoping he would. That few seconds when she'd managed to let him discover what a strawberry really tasted like had hit him hard. She'd seen it, felt it. But he'd been a little more distant and wary of her ever since.

He looked at her hand and shook his head. "No, but I would like you to put on some sunblock. Your lily-white skin is getting as red as the rocks." He took off his light pack and brought out a spray can. "Come here."

"But, Demetrius, if I get a sunburn I'll heal overnight."

"You'll suffer in the meantime. I know, I've made that mistake. Even for me, it was unpleasant in the extreme. Come here."

She did, holding her arms out to the side. Demetrius sprayed her liberally, and she sucked air through her teeth when the cold mist hit her sun- and exertion-warmed skin. He crouched to get her legs, then rose again and sprayed himself.

"What else is in that pack?" she asked, standing on tiptoe to try to peer inside as he put the sun block away.

"Water. A cell phone. A camera."

"You brought a camera?"

"I guessed you'd want one. I see all this every day, but it seems special to you." He took the camera out and handed it to her. "I would have taken it out sooner, but I would like to get to the top before it gets much hotter."

"Good idea. I can photograph anything we've already passed on the way back down." She took it from him, looping the strap around her neck, then looked it over and saw that it was going to be simple to operate. Then she accepted the water he offered and took a long drink.

She felt his eyes on her, then lowered the bottle and met his intense stare. It was intimate, a look she remembered very well, though it had been centuries. A woman didn't forget that expression in her man's eyes. He wanted her.

He turned away, though, slinging the pack over his shoulders once more.

They continued their journey, speaking very little. She suspected he was silent because talking to her felt dangerous to him. A threat to his determination to remain the unnatural, unfeeling, not-quite-human being that he was. And she was silent because she felt as if she were inside a church, in a place too sacred to speak.

They were going up now, up and up and up, following a trail marked by hollow wire pillars filled with red stones. They'd left behind the groomed part of the path, and aside from the occasional trail marker the way was wild, but still easy.

She climbed from boulder to boulder over a particularly steep patch, going ahead of him at his insistence, and then found herself on a wide, very flat spot in the side of Bell Rock. She walked nearly to the center before pausing and turning slowly.

The vista spread out before her like something in a painting or a dream, too beautiful to be real. She could see forever, it seemed, and everywhere there were towering red rock formations. Wide ones, narrow ones… all of them looking as if the Gods themselves had decided to make some sculptures out of rusty-red clay, and the sun had baked them. Giants, megaliths, everywhere she looked, and far, far away, beyond the giants, shaded by the veil of distance, still more formations fading into invisibility.

The sight took her breath away and literally brought tears to her eyes. "Oh, my Goddess," she whispered. Pressing a hand to her chest, she said it again. "Oh, my Goddess."

Demetrius came up to stand beside her, and she realized that she'd lost track of him—him, the man she couldn't stop noticing or feeling or wanting. She'd actually forgotten all about him for a moment. That was the power of the natural beauty around her. No matter which way she turned, they were there, ancient guardians, distant rock formations, massive and barren and beautiful. She felt as if they were alive.

They are alive, her heart whispered. *Alive and aware and as old as time.*

"Lilia?" Demetrius asked, looking not at the vista but at her face. "You're crying. What's wrong? Why are you crying?"

"Don't you see? It's so beautiful."

He looked, too. She managed to tear her eyes from the scenery long enough to look at him as he scanned the view. But what she saw there was only emptiness and a powerful longing. He wanted to see it as she did. He *wanted* to. Not enough to accept his soul back, perhaps. Not yet. But enough that his hand crept around hers as if of its own volition. He tightened his hold, and she closed her eyes in pleasure at his touch.

She wasn't even sure if he was aware of what he was doing, what his fractured human soul was silently asking for. But she didn't wait for permission. She willed his missing soul-piece to touch its host as it had at breakfast, felt it flow through her and felt him stiffen as he sensed what was happening. He shot her a look, surprise, maybe a little anger, but she only shook her head in silence and lifted her free hand to point.

Tearing his eyes from her as if by force, he turned his head and looked out at the vista once again.

A change came over him, a powerful wonder filled his eyes. They softened, and his features relaxed. His tight jaw eased, his mouth opening slightly as the breath rushed out of him.

"I don't understand," he whispered.

Whispered, just as she'd been doing. He felt it now, the holiness of this place. "What, my love?" she asked softly. "What don't you understand?"

He was still drinking in the view, holding her hand and turning slowly to take it all in. "I've seen this before. A hundred times. Not from this vantage point, but surely it's not all that different. I've seen it before. And it's just the same. Red rock formations, that's all it is."

"Yes, that's all it is."

"Then why does it feel so much...*more* this time?"

"Because you're seeing it through the eyes of your soul, Demetrius. And your soul is an extension of the energy that created all this. You're seeing a painting through the eyes of its artist. Understand?"

"I think perhaps I'm seeing it through your eyes," he said softly.

There were tears in his eyes. They didn't spill over, because he kept blinking them back, but she saw them there, and it made her own well up all over again.

He kept holding her hand as he walked forward, closer to the edge, and gazed down. And then he gasped sharply, and there was a sudden horror in his expression. His hand clasped hers more tightly, almost to the point of pain.

In a brief flash she saw what he was seeing instead of the other way around. She saw herself standing on the edge of a darker cliff, her sisters alongside her, their arms bound behind them, their backs welted and bleeding from the lashes of Sindar's whip. She saw it all from his point of view, felt his pain, his anguish, his fury at being unable to save them. Even then, beaten near to death, bound and guarded, he struggled to get free, argued, cursed, pleaded for mercy. And then she saw the hands that pushed her over, and suddenly her vision was no longer his but her own as she plummeted down, down, down, her sisters beside her. She heard her beloved Demetrius's agonized scream as he was forced to watch her die.

He yanked his hand from hers, and the vision, the memory, blinked out.

It took her a moment to get her bearings, to remind herself that she was here now, in the Sonoran Desert in Arizona, not the Syrian Desert in what had once been Babylonia. She turned slowly away from the cliff at her feet, astounded at the memory, at the knowledge that it had been real. It had happened. And yet here she was, thousands of years later. Alive and well.

She looked for Demetrius and found him sitting on the ground with his knees up and his back against the rocks that rose behind him. His head was down, almost hidden by his hands, and she felt a sudden certainty that his scream had been real, here in the present, not a part of the vision from the past.

Lilia crossed the expanse between them, wishing her feet were bare. It felt wrong, wearing shoes in this sacred place. She knelt in front of him, her hands on his bent knees. "I'm sorry. I'm so very sorry, Demetrius. I didn't know that would happen. I only wanted to share this beauty with you."

He lifted his eyes to hers. "I tried to save you," he said. "I tried—"

"I know you did, my love."

"I don't want to remember this. I don't want it!"

She bit her lip. "I don't blame you. It's a horrible memory. But that's all it is. A memory. It's over. I'm here. And so are you. We survived it, both of us. All of us."

"You died," he whispered, and it felt like an accusation.

"But I came back. I'm right here with you now."

He clenched his fists in his hair, and his breathing was ragged.

"Demetrius, listen to me," she said. "That tragedy you don't want to remember and I will never be able to forget is not the end of our story. The ending can be whatever we choose to make it. But you have to let me restore your soul for that to happen."

"And that memory with it? And the pain of it all the time, not just in a brief flash? No. No, I can't let it in. You don't know how painful it is."

She slowly stood upright, propping her hands on her hips, her patience with him wearing thin. "I don't know how painful it is? I'm the one who got thrown off that cliff, you know. For the love of the Goddess, Demetrius, if I can deal with the memory, surely you can." Then a phrase she'd heard Indira utter sprang from her lips without permission. "Dumb-ass."

He looked up at her, blinking, apparently stunned by her words.

"You're…" She clenched her fists and made a sound like a frustrated growl. "Maddening!" Then she turned away from him and continued her climb, trying to vent some of her frustration by clambering over wild and unmarked terrain that would have given a mountain goat pause.

All right, he thought, it had been a stupid thing to say. Of course she knew the pain of it. She'd lived it. But she'd been living with it for more than three-thousand years. For him it was fresh. For him the horrifying event had flown through his mind as if it had happened only seconds ago. As if it were happening right now.

Anguish, heartache, loss, horror…he couldn't shake them. He'd just seen someone he'd loved more than his own life being tortured and murdered, torn from him by a man who was supposed to be in touch with the Gods. A man who was supposed to be holy and wise.

And powerful. That, Sindar had truly been. Not physically, but he'd had…abilities. Demetrius knew that now, having seen the hated face that had been burned into his mind so long ago. Sindar had a cupid's bow mouth, small pouting lips always stained red, and round cheeks like a toddler that were always as rosy as his lips. He'd never been seen without his eyes darkly lined in black, their lids coated in gold powder. He'd kept his long black hair pulled tightly back or braided, and his body had been plump and weak. Flabby, no doubt due to the number of slaves and servants who attended to his every need. He wore only the finest garments in the brightest colors, and he was always laden with golden baubles, like the symbol of the God, Marduk, on a chain around his neck and the matching bands on his arms.

Demetrius remembered his hatred of that high priest, along with the unbearable pain of watching Lilia and her sisters die. And then nothing. Numbness. A dark void, where the emotion attached to the memories had vanished like a droplet of moisture in the desert sun. But the memory of the memories remained. He knew the pain of that moment even though he no longer felt it. And he did not want to feel it again.

The powerful love for her, though? That, too, had been real, vivid, overwhelming in its intensity. Surely that wasn't what most people felt when they loved another. Was it? Could it be common, that emotional fire-

storm? And since she was here, not lying dead at the
bottom of some cliff—a thought that sent a finger of
ice up his spine—he presumed that that, at least, could
be a good feeling to experience again.

Unless, of course, he lost her once more. In which
case...

No, that was a risk too big to take. He was better
off in his current state. Powerful, immortal, rich, comfortable if not precisely happy. It was good. Why risk
agony in pursuit of ecstasy?

Decision made.

He pulled himself together, shook off the remaining
aftershocks of emotion and continued up the trail in the
direction she had gone. But after a few steps he paused
and looked back at the panorama that had brought him
close to tears moments ago.

It looked like red rocks. Just a bunch of red rocks.
He could not, for the life of him, figure out what the
big deal had been. Why he'd reacted the way he had,
or why she had.

Shrugging, he started after her again.

She'd gone beyond the trail markers now, he realized as he reached the end of them himself and saw
her ahead and above him, standing precariously on a
boulder, reaching up for a ledge above her head. The
sight sent fear coursing through him. "For God's sake,
Lilia, be careful!"

She paused, stuck to the stone face like a fly on a
wall, and turned her head to look down at him. "What
do you care? You won't feel a thing if I die. You're incapable of it." And then she continued pulling herself
up, hitching one knee onto the ledge above her and le-
veraging the rest of her up after it. Only a single layer

cake level and a pinnacle rock were above her now, neither of them climbable, he thought, at least not without professional gear. She must have thought so, too, because she sat down where she was, crossed her legs and closed her eyes.

"Now what are you doing?" he asked.

"I'm feeling the energy of the vortex," she replied. "So either be quiet and let me be, or come on up and join me."

He joined her. He didn't think she had expected him to. She seemed both surprised and happy about it when she opened her eyes and saw him sitting down close beside her. Closing her eyes again, but unable to quite control her smile, she said, "Sit like I'm sitting, but keep it loose. Comfortable."

"Comfortable, while sitting on a rock while the sun bakes me from above? Is this some magical skill I haven't yet learned?" She opened one eye, and he sent her a teasing grin before he realized what he was doing and bit it back. That wasn't a good sign, wasn't it? He was starting to like the woman and to feel badly that he'd so angered her earlier, and wanting to try to make it up to her in some way. No, this couldn't be good.

And yet he complied, and for no other reason than because he knew it would please her. He quickly mirrored her position. She closed her eyes again. "Holding your hands the way I'm holding mine is one of many postures called mudras," she said, her voice low and soft, but steady and confident. "This particular mudra helps the energy flow. Let the backs of your hands rest easily on your thighs or knees, thumbs against your second fingers. Keep the touch light, relaxed."

He did as she asked, not sure if he should or not, but

not thinking too hard about that. It was her smile on his mind, the way his joining her up on this rock had put it there, and his sudden and inexplicable eagerness to give her even more reason to beam. How brightly could she shine? he wondered.

"Keep your elbows close to your body, your chin slightly down, and kind of tuck your butt under a little to straighten and lengthen your spine."

He shifted slightly. He was so aware of her, of her nearness, of her energy, her mood, of her voice soft in his ears.

"Breathe in through your nose, filling your lungs. Slow and deep." She inhaled with him, guiding him as he took what had to be the deepest breath of his life.

"Now breathe out through your lips, but very slowly. Empty your lungs all the way." She exhaled with him, too.

"Breathe in," she said softly. "Sink your spine down into the earth, like the roots of the great Tree of Life." Her voice was deeper, softer, a silken whisper. "Breathe out. Feel your spine lengthening, as if a string attached to the top of your head is gently pulling you upward and your spirit is reaching into the heavens like the limbs of that same great tree."

He could feel it. He could truly feel it.

"Breathe in. Thoughts will come. Gently push them aside and focus on your breath as it swirls around your nostrils, over your lips, into your lungs. Breathe out."

He felt himself relaxing. She continued coaching him a bit longer, but he soon fell into the rhythm easily, naturally, until they were breathing as one. Time ticked by unnoticed as they sat in silence.

Demetrius fell into himself, into a memory. But

there was no panic this time, no pain. He watched it play out as if he were watching a movie, without the detriment of wild human emotions to distort it. There was the soldier, once the King's most trusted friend, now his murderer.

Could that really have been me?

He'd been beaten nearly to death, and now he lay on a cliff top far from his home.

Babylon…

The city gleamed like a jewel in the distance, across the desert, beneath the brutal, red-eyed sun. A stone wall rose behind him, and there was more stone beneath him.

Nearby, but beyond his reach, his beloved stood on the cliff's edge. She and her sisters were lined up, each with a novice priest at her back, ready to push on the High Priest's command.

Sindar!

His gaze found the unholy bastard who was to blame for all this. Since that day in the harem, Demetrius had learned that Sindar had long suspected Lilia and her sisters of witchery. Their mother's powers of healing and sorcery were spoken of in whispers, and where the tree grew, the fruit was soon to follow. Sindar had little power over what the common folk did, though. And Balthazorus was a tolerant king; the superstitions of the masses bothered him not at all.

And he was my friend. A good man. A good king.

But the practice of magic was the right of the High Priest alone. Sindar saw the notion of anyone else using it as a personal assault. And he struck back.

When his snooping had uncovered Demetrius's love affair with the King's favorite harem slave, Sindar had found the perfect weapon to punish the women, their mother and, in a way, the King, whom he blamed for not taking action himself.

He stood there, that pregnant-bellied man with his cheeks as fat as if he were preparing to blow a trumpet, his white-and-purple robes wafting in the mountaintop's searing winds. His eyes glistened as he stared at the women about to be murdered on his command. Already he'd been delighted as they were scourged for their crimes.

The fat bastard didn't have the stuff in him to wield the whip himself. Only to watch in secret, sexual pleasure.

The priest's small tongue darted out to moisten his berry-stained lips.

"I'll kill you for this, Sindar," Demetrius said, mustering the strength to form words.

"How? You won't have a body. You will be a formless mass, imprisoned forever in the Underworld. Stripped of the immortal soul you never deserved."

"I'll save you, my love!" Lilia cried. "I swear to you, I will find you, and I will save you."

Sindar smiled sickeningly. "You have no power, witch. The power of the Gods belongs only to the High Priest of Marduk."

"It's not Marduk you need to fear," Lilia said bravely, despite the fact that she was about to die. "We are the Daughters of Ishtar, my sisters and I. Ishtar, Queen of Heaven. You'll know no peace until this is made right. So sayeth the Goddess."

For an instant the High Priest's smile wavered, and his eyes betrayed his fear. Shaking his head as if to rid himself of weakness, he allowed hatred to replace the fear and lifted his hand. "On my command," he said.

"Sindar, don't! I beg of you!" Demetrius struggled, but soldiers held him back.

Do not beg anything of this pig, my love. Lilia's voice rang inside his mind, louder than the incantation Sindar was speaking, asking Marduk to accept this offering of three witches.

All will be well, she said gently, softly, inside his mind. *Death is but an illusion. Hold on to your true self. He cannot take from you the man you truly are, only separate you from your higher self for a while. And that will be torture, but it will end. I will find you— I'll make it right again. I—*

The high priest dropped his hand, and Demetrius heard Lilia's sharp gasp as she was pushed over the edge. She and her sisters began chanting together as they fell, words he could not make out. But in his heart, he heard her final thoughts. *I will love you beyond the end of time, Demetrius. No power on earth can be greater than what I feel.*

Pain rocked through him, more powerful than any explosion, but brief. Shattering, then gone. He knew he'd felt exactly what she had suffered on impact. He could only hope her agony, too, had lasted no longer than an instant.

Lilia had to force herself to stop wondering what he was feeling, what he was experiencing in the ultra-relaxed, ultrareceptive state of meditation, the only time when a person could hear her—or his—higher self through all the white noise of the human mind, all the to-do lists, all the worries about tomorrow and regrets over yesterday. Meditation was being, just being, existing wholly and entirely in the eternal present, connected fully with one's truest self. Which was…well, everything, really.

As she stopped thinking of him, and focused only on her breathing, on her being, she felt the warmth of peace surround her and flood her with the certainty that everything was going to be all right. Everything would unfold exactly as it should. She would live and find happiness with Demetrius. Or she would die and move on into blissful oneness with the Whole, achieving perfect understanding of why things had happened as they had. Either way, all would be well. It already was, in fact.

Eventually she opened her eyes as she felt the heat of the sun increase. She looked at him. He was sitting still, eyes wide open, looking stricken.

"What is it, Demetrius?" She put a hand on his powerful biceps, felt them tighten in reaction to her touch. "What did you experience?"

He met her eyes, and his were roiling. But he only shook his head. "Nothing."

"I can see there was something," she said.

He ignored her and got to his feet. "We should climb down now. It's getting hotter by the minute." He extended a hand to her, and she let him pull her to her feet, relishing the feel of his hand around hers, strong and firm.

Then she was up and standing beside him, and he was still holding on, staring down at her. She looked up, met his eyes. They were troubled, but there was more. Something unfathomable but real. Powerful.

"You remembered something."

"Someone."

"Did you remember me? Us?"

"No."

"You lie."

He shook his head, tugged her toward the way down. But she pulled back. "Do something for me, Demetrius."

He looked back at her. "I let you stay in my home. I came here with you. I sat through your silly ritual. What more can I possibly do for you?"

"You can kiss me," she said softly.

She saw his eyes flare wider, and she stepped a little closer to him. "Kiss me here, where we're wrapped in the vortex. Kiss me, just once, in this sacred place."

He narrowed his eyes as if he suspected her of trying to trick him in some way.

"No magic, I promise. Just a kiss."

Her gaze strayed to his lips, and his tongue darted out to moisten them—involuntarily, she was certain.

"Please?" She moved even closer and slid her hands up his chest, over the shirt she wished would vanish at her touch.

He slipped his arms around her waist, then pulled her close, bent and kissed her. His mouth was gentle, tentative at first, then gradually he became more demanding, pressing her lips apart, tasting her with his tongue. She felt his soul-piece leap in her heart. She felt it swell and grow, and begin to spill out of her, as if it wanted to flow into him but was meeting a dam that held it back. Even so, bits seeped through. She was sure of it, because his reactions told her so. He kissed her more deeply, bending her backward and tangling his tongue around hers. She felt him grow hard against her belly, and she longed for more and knew he did, too.

When he straightened, he stared at her, his eyes spitting fire. And she felt his yearning, his need to consummate, and also his fear that it would mean accepting the remainder of his soul, that it would enmesh him with her past the point of escape. She also sensed relief in him and somehow knew he was relieved to know that his body did indeed function properly. He had never been able to achieve this state of arousal with another woman, though he had tried many times before giving up in embarrassment and frustration.

She read all of that before he closed his mind to her just as if he were slamming a steel door in her face, and all simply by averting his eyes.

"Demetrius?" she whispered.

"What?" He didn't look at her. It didn't matter.

"I love you. I've loved you for three-thousand, five-hundred years. I've loved you beyond life, beyond death, and back again. And I will love you forever, no matter what happens between us now."

He turned and met her eyes again, but his were sheltered, protected. "And if I reject you, send you away the instant we return to the mansion?"

"Love isn't conditional. I don't love you when you act the way I wish you would and stop loving when you don't. Love is pure. It's consistent. It's deep. It matters not one bit what you do. I loved you when your raging hatred brought death to the innocent at that interfaith conference. I even loved you when you tried to evict the soul of my baby niece from her body so you could take it for your own."

"I was misled." He couldn't meet her eyes. "And I

would bet all I have that you wouldn't have continued to love me had I succeeded in that attempt."

"I would have killed you," she told him flatly. "But I would still have loved you. I will love you whether you embrace your humanity again and love me back, or whether you remain this uncaring being you think you are. I love you." She shrugged. "I thought you ought to know that."

And on that note she started back down, climbing from boulder to boulder until she reached the marked part of the trail again, while he followed in brooding silence.

Father Dom didn't seem surprised to see Demetrius when he climbed the spiral staircase to the observatory. The old man was standing at the window, gazing out at some distant point, and he spoke without turning around. "Did she get to you, then? With her wiles and her magic? Has she convinced you to give up your power, your immortality, your very life, for her…again?"

"I don't think she tricked me in that past lifetime," Demetrius said softly. "I think I truly loved her."

The priest turned slowly. Truly, his health was improving by leaps and bounds. Daily, he looked more robust. His cheeks were plumping, growing pinker, and his body had taken on an ever-thickening layer of fat that didn't seem possible in a few days' time.

"Of course you loved her, fool. You were under her spell."

"What if I wasn't? What if it was real?"

The old priest rolled his eyes and faced the window again. Demetrius paced forward, searching for words to explain what he was feeling to the man who had somehow become his confessor and confidant. As he passed the telescope, he paused to peer down through the eyepiece, and then he jerked back, surprised. It was aimed not at the sky but much closer, on some of the red rocks in the distance. In fact... Demetrius adjusted the focus.

Bell Rock. Clear as day. Father Dom had been watching him and Lilia this morning.

"Perhaps if you could read the journal for yourself, you would believe me," Father Dom was saying in the background. "But since you can't read any of the ancient Babylonian dialects—"

The old man turned, and Demetrius sidestepped away from the telescope, starting forward toward the windows as if he'd never paused. He wasn't sure why he tried to hide what he'd seen, but he felt it was somehow important to keep his discovery a secret. "No," he said. "I can't. I'll just have to trust you to translate for me."

"That's what I have been doing. But apparently the succulent flesh of a witch holds more sway with you than any wisdom I have to share."

Demetrius shook his head and noticed a bundle of fabric in the corner, near Father Dom's cot. Purple and red. "What's that?" he asked, nodding toward it.

"Linens," the priest snapped. "I like color in my bed sheets, so I went shopping today."

"How did you—"

"I slipped out the gate while your friends were busy elsewhere. Soon enough a passerby stopped to offer me a ride. When you wear the collar of a priest, people are eager to help you, I've discovered."

At the mention of his wardrobe, Demetrius noticed that Father Dom now wore a pair of lightweight off-white trousers and a button-down shirt, white and completely covered in purple cactus blossoms. A chain dangled from around his neck, and it wasn't a crucifix at the end but some sort of serpent-shaped dragon.

Something flashed bright and painful in his head, but too brief to make sense.

"Did you pick that up today, too?" Demetrius asked, indicating the pendant.

Father Dom smiled. "A gift from an old friend," he said, lifting the thing for a loving look before dropping it beneath the shirt he wore. "I had to wear it at least once."

"And you've given up your cleric's clothes, despite how helpful people are when you wear them?"

"I'm growing fat under your hospitality, Demetrius," the priest said with a pat to his belly, which really was beginning to protrude. "They no longer fit, and it's not as if I can go find a new set at the local Kmart, now is it?"

"No, I guess not."

"Tell me. What has you doubting, my son?"

"I don't know."

"It's the witch. I know it's her."

"I don't think so." Demetrius studied the old man's eyes. "I've recalled some things. You told me that she and her sisters got away and left me to my fate. But that's not what I remembered."

"No?" Father Dom moved to his cot and sat down. "Tell me what you *did* remember."

Demetrius nodded. "It was an…execution. She and

her sisters were thrown from a cliff while I was forced to watch."

"I see." Dom took a deep breath, rubbing his chin with one hand as he seemed to think. "Tell me, did she touch you before you had this…memory? Did she take your hand, anything like that?"

"Yes. Yes, she did."

"Amazing to me, the extent of her power. That she could create a false memory in you just by taking hold of your hand…" Dom shook his head slowly. "Oh, she's good. She's very, very good. And far more dangerous than even I realized. I think you should send her away. And soon. Before Beltane, certainly. She'll experience a boost in her powers then. All witches do. It's a powerful time, and if she realizes that it's also her final chance to make you surrender your power to her, then God only knows what she might do."

Demetrius nodded slowly. "But what about the binding spell?" he asked, even though he had no intention of sending Lilia anywhere, even if he could. Not until he was sure which of his two houseguests was lying.

"Ahh, the binding. I'll study on that overnight. I might be able to come up with a way to break the spell, my son. In the morning, all right?"

"All right. Thank you, Father Dom."

"You're welcome, my son."

Demetrius left the man, heading back down to his own quarters. Something was niggling at him, something that felt urgent, and yet he couldn't quite get a handle on what it was.

He needed privacy. Privacy and his magical tools. The dagger and the chalice. Maybe he could figure out a way to use them to find the truth.

* * *

Lilia's cell phone showed five missed calls when she thought to turn it back on that afternoon, along with several voice mails, all from her sisters. She was lounging poolside with Gus and Sid, relishing the relative solitude. She hadn't yet ventured into the water, but she intended to. She even had a bathing suit in her room and had been thinking about changing into it.

But first she decided to call her sisters back, so she dialed Lena, who had been the first to leave a message, then lay back in her chaise.

Magdalena answered on the first ring. "Where have you been? I've been trying to get you all day!"

"With Demetrius," Lilia said softly. "We hiked up Bell Rock, meditated together in the midst of all that vortex energy. I think he's starting to remember. I think he's starting to…to become himself again, even without the missing piece of his soul. It's only a matter of time before he asks for it."

"Yeah, well, while you've been playing tourist, I've been scrying, and, sis, the source of that evil you've been sensing is still there in that house with you."

"In the house? Are you sure?"

"It's bad. And it's there. I printed up satellite photos of the entire area, and the only place I'm getting a positive response—a violent one—is the house itself."

Lilia sat up straight and looked at Gus, who was sitting in his bright blue bathing trunks with his swirls of gray chest hair protecting him from the sun, grinning like a loon and sipping a beer. Then at Sid, who, though poolside, was apparently still on duty. He wore cargo shorts, a white T-shirt and a baseball hat that failed to contain his red curls, and had a laptop open beneath an umbrella-shaded table, clicking away.

"We've sent everyone away. Even the staff took the day off after breakfast, at my request, so I could pinpoint the source of the evil I've been sensing."

"Leaving who?" Lena asked.

"Sid, who sort of came with the place. He's the limo driver. But it's not him. I'd know if it was him. And Gus."

"The homeless guy who's become Demetrius's BFF?" Lena said.

"Right. And it's not him, either. Which only leaves me and Demetrius."

"Well then maybe—"

"He's not evil. I'm telling you, he's the victim in all this."

"Forgive me if I still have a little trouble swallowing that after his brain-dead zombies tried to have me killed while giving birth."

"Forgiven," Lilia said, choosing to ignore the sarcasm.

"Scry, sister. Get your freaking pendulum out or get Demetrius to loan you the chalice, and scry that house like a ghost buster. Find the source." Lena softened her tone as she went on. "I'm scared for you, little sister."

"You don't have to be. I think it's going very well. But yes, I'll figure out who it is. I'll keep you posted, okay?"

"All right. Have a good day, then."

"You, too. Kiss Ellie for me."

Lilia hung up the phone, saw Sid looking at her with concern from his shaded table. "Everything all right?" he asked.

She nodded. "Sid, are you sure there's no one here but us?"

He lifted his brows. "Not unless someone's hiding out in the wine cellar." He grinned, but she didn't. "What's the matter with you?"

"I don't know. I think I'll go inside. Maybe I've just had too much sun today."

He nodded, and she got up and headed in, going straight up to her room to grab her scrying crystal, a flawless amethyst point suspended at the end of a silver chain. It had a silver band around its thicker end decorated with a sodalite cabochon like an all-seeing eye, and tiny silver arms extending from either side to form the ring that connected it to the chain. It was a powerful tool. Not as powerful as those Demetrius had, perhaps, but powerful.

After all, magic wasn't about the tool. It was about the witch who wielded it.

She changed into a long turquoise tie-dyed sundress with crocheted cotton trim and spaghetti-thin straps, and took enough time to center herself and breath her way into alpha state. Then she lifted the pendulum and, holding it before her, walked out of her bedroom and into the hall. "By flesh and blood, by hair and bone, the evil here shall soon be known."

9

The pendulum began quivering as soon as Lilia left her bedroom. She moved left, down the hallway, but very soon saw its motions easing slightly. So she turned around and went back the way she'd come. The little stone seemed to vibrate, as if it was reacting to a musical note high enough to shatter it.

At the head of the stairs she started down. One step, then two, three.

No, it wasn't downstairs. The stone grew calmer the farther she went. Turning, she frowned. There was only one door on the other side of her own room—the one to the private stairway that led up to the third floor, where Demetrius lived in solitude.

Oh, hell. Was it true? Was he evil? Had it taken too long to free him from the Underworld, so long that he was already on his way to becoming…

"A demon," she whispered. "Goddess, no. It can't be."

Devastation tasted like bitter root in her mouth. But she had to follow through. She had to find the source of the evil, and if it was him…well, if it was him, she might as well go back to the Finger Lakes, go back to the wine country and her sisters, and spend her remaining time with them. Goddess knew there would not be much of it.

She mounted the staircase, moving slowly upward. And there was no question she was getting closer. The pendant continued to vibrate as it began swirling in ever widening circles.

At the top of the stairs she opened the door without bothering to knock first. She heard something, another door closing, and snapped the chain up and caught the pendulum in her palm all in one quick motion. She didn't need him knowing what she was up to.

There was no one there to catch her scrying, though. The rooms were empty. She checked the bedroom first. His bed lay rumpled and unmade, since the staff had taken the day off. She could feel his energy in the air, but he wasn't there. Moving all the way through it, she peeked through the open bathroom door, then gasped at the size of the tub, and imagined herself in it with him.

Not if he was too far gone. It would never happen.

Next she checked the kitchenette, with its tiny fridge and granite counters. But no, Demetrius hadn't even been in there today.

And then she heard something. The sound of voices coming from behind the closed door of the one remaining room. So there was someone else here! She pocketed her pendulum and went slowly to that closed door, tightening her hand around the knob, mentally preparing herself for battle as she pushed it open.

The giant room was dark, except for the moving images on the wall-sized screen at the far end. A movie?

Yes, a movie, and Demetrius was sitting all alone in

an oversize lounge chair, staring at the screen, frustration knitting his brow.

The film was a comedy, and the reason for his frown was completely clear to her. He didn't get it. Her heart ached for him as he stared, obviously trying to figure it out.

Moving softly forward, she put a hand on his shoulder. He didn't look up, didn't start in surprise. It was as if he'd felt her presence. "Gus says this is the funniest movie he's ever seen. Sid agrees with him. And I just… I don't…"

"I know." She squeezed his shoulder.

He lifted the remote control in his hand and paused the movie. "Is this the same as the view from Bell Rock?" he asked.

She smiled down at him. "Could be. Want to try and see?"

His nod was immediate. "I do. It's such a petty thing, but…could we?"

"Of course, on two conditions." She nodded toward the antique popcorn cart in the corner. "Does that thing work?"

"It's loaded and ready." He sprang from his seat, hurried to the machine and hit a button to start it up. "What's your second condition?"

"Start the film over from the beginning?" she asked. "I hate coming in halfway."

Demetrius laughed until his sides hurt, sometimes fighting to catch a breath between gusts of hilarity. Sitting beside him, Lilia was laughing, too. She kept slapping his shoulder and clinging to it as if the film was too funny to bear, and he loved every single touch.

And they ate popcorn, hot and buttery and salty, and it was so good.

He found himself wanting to experience more things in this new, enhanced way. He wanted to soak in the bubbling cool-water tub in his private gardens and smell the blossoms there as he felt the jets massaging his muscles.

And sex. He really wanted to have sex and discover what it was supposed to feel like.

By the time they finished the movie their hands were cramped from holding on so long, and yet he hated to let go, because it would return him to that state of not quite being alive. Not quite experiencing what life truly had to offer.

Damn. She might have a point. Endless time just going through the motions? Or a limited time feeling everything to its fullest?

Maybe her offer had merit after all.

As the credits finally scrolled down the screen he said, "I was thinking about a soak in the spa down in my private gardens." He didn't want to ask again. It seemed like cheating, feeling things this way but not making the commitment to humanity.

But she didn't make him ask. She just smiled and said, "I'd love to join you."

He nodded and led the way.

Following him, Lilia took the pendulum from her pocket and, pausing for a moment, let it dangle. It was calm.

Relief surged through her. Demetrius wasn't the source of the evil. But her relief was short lived. Because if it wasn't him, then who or what could it be?

He turned, caught her holding the long chain with its dangling crystal, and she quickly looped the chain around her neck. The amethyst lay still and cool on her skin.

"Pretty," he said. Then he led on.

He opened a door at the end of a tiny corridor, a door Lilia had presumed led to a closet. Instead it opened to reveal a curving stairway she'd had no idea was there. Redwood, as if it was meant to be outdoors. And after a few steps down it, she realized that was exactly where it was leading: all the way down to a private garden tucked behind the house.

When they reached it, she blinked to adjust her eyes to the darkness that had descended while they were watching the movie and found she could hardly breathe for the beauty. A natural boundary made of thick vines enclosed it. No one would ever find a clue to its existence from the outside. Inside the small private Eden there were flowers, cacti, red rock walkways and a bubbling kidney-shaped spa that was big enough for half a dozen people. But only two people would be using it now.

Demetrius peeled off his clothes and stepped into the water, ending her view of his nude body entirely too quickly for her liking as he sank down onto a built-in seat. He leaned his head back against the side, closed his eyes and absently stroked the amulet that rested on his broad chest. There were fine lines of strain around his eyes and right between his brows.

"It's not doing what you want it to?"

His eyes popped open. "I don't know what it's supposed to do, and it's not giving me any answers."

"What were you *hoping* it would do?"

He frowned as if trying to come up with an answer, which told her he wasn't intending to tell her the true one. She moved closer, pulling the long edges of her dress up around her hips, and then stepping down into the hot tub.

"Ooh. It's not hot at all," she said, surprised.

"No. Makes no sense to have it hot in the desert. It's more of a cool tub. I was thinking of having a system installed to keep it even cooler."

"Nice." She eyed him, tilted her head a little.

His eyes moved up and down her, then met hers. She read the anticipation in them, though he said nothing. So she peeled the dress over her head, then stretched to lay it across the largest of the boulders that had been placed around the tub to make it look like a natural pool. The illusion was a good one. A little waterfall spilled from the stacked-up rocks into the tub. "This is really beautiful," she said, sinking into the cool water in her pink demi bra and matching panties.

"Is it?"

"Take my hand and I'll show you."

He was looking at her, though, as if he'd figured out how to appreciate visual beauty all by himself. She swallowed past the dryness in her throat and sat down, then slid along the bench seat to get closer to him, finally slipping her hand inside his.

He emitted a soft, stuttering sigh, and then he hit a button and the jets came on, blasting her almost off the seat. She gave a little yelp and grabbed his arm to hold herself down.

He was smiling now. It was an improvement over the scowl he'd worn before. He hit the button again, turning the jets down a notch. She relaxed, positioning her lower back over one of them and closing her eyes. "This is nice."

"Yes, it is. I had no idea how nice until now. God, that smell. Do you smell that?"

"It's the flowers. I wish I knew their names, but I don't. They're luscious, aren't they?"

"Yes."

"And this private garden is like a paradise."

"It is," he said. "No one else knows it's here. I'll have to trust you not to tell."

"Your secret's safe with me." She stayed where she was. "I know what the amulet does, Demetrius."

"You do?"

"Of course I do. My sister Indy wore it. She kept a piece of your stolen soul safe within it until she returned it to you."

"How did she get it in the first place? How did any of you—"

Her eyes opened, and she straightened, so excited to hear him actually asking. But she forced herself to relax back. To take it easy. He might still be evil, since she'd seen no one else up there, and her pendulum wouldn't lie. Maybe he was shifting back and forth between good and evil or something, and that was why the stone hadn't reacted to him a few minutes ago. She had to remember that it was possible, and not even all that surprising, given what he'd been through these past thirty-five-hundred years.

"My sisters and I—"

"Wait," he said, looking down at their clasped hands. "I think I should hear this without..." He looked from their hands to her eyes.

She nodded, taking her hand away when he released

it. "That's for the best, in case any painful memories come up in my story."

He nodded, but she didn't think that was the true reason why he'd wanted to let go. She didn't think he trusted her not to cast some kind of spell on him that would make him believe her, and that hurt. She deserved his distrust, she supposed. She had slapped that binding spell on him without warning, after all.

But she shook off her thoughts and began her story, not missing the way he looked at the garden around him with a sad expression. No doubt it was like seeing it through a smoky mirror.

"My sisters and I were slaves in the harem of King Balthazorus of ancient Babylon. And we were witches, Indira, Magdalena and I. I was the King's favorite, though I didn't love him. I loved his First. His most highly placed soldier. A man completely forbidden to me. You."

She glanced up at him to find him rapt. Good.

"And you loved *me,* too. Someone found out and told the high priest. Or maybe it was Sindar's own constant snooping that uncovered the truth."

"Sindar," he whispered.

"That was his name. Evil bastard. I never knew a man quite that purely rancid. He was made of hate, I swear. I still can't think of a single redeeming quality in him. Jealous, he was always so jealous. He knew our mother was a witch, hated us for that, but she was beyond his reach. She still lived in the outskirts, far from the city itself, and the King was tolerant of the superstitions and ways of the country dwellers. We, however, were closer. Sindar could get to my sisters and me." She shrugged slightly. "And you. We probably should have been more careful."

"So we were found out."

"Mmm." She nodded. "And then we were caught naked, wrapped up in each other's arms. You tried to fight them off, but they beat you down and took me away, and my sisters with me. We were arrested, locked up in underground cells in different parts of the city. That's how afraid Sindar was of us. He must have sensed how powerful we were." She sat up a little straighter. "Are."

"Somehow I don't doubt it," he muttered.

Lilia met his eyes, reminded herself that this was the here and now. Sindar was long dead. No longer a threat to her or those she loved. "Sindar declared that my sisters and I would be sacrificed to the chief god, Marduk. You were arrested, too. When they had you brought before the King and you learned what was to become of us—of me—you broke into a rage. They couldn't hold you, nor could the shackles in which you were bound. You killed the King, slashed his throat with his own blade, and then killed two of his guards before they subdued you again."

He was watching her intently. Really hearing her, she thought—and for the first time. Maybe there was hope after all. "Sindar was furious. We had always suspected his affection for the King went well beyond friendship. He loved the man. Maybe that counts as his single redeeming quality. He loved Balthazorus, and in truth, the King was a good man."

"A good man wouldn't have sentenced you to death."

"Even a good man has bad moments, Demetrius."

"I guess I'm the last person who could argue with that."

"He'd been betrayed by a woman he trusted and thought of as his own. And he was very heavily influenced by Sindar, who was, after all, his most trusted advisor as well as his conduit to the Gods."

Demetrius nodded slowly.

"Sindar was enraged at the death of his love. Maybe that's why he decided to murder yours. He visited me in my cell that night, telling me what would become of you. That he would strip you of your soul, using the blackest of magics." She closed her eyes against the pain of memory. "That he would imprison what remained of your spirit in the Underworld, there to remain for all time."

He was staring at her when she opened her eyes, and she slid closer, one hand cupping his cheek. "But my sisters and I made a plan of our own, and thank the Gods our plan worked. We got you out. You're here. Even if everything else fails, we have this. We have these moments together. This morning on Bell Rock. Our precious few days here in this beautiful place you've created. We have this."

She closed her eyes, but tears seeped out all the same. His fingertips touched one of them as it rolled down her cheek.

"What was your plan, exactly?"

"That we would not cross into the afterlife when our bodies were dashed against the rocks below that cliff where so many of Sindar's victims had died before us. We vowed that, together, we would find you in the cave where Sindar secretly performed the darkest of his rites. He was never a holy man, this we knew. But what could we do?"

"How did you know?"

"A witch knows good from evil, Demetrius. She just does."

Yes, she thought. A witch knows. So why wasn't she sensing evil now? Demetrius was good. He had to be.

"So your spirits somehow floated to this cave…"

"Yes. He was tearing your soul from your body. But we snatched it from him. We stole some of his tools, whatever we could grab, powerful tools, imbued with magic. Indy took the amulet and bound a part of your soul within it, at the same time binding it to her own, so no one could ever find it but her. Lena took the chalice and the blade, which Sindar had confiscated from our quarters, and did the same. I had no tool, only one part of you, the part that loved me, the part that was already bound to me. Your heart…" She put her palm on his naked chest and smiled. "The essence of it, not the organ."

"So you had no tool. Where did you hide it?" he asked.

She closed her other hand around his wrist and brought it to her chest. "You know where," she whispered. "Right where it's always been."

He was so close to her, touching her, naked, in the bubbling pool. She sat there, her palm to his chest, his to hers, just basking in this moment. In touching him. In being so close. His scent, his energy, his essence. No, there was no evil here.

"Are you doing this?" he asked softly, his voice gruff and coarse.

"Doing what?"

"Making me want you?" She met his eyes. "I'm trying my hardest. But not by magic, if that's what you mean."

His lips tightened, as if he wanted to smile but was resisting. "I'm not ready to give up my immortality for you, woman."

"I'm not asking you to. Not here, not now." She was closer to him now. She had no memory of moving, but she had. Her smooth thigh brushed against his broad, hairy one. Her shoulder pressed up tight to his arm, and when she turned her head to gaze at the face she so adored, she found his eyes gazing right back at her. Mere inches lay between her lips and the ones she longed to kiss.

"I was captive in a void for so long," he whispered, breath warm on her mouth. His eyes roamed her face until they seemed to get stuck on her lips. "I'm enjoying being alive too much to give it up."

"You've only been half alive," she whispered. "As I've been trying to show you."

"You *have* shown me. I understand what you were trying to tell me now. It's true, my entire experience has been filtered, dulled. It's amazing how different it is when I see it through your eyes."

"Through your own soul," she corrected him gently.

"Yes. I just…I don't know if it's worth giving up my immortality for. I may be missing a lot of the sensory pleasures of life, but I *am* alive, and I will be forever."

She leaned in closer, lifting her chin and putting her mouth so close to his that their lips were almost touching. Hers brushed his mouth as she said, very softly, "Why don't you let me show you a few more of those sensory pleasures you've been missing, Demetrius?"

He gave a low, growling consent, and then his lips captured hers and his arms wrapped right around her. He slid his big hands beneath her and kneaded her backside as he lifted her to straddle him. And then he tore her panties, first at one hip and then the other, and pulled them free. She barely noticed the friction, she was so lost in the feel of his chest against hers, his mouth feeding from hers, his hands all over her.

Her breath came faster, shorter, as she moved against his familiar hardness. She'd missed this beautiful part of being human. Of being physical. Loving was the best part of living, she decided. And she wondered why it was so powerful, and then stopped wondering and gave herself over to simply feeling.

He'd unfastened her bra and tugged it down her arms, forcing her to let go of him long enough to pull her arms through the straps. And then he bent and tasted her breasts, one and then the other, lapping lovingly, tugging playfully, nipping and making her gasp when she least expected it. She looked down at him, watching his dark head as he sucked and nibbled, until the pleasure was too much to bear and her head fell backward.

"Are you feeling it, my love? Is it above and beyond?" she whispered brokenly. He nodded, because he couldn't speak with his mouth full of her. And then he gripped her butt again, lifted her up a little and settled her over him, so the tip of him was just nudging into her. Then he brought her down all at once, sheathing himself inside her to the hilt.

His invasion drove every bit of air from her lungs, and she felt a moment of absolute bliss at the union. For an instant she gripped his shoulders, willing him to hold still and just feel. It was nearly an orgasm in itself.

They were together again. He was with her; they were one. After thirty-five-hundred years of longing for him, that instant when he slid home was sheer heaven.

And it only got better from there. He moved, despite her attempt to keep him still. He was too strong for that, his hands too demanding. He lifted her up and brought her down again over and over. She moved with him as much as those commanding hands would allow, and they twisted and arched against each other, yearning, reaching, uniting. Over and over he pushed her near, then relaxed away, built the passion, then eased it back, teasing, taunting, tempting, making her burn hotter with every round, like waves rolling up over the beach, then retreating back to the sea, reaching further inland each time as the tide rose higher and higher.

For an hour he played with her, teased her, until at last he held her close when she expected him to pull back yet again. He gripped her against him and drove deeper, faster, again and again. There was no resisting the climax this time. Like water surging through a broken dam, it hit hard and swept them both into its torrent, rolling over them, carrying them, until at last they crashed onto the shore together, clinging, panting. Her heart was pounding so hard she didn't think she could survive, and his pounded even harder against her chest. She rested her head on his shoulder, her entire body relaxed, almost limp with satisfaction. She closed her eyes and thought this was the happiest she had ever been. And if this was all she ever had with him, then it was worth all the time she'd worked toward it.

Demetrius held her and felt her trembling against him in the aftermath of the storm. The physical release, the pleasure—too small a word—the *ecstasy,* had his body shivering and his brain completely numb. He was weak in the wake of it. Content. Blissful. Basking. Completely alive for the first time in his memory. He had to admit that.

When she held him and allowed him to feel things through that connection with her, he realized that she wasn't lying when she said he was normally only half-alive. Food had tasted a thousand times better. The natural beauty around him had become more vivid, so much so that it had made his heart sing. He'd finally understood why people laughed so hard at comedy, had laughed with her until tears filled his eyes. But this—the sex—had been beyond any of it. Beyond description, really. He couldn't put words to how it had felt.

And now something else was filling him. Something he recognized, because he'd remembered feeling it in those glimpses of memory, those mind-journeys back in time. So he was fairly certain what it was, and it terrified him. He thought the feeling might be love. And if he loved her, then lost her again, he knew in his heart it would be over for him. He would just end. Even an immortal couldn't possibly bear that kind of pain twice.

He lifted her off him and set her gently beside him on the seat. Taking the hint, she broke the connection, and his world returned to one of muted colors, tasteless foods, passionless sex. It was like dying a little bit. It was frighteningly akin to the void where he'd been imprisoned. Too empty to bear.

"It can be like that again," she whispered. "It can be like that every single night if you will let me return the final piece of your soul to you, Demetrius. If you will accept your humanity—"

"And vulnerability. And mortality. And powerlessness."

"Yes, to the first two. But humans are far from powerless. I can show you. I can teach you."

He sighed deeply, for the first time truly torn about the decision. She was convincing him, he realized. She was getting through. And he thought he liked it.

But not yet, not now. He needed a clear head, some distance. And yet he didn't want her to leave his side. Didn't think he could stand to have her too far from him at this moment. Was that a part of her magic? The effect of the binding spell? Or was it something much more? Something as old as time itself, perhaps?

He didn't know. Couldn't know. Time for a new subject.

"You never told me what the amulet does."

She sighed, looking crestfallen, but only briefly. Wiping the disappointed look from her eyes, she put her palm over the amulet where it rested on his chest. "Try to open yourself up to it. Invite its power to course through you, to channel its energy into your body, into your heart and up into your head." She took her palm away but pressed a forefinger to the amulet, and then traced a path up over his neck, chin, nose, to the very center of his forehead. "Visualize it beaming its light into you, and then direct it up and focus it all right here," she said, pressing again on the spot in the middle of his forehead slightly above his brows.

He tried, until the spot where the amulet rested seemed to grow warm and he was pretty sure the place between his brows was beginning to tingle. That might have been from her touch, however.

She looked around, pointed. "That potted palm over there. Move it."

He started to get up, but she put her hands on his shoulders and pressed him back down. "Move it from here."

He frowned at her, then raised his brows as he finally understood her meaning. "Without touching it?" he said softly.

She nodded.

"That's what the amulet does?"

Again she nodded. "Try."

He closed his eyes and visualized the energy of the pendant traveling through his chest, up his body, into the center of his forehead. Then he opened his eyes and stared at the plant, pushing it with his mind.

It moved. Only an inch or two, but there was no question that the entire pot, palm and all, had slid away from him.

He was so stunned that he dropped his focus, and after that he couldn't repeat the feat no matter how much he tried.

"Indy, my sister, picked up martial arts skills during one of her many lifetimes, but with the amulet's power, she didn't need to make contact to send her enemies flying. She moved to direct the energy, and her enemies went down without her putting a hand on them."

Demetrius blinked, fingering the amulet and staring down at it.

"With practice, you'll master the way it works best for you."

"But I'll lose the ability to use it if I accept your offer and become mortal again?"

She nodded. "Those are the rules as I understand them."

"Who taught them to you, these rules?" She shrugged, gazing upward at the dark, star-dotted sky far above. "I don't know. I sort of…absorbed the knowledge during my thirty-five centuries between the worlds. And I have the feeling there's more I don't know—I'm sure of it, in fact—but I was only given what I need in order to accomplish what I've set out to do."

"The Gods…want you to succeed, then."

She shrugged. "Or maybe they only want me to have the chance to succeed. They have a sense of fairness, you know? You and I were robbed of the lifetime we might have had together. It was taken from us in the name of the Gods by Sindar's evil. So the Gods, for whatever reason, have granted us the chance to make it right."

"And your sisters, too."

"Their lives and loves were stolen from them the same way. So yes, my sisters were permitted to incarnate lifetime after lifetime with access to the memories they would need to help you when the time was right, and to remember their lost loves and find them once again. I was permitted to remain in between the worlds to watch over them, to call them into action when the stars aligned and the Veil thinned, and your opportunity to escape that Underworld prison came at last. And now it's up to you."

He nodded. "What about the chalice and the blade? Will I lose the powers they possess, as well?" It worried him that he'd said "will I" and not "would I." Was he that far gone?

"The blade that shoots fire probably won't shoot

fire anymore. But any witch worth her salt can direct
energy through an athame, a dagger. It's just a matter
of learning how. And any witch can scry the future in
a chalice of water. The visions won't be as big, as dra-
matic, but the true power of the witch is in *her,* not in
her tools. I can teach you."

"And what about what happens when I use the two
together?"

"Manifesting your dreams as reality?"

He nodded.

"That's what life as a human being is all about.
Those who understand that are able to manifest their
dreams every day of their lives. All it takes is the belief that you can make things happen."

"Then why are there poor and sick and miserable
humans everywhere you look?"

She shrugged. "Each for his or her own reasons.
They don't know any other way to be. Or they don't
believe it's within their power to change their lives. Or
they're so disconnected from their own higher selves
that they can't find their way back. Or they're on a journey of their own for reasons I can't begin to guess."

"And you can teach me this, too, I suppose."

"I can help you learn. But what you choose to believe is too personal for anyone to influence other than
you."

He sighed. "You didn't have to show me the power
of the amulet. It makes me even less likely to accept
your offer."

"I didn't have to make love with you, either. I want
you to make a fully informed decision." She lowered
her eyes. "As fully informed as I'm permitted, at least."

He frowned. "Is there something I'm not allowed to know?"

She met his eyes, longing with everything in her to tell him the truth. That choosing not to accept his soul would mean death not only for him but for her, as well. That information would be too prejudicial. It would effectively remove his ability to make the choice he truly desired.

He had to want his humanity again in order to receive it. It was a gift. He had to see it as such, to truly appreciate what being human meant, before he could choose to accept it.

She caught her breath as the pendulum around her neck began humming against her skin, and her eyes were intuitively drawn up to the upper stories of the house. "Someone is up there. Someone is watching us."

Father Dom closed the door at the top of the stairs above the private garden and backed into Demetrius's rooms. He glanced back up at the spiral stairway that led to his own temporary abode but knew he could no longer stay there. Not now. They would be looking for him soon. Demetrius had fallen prey to the witch's charms. He would surrender soon, if he hadn't already. It was only a matter of time.

Not a lot of time, at least, and that was in Dom's favor. If Demetrius didn't accept the final piece of his soul by Beltane, he would die, and so would the witch—but Dom hoped to get his hands on both of them just before they expired and ensure that they suffered a fate far worse than mere death. He wanted Demetrius destroyed utterly. If he could kill the witch in mid-ritual, while the last remnant of Demetrius's soul remained within her, it would die with her and he would cease to exist.

But short of that, death would suffice. If he didn't accept his soul by Beltane, he would die a more normal death, one that came with an undeserved afterlife and more lifetimes to come. So would the witch. Her cursed sisters would expire with her, though he didn't think that even Lilia knew that part of it yet.

All of those who'd murdered, directly and indirectly, King Balthazorus so long ago would finally pay the price for their crime. His hatred had been festering and growing for a long time. He hadn't been content with Demetrius's suffering in the Underworld. And the women…well, they'd barely suffered at all. Look at the way they'd worked their dark spells and averted their deserved fate. Look at the way they'd reincarnated and found their illicit, unholy lovers again. Indira and Tomas—he'd been a novice priest, forced to push her to her death for Marduk's sake. Magdalena and the King's own son! They'd even had a child together.

A child…

Now there was a thought.

He needed only a few more days. Just a few more days to delay Demetrius from making the final decision and accepting the return of his soul. Then they would all die, and perhaps he could have peace of his own, a peace he had never known since the murder of the King. But they would realize his true identity at any time now. So he needed to delay them, and then to distract them from trying to stop him. He needed to slip away while they were distracted as they were now, and then he needed to provide a reason for the temptress to want Demetrius to stay just as he was, with his soul fragmented and destined to die.

And an innocent baby would make a very good reason indeed.

If he did everything just right, before that became necessary he might even be able to destroy Demetrius as he longed to. Utterly. Because if the witch died with his soul still inside her, and if her body was then destroyed so she could not revive, then Demetrius would cease to exist.

He'd never burned a witch before. He found himself looking forward to it.

10

"Someone is watching us," Lilia said.

"Probably just the old priest," Demetrius muttered without thinking, unable to take his eyes from Lilia, his mind still on the amazing sex they'd so recently shared.

She was rising from the tub, water trailing down her beautiful flesh, her eyes troubled as she stared up at the stairs. But when he spoke, her head snapped toward him. "The old priest?"

He didn't like the alarm he saw in her eyes. "He's been staying here, but he's asked for privacy, so I've indulged him. But he's harmless, Lilia," he said, cursing himself silently for erring and mentioning Father Dom's existence. "He just…he found some bad information. Stories change after being passed along for so many centuries."

Her eyes narrowed on him. "What stories? What misinformation has he been telling you, Demetrius?"

He shrugged. It was clear to him now, knowing Lilia as he had come to, that the old man was confused, obsessed, perhaps even a bit insane. "I promise you, he's just a harmless old man who thinks he's trying to help. He believes you're trying to trick me. He's the one who told me you and your sisters wanted me to become human again so you could steal my powers for yourselves." She was looking angrier with his every word. "But I know he's wrong. I know that now," he said, hoping to ease the fury in her eyes.

"Demetrius, I need you to start at the beginning. What old priest are you talking about? Where did he come from, and how long has he been here?"

He sighed, realizing their respite was over. She was all business now, turning to pick up a towel from the rack nearby and rubbing herself dry.

He supposed he should do the same, so he got up with a heavy sigh and helped himself to a towel, though he suspected he would feel much better if he were holding her hand.

"All right, from the beginning," he said slowly. "He arrived here a few days before you did and he told me you were coming. He said you would try to trick me into accepting the final piece of my soul, so that you could take my powers for your own."

"And you believed him." It wasn't a question. "That's why you've been so suspicious of me, so resistant to me, this entire time?"

He nodded, hating to admit it. "Yes, it's part of the reason. But he was very convincing, Lilia. He knew things he shouldn't have known, not only that you were on your way here but that I'd spent thousands of years in an Underworld prison. And that if I accepted your offer, I'd lose my powers. It all turned out to be absolutely true. So when he said that you'd tricked me before, made me fall in love with you through black magic, then used me to kill the King so that you and your sisters would be free of his harem, it…it seemed to make sense."

"My sisters and I were executed, Demetrius. Not freed. And we've spent the past three-and-a-half millennia trying to set you free."

"I know that…now. Believe me, Lilia, I do."

She draped her towel over the rack to dry, then reached for her sundress and pulled it over her head, not bothering with her wet bra or torn panties. He finished drying off and pulled on his own clothes.

"Where did he claim to have come by all this ancient knowledge?" she asked. "It's a story only a few living beings know."

"He said he had scrolls, that they'd been handed down through the priests of his line for centuries."

Her brows bent deeply, and she looked at him intently. "I think I already know, but what's his name, this old priest?"

"Father Dom. He's—"

"The same Father Dom who tried to kill my sister Indira to keep her from helping you escape through the Portal in the first place?"

"Am I supposed to know the answer to that?" But he was suddenly alarmed. Was the priest in his observatory more than he'd seemed?

"You were there, raging and manipulating and—" Her eyes were blazing, but then she bit her lip and looked into his eyes, and the fires were banked. "I'm sorry. I know that wasn't you, not really. It was just the energy mass that had once been you, robbed of its soul and tortured past the edge of sanity."

"I don't remember a lot of what happened while I was…in that state."

"I know." She moved closer, sliding her hand around the curve of his neck, moving as if to kiss him again.

But she stopped, and he did, too, because the necklace she was wearing had begun to shake, practically jumping up and down on her chest. Backing up a step, she removed it, then held it by one end of its long chain, letting the crystal dangle and staring as it began to spin.

"What is that?" Demetrius asked, mesmerized by the winking light reflected by the gleaming stone.

"It's a pendulum. I use it to...find things, or to answer simple yes or no questions. I've been sensing evil in this place, and my sister Lena, the one with the most powerful scrying ability, said it was here. Inside this very house. I brought out my stone to try to track it down, and it led me upstairs, to you."

"You think I'm evil?"

She shook her head. "No, Demetrius. Not you. It's that priest. He's evil. And there's something else," she said, looking down at the madly spinning amethyst. "Something big, but I don't know what. The stone is going crazy." She started up the stairs, and he followed.

"What else could there be?" he asked.

"I don't know." Reaching the top of the stairs, she tried the door. "He's locked us out. He's up to something."

"I can break it—"

"You don't need to." She caught the stone in her hand and stepped aside, making room for him on the top stair. "Channel the power from your amulet and turn the lock on the other side."

Doubtfully, he focused on the doorknob, thinking past it to the lock. She kept talking as he tried to focus. "Father Dom has been in a coma for months, even since

Indira managed to bring you through the Portal, freeing you from the Underworld. They didn't expect him to recover. Focus harder, my love, he's getting away."

"I don't know what he would have to get away from," he said, but he tried to focus harder.

"He awoke from his coma the very day I returned to physical being. The very first time you used the magical tools you received from my sisters. He was not expected to recover, but he woke up and walked out of the hospital."

He frowned and forgot about the lock—and heard it snap open at that very instant. "What are you saying?"

"I'm saying he isn't finished with us yet." She reached past him, opened the door.

"He said he wanted to help me," Demetrius said. "I think he's sincere, just misguided."

She stepped into the bedroom, looked around and felt that it was empty. Then she turned to him and lifted the pendulum. "I asked the crystal to lead me to the evil I've been sensing in this place since I came here. It led me up the stairs, into your suite. I checked and found you watching a movie. For a moment, I was afraid…"

"That I was the one who was evil." He lowered his head. "I can't even say that I blame you."

She sighed, but nodded. "But it wasn't you. The pendulum didn't react to you. Where was he staying?"

Demetrius nodded toward the narrow spiral staircase. "In the observatory."

She pocketed the crystal, headed through the hall and started up the spiral stairway, but he snapped his arms around her waist and lifted her back down. "I'll go first, just in case you're right and he really is dangerous."

"I know I'm right."

Protecting her. It was an instinctual thing, one he couldn't resist and didn't particularly want to. He'd been unable to protect her before, in that past life he was starting to remember in bits and snippets, and the pain of that was not something he wanted to recall, much less relive.

The love they'd had just might be, though. In fact, he felt as if he didn't have much of a choice about that. It was coming back to him, maybe not in vivid images in his mind, but in feelings, powerful feelings, that he now knew were only dull echoes of the true ones.

He reached the top of the stairs, pushed up the trap-door and stepped up into the observatory, which appeared empty. Then he turned and reached down for Lilia, taking her hand and helping her up to join him. When he let go of the trapdoor it slammed closed with a bang that sounded like a gunshot.

"That's not how it's supposed to work," he muttered. "I'll have Sid take a look later on."

She looked around the circular room, but he already knew she wouldn't find the priest. There was nowhere for anyone one to hide up there. It was one large open room, with the powerful telescope in the middle and the glass dome above. Father Dom's make-shift cot stood as close to one curved wall as it would go, made up none too neatly, with his things scattered on top of it.

"He's not here," Lilia said, her tone disappointed.

"He can't have gone far, and he'll surely be back. His things are still here." He nodded at the black suit Father Dom had been wearing when he'd first arrived, which had been tossed carelessly into the corner. There was a battered old suitcase on the floor, a shaving kit on the bed.

"We don't need his things."

"But he said he had a book—an old journal that told the story of our past together."

He was already bending to open the suitcase, while Lilia went to the glass to look outside, slowly circling the room so she could explore in every direction.

In the case, he found a book, large and old, and bound in black leather.

"There he is!" she shouted.

Demetrius tucked the book under his arm and hurried to her side, staring down at the man who had paused just beyond the front gate to turn and look up at the house, a man who didn't look like Father Dom at all, not even the Father Dom who'd worn the gaudy cactus shirt.

He was wearing a white tunic with swaths of purple fabric draped around it and over one shoulder. His hair had lengthened and thickened and grown darker, far darker, and his belly thrust out like a woman late in pregnancy.

Demetrius shook his head. "That's not him." But he recalled the purple fabric he'd glimpsed in this room before. He snatched one of the small secondary lenses from a stand near the telescope and peered through it.

Father Dom—and it *was* Father Dom, Demetrius realized—had changed more than his clothes. He'd lined his eyes and reddened his lips. But it was more than the makeup and more than the clothes. His cheeks were plump and pink, and he'd developed a double chin, when a few days ago his face had been drawn and gray. And that pendant with the dragon on it was still around his neck. Father Dom looked up, and Demetrius could have sworn that the old priest was looking right back at him, straight into his eyes.

"Let *me* see," Lilia said. He handed her the lens. She held it to her eye, then gasped and staggered three steps backward. Her eyes were wide. "You're right, that's *not* Father Dom," she whispered. "It's Sindar."

Everything in him went icy cold as the name turned a lock in his mind and he remembered the high priest he'd vowed to take vengeance on, the man who'd tortured and murdered the woman he'd loved. He remembered the dragon pendant, symbol of the Babylonian god Marduk.

"The same man who had you killed?" he asked, though he already knew.

"The same man who stripped you of your soul," she said. "He hates you, Demetrius. He hates us all."

"I don't understand. If he hates me, why would he want me to keep my powers? To remain immortal?"

She opened her mouth, then closed it again and, frowning, sniffed the air. "Demetrius," she whispered. "Do you smell smoke?"

Lilia turned panicked eyes on Demetrius as sooty gray smoke began puffing up around the trapdoor. He saw it, too, and dropped the leather book he'd been holding, moving her gently aside. Then he bent toward the trapdoor and reached to yank it open. But it didn't move, making her blood run cold.

"He must have rigged the door to trap us in here." He continued yanking vainly on it.

Lena backed away, then spotted the book he'd

dropped and she grabbed it. Something told her it might be important.

"The amulet, Demetrius. Use it."

He nodded, straightened and focused intently on the trapdoor. Then he suddenly thrust one fist at the door and it exploded, letting the smoke come rushing in at them.

"Grab the blanket!" he shouted.

She did, holding it around her mouth and nose as they scrambled down the spiral stairs. Demetrius ran to the door that led down to the second floor and pulled it open, only to see a wall of red-orange flames licking at the ceiling. It had happened so fast!

He slammed the door closed again. "He must have set the place on fire before he left," he said. "Sid and Gus—" He was choking on the smoke and couldn't finish the sentence.

Lilia ran to the far end of his bedroom to open the French doors. Stumbling onto the balcony, she sucked in great greedy gulps of air and wiped the tears from her stinging eyes.

Demetrius was beside her a moment later, pulling the doors closed behind him. They both leaned over the railing, looking down at the beautiful mansion. Flames were leaping from an alarming number of windows.

"We're going to have to jump," he said.

"What about the stairway to your private garden?"

"The smoke would get us before we got that far. And we could burn to ashes before we revived."

"If our bodies are destroyed, it's over. We won't come back from that," she told him.

He looked back into the increasingly smoke-filled

bedroom. "I've got to get the chalice and the blade from the safe."

"Don't be insane! You'll be killed!"

"At the moment, I'm still immortal," he reminded her. "I know I can make it. We might need those tools, Lilia. We have no idea what Sindar's intentions are."

He clasped her shoulders, kissed her forehead. "Don't wait for me if it gets too—"

"Just go!"

Nodding, he flung open the doors and ran into the smoke. Lilia didn't close them behind him. She stood trying to peer through the smoke to see him, the blanket over her face, coughing now and then. Moments ticked past, then still more.

"Demetrius?" she called. "Demetrius, are you—"

He emerged from the smoke so suddenly that she jumped backward, and then he was with her once more, shutting the doors and trapping the smoke inside. He had a small leather satchel in one hand, presumably with the chalice and the dagger inside, and his cell phone in the other.

Holding the phone out to her, coughing so hard he could barely speak, he managed, "Sid. Gus."

"Nine-one-one first?"

"No, the security system will already have notified them."

Nodding, and moving to the edge of the balcony, she quickly scrolled to his phone book, cursing her slow fingers but finally hitting the entry marked Sid.

It rang and rang.

She switched to the entry for Gus, praying, while Demetrius took out the blade and strapped its hand-tooled leather sheath and belt around his waist. Neither of them took their eyes from the closed glass doors for long. The room beyond them was black with smoke by now.

Demetrius took the old book from her and added it to the satchel. Then held out his hand. "Give me the phone. We have to go."

"Just one more minute."

Gus's phone rang endlessly. She shook her head. "Gus, please... Answer, dammit."

His face was grim. "We can't get to them from here. The stairway's engulfed." Then he took the phone from her hand and put it into the satchel, buckled it up and tossed it over the railing.

Lilia watched it fall into the hedges near the house.

"Jump out as far as you can, aim for the pool," he told her.

She stared down. Three stories, and the pool was far too shallow. She would recover, but it was going to hurt like hell.

"Come on, we don't have a choice."

She looked down at the dizzying distance and stepped backward. She'd had no fear up on Bell Rock. But she hadn't been about to jump off it, either. Her history with falling from high places was not good. "I...I can't."

"We have to save Sid and Gus. Go."

She nodded and, bracing one hand on his shoulder, got up on the railing. Then, with a deep breath and a silent prayer, she jumped. She screamed all the way down—a distance that took about three seconds to descend—and hit the water feetfirst, shooting like a missile all the way to the bottom. Her feet hit, her knees bent, and she absorbed the impact. It was just that easy.

It didn't even hurt all that much. She pushed herself toward the surface and emerged spluttering. Demetrius was already splashing down into the pool beside her. Then he surfaced, shook the water from his head and looked at her. "You okay?"

"Yes. Fine. You?" She pushed her wet hair back from her face.

"I'm fine, too." Then he looked back at the house, and his eyes went frantic. They swam to the edge. He climbed out, then reached down to pull her up beside him, grabbed her arm and drew her away from the heat. A window exploded, and flames licked out the opening.

He pointed. "Get the satchel. See it there? In the bushes? Get it, and then go open the gate. Do it fast. Don't wait for me."

"Demetrius—"

He strode back toward the house, and she went after him and gripped his shoulder. "It's possible you might have accepted the final piece of your soul already and not even be aware of it, because you asked subconsciously, not out loud. And if that happened, then you could be mortal right now and not even know it."

"Get the satchel and get out of the way, Lilia."

He pulled free, but she lunged after him again, still trying to stop him.

This time he turned on her fiercely. "Dammit, Gus is my best friend. And Sid's barely more than a kid." Angrily, he aimed a forefinger at the satchel in the shrubs near the house and then swung his arm toward her. The satchel launched like a rocket, landing at her feet. He still had powers. He wasn't mortal, then. She bent automatically, picked up the satchel and held it to her chest. Demetrius was jogging away before she even managed get the strap over her shoulder.

"If your body burns, it's over, Demetrius! Please!"

He ran right up to the front door, and she knew it had to be searing hot that close to the fire. She could feel the heat from here. Yanking the dagger from its sheath, he blasted the doors open, and then he was gone, vanishing into the flames and smoke.

"Demetrius!" she cried.

Sirens wailed. The gate closed. She had to let the firemen in. They were her love's best hope now. She carried the satchel to the gate and tucked it behind one of the pillars, out of sight. Then, as the fire trucks rolled nearer, she pressed the keypad and let them in.

The trucks rumbled through, rolling toward the house, and Lilia ran behind them. By the time she caught up, the fire crews were already pouring from their vehicles and swarming over the lawns of the once-beautiful home.

She started toward the house, but three men rushed over to her, the apparent leader clasping her shoulders and shouting questions over the roar of the flames, the whoosh of the hoses, the rumbling motors, and the shouting of the firefighters. The trucks' flashing lights hurt her eyes.

"Are you hurt?"

"No, no, but—"

"Is anyone inside?"

She nodded. "Three men. One of them is older. Gus. Please, I have to help—"

"We've got this, ma'am." He nodded to one of his subordinates, who took her arm and kept her from running back toward the house as the chief jogged toward the others shouting, "We have three adult males inside! Let's do this!"

Meanwhile, her captor was tugging her toward an ambulance. "Were you inside?" he was asking. "How did you get all wet?"

She couldn't drag her eyes from that inferno as the flames grew fiercer, hotter. God, where was Demetrius? Yes, he was immortal, and yes, he would recover from any injuries with rapid speed, but what if his body was destroyed? And what about Gus and Sid? God, had Sindar murdered more innocents today? Had her attempt to reclaim the life he'd stolen from her only brought about more death?

"Ma'am?"

She shook herself. "We were upstairs. We jumped from the balcony into the pool."

"We?"

"Demetrius and I. He went back inside after Sid and Gus."

"Did you inhale any smoke, ma'am?" He pressed her to sit on the back edge of the open ambulance.

In seconds an EMT was leaning over her and pressing a stethoscope to her chest. "Take a deep breath for me," he said, as the firefighter raced back toward the blaze.

"I'm fine." She pushed his hands away, rising as something moved behind one of the second-floor windows, a shadow in front of the eerie red-orange backlighting. "Is that—"

The shadow smashed through the window, plunging into the hedges and vanishing. But she'd seen enough to know it was Demetrius, with one or maybe both of the other men entangled in his arms.

She lunged forward, but the paramedic blocked her. "Ma'am, you really can't—"

"You really don't want to get in between me and the man I love," she said. Her eyes met his, and she willed him to move. And he did, his face going as blank as a sleepwalker's.

She raced toward the hedges where firefighters were already pulling the men free. It was hot this close to the fire, so hot it seared her face. Demetrius emerged at last, nearly falling to his knees before she reached him, grabbed him and, pulling his arm around her shoulders, half carried him away from the danger. The firefighters followed with the other men.

When she reached the far side of the pool she eased Demetrius onto the grass and knelt over him, cradling his head in her hands. His face was sooty, his eyes watering as he stared up at her, and then he looked back toward the rescuers who were tending to his friends. She followed that gaze and saw that neither Sid nor Gus were conscious.

"They were trapped in the game room on the second floor," he said. "They didn't have a chance. I tried...."

Then his eyes fell closed and there was only the sound of his lungs, wheezing with every breath.

The medics closed in, and Lilia had the presence of mind to slide the blade from its sheath and beneath her skirt, away from prying eyes, before they shoved her out of the way and she lost sight of her love.

11

When Demetrius came around again he was in a hospital bed. He'd been bathed and no longer stank of smoke, and he was wearing a clean blue hospital gown and was resting between crisp white sheets.

As memory returned, his eyes widened and he sat up with a sudden start and a grunt of horror.

Soft hands pressed him gently back onto the mattress. He knew that touch. And the voice that came with it. "It's all right. It's over. We're safe."

He blinked away the nightmare images of Gus, of Sid, slumping in the corner of the game room, coughing, barely breathing, as he blasted through a wall to get to them. And then so limp, so lifeless, as he'd carried them to the closest window and launched the three of them through it.

"What about the guys?" he asked softly, his eyes searching hers. So blue. So beautiful. So very sad.

"Gus has some burns on his hands and arms, but it was mostly smoke inhalation. But he's going to be all right."

He blinked slowly, knowing already that he didn't

want to hear the answer to his next question, yet asking it all the same. "Sid?"

She closed her eyes, but a tear squeezed through anyway. "Sid was gone before you hit the ground. He had an undiagnosed heart condition, they said. The smoke was just too much. They tried to revive him, but—"

"Dammit!" He sat up in bed, and no amount of pressure from those tender hands stopped him this time. "I need clothes."

"Demetrius, wait."

"I need my damn clothes. I'm going after that bastard who calls himself a priest, and when I find him—"

"You'll do what?" she demanded.

He went still, staring into her tear-filled eyes.

"You'll do what?" she asked again, her voice softer now. "Act like the demon he tried to force you to become?"

He stared at her. She was clean, too, wearing a dress someone must have donated, because it was a size too big and not her usual style, green, with a tank-style top and flared skirt. Flip-flops on her feet.

"It would be poetic, wouldn't it?" he asked her slowly. "If I murdered that animal because of what he made me?"

"It wouldn't hurt him a bit, Demetrius. Death is an illusion. No more than a release from the constraints of the physical body. You know there is life beyond it. You know this."

He sat there with his legs over the side of the bed, feet on the floor, itching to get out of there and wanting to argue with Lilia's calm logic. But it was true, what she said. It was true, and he knew it.

She was still talking. "If you kill him, all you do is release him into wholeness and oneness and bliss, and he can then process what has happened and perhaps, return a better man. While you? You stain your soul with the mark of murder. What good would killing him do?"

"Maybe keep him from hurting anyone else," he said. "Maybe avenge that kid who befriended me when I had only one friend in the world. He would have taken a bullet for me, you know."

"I know." A tear slipped down her cheek. "I know. But Sid is fine, I promise you. He had a few minutes of fear, then he closed his eyes, and when he opened them again it was to a world of beauty and understanding the likes of which he had never even imagined."

"That's not what the afterlife was like for me."

"You were in a realm created by hatred and dark magic. That wasn't the afterlife. It was something altogether different, completely unnatural. And I think you know that."

He sighed. "I'm still going after Sindar."

She nodded. "I know you are. And I'm going with you. Would you like to see Gus first?"

Grunting, he nodded. "If you would please get me some clothes."

She picked up a plastic bag from the floor. He looked up, sending her a question with his eyes. "The hospital found something for me to wear and provided these for you. Right now these are the only clothes you have."

Then he lowered his head. "How bad?"

"The house is a total loss. The garage survived, and the limo and the Jeep are all right. But everything else is gone."

"How long have I been out of it?"

"Three days. You missed the funeral, I'm afraid."

Heaving a deep breath, he blew it out slowly. "I'm really sorry about that," he said.

"He knows you are."

Blinking slowly, Demetrius tried to take stock. His life had turned upside down in the space of an hour, it seemed. "So I'm back where I started. Homeless."

"Your home," she whispered, taking his hand and laying it over her heart, "is right here."

Oddly, he believed her. The feel of her heart beating gently beneath his palm filled him with…something. Something he'd been determined not to feel. Something he knew he could feel a lot more powerfully if his soul were intact.

But if he accepted her offer he would lose his powers. He wouldn't be able to fight the powerful high priest who'd somehow take up residence in the body of a comatose old man after thousands of years. He could not fight the powerful, maybe immortal, dark magician without his powers. So he couldn't let Lilia restore the final piece of his soul. Not yet. And if he didn't succeed in his mission to subdue Sindar in time, maybe never.

And yet Lilia had made a very good point. What good was vengeance going to do any of them?

"We can return to my sisters," she said softly. "They'll give us a place to stay for now. We can be there in time to spend Beltane with them."

Beltane. The deadline for his decision to be made. One more day, he realized. Nodding slowly, he got to his feet. "I'll get dressed. Will you let them know I'm discharging myself, get the forms I need to sign so we can get all their arguing over with and be on our way?"

"Of course. I've already phoned my sisters—your phone, not mine. Mine burned with the house."

That reminded him of his magical tools.

"They're safe," she said, before he could even speak, and then she nodded toward the chair in the corner, where the satchel sat undisturbed. "The blade, the chalice and even your amulet are in there."

She'd taken care of his most cherished possessions. She'd made sure he had something to wear. She was trying to take care of him. Had been, he realized, for thirty-five-hundred years. Had anyone ever been that devoted to anyone before?

Gus lay in his hospital bed looking pale and pain-racked. He wore mittens of gauze and padding that reached to his elbows, and his ankle was in a cast and elevated in a sling. IVs pumped him full of drugs and fluids, but if pain meds were part of the mix, there were clearly not enough of them.

Demetrius sat in the chair beside the bed, feeling for his friend. Hurting for him. And certain his empathy would be far worse if he had an intact soul. Yet another mark on the con side of that decision. "I phoned Ned Nelson before I came in," he said. "He's been here, but I was still too out of it to talk then. Anyway, he's going to have his lawyers handle everything for me."

"What's to handle?" Gus asked, searching Demetrius's face.

"I'm selling enough stock to take care of Sid's family. It's the least I can do."

Gus nodded. "He was a good kid. Damn good kid. Should've been me dying in those flames, but

I guess I'm...not done yet. There's still something I need to do."

"There are a lot of things you still need to do, my friend." Demetrius moved to pat Gus's hand, then stopped, because they were so thickly mittened.

"You saved my life," Gus said softly.

"You would have done the same for me."

The old man's lips thinned, and he looked away. There were tears in his eyes. "We had a good run, you and I."

"Don't talk like you're going anywhere soon, old man. You were right just now. You *do* have more to do." Demetrius found a spot to touch, Gus's shoulder. "I'm keeping enough to live on for a while, but I'm signing the bulk of the stock and what's left of the property over to you."

Gus's pale blue eyes widened, and he moved as if to sit up but only managed to raise his head from the pillows a couple of inches before it fell back down again.

"The house is a total loss. But the property is still a prime piece of real estate. Worth several million, given that location. And there's the limo, the garage, all still intact. I'm taking the Jeep."

"But—"

"It's the least I can do. I'm the cause of this, Gus. I cost a young man his life and nearly got you killed."

"No. No, listen, D-man, Lilia says Sid was ready to go or he wouldn't have gone. And that I wasn't, or I *would* have. She told me about that priest. It's *his* fault, not *yours*."

"Lilia is wise about many things, but not everything, Gus. I let that old priest in. I listened to his lies, agreed to keep his presence secret. I trusted him, a stranger, more than I trusted Lilia, or Sid, or you—*you,* Gus, my best friend. I betrayed you and almost got you killed."

It hit him then that he'd done this before. Betrayed his best friend by his secret love for Lilia. That time his best friend had been a king, and the betrayal had led Demetrius to kill his friend with his own hands. For a moment he sat there awash in a sense of déjà vu that was almost dizzying. And then it passed, though he was left shaken in its wake.

Gus saw that he was upset and changed the subject. "Who was that old priest, anyway? Why would he want to do something like that to you? To us?"

Averting his eyes, Demetrius shrugged. "I think he was deluded, and for some reason he chose me to obsess over, and it got worse when Lilia appeared. It was just…random."

"That little witch of yours," Gus said, "She says nothing is random. She knows things, D-dog. You should listen to her."

"I've figured that out already. That's why I'm going home with her. Back East. She's got family in New York state, near Ithaca. Once—"

"You're leaving me?" Gus whispered. "But, D, we've been together for—"

"You didn't let me finish. As soon as you're well enough to travel, I'm bringing you out there, too. If you want to come."

"Damn straight I do."

Demetrius nodded. "I'd stay until then, but we need to find that priest, before he hurts someone else. And Lilia thinks her sisters can help us do that. You just get well, Gus. And let me know if you need anything." Demetrius reached for the notepad near the phone on

Gus's nightstand, which, he thought, was rather ironic, since the man would have had to dial with his nose. After jotting a number, he set the pad down again. "That's Lilia's sister's number. That's where I'm heading. And I've still got my cell phone. You remember that number?"

Gus made a face. "My new cell's in the drawer. Lilia bought it for me. Don't know where she got the scratch, but—"

"One of her brothers-in-law is nearly as wealthy as Ned Nelson."

"That must be it, then," Gus said. "So, do you mind programming the numbers into that new phone for me?" He held up his hands and shrugged sheepishly. "Kinda hard with my fingers all wrapped up like boxing gloves."

Demetrius found the phone and turned it on. "It takes vocal commands," he said as he entered both numbers.

"That Lilia. She thought of everything." Gus sighed. "I'll be on my way to you two just as fast as I can, D-dog. You better believe it."

Demetrius smiled. "I'll hold you to that, Gus."

After Demetrius left the room, Gus sat up in the bed and began unwrapping the gauze from his hands. He wasn't healed yet. Not completely. But nearly. His friend had been right. He did have things to do. He'd only just come to realize—to remember—what things when he'd been overcome by the smoke. It was all coming back to him now, though.

It didn't taken Sindar long to track down the witches. Like so many other things, such as the language and customs of this time and place, the location of Lilia's sisters had been waiting for him in the memory of the old priest whose body he wore like a suit.

A cheap and ill-fitting suit, at first. But it was changing rapidly to reflect the soul it now held. For someone with his abilities, bodies were mutable, and he was enjoying the sensation of familiarity his newly changed body aroused.

Indira and her husband, the fallen priest Tomas, had been with Father Dom at the end, when he'd fallen to his death. Well, "fallen" wasn't precisely the right word. He'd been pushed. Not by the witch or her consort, but by the demon Demetrius himself. He'd been using wildlife as his eyes and ears to keep tabs on the witch while he'd still been imprisoned in the Underworld. When a wolf had appeared, attacked Father Dom and sent him tumbling from the cliff in a beautifully ironic repetition of the way the witches had died so long ago, the old priest had never doubted that Demetrius had been behind it.

Demetrius probably didn't even remember saving that witch's life, but Sindar knew, because he still had access to Dom's memories.

Not that it mattered. However, something about the poetry of Dom's end appealed to Sindar, and he began to alter his plan to make room for something similarly fitting. Full circle. Yes, that was the way it had to be.

He was going to give Demetrius a reason to refuse to accept his humanity a little bit longer, then kill him. He intended to kill the witch first, though. She would die as Beltane, the deadline, began, just as the clock ticked the hour, so that she would not return. And if she died with the piece of Demetrius's soul still inside her, he would be destroyed utterly. No afterlife, no heaven, no chance to live again. It had to be very precisely timed. And before he killed Lilia, he would take as much from her as he could. Like the skin of a snake or the feathers of certain birds, the blood of a witch had power. Power he could use.

But first he needed to bait the trap.

He'd stolen a car, then switched its license plates with a set taken from a broken-down relic at a junk-yard. Driving had been exceedingly difficult at first, even with Father Dom's muscle memory mostly intact. However, by the time he'd driven the thing all the way from Arizona to the Finger Lakes region he'd mastered it.

He had a cell phone he'd taken from Lilia's room on his way out of the burning mansion. He had cash, picked from an old man's pocket at a highway rest stop. And he had a detailed geological map of the entire area around Milbury, which had allowed him to choose the perfect spot to execute the rest of his plan. The army he intended to raise would wait a few more hours. In the meantime…

Ahh, there they were.

For the second day in a row he'd left the car parked out of sight, just around the bend from Havenwood's long drive, where he could stand and watch through the trees to see if anyone was coming.

Now his patience had paid off. And none too soon, either. Lilia and her demon lover were on their way even now.

But his time was at hand. The man who was, as far as he could tell, the family guru was pushing a baby stroller along the driveway. He, too, wore robes, but not makeshift ones like Sindar's own, pieced together from swatches of fabric, but real robes, white and red. Beneath them he was barefoot. He had dark skin, weathered but not lined, and hair the length of his torso, all twisted and matted in what the old priest's brain told him were called dreadlocks. *Dread* was a good word for them. His beard was just as long and just as tangled. Dark brown, with white tufts here and there.

Sindar hoped the man wouldn't turn the stroller around at the end of the drive and head back the way he had come. *Turn left at the end instead. Come toward me, just a little bit. Just until you're out of sight of the house.*

The guru stopped at the end of the drive, tipping his head as if he'd heard something. And then he turned in the direction of the man who'd just summoned him. He must be in tune with the more subtle forces, Sindar thought as he waved a hand in the air. The guru continued toward him, still pushing the stroller.

When they reached the car, Sindar smiled—beamed, really. "I'm sorry to disturb you on your stroll, friend, but I find I'm in need of assistance."

"If the problem is a mechanical one, I'm afraid I'll be of little help. But you're not far from real aid. You can walk back with me if you like."

"Oh, I think I can take the car that far. Can I give you two a lift?" He opened one of the rear doors as he spoke.

The guru frowned, glancing inside. "It's not far," he said. "I wouldn't want to leave the stroller behind."

"We can put it in the trunk. It folds up, doesn't it?"

"You don't have a car seat."

Sindar could see the suspicion forming in the man's eyes as he began to turn around.

"Wait!" Sindar smiled to ease the power of the command. "Wait. At least let me get a glimpse at the little angel, hmm?"

Sindar could see that the other man didn't like it. He would have to be quick or risk losing them. As he leaned over, reaching as if to move the blanket aside, he grabbed the pink-clad infant. Startled, the baby began to wail, and the guru leapt to her defense.

"What do you think you're—"

"Stay back." Just that quickly, Sindar had a knife in his free hand, holding the screaming infant anchored to his chest with the other arm. "Stay back or she dies."

The guru held up both hands, his dark brown eyes wide. "Don't harm the child, I beg of you. Whatever you want, I'll get for you. Anything, just don't—"

"What I want is the witch's child." Still brandishing the knife, Sindar leaned toward the car and dropped the baby on the floor in the back, where she continued to bawl.

"No." The guru's eyes were on the infant. "No, please, not like that. It's not safe."

"I won't harm her—providing she shuts up within a reasonable amount of time. She's only the means to an end for me." He slammed the door on the screaming baby and opened the driver's door.

"Take me, as well, then!" the guru shouted. And he opened the rear door and dove into the car beside the child, quickly gathering her into his arms.

Miraculously, she quieted.

Sindar nodded as he slid behind the wheel. "All

right, then. That seems like a very good idea, in fact."
He slammed his own door shut and started to drive.

Indy had just gotten off the phone with Lilia and
had delivered the biggest part of her news to Lena, who
was now staring at her as if she had lobsters crawling
out of her ears.

"She's bringing Demetrius here?" Magdalena stood
in the middle of her living room, at 6:30 p.m. on Friday,
May fourth, staring at Indy as if she'd lost her mind.
"What the hell do you mean, she's bringing him here?"

"Easy, Lena," Indy said, trying too soothe her sister by clasping her shoulders, but Lena had fire in her
eyes that matched her hair.

"I'm not going to take anything easy," she said,
shaking Indira's hands away.

"Fine, be difficult then." Indy flung out a hand,
knocking her sister onto her ass in the nearest chair
without even touching her. "But you are going to listen."

Lena surged to her feet, but Indy shoved her right
back again, still hands-free. "Sometimes I hate your
guts," Lena muttered.

"You're supposed to. I'm your sister." Indy turned.
"I'll make some of Mom's tea. Chamomile, I think.
Maybe with some valerian mixed in." She glanced
back at her furious sister. "And maybe a Xanax," she
added. "It'll just have time to kick in before they get
here from the airport."

Her sister scowled at her. Indy scowled back.
"Where's Ellie?" she asked.

"Bahru took her for a walk," Magdalena said. "It's
such a nice day. And since I'm sending her and my

husband away first thing tomorrow morning, thanks to that pain-in-the-ass Demetrius and his stupid Beltane deadline, Bahru wanted one last walk."

Indy's gaze shifted toward the window, but Bahru and the baby were not in sight. Selma was on a cruise with her witchy friends Betty and Jean. And Lena had convinced Ryan to take Ellie away, too. She'd found a father-daughter retreat designed to encourage a more powerful bond and had nudged her husband to attend, using the old "Mommy needs a break" excuse, which he'd bought, hook, line and sinker. The truth, of course, was that they were trying to get their families out of harm's way before Beltane, as Lilia had warned them to do. Beltane was near. It was already Friday afternoon. Beltane would arrive on Saturday morning at 9:05 a.m.

Tomas had seen through Indy's attempts to send him out of town and was refusing to go anywhere. And frankly, Indy was glad.

She pulled out her cell phone and tapped "Home" in the directory. Tomas answered on the first ring, and as always her heart turned into a pathetic puddle of pudding at the sound of his sexy voice. "Where are you guys?" she asked.

"Doing what you asked us to, of course. Erecting a Maypole in the clearing near the lake for Beltane. Even though Ryan's spending most of his time complaining that he won't be here to dance around it with his wife."

Indy smiled. "Tell him he can dance with Lena when he gets back. Beltane celebrations can last for days. Did you remember the ribbons?"

"Alternating red and white. Got it. What's up, hon?"

"Bahru and the baby went for a walk. I need you to go get them and bring them back here, okay?"

His tone grew worried. "Something's wrong."

"Maybe. Do it quick, all right? I'll fill you in when you get here."

"On the way, babe." He was hollering for Ryan before the connection was broken.

Indy looked up and her eyes were immediately held hostage by her sister's, but she broke the gaze when the teapot started to whistle. "I'll get that."

"Hang on, sis. Tell me what's going on. Tell me *now,*" Lena said. "We haven't heard from Lilia for a couple of days, and now she not only called, she's on her way here. Something happened, didn't it?"

Indy nodded, cleared her throat. "Lilia and Demetrius found Father Dom. Apparently he tracked Demetrius down at his playboy pad in Sedona and convinced him to let him hide out in the attic. He's been playing the priestly confessor and trying to undermine Lil's mission this whole time." She walked into the kitchen as she spoke, made their tea and added cream and sugar to her own cup.

"And Demetrius didn't know who he was?"

Indy shook her head. "When Dom realized he was going to fail, he burned the place down with them in it—but they're both fine." She added that last bit fast, before Lena could panic.

"Why would he do that?" Lena asked. "Unless he doesn't realize they're immortal."

"Temporarily immortal," Indy said, carrying her teacup to the front door and opening it. "It's a nice day. Let's sit on the porch for a while."

Lena followed her outside. "If Demetrius doesn't accept the rest of his soul by Beltane, they both die," she said, as if trying to work through the whole thing out loud. "So I guess Father Dom knows that somehow? And that's why he wants to convince Demetrius not to take it back." She held her cup in her hands, blowing on the surface to cool it off.

"It wasn't Father Dom," Indy said.

Lena frowned, lifting her gaze. "But you just said—"

"Lilia saw him running from the mansion after he'd torched it. Got a good look, she said. And she has no doubt. The person occupying Father Dom's formerly comatose bod is Sindar."

Lena dropped her teacup. It hit the floor at her feet and shattered. She didn't even jump when the hot liquid spattered her legs. "How?" she whispered.

It was at that moment that Ryan's big black pickup truck skidded to a stop in the driveway, sending up a dust cloud. Lena noticed the baby's stroller in the back as Tomas and Ryan dove out of the front. She shot to her feet, sensing disaster. Both sisters raced off the front porch, Lena going straight to Ryan, clasping the front of his shirt and searching his face.

"Where's Ellie? Ryan, where's the baby?"

His stricken expression said it all, but his words, hoarse and choked, confirmed it. "I don't know, honey. We found the stroller on the side of the road. Bahru and Ellie were nowhere in sight."

12

"Oh, no," Lilia whispered as Demetrius pulled the rented Jeep Wrangler to a stop. The century-old farmhouse where Lena and Ryan lived had been freshly painted, and the vineyards around it were in the process of being newly planted. A state police car and a sheriff's SUV sat in the driveway, lights flashing, doors standing open.

It was an hour before sunset, and the temperatures there were far different from an early May evening in Arizona. It was cool. Almost cold. The air was damp on her skin as she got out of the car, sensing all sorts of discord in the air and hurrying up the front steps, her heart in her throat.

She walked in without knocking, leaving the door wide open behind her, and was dumbstruck by the tableau before her. Her sister Magdalena was sobbing and barely able to stand upright as Ryan held her, his face pale, his eyes devastated. Indy was pacing like a caged tiger, while Tomas stood listening intently to one of the cops, a man far too young, Lilia thought, for the sheriff's badge pinned to his shirt.

"What's going on?"

Lena looked up at her, her eyes so puffy and red she seemed to have aged ten years overnight. "He took her. He took Ellie!"

The room seemed to waver in and out of focus. Lilia didn't have to ask who. But it didn't make sense. Little Ellie? "But…but…"

Demetrius laid a strong hand on her shoulder, but only for a moment, because Magdalena tore free of her husband's gentle embrace and flew at him, hitting him like a battering ram, driving him right back out the door onto the front porch and shrieking like a banshee the entire time. "This is your fault, you bastard! I'll kill you for this. I'll kill you!"

"Lena!"

Demetrius sent Lilia a quelling look that seemed to say *Let her be,* as Magdalena pummeled his chest, driving him backward across the porch. He let her keep hitting him until she'd spent herself, and then he put his hands on her shoulders and held her gently. Lilia saw his lips moving, knew he was whispering something, but she couldn't hear what he was saying.

Then Ryan was there, pulling Lena gently away. Before she let him take her back inside she lifted her head, looked Demetrius in the eyes. "It's you he wants," she whispered.

"I know," he said.

The young sheriff and the state police officer were looking at them oddly. "Bad blood between those two," Tomas said. "It's a family thing, you know how it is. It goes back a ways. A long ways."

The sheriff, whose name badge said "William Tucker," shrugged and looked down at his notepad.

"So you say you're sure this Father Dominick is the one who snatched the baby?"

"We're sure," Ryan said. "He's the only one who would have reason."

"That reason being...?"

Ryan looked blankly to Tomas for help, and Tomas took the hint. "I was once a priest. His protégé," he said, not bothering with the details. They didn't matter anyway. "He blames my wife for luring me away from the church, and he's trying to hurt her by taking the baby he knows she loves more than life from the woman he knows she loves like a sister."

"That's a bit of a leap, don't you think?" asked the state trooper.

"He's sick," Tomas went on. "Just awakened from a six-month coma, checked himself out of the hospital—"

Stepping back into the house now that Lena had given up trying to kill him with her bare hands, Demetrius picked up from there. "Then tracked their other... friend—" he nodded toward Lilia "—to my home in Arizona and burned it to the ground with us inside," he said. "We saw him running away from the scene. There's no question."

"Good God, and you say this guy's a feeble old man? And a priest, for God's sake?" Sheriff Tucker asked.

"Maybe he's on something," suggested the trooper. "Meth. PCP. Maybe bath salts." The sheriff nodded his agreement with the theory, and the trooper went on. "Was anyone hurt in the fire?" he asked.

Demetrius nodded. "A friend and employee was killed, a kid still in his twenties. And my best friend in the world remains in serious condition. You can verify all of this with the Sedona Police Department, or just call Ned Nelson. I have his private number."

"*The* Ned Nelson?" asked the trooper.

Demetrius nodded, and the cops looked impressed.

Lena turned her face into Ryan's shirt and muttered, "Make them leave now. We have to go after Ellie."

He nodded, cradling her head. "I'd feel better if you were out looking for our daughter," he told the police. "We've been over everything twice."

"We've got every resource already on it, sir," said the trooper. "The New York State Troopers, the Tompkins County Sheriff's Department, along with the sheriff's departments from every nearby county, Cayuga, Cortland, Tioga, Chemung, Schuyler and Seneca. And we alerted the Ithaca PD first thing, in case he heads that way. An Amber Alert has gone out, as well."

"In fact," Sheriff Tucker put in, "we're about the only two cops not out looking for her. And we're headed that way next. We'll find your baby, folks. This guy's crazy, yes, but at least he's not a pedophile."

Lena released a horrified gasp, and the trooper elbowed the young sheriff, then tried to say something helpful. "Your friend, this—" he consulted his notepad "—Bay-roo—"

"Bahru," Indy corrected.

"You say you believe he's with the baby?"

Ryan nodded firmly. "He never would have let anyone take Ellie, except over his dead body. And since we didn't find that, I'm convinced he's with her. Wherever she is." His voice broke at the end.

"That should give you comfort," Sheriff Tucker said. "At least she's with someone familiar."

"Yes, and from your description, he's going to be

easy to spot. The guy stands out, you know?" The trooper flipped his notebook shut. "You'll want to call the press, get them to let you make an on-air appeal. Start recruiting locals to help in the search."

"Right," said the sheriff. "My department will start organizing that at first light, downtown at the Milbury Town Hall."

"Call everyone you know, and the Center for Missing and Exploited Children, as well." The trooper handed Lena a card he'd fished from his wallet while speaking. "They can be a huge help at a time like this."

"We're very sorry for your trouble, folks," Sheriff Tucker said. "I promise you, we are going to do everything in our power to bring your baby home safe."

"And we'll do everything in ours," Indy said softly. And there was blood in her eyes.

As soon as the door closed on the cops, Lilia yanked her pendulum from around her neck and raced for the kitchen table. "Map!" she said, snapping her fingers repeatedly.

"Right here." Indira snatched a street atlas from a shelf and opened it to the page that included Havenwood, then slapped it onto the table. Magdalena leaned closer as Lilia held up the pendulum. It was hard for her to keep it still, because her hands were shaking.

"I'm the one with the supercharged scrying skills, sister. Let me." Magdalena held out her hand.

"I figured you'd be too distracted." But Lilia handed her the pendulum.

"What the hell does Sindar want with my baby?" Lena whispered, dangling the stone over the map with surprising stillness.

"I don't know," Lilia said. She tried to quell the horror of knowing that the man who had had the three of them brutally murdered now had his filthy, blood-stained hands on Eleanora. She could only imagine how much worse the knowledge felt to Magdalena. They had to get the baby back—and soon.

"I think we need a bigger map," Indira said with a nod at the pendulum, which wasn't even wiggling.

"Sweet Mother, how far can he have gone?" Lena asked. "It's only been…" She looked at the clock. "Over an hour. It's been over an hour." The pendulum fell from her hand, and she sank toward the floor. Lilia scrambled to grab her, but Ryan beat her to it.

"I'm calling Doc. She needs something," Indira said.

"I won't take it. I want to be awake and alert enough to kill that bastard when we find him."

Demetrius met Lilia's eyes, and she knew he was recalling their recent conversation in which he'd said that he wanted to kill Sindar for murdering Sid and nearly killing Gus. She'd talked him down. Explained that death wasn't really a punishment. But she wasn't even trying now. Not this time. Death could be paradise with whipped cream on top for all she cared. If she got the chance to kill Sindar, she was damn well going to send him there.

Demetrius observed the pain in the eyes of the three women, especially the mother of the missing child, with a mixture of wonder, fear and something that felt like sympathy. The idea that he could ever find himself willing to ask for the ability to feel that much pain was almost unimaginable to him. The thought of never being able to feel it, however, was just as unimaginable. And the guilt…God, the guilt over the soulless monster he had been, a being intent on taking this very same infant from its mother, thinking to somehow expel it from its body and take that body over as his own...how could he? How could he ever have been that vile creature?

Seeing the women hurting hurt *him*. And he was afraid of that, because it might mean the missing part of his soul was starting to seep back into him a little bit at a time. He didn't recall feeling this sort of empathy for anyone before, hurting because they hurt. Not in this lifetime, at least. So that must be the explanation. He was changing, the remainder of his soul finding its way back to him, even though he hadn't asked, as Lilia said he must. If that happened, there would be no going back. No more powers.

Hell, he needed his powers now more than ever. He needed them to help get the child away from Sindar, back into the loving arms of her parents, where she belonged.

He needed his powers to put a smile back on the face of his beautiful Lilia.

And he needed them, too, to rid the world of Sindar and his evil, once and for all.

Bahru held Ellie close to him, walking along in front of the man he knew was not Father Dom but someone—no, some*thing*—else, something evil, wearing the old priest's former body and stretching it out of proportion. Bahru had never met the old priest, Tomas's former mentor, but he'd seen photographs, and had heard Tomas and Indira tell stories of the good priest gone bad. Those stories had troubled him greatly, because he knew the true power of the forces working against them. He knew, because he, too, considered himself a holy man. And he, too, had fallen prey to the spell of darkness.

It was Ryan, who'd never liked or trusted him, who'd saved him. Saved them all. And Bahru would spend the rest of his life trying to make up for his own role in the near disaster.

Besides, little Ellie had won his heart. She was special. She was his life's calling. He'd known that the first time he'd looked into her newborn eyes.

"It'll be all right, little one," he whispered, holding her close, letting her tug his beard as much as she liked. Not even three months old yet. And already a beauty, with bright knowing eyes of chocolate-bar brown. She smiled and burbled at the sound of his voice. The man behind them gave him a shove to get him moving faster, and Bahru picked up the pace. So far he'd offered nothing but compliance. He didn't want to give the lunatic reason to send him away—or kill him— leaving Ellie all alone.

They'd exited the car and entered what had at first appeared to be a cave in the side of a mountain. He'd quickly realized that it was man-made, perfectly arched overhead, lined in brick. The railroad track that remained in places showed him what it was. A tunnel through the mountain, long since abandoned and left to fall into disrepair. It didn't feel safe, and it was damp, dripping. Their footsteps echoed in the emptiness.

"Stop," said the priest.

Bahru watched the man move past him and over to one side of the tunnel, where a metal door was built into the brick. He opened it and beckoned Bahru closer.

"This way. Hurry." He flicked a switch, and lights came on beyond the door.

Nodding, Bahru obeyed, and he was soon carrying the baby down a flight of steel stairs that creaked and groaned and rattled under his feet. Their green paint had mostly flecked off, and rust was feeding on them. They shuddered with every step, and he clung to the baby with one arm, gripping the rail with his free hand and praying the stairway would hold out.

"It's fine. They won't give way. Go down."

"Yes, sir. I'm going." He tried to hurry enough to please his captor while moving slowly enough to keep the baby safe, and blessedly soon they were at the bottom, standing in a huge concrete room. There were twin pillars every twenty feet or so, with arched concrete supports on top, holding up the mountain above. There were swirls in the footers, grooves in the pillars. They'd been made in an era long past, when things were built to be beautiful as well as functional.

"What is this place?" Bahru asked.

"It's where I'm going to keep you and, soon, the witch until I can end all this, once and for all, at the moment of Beltane." The man nodded at a deep niche in one wall. "That's where you're to stay. There are shelves, with some blankets stacked up on them. Keep the child quiet, or you will have outlived your usefulness to me, Bahru."

"Babies cry from time to time. It's their nature. But I'll do the best I can." Bahru moved quickly to the "room" and found the shelves lined with canned food, and plastic bags of salt and sugar that looked to belong to an era long gone by.

The place must have been some sort of bomb shelter, forgotten and abandoned to time, he realized. He located the blankets, also plastic-wrapped and therefore clean, or so he hoped. Then, even better, he noticed a cot, folded in half and standing against the back wall. The mattress was ancient, but there was nothing nesting in it that he could see. Anchoring the baby on one hip, he managed to unfold the thing and spread several blankets on top. He laid Ellie down on the mattress and sat on the floor close beside her.

Something metallic scraped loudly behind him, and he turned to see a barred door sliding closed. It hit with a bang that startled the infant. She went stiff and wide-eyed, then began to wail.

"No, no, no," Bahru cooed. "It's all right, little one. It's all right." He gathered her close and jounced her gently. She stilled again, and he realized she'd fallen asleep. Good. The more of this nightmare she could sleep through, the better. He laid her on the cot again, tucking a blanket securely around her, and then relaxed on the floor, his back against the cot, turning his attention to the room beyond the bars of his cell. The barred door must have been someone's notion of keeping what might be a crucial supply of food safe from anyone who might try to take more than his share.

He was glad society's notion that such places as this were necessary had fallen out of fashion. The world had gotten better.

Meanwhile, though, there was magic afoot in this bomb shelter. Dark magic.

The man in the purple robes stood in the center of the room, arms extended, chin up, chanting in some foreign language that Bahru had never heard before. It sounded not just old but ancient. His voice grew, echoed, took on a resonance that was unnatural. Otherworldly. And his eyes rolled back in his head as a dark column that looked like smoke, but wasn't, began to spiral around him.

"Come to me," he said, speaking in English now. "Come to me, all of you whose minds I can and do command. Come to me, as many as are close enough to hear my call. In black shall you dress. And your faces shall be covered, the better to strike fear into the hearts of my enemies. Come to me, and I will give you everything you have ever desired. I shall smite your enemies with vengeance, and shower you in riches and glory. Come to me. Come to me, my minions. Come."

Then he dropped to the floor, just as if his legs had turned to water, and at that same instant the black smoky ribbon shot upward, hit the ceiling and vanished as if it had gone straight through.

An hour later they started arriving, a few at a time.

They were all dressed in black, some in jeans, some in sweatpants, some in dress pants, others in monks' robes. And their faces were covered. Ski masks. Halloween masks. Surgical masks. They gathered around the old priest and said nothing, clearly waiting for his command.

The sense of evil was overwhelming as the one who'd taken them, a man whose body was becoming more grotesquely swollen by the minute, moved among them. He welcomed them, patted their shoulders and backs, spoke softly to them, probably reiterating the promises he would surely never keep.

Eventually he moved to stand on a slightly raised platform between the two pillars on the far end of the room.

"Welcome, new followers of Marduk," he said. "I

am the one who called you here, the one who will re-
ward you so richly for your loyalty to me and to the
chief god of all Gods. I am the high priest Sindar."

Sindar!

Bahru felt his heart begin to pound in alarm. Sindar was the name of the high priest who'd murdered
Magdalena, Indira and Lilia so long ago. But how could
that be?

"I have a plan, my friends," Sindar continued. "Tomorrow we will spill the blood of the most powerful
witch of a witches' triune, for her heart holds a piece
of her demon lover's soul and her blood holds power
untold. We will not kill her until the moment of Beltane, so that when she dies the piece of the demon's
soul she holds will die with her. And then he will cease
to exist, her sisters will die, and their progeny will die.
At last this curse will end, and my King, Balthazorus,
will at last be avenged."

No. Bahru looked at the sleeping infant and thought
of her mother, and his heart clenched tight in his chest.
He closed his eyes, sinking into a meditative state
while keeping an ear attuned to Ellie. And he whispered, "Magdalena, if you can hear me, listen well.
There is evil afoot. You must not allow Lilia to come
here."

"It's no use." Lilia dropped the dangling amethyst
pendulum onto the map and tipped her head back in
frustration. "Sindar must be blocking us somehow. His
magic is just too strong."

"No, it's not too strong, not for us," Indy said.

Magdalena said nothing. Her eyes were vacant, her
soul bleeding. Her body still moved, but it was act-

ing on autopilot, Lilia thought. "He'll contact us," she promised her sister. "He took the baby for a reason. To force us to do what he wants. He's going to have to tell us what that is, sooner or later."

Indy nodded. "I agree."

Magdalena looked around, blinking her swollen eyes. "Where are the men?"

"Upstairs in the temple room," Indy said. "Tomas is trying to translate a journal written in Akkadian."

"Journal?" Lena looked from one sister to the other.

"We found it in Sindar's room before he set the house on fire," Lilia said.

"It belonged to Father Dom," Indy said. "He'd been studying our history for years, so I suspect it's some warped version of our past."

"Sindar. That bastard. He killed my baby then, and now he has her again."

All eyes shot to Magdalena.

"I was pregnant then, too," she told them. "Don't you remember? When he had us thrown from that cliff, he killed my child with me. And now he has her again. My Ellie…" Turning, she ran out the front door, nearly knocking over a chair in the process.

"Let's leave her alone for a moment," Lilia said, when Indy moved as if to go after her. "Let her cry in private. Why don't we go upstairs and see how Tomas is coming with that old journal and give her a little time to process all this?"

"He's not going to win this time. Dammit, he's not," Indira said. Then she shot Lilia a searching look. "Is he?"

"No," she said, simply and confidently. "No, he's

not going to win." Not even, she thought in silence, if it cost her everything. Her second chance. Demetrius's. Everything.

Demetrius leaned over the journal, side by side with Tomas, managing to translate a symbol here and there as his memories of his ancient past life became steadily more and more vivid.

Tomas read what they had so far. "'And if the demon refuses his final soul-piece by the High Holy Day that marks the halfway point of the Sun God to His power, then shall he die, and then shall the time of the witches expire. But they deserve far worse than death and renewal. They deserve far worse than crossing the Veil to bliss and returning again as all human souls must.'"

"Wait, wait," Demetrius said. "If I don't accept the rest of my soul, I die?" He looked up from the journal to meet Tomas's eyes. "Why the hell didn't Lilia tell me that?"

Tomas looked at him steadily. "She wasn't allowed. You're supposed to decide based on wanting to live rather than not wanting to die."

"It makes little difference," Demetrius said, lowering his head. "I can't accept it now."

"Demetrius, maybe you're not seeing the point here," Ryan said.

"You're not seeing the point. If I accept my soul, I will lose my powers. If I lose my powers, how am I going to fight Sindar and get your daughter back?"

"So that's why he took her." Lilia's voice came from the doorway, and she was clearly stunned to the bone. "Truly the man is far more conniving than I gave him credit for being."

Demetrius went toward her, intending to fold her into his arms, but she held up a hand and lifted her chin. "We have to find a way to rescue Ellie."

"And Bahru," Ryan put in.

"Before the deadline."

"When the Sun God reaches the halfway point to his power?" Demetrius asked. "What does that mean?"

"Beltane is halfway between the Vernal Equinox and the Summer Solstice, which is the longest day of the year, the sun's point of maximum power. At the moment of Beltane, the sun is halfway to its strongest point," Indy explained.

"But isn't that…tomorrow?" he asked.

Lilia looked at the clock on the wall. "Given that it's after midnight, no. It's today. 9:05 a.m." Blinking, she turned to Ryan. "Lena needs to pull herself together enough to try scrying again. She's got the strongest bond to Ellie, and she's got the most skill at divination."

"If it didn't work before—" Ryan began.

"Demetrius, we'll need your chalice."

"I'll get it," Demetrius said, jogging out of the room and down the stairs.

"And I'll get Lena." Ryan followed him.

Lilia nodded at Tomas and Indy, who entered the room just then. "We'll cast a circle. Scrying within the circle will give it added power."

Indy moved to the cabinet with a sharp nod, taking out incense, herbs, candles. Soon Demetrius was back with the chalice, which he handed to Lilia. His hand brushed hers, and their eyes met. She wanted to whisper, "I love you," but she was afraid to. Goddess, if he opened to her now, all would be lost.

Amazingly, he closed his hand around hers and

whispered, "Don't worry, Lilia. I would rather die myself than risk the life of an innocent child. I know what this means. I'm choosing to remain as I am, but this time for the right reasons."

She closed her eyes. He did not yet know that she would die with him. And she wasn't going to tell him, because that might change his mind. She, too, would willingly give her life to save Ellie's. And crossing the Veil with him by her side didn't seem all that much of a sacrifice to her. She'd died before. It wasn't so bad.

Noisy footsteps pounded up the stairs, and then Ryan and Lena were coming into the room, holding hands. Lena looked stronger, with a new determination in her eyes. Perhaps a new hope. She'd seen the power of the chalice before, after all.

Lilia nodded, then glanced at the window, at the stars dotting the midnight sky. "Your abilities will gain more power from nature. Let's go outside."

Lilia walked a circle with her hand held palm-down as the rest of them waited and watched. Demetrius could not takes his eyes from her. She'd donned ritual robes, golden and flowing, and they moved in the breeze with her silvery-blond hair. She was slight and fairylike, and yet so very powerful.

"I conjure thee, oh, circle of power. Three times 'round I walk this hour. Once to draw thee on the ground. Twice to raise the ring around. Thrice to close, above, below. Stomp to seal, and make it so." She stomped her foot at the end of her third circuit and declared, "The circle is sealed."

Then she used her forefinger to trace a "doorway" in the invisible sphere of energy she'd created and gave her sister a nod.

Indy was holding a conch shell filled with smoldering sage leaves in one hand and a vulture feather in the other. As each of the others approached the circle, she wafted the smoke over them, head to toe, front and back, before allowing them to pass. They entered and then walked clockwise, far enough around the circle to make room for the rest. Indy wafted the smoke over herself last of all, then entered and took her position. Lilia then traced a line over the ground where they'd entered, closing the door.

The stars twinkled above. Demetrius watched Lilia, mesmerized, even though her sisters were taking over some of the action now. On the eastern side of the circle, Lena raised her arms and called out, "Powers of Air, winds of change, elemental energies of the east and all those in the fairy realm, I summon, stir and call thee forth." She paused, eyes closed, then with a nod said, "Hail and welcome."

Everyone repeated the phrase. All the women, at least, and Ryan and Tomas, who seemed to know what was expected.

Indy's short blond hair riffled as she opened her arms. "Powers of Fire, flames of passion, elemental energies of the south and all those in the fairy realm, I summon, stir and call thee forth. Hail and welcome."

This time he repeated "Hail and welcome" with the others.

"Powers of Water, waters of transformation, elemental energies of the west and all those in the realm of the fay, I summon, stir and call thee forth." Lilia said from the western side of the circle, her voice like a song. "Hail and welcome."

Almost before the answering echo died, Indira walked across the circle and called out, "Powers of

Earth, foundation and strength, elemental energies of the north, and all those in the fairy realm, I summon, stir and call thee forth. Hail and welcome."

"Hail and welcome," said the others.

The three sisters then moved to the very center of the circle, facing one another, palms pressed one to the other. "Powers of Spirit," they said in unison. "Energies of the great below, all that's come before, ancestors, beloved dead..." Slowly they raised their hands high overhead, palms still touching. "Energies of the great above, enlightened beings, angels and guides, we summon, stir and call thee forth." Their hands parted like a starburst, out and down to their sides again. "Hail and welcome."

They all repeated it. Then Indira and Lilia backed up to resume their places in the outer ring of the circle, leaving Magdalena alone in the center. She rose, opened her arms wide, feet apart. But she didn't speak. Perhaps she couldn't. Her tears were flowing. Slowly she crossed her arms over her chest, lowering her head. Again, no words. Then, nodding in apparent satisfaction, she whispered, "Hail and welcome."

The echo was melancholy this time. Magdalena sought out Lilia and whispered, "Water."

Lilia nodded, picking up the tiny jug that sat on the ground beside her and carrying it forward. Uncorking it, she poured water into Demetrius's chalice, and then the two women knelt and looked into the water together for a very long time. Indy began to hum a tune that was somehow mystical, somehow magical, yet short and repetitive. She nodded at Tomas, and he joined in, followed by Ryan. And when they all looked at him expectantly, Demetrius added his own voice, an octave lower.

Finally, after a great many minutes had ticked past and the humming had lulled his brain into a sort of a daze, Lilia and Magdalena looked up from the chalice and into each other's eyes. It seemed to Demetrius that they exchanged some silent message. They were both crying, tears streaming, and then they hugged hard and long before finally getting to their feet.

"What did you see?" Demetrius asked.

Lilia looked at him, then at her sister, who spoke for her. "Nothing," Lena said. "The chalice showed us nothing."

Lilia started to turn away, but Demetrius stepped forward, gripped her upper arms and held her, gently but firmly, so he could search her face, her eyes. "You saw something."

"There is nothing we can do right now, Demetrius. Sindar will contact us when he's ready."

He frowned, wounded to the core. "You told me once that you couldn't lie. Has that changed, Lilia?"

She lifted a palm to his face, sliding it over his cheek, and he closed his eyes at the gentle touch. "Then believe me when I tell you that I love you like no human being has ever loved another. Believe that. Because it's nothing but the truth."

He wanted to kiss her, but the moment he thought it, she stepped away, picked up the cup and emptied it onto the ground. "Close up the circle, Indy. We're finished here."

He knew, with everything in him he knew, that she was lying. They had seen something in that chalice, and it terrified him that she refused to tell him what.

13

"I don't want to let you go," Magdalena whispered.

They were in the kitchen, cleaning up dishes. No one had eaten, but the coffee and tea had been flowing all night. Lilia and Lena were alone together, but only for the moment.

"Watch what you say, Lena. If Indy or, Goddess forbid, Demetrius finds out, no one is going to let me go. But you know and I know that this is the only thing to do." She was scared. Hell, she was terrified. She had no idea why he wanted her; she'd assumed Demetrius was his quarry. Her plan could be terribly dangerous. But he had Ellie. She had no choice. "Sindar said I had to come alone."

"How did he manage to send a message through the chalice, anyway?" Lena asked, keeping her voice very low.

"He's a powerful magician. You know that." Lilia put a hand on her sister's shoulder. "At least we got a glimpse of Ellie. Enough to know she's okay, and that Bahru is with her."

"Thank the Gods." Lena brushed tears from her eyes. "It's not fair that I can't tell Ryan even that much."

"You can—just as soon as I get out of here and have enough of a head start."

"You could tell where it was?" Magdalena asked.

"You couldn't?" Lilia returned, surprised.

Lena shook her head slowly, left then right, her eyes probing her sister's.

Lilia only nodded. "Then you must not have been meant to know."

"Lil—"

"Shh." The others were coming into the kitchen now, bringing more dirty cups to be washed. The two sisters parted almost guiltily. Indira's sharp gaze didn't miss it, but she didn't ask.

There wasn't a person in the house who wouldn't do anything necessary to save Eleanora. Not even Demetrius, Lilia thought.

Demetrius. If she went to Sindar, surrendered to him, he was undoubtedly not going to let her live. Demetrius had to ask for the last piece of his soul before she died because if she died before Beltane and could not revive, his soul would die with her. As would he. And then, if he died, it would be a true death. He would cease to exist. There would be no afterlife, no reincarnation, no blissful release. And that, she suspected, was Sindar's goal. Keeping Demetrius from accepting his final soul-piece, so that he died and went to the afterlife, was not good enough for him. He wanted to destroy Demetrius utterly.

That meant, she realized, that he had to kill *her* in a way that would not allow her to revive. Which meant either destroying her body entirely, or killing her just before the moment of Beltane, so her time would run out.

But either way, it wasn't up to her. To receive his soul-piece, Demetrius had to ask for it. Deep down in his heart ask for it. He had to want it. But not too soon. His powers might be the only chance any of them had, and he would lose them when his soul was restored.

"Are you all right?" His deep voice came from close behind her and sent a shiver down her spine.

She turned to face him, nodding once. "Fine." Her hands started to rise, and she stopped them, realizing she'd been about to slide them up his chest, around his big neck, to thread her fingers into his hair.

He saw it, she knew he did by the reaction in his eyes. Fire flared up, but he forced it back down. She had to be at the meeting place at sunrise. That was less than six hours away. And it might very well be the last sunrise she ever saw in this life. It might be the end of her physical existence. More than anything, she wanted to spend those six hours wrapped in her true love's arms.

"It's 2:00 a.m.," Magdalena said, closer to them than Lilia had realized. "I'm going to be up pacing all night. No one in this house is going to get any sleep tonight. You two might as well bunk in Bahru's cottage. In the morning we'll pick up the search."

Indy rolled her eyes. "No one is sleeping. We're gonna work the night through if that's what it takes."

"It won't matter," Lena said. "Look, I didn't see anything in the chalice, but I felt something. I felt a knowing. Ellie's all right. She's with Bahru. She's not in immediate danger. And this thing will not be over until Beltane, just over five hours from now. That's when it all has to happen, whatever it is. We should get some rest, so we'll be ready."

Indy frowned at her, then snapped her gaze to Lilia's. "Did you get any of that from the chalice?"

"All of it," she said with a nod. "I've just been try-ing to…process it. Figure out if it was real. It was much more subtle than a vision would have been."

"So we should get some rest, even just an hour or so," Magdalena said. "We're going to need to be sharp and on our toes for whatever tomorrow morning will bring."

Indy looked from one of them to the other, then slid her gaze to Tomas's. "Are you buying this?"

"I don't think it matters who's buying it," he told her. "It's Lena's baby. She wouldn't do anything to put her at risk. This whole thing has to be her call. If she says we sleep, then I suggest we sleep."

Indy clearly didn't like it. She drew a breath, pursed her lips as if to keep harsh words from escaping, then turned and headed out the door, grabbing Tomas on the way. "Fine. We're quitting for the night."

He let her tug him in her wake.

Lilia took the stack of bedding Magdalena had brought out for her, then hugged the woman who had once been her sister and, in every way that counted, was her sister still. She inhaled the scent of Lena's hair and wondered if this would be the last time she would see her in this lifetime.

Lena hugged her back just as hard, and then Lilia and Demetrius went out the door together. He looked down at her as they walked along the driveway side by side. It was late, and the sky was a deep purple, as dark as it would get before beginning to lighten again. Night birds called; an owl hooted three times. Not a good omen. Crickets, a sure sign that spring had arrived, were singing a noisy chorus. The air smelled rich with the earliest of the apple trees already beginning to blossom, and some hyacinths, as well. It was beautiful. It was romantic. It was heartbreaking. Because it was, in all likelihood, the end.

"Your sister presumed we would want to spend this night alone together," Demetrius said softly.

"Not such a leap of logic, really. You were the love of my life."

"I was?"

"You still are, and you know it. Everything I've done for the past three thousand years has been for no other reason than to bring you back to me again. I've defied death for you. I've defied nature, commanded it to do my bidding, just so I could be with you again."

"I know," he whispered. "I know that now. And I'm grateful, more grateful than I'll ever be able to express. You freed me from that Underworld prison, gave me a chance to know life again. But, more important, Lilia, you gave me a chance to know *you* again. To remember what we had."

She smiled, tears leaking onto her cheeks. "You remember."

"Enough to know that it was something far too precious to forget. But, Lilia, I can't take the rest of my soul-piece back from you now," he said. "You have to know that. As much as I might want to, I—"

"Shh. Don't say you want to. Don't even think it, or it will be done. You need to keep your powers a little bit longer. Rescue the baby. And then, if we're lucky, there might still be time."

"And if we're not?"

"Then you and I will pass into the afterlife together,

my love. And it will be all right." She prayed it was true, feared it might not be, but told herself it wasn't a lie. She wouldn't let it be a lie.

He stopped walking when they reached Bahru's cabin, turning her to face him, his eyes delving into hers so deeply she could feel them like a physical touch. "You saw more in the chalice than you've told me."

"I only know it will all end by the hour when Beltane begins."

"And when is that, exactly?"

"A little after 9:00 a.m. An hour after sunrise."

His eyes widened. "That's just over seven hours. We can't sleep."

"No. But we can make love. And then we can face whatever it is we *must* face."

He stroked her hair back from her face. "I'm sorry. I'm sorry I didn't listen to you to begin with. It wouldn't have come to this."

"Things happen the way they're supposed to, my love."

"I lo—"

She pressed her forefinger to his lips. "Keep it for later. Don't open your heart too far, Demetrius, or it will cost us everything."

"I don't know if I can stop myself." He bent his head, taking her mouth, kissing her deeply and building an inferno inside her that rose through her body and threatened to burn it down.

She clung to his broad shoulders as he stumbled with her up the three steps and through the cabin door. This was risky, but she couldn't deny herself this one thing, not when she'd ached for him for so long. She vowed she wouldn't let his soul-piece go as she fumbled for the light switch just inside, then found it far too bright once she'd flipped it on. But he stopped kissing her then, lifting his head, tearing his gaze from hers to look around, to get his bearings. He'd taken the stack of bedding from her. She'd forgotten all about it. The sheets could have been lying on the ground outside for all she knew...or cared.

Demetrius spotted the only bedroom and stepped into it. He swept the existing bedding to the floor, kicking it into a corner to be taken care of later. Then he spread the fitted sheet over the small bed while Lilia leaned in the doorway, watching him with love pouring from her eyes. He added the second sheet and a light blanket. Then, turning, he held out his hand.

She peeled her blouse off over her head. She'd skipped a bra.

He took *his* shirt off, too, and she stared at him and thought she would wear bras twenty-four hours a day if it meant getting to experience this delicious rush of desire, of wanting, this rippling excitement at the sight of his beautiful body. She went to him, loving the way his eyes devoured her, and then his hands were on her shoulders, sliding up and down her arms, wrapping around her waist, and her palms were skimming his chest, sliding up, around his neck. Their bodies pressed against each other, naked flesh to naked flesh, her chest to his, warm skin to warm skin. It felt as if she were absorbing him into her, letting his essence fill every part of her just through this contact. She tipped her head up, caught his eyes blazing down into hers, and then he kissed her again and lowered her to the bed.

When he touched her breasts she felt alive. When he kissed them she lost every other thought. There was only feeling now, only sensation. Delicious physical sensation, shivers of pleasure up her spine, the response of her body to his, the taste of his mouth, sweeter than honey wine, the scent of his skin, like sandalwood and myrrh. And the way his muscles rippled beneath it, firm and hard, powerful and strong. He was big, so big. His hands seemed huge on her small body. But she relished their touch, and shifted around beneath him until she managed to wriggle out of her remaining clothes, soft white draping pants and panties.

He slid his hand between her thighs as soon as her clothing was out of the way, finding her wet already, teasing her with his fingers before delving inside. She gasped in pleasure. Sex was one of the most amazing and wonderful parts of being human, she thought, and she relished every second of it as he drove her wild, made her want him even more than she already did. She reached for him, found his jeans in the way and tugged impatiently at the button, the zipper.

Her lover complied with her unspoken demand, shoving the jeans off, kicking them to the floor, lowering himself over her again. He stared down into her eyes, and she gazed right back up into his. What she saw there made her heart go soft, then jump in fear, and she had to force words and a tune to her lips, though they trembled with bittersweet joy.

"Hold your love," she sang softly, in a song barely more than a whisper. "Hold it tight. Close your heart, for tonight. Be thou strong, love me not, let the past be forgot. Keep your warrior soul at bay, till the shining light of day."

She didn't know if he heard her with his ears, but

his heart heard. She knew it. She felt it. Her enchantments were all but irresistible.

And then she was no longer capable of coherent thought, because he was settling over her again, nudging her open. When he filled her she gasped, because that moment of joining, that first instant, felt so powerful to her. Always had. The sensation of being one with him, of uniting with her soul mate in this most intimate way, was magic.

Her heart cried out, *I love you!* but she bit her lips to keep the words inside. Later, she told herself. Later, when the baby was safe and they were together again, be it in this life or the next. And then she prayed it would be one of those two options and not the third, unthinkable one where he simply was no more.

Demetrius lay in a tangle of sheets, satisfied to his toes. Making love with this woman was beyond anything he'd experienced in this lifetime. Or, he was certain, in the one before. And likely in every lifetime to come.

She hadn't lied when she'd said that what they had was unlike any other relationship in the realm of mankind. He believed her completely. She felt like home to him. And soon, he thought, it would be that way all the time. Because he didn't intend to stay soulless any longer. Once the rescue had been completed, he would ask Lilia to restore that final piece of his soul to him, because she was worth far more than his powers, more than his immortality, more than anything, really. Being with her again, loving her again…it was all he wanted from this life. He couldn't believe he had ever wanted anything else.

She kissed his chest, and rolled out of the bed. "I'll make us some tea."

"We only have a few hours," he told her, sending a worried glance at the bedside clock. 4:30 a.m.

"I know." Naked, she walked to the tiny kitchenette, still in full view from the bedroom and he feasted his eyes on her. She filled a teapot, then set it on a burner. He drank in every movement of her nude form as if she were performing some erotic dance just for him. She was humming. His Lilia was always humming some tune or another. And then a few words, too soft for him to hear clearly, but she was singing. Happy, he thought. He'd made her happy, despite all that was happening. He must have, because she wouldn't be singing otherwise.

His eyes felt heavy, and he caught them falling closed and forced them open again. Then it happened again. His head sank into the pillows, eyes closing as the velvet embrace of sleep reached up to enfold him.

"Master Sindar," Bahru called, addressing the ego-maniac in the way he'd been instructed, while peering between the bars of his makeshift cell. "Master?"

It wasn't Sindar but one of his minions who responded by coming over. He wore black from his head to his feet. Loose-fitting black pants of thin cotton, a shirt that matched, and a sash, also black. Did that black belt signify a martial arts ranking, or was it purely decorative? Bahru wondered. And why were they all wearing masks? Ridiculous masks. This one wore a half mask that covered only his eyes and nose. It was black, like everything else.

"He's busy," the man said. "What do you want?"

"The baby needs to eat. Baby formula. Goat's milk. Something."

"There are only a couple of hours until her aunt arrives and we can let it go. It won't starve in a couple of hours," the man snapped, his tone hateful.

Bahru tilted his head, locking his gaze with the other man's. "I am not your enemy. I only came along to care for the baby until Sindar has no further use for her. He doesn't want her screaming for her mother, as she surely would be, were I not here."

He was speaking to the man's soul, trying to reach it with his own. But a man like this one was unlikely to be in touch with his higher self, so it might not do a lot of good. Still…

"What's your name, my friend?"

The man blinked. "Jarred."

"Jarred, if I don't have a bottle of warm milk for this little girl soon, she'll be wailing like a howler monkey." He looked past the man, up at the domed ceiling. "In this concrete room, it will echo enough to drive us all mad. Believe me when I tell you, it would be far better to keep her content now than try to quiet her once a full-blown fit is under way."

Jarred's eyes shifted to the baby, wrapped in a blanket and sleeping on the cot, then moved quickly back to Bahru again. "She seems fine now."

"She won't be for long. But that's all right. Just let it happen. Once we're all covering our ears to avoid her screaming, I will be sure to tell your master that you were warned and chose to ignore it."

The eyes peering out though the holes in the mask seemed to narrow. "I'll send someone out. Where we're going to find formula at this time of the night, I can't even—"

"True, there's no place open. The mother's home, however, would have bottles filling the refrigerator. Surely one of you is skilled enough to slip inside undetected and bring back a bottle of baby formula?" He knew they were close. Sindar had only driven for a couple of miles before they got out and headed for the tunnel on foot.

Jarred didn't say no immediately. He was considering the suggestion.

"And, if you can, the little teddy bear sitting on the fireplace mantel. That would soothe her a great deal."

"I don't think—"

Ellie chose that moment to begin to cry. And not just any cry, but a lovely loud shriek of a cry that made the would-be ninja's brows rise in alarm, "Quiet her!" He looked behind him toward where Sindar was gathered with several others on the far side of the room. They were pounding and drilling and rattling chains over there, and despite all the noise, they were starting to look this way.

Bahru gathered Ellie up into his arms and held her close. "There, there, little one."

She paused only for a breath and cut loose with another wail.

"All right, okay, I'll go. I'll get what you need. Just keep her quiet in the meantime."

Bahru smiled as the man raced across the room, spoke quickly to Sindar and apparently, gained his consent. Of course, Eleanora was still howling.

But as soon as the man started up the stairs she stopped. Just like that.

Bahru smiled down at the baby. "Well done, little witchling. Very well done." She only clasped a fistful of his beard and tugged.

Lilia gazed at her beloved, lying asleep in the bed. She hated to leave him, especially since she might not see him again in this lifetime. But she had no choice. The message in the chalice had been very clear. She must come alone, and only then would Ellie be released. As she'd stared down into the chalice, it had become more like a video chat than a scrying device. She'd seen Sindar as he'd been before. Fat and mean, effeminate and powerful. She'd asked silently how she could believe that he would release Bahru and Ellie upon her arrival, and he'd sworn in the name of Marduk, the God he served.

She didn't think he would break a vow to Marduk, so she had agreed. When she'd asked what would happen to her, he'd shown her nothing at all. But she knew. He was going to kill her close enough to Beltane so that she wouldn't have time to revive and Demetrius had a chance to reclaim his soul-piece, and it would die with her. And then Demetrius would die, as well. Forever. Unless she figured out a way to save him.

One last kiss, she thought, leaning over the bed, whispering in song to him. "Sleep my love, a little more. Till the babe is safe once more. Then come find me, where I wait. I'll sing you right up to the gate. Listen for my song, my heart, and never more we'll be apart."

She leaned down and kissed him. Then she put her clothes back on, donned a jacket and good walking shoes, and slipped out of the cottage, walking briskly

and unerringly through the night to the tunnel she'd
been shown in the vision.

It was part of an abandoned railroad track. A tunnel had been blasted through one of the mountains in
the area and track laid straight through, to save the
time it would have taken to route the train around the
mountain and through the pass. This stretch had been
abandoned decades ago, deemed unsafe after repeated
cave-ins. One train had barely escaped as part of the
cave collapsed behind it. The tunnel had been cleared,
shored up, repaired, and then a second cave-in, trig-
gered by a roaring engine, had crushed a passenger
train, burying three cars inside the mountain.

By the time the workers had dug them out, fifteen
passengers were dead. Thirty-three survived with various injuries. From then on, the track was never used
again.

In the sixties, while schools were training children
to line up against walls and shield their faces with their
arms in case of nuclear attack, the government had created a bomb shelter in the mountain underneath the
cave. It was supposed to have been a secret.

She received all this information as she approached
the cave. It filtered down to her from the vast pool of
knowledge stored in the Akashic Records, the universal
library where all knowledge of all things for all time
was stored. Apparently she'd tapped into it simply by
asking, *What is this place?*

And now she stood before it, facing the tunnel's
dark maw and feeling as if she were facing the jaws
of death itself.

A man in black stepped out of the shadows. "Who
are you?" he demanded.

"I'm Lilia."

He moved closer to her, then turned her around, lifting her blouse to check her lower back. She knew what he saw there: the cuneiform symbols that said "Daughter of Ishtar." Apparently satisfied, he nodded and took her by one arm.

"I'm not setting foot inside until Bahru and the baby are set free."

She was unafraid, even though she knew she was facing probable death. Her mind was completely focused on saving Ellie. The man lifted a hand and three others appeared, closing around her on all sides. "You will do as you are told, witch," said the first man. Two of the others clasped her arms and pulled her bodily forward. She could either move her feet to keep up or she would be dragged. So she tried to keep her feet moving.

They pulled her into the bowels of the tunnel, into utter darkness, and then there was a door, and it opened, and there was light, a metal staircase, more men in black. At the far wall, as she descended the stairway, struggling not to fall, since the bastards were still pulling her, she saw Bahru holding Ellie in his arms, a bottle to her little mouth as she sucked happily. A teddy bear was on the floor near him. She recognized it and frowned, then snapped her eyes up to his.

He held her gaze. His was very sad. He was not happy to see her, nor was he surprised. He must know, then, what Sindar had planned.

"Well, I'm so glad you finally arrived. Time is short, you know."

She knew that voice, and she turned her head toward it. Sindar. The evil priest's soul had further contorted

Father Dom's vacated body. He looked more like he had in the past than when she had last seen him. His skin was still a shade lighter than before, and he was taller, as Father Dom had been a tall man. But aside from those details, he was all Sindar. He'd even gotten his hands on some eyeliner somewhere.

"What became of Father Dom when you stole his body?" she asked.

Sindar's eyes sparkled, just like a man on the brink of victory. "He'd already vacated the premises, so to speak. Of course, he couldn't move on into the afterlife while the machines kept his body alive. The bonds, you know."

"I know."

"I imagine he's in a place much like the one where you've been these past thirty-five-hundred years. Limbo."

"The world between the worlds," she said, nodding. "I hope he's free soon."

"That can only happen if I die."

"In that case he will be free soon."

He scowled at her, a look of disgust.

"I'm here, just as you asked me to be. You have to keep your vow to your God and let Bahru and the baby go," she said. Because as soon as he did, she was going to attempt to sing Demetrius here to her. She would sing them all here to her. They would make it in time. They would save her. And she would return the last piece of Demetrius's soul to him, and everything would be all right again. Just as soon as the baby was safe, she would—

"I will let them go," Sindar said softly. "Just as soon as you're dead and that demon's soul is dead with you."

"If you kill me, I'll revive."

"You can't return his soul to him while you're dead. And I'll make sure you are, before Beltane has arrived, at which point you will stay dead and his soul will die with you. And he will be no more." He nodded to his men. "Dress her, then chain her."

The men who still held her arms were joined by others who tore off her clothes. She twisted and kicked, but there were too many of them, and she didn't possess the supernatural fighting skills Indy did. If she'd had the amulet, maybe, but not on her own.

When she was naked except for her panties, they released her, and she stood there exposed and furious. She saw Bahru in the cell, his gaze respectfully lowered, but he was the only one. The others leered their fill. Sindar's gaze was on her, too, but his wasn't lecherous. It was disgusted. He threw a garment at her chest. "Cover yourself, witch."

She held the soft white garment in front of her, shaking out its folds and finding it was little more than rectangle of fabric. She wrapped it around herself, back to front, then crossed the corners in front and tied them behind her neck.

"You have to release them, Sindar. My sisters will come, and they'll kill you. You can't win."

"I've already won." He nodded to his men, and they were on her again, clasping her arms and lifting her off her feet, carrying her backward. She kept twisting her head around, but she could see only a concrete slab and few scattered support posts.

"You swore by Marduk that you would keep your word."

"Marduk knew fully what I intended."

"Damn you, Sindar!" She yanked one arm free, made a fist and punched one of her captors, who dropped the other, but they grabbed her again before she could get her legs loose. "The Gods allowed me to remain between the worlds," she said, speaking rapidly to keep her panic at bay. "For three-thousand, five-hundred years they allowed it. And my sisters—"

A shackle was snapped around each of her wrists, and the men stepped away to the nearby pillars, where they picked up heavy chains and snapped them to her cuffs. She followed the links up and saw pulleys at the top, and as the black-clad thugs pulled the chains, they raised her arms with every tug.

"The Gods allowed my sisters to reincarnate, lifetime after lifetime, Sindar. To remember, to bear the same names, to find each other again. Do you really think— Unh!" The chains pulled her arms all the way overhead, and then farther, so she was lifted off her feet. It hurt. She gripped the chains in her hands to take her weight off her shoulders, but it wasn't easy. "Do you really think..." She grunted, forcing the words past the pain of her shoulders being so painfully wrenched and the burn of her hands on the chains. "Do you really think that the Gods gave us all of that only to see us fail now?"

"You're witches. The Gods gave you nothing. Your demon overlords, perhaps. But not Marduk."

"Not Marduk," she agreed, holding her head up when she wanted to let it fall forward in pain. "Ishtar."

The flash of fear in the ancient high priest's eyes was enough to tell her that she was on the right track. "Even Marduk himself doesn't dare defy the wishes of the Queen of Heaven. Ishtar will exact a huge price from you, Sindar."

He held up a hand, and the yanking of the chains ceased. Then the men pushed a concrete slab, a dais of some kind, forward. It scraped loudly against the concrete floor, but soon it was beneath her, supporting her feet, taking the burden from her hands and shoulders. She pressed her feet down and sighed in relief.

"Fetch the vessel," Sindar barked.

Vessel? By the Gods, what was he up to?

A man scurried off, then returned with a large pottery urn, wide at the top, narrower at the bottom, and inlaid with semiprecious stones in the image of a golden rearing lion and lapis bull, just as they'd appeared on the city gates of Babylon.

She couldn't help but marvel at the beauty of the piece from her own former time. And yet it didn't bode well. It was very much like one that had been routinely used to hold the organs of victims who'd been disemboweled for scrying purposes, one of the high priest's specialties. The heart and liver, sometimes other organs, would be stored inside it for use in future spells and rituals, while the intestines would be examined for signs and omens of the future.

"Is that for my heart, then?" she asked him. Her shoulders still hurt, but at least the pressure was off them now. She tried to relax her still-raised arms, to let the manacles at her wrists support their weight.

Sindar smiled. "The blood of a witch has powerful magical properties, my dear. Especially if we drain it from you during Beltane. Timing is everything, you know." He nodded once more to his men, and they approached her feet. Lilia tried to avoid the bastards, kicking at them, gripping the chains in her hands and pulling her legs up out of reach, but it was no use. She couldn't move far enough or fast enough. There were too many of them. And now they shackled her ankles, then began pulling her chains again.

This time her legs were pulled right out from beneath her, backward, and she fell forward, her shoulders jerking painfully when she reached the chains' limit. They pulled her legs higher, until she was suspended by her wrists and ankles, facedown over the urn. Her spine was curved painfully from the unnatural position, and she was crying softly now.

"It's not B-Beltane yet," she said.

"Close enough for this. Besides, I can use a little of that extra power now." He nodded at one of his men. "Cut her."

"No. No!"

But a man jumped up onto the dais, ignoring her cries, and his blade flashed, slicing her inner arm near the elbow. Pain burned when the blade slashed her skin, and warm blood ran down toward her shoulder and began dripping to the concrete below.

Sindar moved the urn to catch the drops as they fell, and soon the drops became a trickle. It sickened her to see her blood flowing into the ancient jar, and she let her head fall forward and closed her eyes. She knew she should call Demetrius, but if he came too soon they would kill Ellie.

And if he came too late? Then he would pay the ultimate price along with her.

14

Demetrius felt her kiss him and vaguely, fighting sleep, heard the remaining words she sang and realized she was casting a spell. She'd cast a spell to make him sleep, and she was casting another one right now.

I cast and bound you tight to me; tonight, my love, I set you free. The spell I cast I now undo; we once were one, but now we're two.

He fought the enchantment. He knew she was going to try to go after Ellie all by herself, whether it cost her life, and his, or not, because she felt the baby was more important. And he agreed with her, but dammit, he hadn't refused to accept the missing part of his soul for nothing. He'd done it to keep his powers intact so he could use them to save Ellie and, he hoped, somehow save Lilia, too. If he died in the effort, so be it. If death was what Lilia had told him it was, then he had little to fear.

Only being without her. That he feared more than anything.

Fight it. Fight the spell.

She'd enchanted him, sung to him, commanded him

to sleep while she slipped away. And it had almost worked.

Remember what she told you, though, he reasoned inside his sleep-addled mind. *She said a spell can't work on a man unless he wants it to on some level. And there is no part of me that wants her to face this alone. Not even a single cell. I don't want to be unbound from her. Hell, I want to be bound to her for the rest of our lives!*

He managed to pry his eyes open, forced himself from the bed, landing on hands and knees on the floor. Groping almost blindly, he found his way into the bathroom, pulled himself into the shower stall, then lifted a hand in search of the knob and twisted without hesitation. Icy water poured over him, and he sucked in a breath and felt his heart pound faster. Miserably unpleasant. But it worked.

The cold shocked the fog from his brain and brought him fully awake. He got himself upright and strode out of the stall, toweling off on the way back into the bedroom for jeans, shoes. He belted his dagger around his waist, snatched up the chalice and grabbed a shirt and his satchel on the way out the door. And then he went to the Jeep, surprised that Lilia hadn't taken it.

She was on foot.

That meant she was close.

He closed his hand around the amulet and closed his eyes, about to ask it to show him where she was… but he didn't have to. His feet were moving all on their own. He was being pulled. It felt as if he were at one end of a rubber band, stretched between them. Just like before.

He'd done it! He'd kept her spell from working. The

binding spell she'd cast that first day was still intact.
He let go of all resistance, let his body be tugged and
pulled in the right direction, even though he stumbled
once or twice.

He thanked the Gods for that spell. He was very
glad that she'd been such a stubborn and persistent
little witch.

She'd told him that the binding spell would work
until one of them died. And that eventuality might be
nearer at hand than he thought.

No, he couldn't afford to think that way. He would
find her in time. After all she'd done for him, he owed
her that much.

Besides, he thought, he couldn't live, didn't want to
live, without her.

Tomas worked steadily over the journal that Lilia
and Demetrius said they'd found in Father Dom's room.
He'd taken it back to the house with him when Magdalena had shocked them all by calling it a night.

There had been something off about that, he thought.
Indy had clearly thought so, too, and that made him
doubly sure.

As he worked, he became more and more certain
with every line he translated that the man who'd written these words had not been Father Dom at all. He'd
claimed to have many ancient texts pertaining to Demetrius and the three witches, and this journal was an
old copy of one of them. But there were newer entries,
too, written in fresh ink, added to the rest.

Dom had known some ancient Babylonian dialects.
But this…this had been written by an expert, using
words and glyphs whose meaning he had to guess at

based on their context, because some of them had yet to be translated by modern-day historical linguists. It was written in a conversational style that only a native speaker could have pulled off.

He had a half dozen reference books open around him, and sometimes he was barely aware of what he was transcribing until he finished a line and went back to reread it, so painstaking was each and every word.

But then he went cold as he realized what he'd read so far, and he closed the journal, took his notebook and headed into the bedroom.

His beautiful Indy was lying on the bed, staring at the ceiling, muttering incantations. "I knew you wouldn't be able to sleep," he said. "Get dressed, hon. We have to go."

"Where?"

"First to your sister's. And then we need to find a bomb shelter built in an abandoned railroad tunnel in or near Milbury. And we need to find it fast."

She flung back the covers, and he saw that she was still fully dressed. The only thing she'd taken off were her shoes. "It's about freakin' time."

Thirty minutes later, Magdalena leaned over the map on the dining room table while Ryan searched the internet on a laptop close beside her. Tomas paced as he skimmed his translation and relayed every pertinent detail. "In the final pages Sindar claims—using the word *bomb* in English, as there is no Babylonian equivalent—that he's found the perfect place," he said, running his finger down the page, then read aloud. "'An abandoned bomb shelter, so close to the witches and yet completely invisible to them. My spells and wards will shield it from discovery. And it's below-ground, so no one will hear the—'"

He stopped there and gave his head a shake, but Magdalena saw the look in his eyes and yanked the notebook from him. "'So no one will hear the demon whore's screams,'" she read, then pressed a hand to her chest and closed her eyes.

"This guy is sick." Tomas took the journal back, before she could read any more. There were things in it she would be better off not knowing.

"We knew that already," Magdalena said. "We knew how much Sindar enjoyed torturing us, even back at the beginning."

"Where the hell are Demetrius and Lilia?" Ryan asked, looking up from the computer.

"Indy went to get them," Lena replied. "Have you found anything on the location?"

"Seven bomb shelters within a fifty-mile radius. I need more to go on."

Ryan kept searching, but Tomas leaned over him. "That's gonna have to be good enough. Start marking the locations on the map. We'll visit every last one if we have to."

"I'll scry them instead," Magdalena said. "I need to go get my pendulum." She raced away, through the living room and up the stairs. She was back so quickly that Tomas and Ryan still had their heads together, marking each of the bomb shelters on the map.

"That's it," Ryan said, as they marked the final spot. "That's everything that came up in my search."

"Okay, give me some room." Lena let her pendulum dangle over the map. Then she shook her head. "No. They're too close together. I need to cut them up. The way we're going through maps around here is going to make the local shopkeepers wonder what the hell we do with them." She went for the scissors, then carefully cut out each section of the map that contained a bomb shelter. When she finished she spread the sections on the table and dangled her pendulum over the first of them and watched to see if it would swing.

"Sindar's journal said he could block you from locating him that way," Tomas said, watching her and watching the doorway, as well, waiting for Indy to return, getting worried. She should have been back with Lilia and Demetrius by now.

"He can," Lena explained. "But the pendulum gives negative as well as positive readings. It will tell me where he's not. What's left will be where he is."

Ryan's eyes filled as he watched his wife work. "Damn, you're smart."

Tomas put a hand on his shoulder and inclined his head. Frowning, Ryan backed away from the table, where Lena was too busy to notice. When they were out of earshot, Tomas looked Ryan in the eye. "If Demetrius doesn't accept the final piece of his soul in time, he's not the only one who will dies."

"I know," Ryan said softly. "Lilia will die, too. She told us that already."

Tomas held his gaze, searching for words. "Not only Lilia," he said at last. And then he swallowed. "All of them. All of them, Ryan. We'll lose Indy and Lena. And…and I'm not sure, but…maybe Ellie, too."

He saw the man pale, saw his eyes widen. But just as quickly Ryan set his jaw and lifted his chin. "That's not gonna happen. We're not going to let it happen."

"Damn straight we're not. I just…I thought you should know."

Ryan sighed. "Should we tell them?"

"I don't know. Indy will probably kill me if she ever finds out I knew and didn't say anything."

Before they could decide, the front door burst open and Indy came rushing in, breathless, her eyes wild. "They're gone. Demetrius and Lilia are gone!"

Magdalena called from the kitchen, "I know where. I found it!"

All of them ran to join her at the table.

"This one," Lena said. "It's the only site that didn't give a negative response. In fact, no response at all. Nothing. The energy's being blocked there, I'm sure of it."

"That's close," Indy said, leaning in. "Maybe two miles from here. Probably why Demetrius and Lilia didn't take their car." She smiled grimly. "I've owed Father Dom a kick in the crotch for a while now," she said. "I'm almost glad I'll have a chance to deliver it."

"It's not Father Dom." Tomas smoothed his palm over her clenched fist. "It's Sindar. You need to remember that."

"Fine. I've owed him even longer."

"It's two-for-one day on priests," Lena said. "Kick one, kick another free." She straightened. "Everyone ready?"

"More than ready," Ryan said.

Tomas's eyes were solemn and lingered on Ryan's a second too long, making Indy look at him with suspicion. He had to tell her. When he could get her alone. *If* he could get her alone. "Just remember," he said to take his mind off that particular problem, "we have two objectives. Get Ellie and Bahru out of harm's way, and make sure Demetrius has the chance to accept the rest of his soul *before* Beltane. It's vital we accomplish that."

Lena rolled her eyes. "Like we'll forget the thing that's going to keep our sister from dying. Let's go already."

Tomas looked at his watch. "All right. Time to go."

"I wish we had weapons," Magdalena said.

"I have a shotgun in the car," Tomas said. "It's loaded."

"And I can kick ass without one," Indy put in. "Let's do this."

They started for the door, but before they reached it there was a soft knock. Frowning, Indy, who was closest, opened the door.

An old man stood on the other side. He had a face like the bark of a hard maple tree, all lines and crevices, pale blue eyes and a face in need of a razor.

"Hello," he said. "I've come a long way. You must be Indira," he went on, after a long look into her eyes. "So that must be Magdalena."

"Yes, but—"

The newcomer looked at the men then, nodding as his eyes roamed their faces thoroughly. What he was looking for, Tomas couldn't have said.

"Look, friend," he said to the visitor, "I don't know who you are, but we're in the middle of an emergency here, so—"

"I know that, son. I know that. It's why I'm here. To help."

Indy looked back at Tomas, who shrugged.

"I'm sorry, bad manners," the man said. "I haven't

even introduced myself." He held out a hand. "I'm Gus."

Ryan moved forward, "Demetrius's friend Gus? Aren't you supposed to be in an Arizona hospital right now?"

Gus waved a hand. "I knew the D-man was going to need me, knew I had to be here. So I booked out of that hospital, caught the first flight and here I am."

Tomas looked the man over, worry in his eyes. "That's decent of you, Gus, but surely you realize you're in no shape to be—"

"I realize. And don't call me Shirley." A grin split his face. "So are we gonna stand here wasting time or get going to whatever emergency you were on your way to?"

"Gus, your life could be in danger if you go with us," Indy told him, one hand tightening on his forearm as if to drive the point home.

The old man's smile died as he covered her hand with his own. His face took on a hard, firm expression. His head lifted higher; his spine straightened. He seemed almost to grow taller before their eyes, and he said, "I'm going with you. You can explain the rest on the way." Then he turned and started across the porch, down the steps, walking in long powerful strides at first, then wincing in pain and limping the rest of the way as whatever had just briefly empowered him seemed to evaporate. He looked at the vehicles in the driveway: Ryan's big black pickup truck with the extended cab and the ancient Volvo that was Tomas's pride and joy. "Which one are we taking?"

"Both," Ryan replied when no one else answered. "Come on, you can ride with Lena and me in the truck."

Indy shot Lena a look. "Has your husband lost his mind?"

"Hey, if he feels Gus has to be here, who are we to question him?" Magdalena replied. "Besides there's something almost…familiar about him."

"Maybe there *is* a reason why he's here," Tomas said. "We don't have to debate it now. Let's go. We have lives to save. And we're very short on time."

By the time Demetrius was pulled by those unseen bonds onto a set of railroad tracks and into an abandoned tunnel through the very side of a mountain, his entire body was on fire. The energy zipping through every nerve itched and tingled, making him anxious and hyperalert. He felt the vibrations of sound coming from below the tunnel and even thought he smelled his Lilia's sweet scent lingering near a rusted metal door.

Placing his hands on that door, he felt the vibrations emanating from beyond it, and heard sounds that seemed to indicate there were several people beyond the barrier. More than just the old priest and his captives. He didn't know if there was another way in, much less whether he could find it. And he didn't want to waste time searching. Lilia might be hurt. He couldn't wait.

He needed to distract the people beyond this door, he realized. Get them to come out so he could go in.

His hand curled around the hilt of the blade at his side, and he drew it silently. Yes. He could distract them.

He withdrew from the cave, aimed the blade and blasted a copse of dying poplar trees. Fire flashed from the tip of the golden athame and exploded the grove

with a blinding flash, a resonating boom, a hailstorm
of splinters flying in all directions. Then he aimed and
fired again in a different direction, igniting another
satisfying explosion.

He ran full speed into the shadows deep inside the
cave and waited there, watching as the door was flung
wide and men flooded through it. Ten or more of them.
All of them dressed entirely in black and wearing a
bizarre assortments of masks. And then came Sindar
himself.

He was even fatter now than he had been before,
and his face was fuller, younger-looking.

The bastard followed his men, shouting orders, then
shoved the slowest out of the way as he shouldered past
and stormed out of the tunnel to survey the damage.
Clearly he thought he was under attack.

Demetrius crept up behind the straggler and hooked
his arm around the man's neck. He increased the pressure until the man went limp in his arms, then dragged
him quickly into the shadows. When he emerged again
he was dressed in the man's black clothes. Dark jeans
that were a bit tight on him, a long-sleeved black
spandex turtleneck, straining at the seams against his
muscles. And the mask, a black handkerchief with eye-
holes torn into the fabric, knotted behind his head.

He quickly ducked through the rusted metal door
and paused as if he were standing guard. Arms
across his chest, his blade concealed, he surveyed the
unstable-looking metal staircase and the large concrete
room below it. His eyes came to a sudden halt and he
almost gasped aloud when he caught sight of Lilia.
She was lying facedown on a concrete table. There
were chains, lax at the moment, attached to her wrists

and ankles, and a length of white fabric was wrapped around her.

His stomach heaved as he saw that there was blood seeping into the fabric from somewhere beneath her body. More had spattered in macabre patterns on the floor.

What had they done to her? By the Gods, was she even alive?

Rein yourself in, his mind told him. *If she's not already dead, you're her only hope.*

Two men stood, one on either side of her, dressed in black like Sindar's other minions. On the opposite end of the room, beyond a barred door, he saw a bearded man in red-and-white robes sitting on the edge of a cot, rocking an infant in his arms. He had to be Bahru, and from the squirming of the bundle he held, it appeared Eleanora was still alive and well.

No other guards in the place. He drew his gaze back to the ones below and, whipping out the dagger, blasted first one and then the other. Then he turned and aimed the athame at the metal door behind him, blasting it along the edge. The metal heated to red-orange and sparks showered as he effectively welded it shut, then he melted the locks and even the hinges with the fire of his blade for good measure.

Finished, he whirled and pounded down the stairway. A quick blast to the cell door sent it sliding open on its own, and then he was running across the room, clasping Lilia's shoulders in his arms. "Lilia. Wake up, Lilia."

She didn't move, didn't even moan. He wasn't sure she was breathing. And in that moment, in that instant of believing her dead, he felt the return of the worst pain he'd ever felt. That same pain of loss, of love destroyed, of utter devastation he'd experienced when she'd been torn from him before. In his mind's eye he saw her again as she'd turned to look into his eyes just before she was pushed from the cliff so long ago. He saw her love for him and knew he wasn't worthy, because he couldn't save her. He couldn't save her then. And he had failed her again now.

He sank to his knees on the floor, his hands going to his head as he howled his pain for the world to hear. It was vivid and real, the past, the present, the pain, the loss. The love. Gods, the love. Memories flooded his mind so rapidly and so completely that he nearly drowned in them. And it was all there. Everything he'd had, everything he'd lost. The horrible crushing guilt of having betrayed his King and friend by loving a woman who belonged to him, and then murdering him when he reacted as anyone could have predicted he would. The even larger weight of knowing that had he never loved her, his beloved would not have died then. Or now.

"Demetrius," said a deep voice from behind him.

He turned to look up at the aging guru, whose weathered face was troubled. "Lilia will revive."

Frowning, Demetrius got to his feet and went to her. Yes, he realized, it was true. She *was* immortal, at least until the actual moment of Beltane. Her heart would beat again, and breath would fill her lungs.

"Pull yourself together," Bahru told him. "We have to get out of here. Sindar intends to kill her, to kill you both."

"Yes." Demetrius shot the blade at Lilia's chains,

cutting through them with fire and letting them fall to the floor with a loud enough clatter to wake the dead.

Then he turned her over, almost crying out at the amount of blood that soaked the gown. "Where are her clothes?" he asked the guru.

The man trotted away, baby in one arm, gathered up Lilia's clothes from the corner where they'd been tossed and brought them back quickly. Then he looked up, his eyes widening as someone began pounding on the door above. "There's no other way out," he said.

"We'll make one." Demetrius strode to the farthest wall and aimed the dagger at the ceiling near what he hoped was the mouth of the tunnel. And he blasted. The concrete shattered, raining down. "Get back!" he shouted to Bahru. "And take her with you."

Bahru grabbed the still-unconscious Lilia by one arm, dragging her off the table. She hit the floor hard, but he kept going, pulling her out of way of the rain of debris as Demetrius blasted again and again.

When he stopped, the men were still pounding on the door. In all their noise, they'd failed to hear his. He had made a hole through which he could see the night sky. And…was that a tree? He hoped so.

Now to get Bahru and the child up there. And then himself and Lilia.

He ran to the concrete table and pushed it with all his might until it stood against the wall. Then he braced himself against it, pushing and lifting. Bahru laid the baby down on the cold concrete floor and came to help him.

They grunted as they strained to tip the thing up onto its end, which would enable Bahru to reach the opening and escape to freedom. But they were not strong enough, and the door above was rattling as Sindar and his minions battered it.

And then he heard Lilia's voice whispering in his memory. He remembered that day in his private garden when she'd shown him how to move a potted palm without touching it. *The amulet, Demetrius. Use it.*

Backing away, blinking at her wisdom and his own apparent idiocy, he closed his eyes, clasped the pendant and visualized the table standing on its end. He was shocked when he opened his eyes and saw it standing just that way. He quickly jumped on top of it. "Bahru, get the baby up here, now."

The old guru hurried closer, sending a regretful look at Lilia as he left her on the floor. Then he held Ellie out to Demetrius.

Demetrius took the tiny girl carefully, holding her while Bahru clambered up onto the table. He stared down into the baby's trusting eyes, and his heart filled with pride. He was going to save her. That much, at least, he would manage this day. "You have to go first," he told Bahru. "So I can hand her up to you."

"Yes, yes. Give me a leg up. The hole is still too high to reach."

Demetrius bent one leg. Bahru stepped onto his thigh and reached for the opening. Gripping the rough and ragged edges, he pulled his head through. He struggled, twisting and kicking, but he finally managed to pull himself all the way out.

In spite of everything, the baby girl smiled and burbled at Demetrius, making spit bubbles and, he could have sworn, giggling. His lips rose at the corners, and his eyes filled with tears. "Be well, little witchling," he said, and without planning to, he bent and kissed her forehead.

Then he straightened and, stretching his arms, lifted her up to Bahru who was reaching down for her.

The door was still being pounded, giving way a bit more each time, as Bahru reached down, his long arms wrinkled and dark. Demetrius stretched, balancing the child on his open palms, and the old man closed his hands around her and gathered her to him.

"Don't wait for us," Demetrius told him. "Take the baby and go. Do not look back until she's safe."

"Yes, yes. Thank you, Demetrius."

And then they were gone.

Demetrius jumped to the floor and hurried toward Lilia. As he went, he gripped his pendant, shot a look at the makeshift cell door and slid it slowly closed. He tried to unbend the bars where his initial blast had altered them. He even plumped the blankets on the cot to look rumpled. And then he was kneeling beside his beloved, gathering her up in his arms. Suddenly, as if by magic, she sucked in a great, gasping breath, arching her back and going rigid in his arms, and then slowly relaxing again as her eyes blinked open.

"Thank the Gods," he whispered. "Thank the Gods." He kissed her, tears falling from his eyes and making her lips taste of salt. All he wanted was more of this, more of her, more time. She breathed, sighed into his kiss, and he felt something—something that felt thick and warm, like heated honey—filling him from head to toe. Soothing, somehow. Right, somehow. Healing and nourishing his body, making him feel more alive than he'd ever been, and almost invincible.

Then the door finally gave way beneath the blows of

Sindar's army. It smashed into the wall, and he knew they had run out of time. But he didn't care. He would die by her side or live with her forever. It didn't matter, as long as they were together.

Lilia lowered herself from his arms and stood tall beside him. He took the amulet from around his neck and quickly put it around hers. "Better we both have a magical weapon for this fight."

"Thank you, my love." She nodded, pressing a hand to the amulet, closing her eyes briefly, then opening them again and standing ready as the dozen or so men in black, all of them masked, tromped down the stairs and assembled at the bottom. Demetrius didn't even look at them but instead marveled at her. His Lilia, poised and ready to fight at his side.

The last few thugs were surging down the metal staircase, causing such a racket that he fought the urge to cover his ears. "Wait for it," Lilia whispered. "Wait."

Finally the entire gang had gathered at the bottom of the stairway. Some had knives drawn, others nothing but their bare hands. But they would be deadly either way. They stood there like a pack of killer dogs awaiting the word of their master.

Sindar alone remained at the top of the stairs, his eyes on Demetrius, glittering with excitement. "I knew you'd come for her," he said. "But where are her sisters? Surely they're not far behind. I was counting on having everyone here for the final execution."

Lilia said nothing, but Demetrius felt the anger surging in her. The heat of it, the energy, was palpable.

"Ah, well, I'm sure they'll be along. In the meantime—" Sindar looked at his goons "—take them."

"Now," Lilia said.

Demetrius pointed the blade into the midst of the slavering pack, and pushed with his mind to fire it.

But nothing happened. Nothing at all.

15

Bahru held the baby close, his arms wrapped protectively around her, and turned from the opening Demetrius had blasted through the side of the mountain, trying to get his bearings. Sindar and his army of drones, men whose minds he'd taken over—Bahru knew it could happen, because it had happened to him just prior to Ellie's birth—had finally broken the door and surged inside. Lilia and Demetrius hadn't had time to escape, and while he was terrified for them, he also knew his task, his sacred mission, was to protect this child.

He'd been led to her. All his life had been about getting him to this place, at this time, to protect this child. He didn't know why, but of that much he was certain.

He stood now on a steep slope beside the long-abandoned railroad tracks. The rails had rusted, and large sections were missing. Most of the wooden parts had rotted away, and weeds had sprung up around and in between what was left. The only logical way to go was down the slope, and he moved as quickly as he could without falling. Stones and pieces of shale slid beneath his feet until he reached a grassier section, and up ahead he saw conifer trees that would hide him from prying eyes.

He looked behind him as he approached those trees, praying he would see Lilia and Demetrius coming after him, but there was no sign of them. No sign of any of Sindar's thugs, either. Perhaps they didn't know yet that he and the baby had fled.

He couldn't wait for Demetrius and Lilia. They'd risked everything to save Eleanora, and it would be a betrayal of them both if he didn't get the child to safety. That was his task. His duty. It was what Demetrius had pleaded with him to do, though leaving them behind was difficult.

So he went quickly into the fragrant pine forest at the bottom of the incline, and from there he kept on going, moving as fast as he could while barefoot. He was often barefoot. It was nothing new to him. But he was usually walking in complete oneness, slowly and calmly, feeling every twig and pebble beneath his soles as he walked in a Zen-like rhythm. Tonight he was racing, not Zen at all but running for his life…no, for her life. For the life of the child he was sworn to protect. And because of that his footsteps fell hard and gracelessly, and the twigs and pebbles beneath his feet poked and stabbed and hurt.

He ran until he could run no farther, then finally stopped and leaned against the sticky bark of a tall pine tree, trying to slow his breathing enough that he could hear something besides the sound of it rushing in and out of his lungs. His pulse pounded in his temples.

Eventually his body quieted and he listened.

There was an owl. Three sharp hoots. An omen of death.

But he did not hear the sound of pursuit.

Perhaps he and the child were safe, at least for the moment. Now all he had to do was figure out where he was and how to get home.

The owl hooted again, another chorus of three in a row, and Bahru shivered. Perhaps the omen was for Lilia and Demetrius.

"Replace the table, and do something with those chains. Repair them. I don't care how." Sindar's men rushed to obey, several of them going to the concrete dais that was standing upright near the hole in the ceiling. They knocked the thing over, straining to get it right side up, and then they pushed it back to its former position between the twin pillars.

Next they approached Lilia.

"No." Demetrius stepped in front of her, gently holding her behind his back. "No, you will not take her from me again. Not again." He still wore the black clothing of one of the henchmen, but he'd discarded the mask. There was no point in hiding his face. Sindar knew him.

The two thugs hesitated, perhaps afraid of the fury in his eyes or the thundering timbre of his voice. They should be afraid. They should be very afraid. They looked to their leader for instruction.

Sindar held up a hand and strolled closer, standing nose to chest with Demetrius, who would have hit him if four goons hadn't jumped into action, grabbing his arms, two on each side, as soon as they'd seen their beloved master moving into harm's way.

Sindar had to tip his head back to look Demetrius in the eye. "She got to you, didn't she, Demetrius? Just as I warned you she would. Look at you. You're weak. You're mortal." He spat the word as if it were something disgusting. "Or haven't you figured that out yet?"

Demetrius's eyes widened as he shot a look behind him and Lilia shook her head. "It can't be," she whispered. "I haven't given it to you."

"The soul knows its home, witch. It strains, always, to return. Your consort's resistance kept it from doing so, but that resistance vanished, most likely when he saw you lying dead on my floor. And when you revived from your temporary death, his soul returned to him."

"But…he chose to wait. To vanquish you before—"

"It need not be a conscious choice, you stupid woman. His love for you, for the child…it left him weak, too weak to even realize what he was asking." Sindar pressed his lips, shaking his head. "I can no longer destroy him forever, as I had hoped to do. But I can kill you both. And I promise you that when it's done, I will kill the rest of your family, including that disgusting little witch's spawn in the cage over there, and her Hindu nanny with her." He stopped speaking, because he had turned to look toward the cell in the back of the room as he'd threatened Eleanora and his eyes narrowed on it suspiciously. He looked at Indy, then at the gaping hole in the ceiling, and then toward the cell again. With a flick of his wrist, he said to one of his minions, "Check on our prisoners."

A man wearing a rubberized likeness of Bill Clinton over his head trotted over as ordered. Two others, both wearing stocking masks, hovered in front of Demetrius, waiting to take hold of Lilia.

"It's nearly Beltane," Sindar said. "I'm going to sacrifice you again, witch. I want you to die knowing your

sisters and their lovers and that child will soon follow."
He looked Demetrius in the eye. "And I'm going to
make you watch again, traitor."

"The guru and the child are gone, master!" shouted
the man who'd gone to check.

The two men waiting to grab Lilia moved in closer.
Demetrius kicked one in the face, sending him crashing to the floor, taking his fellow with him, then Demetrius twisted and stomped the foot of one of his
captors. That man let go of his arm and fell, knocking
over the other thug on that side. Demetrius cocked his
newly freed arm and punched one of the men on his
other side in the face, while Lilia locked her fists together and brought them down on the head of the last
man still clasping Demetrius's arm.

But more came, and soon they were surrounded.
Lilia punched, kicked and fought as hard as she could,
but despite the amulet she wore, there was no more
supernatural boost to her fighting than there was to
Demetrius's.

It was true, Demetrius realized, as he threw himself
at yet another black-clad minion. Their powers were
gone. His soul was intact. Even amid all the chaos, he
knew it. Colors were brighter, and he could smell the
air, musty and old with hints of the thugs' stale sweat.
Lilia was more vividly beautiful than ever, his love for
her more poignant and potent than it had ever been.

He met her eyes, and she sent him a slight smile.
Yes, she knew it, too, knew his soul was intact, that
he was once again the man she loved. The man she
still loved.

Then a sudden crack split the air and silenced them
all. Sindar was standing there with a gun in his hand,

smoke ribboning from the barrel. The men who'd been all over Demetrius backed away, and he saw Lilia's gaze turn horrified. And that was when the pain finally made its way to his awareness. He looked down and saw that his hand was pressed to his belly, and there was blood seeping through his fingers.

Lilia lunged toward him, but she was immediately caught by the guards and could only watch as he sank to his knees. His eyes found hers, and his lips formed words. *I love you,* he tried to tell her, but no sound emerged. And then he fell facedown into darkness.

"Such a vile little device, isn't it?" Sindar asked, looking contemplatively at the gun as Lilia screamed and struggled against the hands that held her. "I much prefer the old ways. Slice the jugular, burn alive, or… oh, I don't know, throw someone from a cliff." His eyes lit, and he gave her an evil smile. "Now, that's an interesting notion, isn't it?"

"Are you just going to let him lie there and bleed to death?" she cried.

"I don't think you're listening to me."

She shot a seething look at him. "Let me help him. Please, I beg of you, let me—"

"Are you not hearing me, Lilia? I'm telling you that we are going to do this exactly the way we did it before. There's a perfect spot not far from here. Black Rock Gorge—one of the many gorges this area is famous for. Students from the local schools fling themselves into it over broken hearts and after too much alcohol, so it's already been purified by blood. A perfect place for a sacrifice. What do you say, witch? Shall we do it all again, for old times' sake?"

She shivered. "We'll be together. You can't stop us."

"Maybe. Or maybe I can strip his soul from him again. I managed it once, after all." Sindar pointed to two men, then to the door. "Go after the swami and the babe. Bring them to me at the top of Black Rock Gorge." He slid a sly look her way. "Yes, I admit it. I planned to kill them the whole time. I know Marduk will forgive me." Then he turned, his robes swooshing with the motion. "Bring her. Bring him, as well. And see to it that he doesn't bleed out on the way. I want him to watch his beloved witch die all over again."

Lilia's tears burned twin paths down her cheeks. She couldn't believe this was happening. She could not believe the Gods had allowed her a chance to make this right and she had failed…again.

There would be no more mercy. No further chances. She only prayed she could somehow prevent Sindar from taking her love's soul again, so they could be together in the afterlife. She prayed in silence for that, and prayed, too, for her sisters and little Ellie, for Tomas and Ryan, for her mother, the mother she hadn't had the chance to bid farewell. *Please let them stay safe. Please.*

The men tugged her into motion. Others brought the mattress from the cell and laid it down beside Demetrius. Then they rolled his big body onto it and carried it as if it were a stretcher.

Like some dark parade, they marched up the creaking, groaning stairs, out the doorway at the top, through the tunnel and out into the dawn.

The vehicles skidded to a halt where the road ended and a footpath following the railroad bed led up into the forest. Lena was out of Ryan's big black truck almost before he'd brought it to a halt, with Ryan and Gus right behind her as she ran to what remained of the railroad tracks. Tomas and Indy got out of his once-white Volvo and hurried to join them. Tomas was carrying a shotgun.

"This way," Lena said. "The bomb shelter was built beneath a tunnel through the mountain where the trains used to run. All we have to do is follow the tracks."

"I don't like this." Indy moved up beside her and clasped her hand. "It's too easy."

"It doesn't matter. We have to go."

"I know that."

The sisters met each other's eyes and then, with a firm nod, began walking. Ryan started out with them, holding Lena's other hand, but fell back when they got to the tracks, because the way wasn't wide enough to walk three abreast. Magdalena knew he understood that she and her sister needed each other right now and she sent him a silent thank-you with her eyes. He acknowledged it with a worried nod as he walked beside Tomas, directly behind them. Gus brought up the rear.

The sun was climbing. If the situation had been different, Lena thought, it would have been a beautiful morning for a walk through the woods. There were birds singing everywhere, and the fragrances of apple blossoms and a few early honeysuckle vines were heavy. But the situation wasn't different, and she had no idea what they were going to find at the end of their travels.

Soon enough the tracks sloped upward and the dark mouth of the tunnel loomed ahead.

"What's the pendulum doing?" Indy asked in a harsh whisper.

Lilia touched the stone where it rested against her skin. "Not a thing."

"I know you two are the super witches and all," Ryan said softly, "but would you mind letting us go first?"

Tomas looked at him sharply. "That's a completely sexist idea. And I concur. Step aside, ladies."

The two men squeezed past them, each one delivering a touch, a kiss, to his woman as he passed. Gus remained at the rear, saying nothing. And then they were moving forward again, the five of them, into the dark tunnel. Lena sensed they were heading for battle. She was as tense and wary as if they were walking into Armageddon. They slowed their steps as every trace of light was left behind them. Each footfall created an eerie echo, and yet they heard no other sound, no indication of human presence.

"We need a light," Lena whispered.

"That could give us away," Ryan said.

"We don't have a choice." Indy pulled out her phone and turned on the flashlight app. "There must be a stairway or something."

Ryan turned and asked, "Can I have that a minute?"

Indy handed it over and he aimed it toward the tunnel's sides, illuminating a metal door that looked as if it had been hit by a train at some point.

Lena swallowed hard and stopped walking. "That could be it. That could be where Ellie is. Goddess, why's it so quiet?"

Tomas shouldered his shotgun as Ryan pulled the

door open. It groaned so loudly there was no way who-ever was inside hadn't heard it.

But as the men moved beyond the door, nothing happened. And when Lena saw Tomas lower his gun her heart fell.

"There's no one here," Ryan said.

"There has to be." Lena pushed past them, hurrying down the unsteady stairway as the rising sun illumi-nated the place through a hole in the domed ceiling. The others followed, their steps banging like cymbals. She crossed the concrete floor at the bottom, then went still, because there was blood. There was a lot of blood.

"Goddess, no..."

Ryan grabbed her shoulders, turning her to him, and she buried her head in his chest to hide the sight of all that blood, but she couldn't stop the thoughts that flooded her mind. Was it Lilia's blood? Was it Ellie's?

The others were exploring the place further.

"There's a cell back here," Gus called. "I think your baby was here, Magdalena."

That brought Lena's head up, and she grabbed Ryan's arm and dragged him over. Inside the cell, an empty baby bottle lay on the floor. Right beside it was a teddy bear, his unseeing eyes staring blankly.

Ryan frowned. "Honey, isn't that—"

"The nanny-cam." Lena let go of Ryan's hand and grabbed the bear. "And it's recording."

"How the hell did it get here?"

"I don't know. It was on the mantel last I— It doesn't matter. We have to see what's on it—fast. Beltane is only—" She looked at her watch. "Goddess, it's only an hour away." She looked around her. "And we have no idea where they are. Ryan I don't know what to—"

"Easy. Deep breaths."

She nodded, gulping air, calming herself again. "We need to see what's on it."

Gus looked at the hole in the ceiling. "If they're not here, chances are that's how they got out. Maybe they escaped."

"Maybe," Tomas said. "But if they did, it's for sure those bastards went after them. Come on, let's get back out and see if they left us a trail."

They all headed up the stairs again, into the pitch black tunnel, and then along the tracks to the far end and back out into the brightening sunlight. "The grass is all beaten down over here," Ryan said, eyeing the slope to the right of the tracks.

"It looks like someone went this way, too." Indy looked downhill on the opposite side. "But the signs are faint. Look, there's a broken stick, a footprint in the wet mud." She turned, met her sister's eyes. "A bare footprint."

"Bahru," Lena whispered, rushing forward. "He got Ellie out. He must have. And he got away from them, too. They all went the other way."

"No," Gus said. "See there? It's another track behind your Bahru's. Someone wearing shoes."

Lena whirled and met Ryan's eyes. "You have to go after them," she said.

"We'll all go."

"No. No, listen to me. Listen to me, and please don't argue. You and Tomas have to follow that trail and save our baby." She gripped the front of his shirt. "I can't go with you. I have to go—" She bit her lip, lowered her head. "I have to take this bear home and see what's on the disc. I'll take the car."

"I'll go with her," Indy said.

Gus said nothing, but his eyes were following the path the larger group had taken.

"All right. Call and tell me what you find." Ryan pulled her close and kissed her. "I'll find her. I promise."

"Hurry, Ryan."

He nodded. Tomas and Indy exchanged a knowing glance as he hugged her close, and Lena heard her whisper, "I'm sorry. I have to—"

And his urgent reply, "I know you do. Be careful, dammit."

"You know I will." She kissed his neck, and then the two men broke away and dashed down the hill after Bahru and the baby.

Gus looked at the women. "If you two don't mind getting home on your own, I'd like to follow this trail."

"We're all following this trail," Magdalena told him.

He frowned, clearly puzzled. "But you just told your husband—"

"He never would have let her go after Sindar without him," Indy said.

Lena took out her cell phone as Indy went on.

"But we have to go, Gus. And you don't. This is our fight—one we've been waiting over three-thousand years to finish. But it's not yours."

He held her gaze steadily. "You're wrong about that," he said. Then he looked at Magdalena, who had pulled something out of the bear and was plugging it into her phone. "I take it you can access the camera footage from your phone?"

"Smart man. There's a flash drive in the bear and a USB port— Never mind." She tapped the screen, waited, then turned the phone sideways. "Here it comes."

The two sisters stood close, and Gus shouldered his way in between them to watch the footage playing out on the small screen. A few seconds later Indy staggered away with her hand over her mouth and tears flowing. "Oh, God, Lilia," she whispered. "Stay alive, baby sister. We're coming for you."

"You, too, Sindar," Lena added, her tone deep and quivering with anger. "We're coming for you, too, you murderous bastard. And this time you're not walking away."

16

Bahru had hiked the Himalayas with Ryan's father. He'd traveled the Amazon by boat and explored the wilds of Peru. Ironic, then, that he would find himself lost in the relatively tame woods of upstate New York. And yet lost was precisely what he was.

Worse, someone was following him. He'd paused twice to cuddle Ellie close and listen. And he'd heard them very clearly, the even, stealthy footsteps of a human being. Animals didn't walk that way, one, two, one, two. A deer would take a few rapid steps, then a couple of slow ones, then stop to sniff or to graze. A rabbit would scamper. A chipmunk would scurry. A bear would lumber and crash. A human kept his rhythm, one, two, left, right.

The baby was fussy. He'd been carrying her through the woods for forty minutes, and he was no closer to finding his way home. Sooner or later he would have to emerge onto a road, wouldn't he?

Ellie squirmed in his arms and wrinkled up her face. He recognized the expression. She was gearing up for an all-out wail. Jiggling her in his arms, he whispered,

"There, now, Ellie. You have to keep quiet now. We're playing hide-and-seek."

She opened her eyes, gazed at him briefly, then squeezed them closed again and opened her mouth. He gave her his knuckle to circumvent the cry, and she frowned and looked cross-eyed at it while gnawing it curiously.

A twig snapped, and Bahru looked around fast.

A man in black, wearing a ski mask over his face, emerged from the darkness of the forest. And then, almost making Bahru gasp in surprise, another appeared off to the right, this one wearing a plastic Halloween mask. A skeleton. How imaginative.

"Hand over the baby now, old man," said the first. "You can go on your way. No one will bother you."

"No one but my conscience," Bahru said, taking a backward step.

"You can't outrun us. And you can't fight us. Give it up."

"I can out-will you, though."

"Out-what?"

"If your faith were the size of even a mustard seed, you could say to this mountain, 'Move from here to there.' And it would move." Bahru sank to the ground, folded his legs and locked his arms around Ellie. "Unless, of course the mountain had faith, too, and said to itself, 'No force on earth can move me.'" Closing his eyes, he willed himself into a deep state of meditation, visualizing himself as a stone mountain and Ellie as a pebble safe within his depths. He heard no more, though he knew the men were speaking, shouting at him, giving him orders, and Ellie had begun to cry. He ignored everything, because he was a mountain. And mountains were not upset by noise.

"What the hell?" Ryan whispered. "What are they—"

Tomas gripped his arm, probably to keep him from rushing forward, and pulled him back into the cover of the dark forest. "Let's just see what's up first, see how many there are. We have to do this right. We can't mess it up."

Ryan knew his friend was right, but every instinct in him was screaming at him to save his daughter, save her *now.* Instead, he forced himself to stand still and stare into the tiny glade, dappled by sunlight that spilled in tiny patches and pools through the trees above, where Bahru sat on the ground with the baby in his arms. She was crying loudly, and two thugs dressed all in black and wearing masks were pulling on Bahru's arms, but they couldn't budge him, couldn't pull Ellie from his hold.

Bahru didn't flinch. His eyes were closed, and he wore an expression of utter serenity.

Ryan shot Tomas a look. "There are only two of them. Can we get my daughter now before they hurt her?"

Tomas nodded. "You go around to the left, I'll go right, we'll count to ten and we'll come at them from both sides, all right?"

"All right." As soon as he was in position he counted quickly and then just sprang. He saw Tomas race in from the opposite side, but after that he couldn't see how his friend was doing. He had his hands full with a skeleton-masked thug who had arms like steel and a right hook like a freight train. The thug pounded Ryan in the face, and he flew off his feet before hitting the ground. He started to get up again, but the thug hit him again, and then again, driving him back down each time. This guy was strong as an ox. Why the hell hadn't he been able to move the old guru's skinny arm away from Ellie?

Ryan scrambled to his feet, ready for more, and the brute was looming over him, about to deliver it, when the baby squealed. Ryan looked her way, and saw her flailing her arms and giggling, when she'd been squalling a few seconds ago. And then something in his peripheral vision grabbed his attention. He scrambled backward just as a huge branch came crashing down right at him. The skeleton saw it, too, but too late, only an instant before it flattened him to the ground, leaving him pinned and helpless.

Nearby, Tomas was duking it out with the second thug. Tomas's lip was bleeding, and one eye was swollen nearly shut. Ryan looked around, spied a brick-sized rock, picked it up and hurled it, only belatedly thinking he might miss and hit the ex-priest.

Fortunately he didn't. The rock hit the thug squarely in the back of his skull. He dropped like an anchor, hit the ground and didn't move again.

Tomas met Ryan's eyes, wiping the blood from his upper lip. "Thanks."

"De nada." Ryan rushed to the baby. She squealed and burbled at the sight of him, as she always did. Then he knelt to shake Bahru out of his…whatever.

"Hey, holy man, it's Ryan. We're here, it's okay. You and Ellie are safe."

Bahru's eyes opened slowly, and his lips curved in a smile. "I know we are."

He unlocked his arms, and Ryan took the baby, hugging and kissing her, flooded with so much relief that his knees were damn near weak with it.

But his joy was short-lived. It skidded to a halt when he heard Tomas talking to the thug underneath the fallen limb. "Where is Sindar taking the witch? Tell me, or I'll leave you under there to die."

"Someone will find me—"

"Yeah, come hunting season. That's in the fall, pal. This is spring. Where did he take her?"

Closing his eyes, the man shook his head, refusing to talk.

"Fine. We'll do this the hard way, then." Tomas stepped up onto the branch, increasing the pressure on the man's chest. "You gonna tell me now?" he asked. And then he started jumping up and down, driving a gasp of pain from the main each time he landed. "How about now?"

"Tomas, for the love of God…"

"This guy was gonna kill your kid, Ry. Don't forget that."

Ryan handed the baby back to Bahru, then walked over and calmly jumped onto the log beside Tomas. "Shall we?" he asked.

"You bet." And this time they both jumped, then landed hard.

The thug cried out, his face twisting into a grimace. "All right, all right. He's taking her to the top of Black Rock Gorge."

Ryan frowned at Tomas. "What the hell is—"

"It's a hundred-foot chasm with a rocky, shallow

creek running through it. The cliff at the top is a popular spot," Tomas said. "Students die there every freaking year. Suicides, accidents and pure idiocy."

Ryan went cold as he stared into Tomas's eyes. "He's going to throw Lilia off the damn cliff," he said, shifting his gaze down to the man under the tree. "Is that what he's planning?" The man didn't answer fast enough, so Ryan jumped again. "Is it?"

"Not just her. All three."

"Over my dead fucking body." Ryan leapt to the ground and went to take the baby from Bahru again. "Come on, Bahru. We need to get back to the truck, and I can't leave you here alone."

Bahru scrambled to his feet, and Tomas fell into step behind.

"Hey! Wait!" shouted the trapped thug. "You can't just leave me here."

"I'll call from my cell and send help!" Tomas shouted back.

"After we save our women," Ryan added.

Ryan glanced up at Bahru as they made their way through the woods. The old man was looking weary. Ryan met his eyes. "You saved my daughter," he said. "You wouldn't let them take her without you, would you?"

Bahru lowered his eyes, trudging on. "Demetrius is the true hero. He risked his life to get us out. Sacrificed it, perhaps."

"And that thing you did just now," Ryan went on. "How the hell could two guys that strong not manage to peel your scrawny arms from around my kid?"

"Because I believed they could not."

"I don't even know what that means."

"Ask Lena."

"Lena," Ryan said softly. "I've got to let her know the baby's all right. Look, when we get back to the tunnel, I want you to take my truck and drive the baby back home. Stay there with Lena and Indy, okay? Tell them we've gone after Lilia."

"I do not drive," Bahru said softly.

"Try believing you can." Ryan said it with a teasing smile, and Bahru smiled back at him. "Thank you for saving Ellie, Bahru. I've been unfair to you for a long time now. That's over."

Pressing his hands together, Bahru paused to bow over them.

And then they were walking again, and Ryan was holding Ellie in one arm and dialing his phone with the other. He called the house, expecting Lena to answer.

Only she didn't.

His eyes widened as he realized his mistake. "Dammit, Tomas, I think they went after Lilia and Sindar on their own."

Tomas nodded slowly. "That's exactly what they did," he said slowly. "And we had to let them. Because this is their deal, and because we had to save Ellie. But now...now we're going after that sonofabitch, too, and he is going to be sorry he ever met our women. Ever."

Sindar made Lilia walk barefoot, her legs shackled with a length of chain he'd salvaged from the bomb shelter and her wrists bound together behind her with rough rope. It wasn't an easy walk, up the steep, stair-like rock face. It was beautiful, though. The trees were green and sweet-smelling. Wild apple trees were awash in blossoms so fragrant the scent made her dizzy. It was almost too strong. The higher they climbed the more she relished the warm spring breeze. It was soothing somehow. And below—farther and farther below—a narrow creek twisted and bubbled and laughed over stones at the bottom of the gorge.

"We're nearly there," Sindar said to one of his men.

He was gleeful over what he was about to do. What a sick and twisted man he was, she thought. And then she looked at Demetrius, still lying unconscious on the mattress as the men who carried him struggled with his weight. So beautiful. So still. Was he dead already? He'd tried so hard to save her.

Yes, he'd done horrible things, but he'd more than made up for them. He'd given his life for Ellie, and for her, Lilia thought. And she loved him more than she ever had, which was saying a lot, because she'd already loved him enough to defy death and linger between worlds for thirty-five centuries.

"Are they coming?" Sindar asked one of his minions. Lilia stopped walking, her attention momentarily distracted from her beloved. "Are who coming?" she asked.

Sindar, who hadn't been paying any attention to her, walked right up to her and clasped her chin in cruel fingers. "Your sisters, of course. We can't have this party without them."

She head-butted him, hard, and it hurt like hell, but when he fell on his ever-widening backside, she thought it was worth it. And the sight of blood spiderwebbing across his forehead gave her the most satisfaction she'd had all day. Then she turned and started running, back down the way she had come. He was not going to kill them. Not her and not her sisters. Not again. If they were following, she had to warn them.

"Stop her!"

She ran, rocks coming loose under her feet, the edge perilously close, and made it past several of his minions before one grabbed her. Dammit!

"Hold her for the rest of the trip. It's not much farther. And answer my question. Are the others following?"

From several yards back a man shouted, "Yes, Master Sindar. The two witches have already reached the base of the gorge. And there's a man with them."

"What man? One of the husbands? Is it the priest or the prince?" Sindar asked, though Lilia was sure his thug had no idea what he was talking about.

"It's an old man, sir. An old man with whiskers and a limp."

Gus? It couldn't be. Gus was in the hospital. There was no way he was hiking up a mountain with her sisters.

"Give me that!" Sindar snapped, waddling down to where his soldier stood and taking the binoculars away from him. "By Marduk's teeth, it's the bum from the alley. What is he doing here?" He handed back the binoculars. "No matter. He's too old and weak to be a problem. Let's get moving. We're nearly there, and Beltane is only minutes away."

Lilia tore her mind away from the puzzle of Gus's presence and paid attention to Sindar once more. "What difference does that make, Sindar? Demetrius already accepted the final piece of his soul. Beltane means nothing now."

"And this from a witch, no less?" Sindar sneered.

"The cross-quarter date is a powerful time, harlot. I intend to make this sacrifice when the Veil between the worlds is at its thinnest, in hopes my beloved King will see and hear and know, and will finally be at peace. I want Balthazorus to know his disloyal concubines and the trusted friend who murdered him have paid the ultimate price."

Just as she reached the base of the trail up the gorge, Lena's cell phone vibrated. She'd long since turned off the ringer, even though the signal was spotty here. She didn't want to give herself away to those bastards who had her sister. Pulling the phone from her pocket, she saw that it was Ryan, and her heart jumped into her throat. "Did you find her?" she asked without preamble.

"She's safe. She's fine. Bahru took her and the truck back to the house."

A wave of emotion washed over her so powerfully that it took away her ability to speak. She tipped her head back, eyes closed, chest spasming.

Indy snatched the phone from her and pressed the speaker button. "Ry? Did you find Ellie?"

"Yeah, Indy. She's fine. Bahru's taken her home. What's wrong? Is Lena all right?"

"Speechless with relief, I think. Thank the Goddess the baby's safe," Indy whispered.

"Why the hell aren't the two of you at the house waiting for him?" Ryan demanded.

Indy met Magdalena's eyes, and it was Lena who spoke. "We had to go after our sister, Ryan. We were following the trail at first, but now we're just making a beeline for Black Rock Gorge. According to the recording, that's where he took her."

"We know, Lena."

"What do you mean, you know?" She looked at Indy.

"We got it from one of the henchmen who came after Bahru. There are probably more with Sindar," Tomas said.

"Ten or so, judging from the bear-cam," Indy told him.

"Babe, Sindar knows you're coming. It's a trap. He intends to throw all three of you from that cliff, just like he did before."

Magdalena met Indy's eyes and said softly, "That's pretty much what we've pieced together, too. He wants us to catch up to him. The trail was way too easy to follow."

"Look," Ryan said, "just wait for us. And then we'll all go up together. We can take them if we work as a team."

Holding Indy's steady gaze, reading it very clearly, Lena said, "All right. I love you, Ryan."

"I love you, too, babe."

"Tomas?" Indy asked.

"I'm here, babe."

"I love you, hon. Everything's gonna be fine."

"I'll be there soon. Wait for me," he said. "I mean it, Indy. Wait for me."

She disconnected, looked at Lena. "We *can't* wait. You know that, right?"

Gus stood staring from one of them to the other. "But you can't face them alone!"

"Fifteen minutes to Beltane," Lena said. "Sindar

might settle for one sacrifice if he can't have all three. We don't have time to wait. If we wait, she'll be dead."

"We're going to win this time," Indy said.

"We win either way, sis. We found each other. We found our loves. I had Ellie. At least she's safe now."

"That freakin' Bahru. Who'd have figured, right?"

"I always liked him," Lena said. She looked at Gus. "This is our fight. I don't want you coming up there with us. Wait for the guys, then bring them along, okay?"

He stared at her, said nothing.

Magdalena took her sister's hand again. "Come on, let's get it done. This showdown is long overdue." And they started together up the trail.

Gus watched them go, shaking his head slowly. "They are so much more than I ever knew, those three women. I was wrong, so very wrong." And then he started up the hill himself, picking a different route and staying out of sight as best he could. At least until he saw the men heading up the trail behind him at a heartbreaking run. All right, then. He would wait for them, and they would go up to the top together and pray they were not too late.

Because, Gus thought, the three beautiful witches were mistaken. This wasn't their fight. It was his. It had been his all along.

Demetrius awoke to a nightmare. He found himself on the ground, hands bound in front of him, propped against a boulder, as he blinked his eyes open and winced at the pain that radiated outward from his belly, burning through his entire torso. But there was worse pain as his vision cleared and a tableau came into focus. A woman in a bloody white makeshift robe stood on the edge of a cliff, her hands bound behind her back, men dressed entirely in black standing nearby.

"Lilia!" He lurched forward as if to get up, only to be slammed by a man wielding a club the size of a baseball bat. It hit him in the chest, and he went down.

"Ah, good," Sindar said, coming into his vision, blocking Lilia from his view. "You're awake. I was so afraid you'd miss it."

"Sindar. What the hell are you doing?" Demetrius demanded. "You failed in your mission. My soul has been restored. It's over."

"It's not over. I could kill you all a thousand times and it would still not be over. My King cannot rest until this is made right."

"What the hell are you talking about?"

"Don't you remember? Think, Demetrius. Now that you have your soul back, think about that day when you murdered your friend."

"That was over three thousand years ago, Sindar. What difference can it possibly make now?"

"All the difference." Sindar turned and glanced behind him, giving Demetrius a brief glance of Lilia. She was looking over her shoulder at him, and there were tears staining her cheeks. For the briefest of instants their eyes met and held.

"Face front, Lilia," Sindar snapped. "I want your eyes on the fall that awaits you, right until the moment I push you over the edge."

"You're a sick man, to delight in torturing an innocent," she said.

"Another word and you go over right now." Sindar

turned back to Demetrius, blocking his view of his beloved again. "We're waiting for the other two, you see. But if they don't get here soon we'll be forced to proceed without them." He looked at the sun and then at his watch. "Ten minutes. That's how long she has to live." He smiled in evil delight. Then he looked at his thugs. "I want two of you to go back and wait along the trail. As soon as the witches pass you, grab them, and don't worry about being gentle. Bind them and bring them to the edge."

"No!" Lilia cried. "Please, have mercy on my sisters. This was all my doing, not theirs."

"I know. And you'll suffer more knowing they will once again die with you for your sins."

"You're a high priest, Sindar." Demetrius sat up straighter, returning his focus to the fat holy man. "You're supposed to represent the Gods. You're supposed to live by their standards. Murder isn't one of them."

Sindar stomped closer, his eyes blazing. "He wasn't quite dead, you know. When you finished with him. He lay on the floor, drowning in his own blood, as the guards dragged you away. But he wasn't quite dead. Hearing the commotion, I raced to his side. I knelt beside him. He could barely speak, and his eyes were filled with pain and fear. He wept, Demetrius. Tears of blood. Because of you."

Demetrius lowered his head, guilt rising up in him. "It was wrong, what I did to the King. I should have reasoned with him, talked to him…." He lifted his gaze and leveled it on Sindar. "I should have convinced him that his High Priest was unfit to serve in the temple of Marduk."

"He whispered to me as he lay there dying. 'I will know no peace,' he told me, 'until this is made right.'"

The guilt rose up in Demetrius's chest. He and the King had been friends. But Balthazorus should never have thought that executing his own harem slaves was justified merely because one of them had fallen in love with another and hurt his pride.

"I promised him, before he died, that I would obey his command," Sindar said. "And then I swore that vow in ritual. Like your precious harlot Lilia, I did not cross over when I died. I lingered, as I knew she would. And I watched. I controlled people like Father Dom and the man who bombed the interfaith conference, and even you, Demetrius. When you were that raging Underworld beast…it was my voice that whispered to you, that told you to take the witch's child in order to manifest a body for yourself. It was I who gave you the power to control the minds of the townsfolk who helped you, and even the Hindu guru."

"Thank the Goddess," Lilia whispered.

"I'm pretty relieved to hear that myself." Everyone turned as one to look back along the trail. Magdalena was standing there, her red curls waving like a battle flag in the wind. "I'm sorry I misjudged you, Demetrius, and I forgive you for everything that happened."

"For the record, so do I." Indy, Demetrius realized. She had slipped around and come out ahead of them.

"Don't stand there like mooncalves!" Sindar shouted at his minions. "Kill them!"

His men split into two groups, one going toward Indira, the others heading for Magdalena. Only one remained to guard Lilia, but not for long. As Demetrius watched, Lilia jumped in the air and kicked the thug in the chin.

He went over the side with a desperate cry that brought Sindar's attention her way. "No, damn you!" He surged forward, but Demetrius got to his feet and plowed into the high priest, his head lowered like an angry bull's, catching Sindar midchest.

Sindar doubled over and dropped to his knees. Lilia ran to Demetrius and pressed against him. She longed to embrace him, but her hands were still bound behind her. Her sisters were fighting for their lives, Indy dealing with four thugs, while Lena took on three.

"Turn around," he told Lilia quickly. As soon as she did, he began tugging at the knots, quickly freeing her.

"Stop!" Still on the ground, Sindar fired a gunshot into the air, then got up and marched over to Lilia. He grabbed her arm, jerking her away from Demetrius and pressing the gun to her head. Demetrius lunged after her, though his hands were still bound, and Sindar pointed the weapon and shot him.

Hot lead ripped through Demetrius's thigh, and he went down hard, bleeding, writhing in pain.

Sindar returned the gun to her head. "Get down here, you traitorous whores!" he shouted to Lena and Indy. "Get down here now, or I'll shoot her and throw her over the side."

"Don't do it!" Lilia screamed. "He'll kill me anyway. Don't let him kill you, too! Think of Tomas and Ryan. Think of our mother, of Ellie."

But they came anyway. Demetrius saw them rushing forward, leaving four thugs picking themselves up off the ground in their wake. Damn, no, seven. Three more were straggling in from behind some rocks.

Demetrius did his best to keep pressure on his bleeding thigh and tried to come up with a plan to save the women. But he was sorely afraid he was out of ideas.

17

Lilia stood beside her sisters on the edge of the cliff. A man in black stood at her back and another was behind each of her sisters, awaiting Sindar's command to push them over. Her hands were tied behind her again. As were theirs. Her love lay on the ground bleeding, straining to help her, suffering more than she was. And she understood why. It would be easier to die herself than to watch him murdered at the hands of a madman. She was sorry for his pain, and even more sorry that they hadn't had the chance to be together as they should have been.

Goddess, she couldn't believe it had come to this... again.

"Cast a circle," Lilia said. "Cast it around all of them. Maybe we can break the spell he put on his minions."

"I don't think there's time," Magdalena said, and closed her eyes. "I love you so much, Ryan," she said, just as if he were standing right there. "I wish you were here so I could tell you how much." Her voice broke on a sob, but she forced herself to go on. "Take care of Ellie. Don't let her forget me. I love you. I love you both so much."

"I love you, too," Ryan said softly. Lilia gasped and almost turned her head, but he added in a harsh whisper, "No, don't look back and give us away."

"No, don't do that," Tomas said from her other side. He was the masked figure standing behind Indira.

"No matter," said a raspy voice in Lilia's ear. "I'm gonna give us away right now."

"Gus?" she whispered, feeling him undo the ropes around her wrists.

"The hour is at hand!" Sindar shouted with delight. "Push them over on my word."

"Ladies, get away from the edge, and do it now," Tomas said, and he wasn't bothering to whisper anymore.

"Now!" Sindar cried.

Tomas and Ryan turned around to face Sindar, yanking off their masks.

Sindar's eyes widened as Lilia clasped hands with her sisters and they raced away from the edge, toward Demetrius. He was on his feet. He'd somehow managed to undo the knots binding his wrists and tie the rope around his leg to staunch the blood flow. But the wound in his belly was still seeping.

Three men stood now against Sindar and his four remaining thugs, though Lilia thought Demetrius looked as if he would collapse at any minute. And one still stood near the cliff with his back to them all.

Gus.

"Kill them all!" Sindar commanded, and the fight was on.

Demetrius, Tomas and Ryan fought side by side.

Just as Lilia and her sisters were about to jump into the battle, Gus joined them, his mask still on, and took Lilia's hand. "Come with me," he told them. "Trust me, this is about to end. Come."

They frowned at each other but followed as he climbed up on top of the boulder Demetrius had been leaning against, then bent down to offer them each a hand up. When they were all standing there with him, he took off his mask at last. Lilia caught her breath, because he looked very different.

His hair was darker, gleaming, and his face had lost its wrinkles but kept its fine chiseled structure, strong jaw, proud nose. His salt-and-pepper brows were jet now, and thicker. He didn't look old anymore. He looked...

"Oh, my Goddess," Magdalena said. "He looks just like—"

"Balthazorus?" Indy asked.

He smiled at them, then shouted in a booming voice that rang from the rocks and seemed to fill the entire gorge with its power. "Sindar! Heed the words of thy King!"

The fighting ceased as everyone below stared up at the spectacle on the rock. Demetrius's jaw dropped, and he took a few halting steps forward. "Gus?"

The King smiled warmly, but his smile died when his gaze fell on the gaping high priest.

Sindar fell to his knees beneath the power of that gaze, then prostrated himself. "My King, oh, my King! I avenged you once, my liege, and now I do so again."

"I never asked you to avenge me, Sindar." Gus— Balthazorus—told the women to remain where they were, then leapt nimbly down from the boulder. He walked right up to Sindar and, staring at him sadly, shook his head. "When my friend and trusted soldier slit my throat, and the life spilled out of me, my final thought was—"

"I'm sorry I betrayed you. I'm sorry I...I killed you, Gus," Demetrius said, lurching forward, but the King held up a hand to stop him, never breaking eye contact with Sindar.

"My final thought was that it was no more than I deserved. I had overreacted. Demetrius was my best friend. I should have given him Lilia with my blessing. But I was an arrogant man with an enormous ego, and I couldn't overcome that. At least not in time."

"B-but, my King, these witches betrayed you."

"They fell in love. That had nothing to do with me, Sindar. But you...all this evil you've done in my name. On my behalf. That has everything to do with me. And it ends now."

"You said you would never know peace until things had been made right!"

"Which is what I'm doing right now." Balthazorus nodded at the four thugs, and then at three more who were coming into the clearing from the brush nearby, wearing Tomas's, Ryan's and Gus's former clothes. "Release these men from your thrall, dark magician."

"B-but—"

"I command it."

Looking stricken, Sindar waved a hand, and the thugs started blinking and looking around as if they had no idea where they were or how they'd gotten there.

"That way," Gus told them, pointing down the trail. "Go."

They hustled to obey, looking as puzzled as if they'd awakened on another planet.

"I thought I was doing what you wanted," Sindar whimpered.

"You knew me, Sindar. I was a good king, a decent man. I never would have condoned the evil you've done in my name. Never."

Sindar began backing away, but Gus kept right on talking. "You killed innocents. You menaced a baby. You stripped a man of his soul. You need to revoke the spell you cast on Demetrius, the spell that has kept you trapped in this darkness all this time. You need to let go, Sindar, and move on into the afterlife your dark magic has kept at bay. And you need to do it now."

Lowering his head, Sindar took one last step backward and went over the edge. The only sound came from his robes flapping in the wind—until the splash when he reached the shallow stream at the bottom.

Lilia didn't feel even a hint of sorrow for him.

Then Gus went to Demetrius and wrapped his arms around him in a powerful hug. "I wronged you, my friend," he said.

"I wronged you far more," Demetrius told him. "I never meant to love her. I never meant to kill you. I'm sorry, Balthazorus."

The King clapped him on the back heartily, then stood back and looked him in the eye. "You saved me from the fire. That put you ahead on good deeds. This one makes us even. And please, for crying out loud, call me Gus." A smile split Demetrius's face as Gus released him and turned to Ryan. "My son," he said. "I'm so proud of you."

The two men embraced, and when they separated

Gus waved a hand toward the women, who still stood atop the boulder, high above the gorge. The wind lifted their hair, and they gazed down lovingly at the men in their lives. In their hearts.

"Are they not the most beautiful women in all the land?" Gus asked.

"And the most powerful," Demetrius said.

"And the most loving," Ryan put in.

"And the most amazing," Tomas said.

"Ahh, that they are. And they are yours. Take good care of them, my friends."

And with that Gus turned away and started walking down the trail.

"Wait, Gus! Where are you going?" Lilia shouted, as she and her sisters jumped off the rock and ran after him.

He turned and smiled at her, at all of them, looking more like the old Gus again. "I am going to live like the king I am, thanks to Demetrius."

He continued on his way. Tomas came up and wrapped Indira in his arms. Ryan swept Lena up for a passionate kiss.

Demetrius and Lilia stood facing each other for a long moment, lost in each other's eyes. And then, together, they moved closer. She lifted tentative fingers, to touch his face. "I—"

He stopped her with a soft, light kiss. And then he said, "I think it's my turn to say it. I love you, Lilia. I've loved you for thirty-five centuries. Maybe longer. I lost myself for a while, but I never lost that. It's what made me rage and rant in the Underworld, though I didn't know it at the time. It wasn't being imprisoned that was driving my fury. It was being kept apart from you. You never held a piece of my soul in your heart, you know. You held *all* of it. You still do. And you always will."

Her tears flooded over. "I've waited so long...so long for this."

"The wait is over, my beautiful Lilia." And then he kissed her the way he'd been wanting to. Long and deep and passionately.

Epilogue

"Anything interesting happen while I was gone?" Selma asked, after hugging them one by one and confiscating Ellie from her adoring daddy, right there by the baggage carousel.

"More than you even want to know," Lilia told her. "But as you can see—" she gazed up at her beloved, who was holding her hand "—it all worked out perfectly."

"Wait till I tell you, Mom. You won't even believe it." Magdalena picked up Selma's carry-on, which was bursting at the seams.

"Hmph, and I missed it all. Still, I brought back a few surprises of my own."

"Souvenirs, right? Is that why this bag is so heavy?" Ryan got the hint and took it from her.

"Well, yeah, that, and… Lena, remember those storybooks you used to write all the time about your past-life adventures? *Lena and the Prince and the Evil Bad Guy, Lena and the Prince and the Little Slave Girl,* and all the rest?"

"Of course I remember. We read them to Ellie every night."

"Well…it's such kismet, I can't even tell you. My

seatmate on the place was this lovely woman, a children's book editor, and we got to talking, and she'd really like to see your stories."

Lena sighed. "We've talked abut this before, Mom. Those stories aren't for public consumption, and besides, I was eight. How good can they be?"

"I know, I know, I just want you to meet her. I have a feeling about this. I just…" She turned to look at the other passengers, and then she spotted someone and waved. "There she is."

The woman, an olive-skinned brunette, came rushing forward, accompanied by her husband, who wore a military uniform. But her eyes were not on Selma. They were on the sisters, and they were oddly intense. As she reached them, she said, "You must be Lilia. I'd know you anywhere." And then her gaze shifted. "And you're Magdalena, and you're Indira. I can hardly believe it." Then a big tear slipped slowly from her eye and down her cheek.

The sisters looked at their mother and then at each other. Selma shrugged, as baffled as they were.

"I'm sorry," the woman said. "I've just…waited so long. And you're finally here. You're really here."

"I'm just…confused," Magdalena said softly. "Do we know each other?"

The woman nodded and looked to Indira, who shrugged. "I'm so sorry. I don't remember you."

Lilia moved closer, though. She stared deeply into the woman's eyes, and then she smiled. "Yes, you do. You just don't remember her being older than us. She was younger then. Slave girl to the slave girls."

"Amarrah?" her sisters both shouted at once. "Oh,

my Goddess, it is! It's Amarrah!" The women hugged and bounced and danced and laughed.

When they finally parted, Amarrah introduced them to her husband, Captain Harry Brockson, U.S. Army. Lena invited them to follow them back to Havenwood for dinner, and they accepted with a smile.

The joyous celebration lasted long into the night. But eventually Amarrah and her husband were on their way. Indira and Tomas returned to their cabin, Bahru to his cottage, and everyone else took to their beds, leaving Lilia and Demetrius alone in front of the fireplace. He was lying on the sofa, staring at the flames—when he could take his eyes off her, at least. She was stretched out on top of him, her head resting on his magnificent chest, listening to the steady pulsing beat of his heat.

"We need to get a place of our own," he said softly, and she loved the way the words vibrated beneath her head. "But first we have to figure out how to make a decent living. I have no skills to offer."

"Oh, I beg to differ." She turned to kiss his neck just underneath his chin, and he laughed with her. But then she grew serious. "Maybe we should sell the chalice and the blade. They're worth a small fortune."

"We could do that." He shrugged. "Or not. It doesn't matter. As long as we're together, it doesn't matter at all."

"I know. I could live in a tent and be happy with you, Demetrius." She shifted so that she could kiss his mouth. It grew from playful to passionate in a matter of seconds, and when he trailed his hand up and down her spine, over the tender skin of her lower back, where the tattoo had been, she shivered.

The mark had vanished, as it had from her sisters' backs. They'd discovered it on Beltane night, when they'd been celebrating their victory.

He kissed her more deeply and pulled her blouse up over her head. She sat up and looked quickly at the stairs. "Someone could come down," she whispered.

"Then let's sneak up to the guest room." He lifted her off him and set her on the floor. Holding her blouse in front of her, just in case, Lilia started up the stairs. She got halfway before she sensed he was no longer behind her, and stopped to turn and gaze back at him.

His eyes were stunned.

"My love, what is it?"

"The mark on your back…it's there again."

Her frown was fast and hard. "It… What?" She twisted her head, trying to see, but she couldn't. While she was still making the effort to see for herself, Magdalena's bedroom door burst open and her sister stood there wide-eyed.

"Look at this!" Lena said, turning to showing her back to Lilia.

"Me, too!" Lilia cried, showing her own back. Seconds later the front door flew open and Indy was standing there, staring from one of them to the other.

"You, too, huh?" Indy asked, and, turning, she pulled up the back of her shirt to reveal the mark of the witch.

"Maybe we'd better not get rid of the chalice and blade just yet," Demetrius said.

"But what can this mean?" Lilia asked softly.

Her sisters shook their heads slowly, neither of them having any clue at all.

"I guess time will tell," Indy said, and she went back to her waiting husband.

"I guess it will," Lena said, and went back into the room she shared with her husband.

Lilia and Demetrius walked in silence into the guest room they would occupy until they found their own place. Inside, Lilia turned to him, running her hands up and down his powerful arms, gazing up into his dark eyes. "What do *you* think it means?" she asked softly.

"I think the Gods only grant special powers when they are needed," he told her softly. "If this means, as I think it does, that our powers have been returned to us, then it must be because they are needed. Somehow. Somewhere. As your sisters so aptly put it, time will tell." He pulled her close, holding her against him and rocking her in his arms. "I hate to think of you having to go through any more battles like this last one, though."

"Small price to pay for the bliss of having you back in my arms, my love."

"I feel the same," he told her. "If the Gods demand our service in return, then I'll gladly do whatever they ask."

"As long as we're together, Demetrius. As long as we're together, I honestly believe we can do anything."

"We've already proven it. You have, anyway." He cupped her head in one big hand and tipped it slowly back so he could gaze down into her eyes. "You're an amazing woman, Lilia. Have I thanked you yet for saving me from the abyss?"

"Once or twice," she said. "But you can thank me again if you want."

"Thank you."

She smiled slowly. "Actions speak louder than words, Demetrius."

His soft laugh was like music to her ears as, bending over her, he kissed her as if there were no tomorrow. Even though she knew there was. There would be many tomorrows. And they would be together for every single one of them.

Finally.

* * * * *

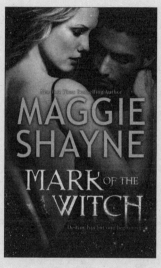

Maria V. Snyder

As the last Healer in the Fifteen Realms, Avry of Kazan is in a unique position: in the minds of friends and foes alike, she no longer exists. Despite her need to prevent the megalomaniacal King Tohon from winning control of the Realms, Avry is also determined to find her sister and repair their estrangement.

Though she should be in hiding, Avry will do whatever she can to support Tohon's opponents—including infiltrating a holy army, evading magic sniffers, teaching forest skills to soldiers and figuring out how to stop Tohon's most horrible creations yet: an army of the walking dead.

War is coming and Avry is alone. Unless she figures out how to do the impossible…again.

Available wherever books are sold.

MMVS1418

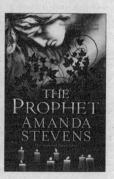

REQUEST YOUR FREE BOOKS!

2 FREE NOVELS FROM THE PARANORMAL ROMANCE COLLECTION PLUS 2 FREE GIFTS!

YES! Please send me 2 FREE novels from the Paranormal Romance Collection and my 2 FREE gifts (gifts are worth about $10). After receiving them, if I don't wish to receive any more books, I can return the shipping statement marked "cancel." If I don't cancel, I will receive 4 brand-new novels every month and be billed just $21.42 in the U.S. or $23.46 in Canada. That's a saving of at least 21% off the cover price of all 4 books. It's quite a bargain! Shipping and handling is just 50¢ per book in the U.S. and 75¢ per book in Canada.* I understand that accepting the 2 free books and gifts places me under no obligation to buy anything. I can always return a shipment and cancel at any time. Even if I never buy another book, the two free books and gifts are mine to keep forever.

237/337 HDN FEL2

Name _____ (PLEASE PRINT) _____

Address _____ Apt. # _____

City _____ State/Prov. _____ Zip/Postal Code _____

Signature (if under 18, a parent or guardian must sign)

Mail to the **Reader Service:**
IN U.S.A.: P.O. Box 1867, Buffalo, NY 14240-1867
IN CANADA: P.O. Box 609, Fort Erie, Ontario L2A 5X3

Not valid for current subscribers to the Paranormal Romance Collection or Harlequin® Nocturne™ books.

Want to try two free books from another line?
Call 1-800-873-8635 or visit www.ReaderService.com.

* Terms and prices subject to change without notice. Prices do not include applicable taxes. Sales tax applicable in N.Y. Canadian residents will be charged applicable taxes. Offer not valid in Quebec. This offer is limited to one order per household. All orders subject to credit approval. Credit or debit balances in a customer's account(s) may be offset by any other outstanding balance owed by or to the customer. Please allow 4 to 6 weeks for delivery. Offer available while quantities last.

Your Privacy—The Reader Service is committed to protecting your privacy. Our Privacy Policy is available online at www.ReaderService.com or upon request from the Reader Service.

We make a portion of our mailing list available to reputable third parties that offer products we believe may interest you. If you prefer that we not exchange your name with third parties, or if you wish to clarify or modify your communication preferences, please visit us at www.ReaderService.com/consumerchoice or write to us at Reader Service Preference Service, P.O. Box 9062, Buffalo, NY 14269. Include your complete name and address.

MAGGIE SHAYNE